HOLLI ANDERSON

Immortal Works LLC
Grantsville, Utah
Tel: (385) 202-0116
www.immortalworks.press

© 2013-2020 **Holli Anderson**
http://www.holli-anderson.com/

AISN B08DYFGKRS (Kindle Edition)
ISBN 978-1-0881-0773-7 (paperback)

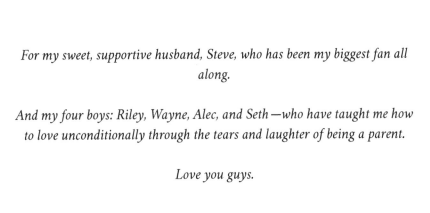

For my sweet, supportive husband, Steve, who has been my biggest fan all along.

And my four boys: Riley, Wayne, Alec, and Seth —who have taught me how to love unconditionally through the tears and laughter of being a parent.

Love you guys.

CHAPTER ONE

L ittle blue sparks of electricity gathered at my fingertips. That should have scared me, or at least aroused my curiosity. But the scene playing out before me pushed away all other emotions except anger. Intense, red-hot anger.

I recognized the three boys from school—future serial killers, to be sure. The trio had Sadie tied to a tree. Her usually silky black coat was covered in dirt and pine needles.

One of the boys—Justin was his name; we had History together—looked up at me. "Hey, look. It's the preacher's daughter. Maybe we can try it on her next." He hocked a loogy and spit at my whimpering dog. They all laughed.

Sadie yelped as one boy held her tail up while a greasy haired boy knelt behind her holding a flaming lighter. He moved it closer to the firecracker they'd shoved in her behind. I could smell the singe of her fur. A fresh flurry of electric anger pushed its way out through my fingertips. My hair flew about my head, gathering more of the little blue bolts.

Then, I lost it. *Completely* lost it. I pointed at the boy with the lighter and let loose all of my anger and fear.

"Get Away!" I screamed, and with those two simple words, that fear and anger formed into something tangible and strong. An unseen force rammed into that sadistic boy with the power of an NFL linebacker. He flew into the tree directly behind him. The breath was knocked clean out of him. His brave, dog-torturing friends looked at him, then at me, then they high-tailed it out of there, leaving their fallen friend in a moaning, gasping heap on the forest floor.

I ran to Sadie. My hands shook as I removed the offending explosive device from her butt. I untied her, all the while keeping an eye on the remaining enemy. I needn't have worried, though. As soon as he was able to breathe again, he crawled away from the little clearing, mumbling something about "a witch."

Sadie rained slobbering dog kisses all over my face as I slumped the rest of the way to the ground. The contents of my stomach exploded from my mouth. When I finished puking, I held my hands in front of me, turning them, examining them. The blue sparks were gone. *Maybe I just imagined it.* I shook my head. No, I *know* I did something to throw that sick creep away from my dog.

What just happened?

The sun slipped behind the trees and the drop in temperature finally forced me to move. I rubbed my arms as my Lab and I walked along the darkened path leading to the back yard of my house.

"Paige, you're late," my mom said when I entered through the back door into the kitchen. "You know your dad's rule, we all have to be home in time to eat dinner together."

"Sorry," I mumbled.

She lowered her head to look into my eyes. "Are you okay, honey?

You're pale as a ghost." She felt my forehead with the back of her hand.

"Yeah," I looked at the floor. "I'm just tired. What's for dinner?" I wasn't lying. I was tired. Exhausted, actually.

She turned her head and scrunched up her brow. "Hmm. Chicken casserole. I hope you aren't coming down with something. Go wash up so we can eat."

Dad said Grace and the three of us dug in. I gulped down my dinner then asked to be excused. "I have some homework I need to get done."

"Okay, sweetheart, go ahead. Love you," my dad said.

"Love you, too." I kissed them each on the cheek and hurried to my room, Sadie at my heels.

The only homework I planned on doing that night was to try to figure out what had happened in the clearing. And, to see if I could do it again.

The first thing I did was flip open my laptop and hit the power button, thinking maybe the internet would have some answers. It powered on for a brief moment before emitting a sick sounding series of beeps followed by a *pop*. The screen went black, the power light turned off, and that was it. It wouldn't power back on.

"What... no, no, no." I growled as I pushed buttons and checked the cord. My dad was not going to be happy. After much begging on my part and studious research on his, he'd finally caved in and bought the laptop for my sixteenth birthday just a few weeks earlier.

I wanted to cry but forced the tears away. I needed some answers, but had no one to go to for them. *Who would believe me? Well, except for those stupid boys...*

Maybe it was all just a fluke. A freak incident where all things in the universe aligned for just a single moment. I picked up a pencil from my desk and balanced it on the palm of my hand. I concentrated on the pencil and imagined it floating. I thought I felt a twitch, but decided it could have just been my overactive imagination.

Flashing back to the earlier events, I remembered saying something out loud when I blasted the boy.

Concentrating on the pencil again, I imagined what I wanted it to do, then I added a word.

"Rise."

The pencil lifted a couple of inches. My heart jumped into my throat and I jerked my hand back. The pencil dropped to the hardwood floor with a rattle. *So much for it being a onetime thing.*

Sadie looked up from where she lay on my bed. She whined, low and brief, before laying her head back down. I picked the pencil up. My heart raced as I concentrated once again.

"Rise."

The pencil rose just inches from my outstretched hand. It hung in the air. I continued to concentrate and lowered my hand down to my side. The pencil stayed suspended in air.

"Are you seeing this, Sadie?" I whispered. She raised her ears at the sound of her name.

A gentle flow of energy formed deep inside my chest. It reached forward and wrapped around the pencil. When I cut the flow with a conscious effort, the pencil dropped to the floor.

Bending to pick it up, I shook my head. I twirled the pencil in one hand, sat on my bed and scratched Sadie behind the ears with my other hand. I laid down and thought about what could have caused my newfound, frightening talents.

Hmm. I don't remember being bit by a radioactive spider. No exposure to gamma rays. I'm pretty sure my parents didn't find me in a field surrounded by the remains of a spaceship. I ran through all I knew about magic and super-human abilities. Which wasn't much—just the comic book stuff. Which wasn't real. *Maybe an alien life force implanted a chip in my brain.*

I drifted off to sleep as chaotic thoughts bounced around my head.

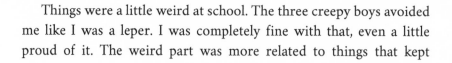

Things were a little weird at school. The three creepy boys avoided me like I was a leper. I was completely fine with that, even a little proud of it. The weird part was more related to things that kept happening around me. Like in the computer lab, when my computer and the one on each side of me sparked and went dead. Lights flickered when I drew too close. My friend's cell phone combusted when she handed it to me to look at a picture she'd taken. The effect I seemed to have on electronics now made school life difficult.

When not in school, every spare moment I had was spent holed up in my room or out in the clearing where the strangeness all began. I pushed myself to see what else I could do. I was scared and thrilled with each new discovery. Being the daughter of a pastor, the thought crossed my mind on more than one occasion that these newfound abilities might be something evil. I talked myself out of believing that with the promise I would use my powers only for good.

One of my favorite spells—I didn't really have another name for them—was uncovered one evening when I was in the clearing. Darkness set in early. Black clouds rolled above, threatening to drop their heavy load. My favorite ring fell into the pine needles blanketing the ground, and it was useless to search for it in the rapidly declining light.

Concentrating on what I wanted, I held my hand in front of me in a cupping motion and said, "Light." What looked like a miniature blue star appeared there, hovering an inch above my palm. It emitted as much light as a flashlight and I found I could increase or decrease the brightness with my thoughts.

Since I was treading in uncharted territory, I knew no names for the spells I uncovered. I named them as I went along. My first thought at seeing the little blue star was the childhood poem, "Star light, star bright, first star I see tonight." So, I called it *star-bright.*

The thrill of discovery was like a drug to me. And, as was the way of drugs, the crash was hard and painful. Of course my parents had noticed the change in my routine, and what, to them, probably seemed like ominous signs. I would run in after school, full of energy and excitement, and go directly to my room or out to the woods. After spending hours practicing, I would show up in the kitchen for dinner, exhausted and blurry eyed.

Friday, after school, I set out for the clearing, thoughts of having all of Saturday to myself running through my head. I reached my destination, and with a rush of excitement, I set straight to work. I'd just figured out levitation using the reluctant Sadie as the levitatee.

"Paige! What… what are you—?"

At the sound of my dad's astonished voice, the spell broke and Sadie dropped to the ground. I whirled around.

"Dad, I can explain." I don't know why I said that. I couldn't explain.

"Paige, what are you doing? How did you do that?"

The anger in his voice scared me.

"I… umm… I'm not sure, Dad. I'm just, magical. I guess."

"No. No." His voice cracked. "This is of the Devil. This is a Dark Art."

"Dad—"

"We're going back to the house right now and you're going to explain to your mother and me what kind of evil you've gotten mixed up in."

Back at the house, my mom cried silently while my dad worked himself into a fit of rage the likes of which I'd never seen. He was convinced I'd made a deal with the Devil or gotten involved in the Dark Arts.

"Dad, I don't even know what 'Dark Arts' are."

"Liar! My daughter is a liar," his voice broke. "There is no other explanation, Paige."

"Dad—"

"No more. No more lies tonight. Go to your room while your mother and I decide what to do."

Before dawn broke the next morning, I learned what decision they'd come to.

I awoke to two burly men in black uniforms looming beside my bed. The sound of my mom's exhausted sobs drifted down the hall. Sadie stood in the doorway, muscles taught, hind legs bunched up, ready to spring; her lips curled back in a snarl, teeth like white daggers dripping with saliva. My dad grabbed at her collar and held her there as she growled at the strangers near my bed.

6

"Paige, these gentlemen are here to take you somewhere to get some help. Your mom and I will visit when we can. We love you." He turned and dragged the furious Sadie from the room.

"I'm Dan. Get dressed. You won't be taking anything with you," said the muscle man on my left.

I made no move to rise. "Where are you taking me?"

"Somewhere safe. No more questions. Get dressed."

My mind raced. I couldn't go with them.

"Could you please wait in the hallway while I get dressed?" I asked.

"I'm afraid not," Dan answered. "We'll turn around while you change."

"No. No way. Dad!" I yelled toward the open door. "Dad! Please! You can't do this. Please! Mom, don't let him do this!"

My mom's sobs increased, tearing at my heart, but she didn't come to my rescue. Her anguished cries grew softer as she moved further from my room.

"Paige," Dan took a step closer to me, his voice gentle but firm. "We can do this the hard way or we can do this the easy way. It's entirely up to you."

I pushed my back up against the headboard in an effort to put distance between us. I shook my head. "Dad!" I screamed. "Don't do this! Let me explain!"

"Your dad isn't going to change his mind. Get dressed, Paige."

Not knowing what else to do, I climbed out of bed on the opposite side from where the men stood. My legs nearly collapsed beneath me when my feet hit the floor. My mind raced, trying to figure a way out of there.

"Turn your backs, please." My voice shook.

I changed my clothes in record time.

"You'll want your jacket, it's chilly outside," Dan said.

I grabbed my pea coat from the hook by my door. The men stood on either side of me. Taking no chances, they grabbed my upper arms, one on each side, and escorted me out the front door.

There was no way I was going to let them force me into the black car parked in the driveway. I had only a few feet to make my move, if I was going to escape. I turned and stared back at the only home I'd ever known. I could hear Sadie's hysterical barking and scratching at the door. The blinds in the living room window twitched and I caught a brief glimpse of my mom's tear-streaked face.

I hadn't practiced any defensive spells—I hadn't thought there would be a need to. But there was one such spell I was pretty sure I could pull off because I'd used it before.

We drew within one step of the car, and I planted my feet, balled my hands into fists and readied myself.

"*Get away,*" I growled.

Borne of fear and anguish, the will with which I infused the spell was strong. The hands that held me tore free of my arms. The large men soared through the air in opposite directions. I didn't know or care how far they flew or where they landed. As soon as I felt the release of their grips, I started running for the thick trees bordering our property.

I didn't stop running for what seemed like hours.

Unsure of where to go, something unseen pulled me. I walked or ran the entire day, never stopping to rest. I tried to stay hidden—not a difficult thing to do in the Pacific Northwest where there are thickly-packed trees everywhere. At nightfall, I found myself boarding the last ferry of the night headed to Seattle—lucky for me it was free for walk-ons going that direction. I curled up on a bench and slept for most of the hour-long ride.

CHAPTER TWO

He found me wandering around the dark, dilapidated Underground of Seattle, three days after my parents had tried to have me carted away. His dark eyes shone with kindness as he approached me.

Exhausted, hungry and thirsty after not eating for three days, my face streaked with dirt and tears... I'm surprised he didn't take one look at my pitiful state and just keep walking.

"Are you okay?" His dark eyes bore into mine.

I shook my head.

"Are you lost? Hurt?"

I shook my head again.

"Can you talk?" His soft voice spoke of infinite patience.

I nodded.

"Okay. Good. Let's start with names, then. I'm Johnathan." His mouth turned up at the corners, revealing a dimple in each cheek.

I stared for a minute before realizing it was my turn. "Paige. I'm Paige."

"Are you hungry?"

I licked my dry lips and nodded.

"Well, I just happen to have some gourmet food to share. Follow me, Paige."

The scant light shining down from the century old glass embedded in the sidewalks above didn't do much to light the way. I tripped every few steps over the rubble strewn everywhere. Johnathan stopped after I almost fell for the gazillionth time.

"Don't be scared, okay? I'm going to... provide some light."

I raised an eyebrow, unsure what he meant. I sucked in a breath as a small blue light appeared on the palm of his outstretched hand.

"*Star-bright*," I said, tears threatening to fall.

"What?"

"*Star-bright*." I was sure he thought I was crazy. "I call it *star-bright*." I held my hand out and produced my own blue light.

His eyes widened and his mouth dropped open.

"You can... you're like... like me?" His voice was barely a whisper.

I nodded. A tear slipped out of the corner of my eye and he reached up and wiped it away. I wasn't alone. There was someone else like me. We stood, staring at one another, for a dozen frantic beats of our hearts. His smile lit up his face—all the way to the sparkle in his dark eyes. Gorgeous eyes. He let out a short laugh and ran his free hand through the loose curls of his almost black hair. In that moment, mesmerized by his smile, I forgot about my fear, hunger, thirst, and desperate situation. The increasing rhythm of my heartbeat in my ears and the jumble of butterflies flapping wildly in my stomach made all other thoughts vanish.

Johnathan shook his head, still smiling. "C'mon. Let's go get you some food and water."

I followed him through the rubble of the Underground street. He ducked into a broken down doorway, stepping over loose bricks scattered around the sidewalk. I didn't hesitate to follow him.

We stood inside an old shop of some sort. Johnathan pulled a mostly intact chair from where it lay toppled over in a corner. He brought it over and sat it across from another chair at a makeshift table he'd apparently set up using bricks and a large piece of wood.

Johnathan made a grand gesture like a waiter at a fancy restaurant. "Your seat, Madame."

I smiled and swiped my dirty hair behind my ear. I sat, still holding the *star-bright* in my right hand.

"Watch this." He placed his *star-bright* into a glass jar that was sitting in the middle of the table, freeing up his hand. "It'll keep going until you release the spell. And, it drains hardly any energy, too."

I added my little blue light to the jar.

"I'll be right back." Johnathan disappeared into a back room. When he returned, he carried two metal cans the size of soup cans. They appeared to be old and had no labels on them.

I raised an eyebrow.

He set one can on the table and took a pocket knife to the top of the other one. "Don't worry. I've been eating these for a couple weeks now, and I haven't been sick once."

"What are they?" I frowned. I wasn't a picky eater, but I had *some* standards.

"Beans. I keep hoping to open one and find something different one of these times. But, so far, they've all been beans."

"Where did you get them?" I raised one eyebrow.

He shrugged. "I found them in that storage room back there." He nodded to the room he'd gone into to retrieve the cans. "It isn't great, but its food. It'll keep us alive."

Handing me the opened can, he said, "Sorry, I haven't found any spoons. You just kind of have to drink it. Be careful, the lid's a little jagged."

I took it from him and sniffed at the contents. The beans didn't smell as awful as I'd thought they would. My stomach growled. I tilted the can to my lips and spilled a few beans into my mouth.

Johnathan worked on opening the other can. "So? How is it?"

I swallowed. "Fabulous."

He snorted. "Yeah." He closed his pocket knife and set it on the table before dumping a large amount of beans into his open mouth.

"You said something about water…" My dry mouth reminded me I hadn't had anything to eat or drink in almost two days.

"Oh, yeah. Of course. I'm so sorry I forgot." He stood and walked to a corner of the room. He brought back two plastic bottles filled with mostly clear water.

I gulped it down then thought to ask, "Where did the water come from?"

"Above. I fill up the bottles at drinking fountains and in bathrooms before I come back down for the night."

Not knowing what else to say, but not wanting the conversation to end, I asked, "How old are you?"

"Seventeen. How about you?"

"Sixteen."

I wanted to hear more of his mesmerizing voice. I had to ask something that would keep him talking—so I could just stare at his face. "Do you know much about this place? The Underground, I mean. I remember learning a little about it in school, but I don't remember much."

He pushed his chair back and propped his feet up on the table. "I just happen to know quite a bit about it. Are you asking for a history lesson?" He wiggled his eyebrows at me.

I laughed. "Yes, teacher. Teach me, please."

He cleared his throat dramatically before beginning, in a scholarly voice, "Well, in 1889, there was a big fire—they called it 'The Great Seattle Fire'—it destroyed thirty-one blocks. The city leaders decided that instead of rebuilding the city as it had been, it would be a good idea to one, construct the new buildings of brick or stone so they wouldn't burn as easily; and, two, build the streets up one or two stories higher than the original street had been in order to solve some annoying flooding problems.

"So, they lined the old streets with concrete walls, leaving narrow alleyways between the walls and buildings and a wide alley where the street was. The business owners wanted to rebuild right away, not wait for the city to finish the sidewalks and streets one or two stories up. So they built at the level of the original street, knowing that the ground floors of their new buildings would eventually be underground and the next floor up would become the new ground floor. Once the sidewalks were complete, these building owners moved their businesses to the new ground floor and mostly used the lower floors for storage and such.

"In the early 1900's—I don't remember exactly when—the city condemned the Underground for fear of the pneumonic plague and the basements were left to deteriorate, except for a small portion that's been restored and made safe and accessible to the public for guided tours. We're in the unsafe and un-restored part."

"Wow," I rested my elbows on the table and my face in my hands. "Either you paid more attention in school than I did, or your teachers went into way more detail than mine."

He grinned. "Neither, actually. I found a pamphlet up above one day. I've read it like a hundred times out of boredom."

As hard as I tried, I couldn't repress a yawn.

"Am I boring you with my vast intelligence and knowledge?" he asked with a haughty, British accent.

I rolled my eyes. "No, no. I'm very impressed, actually. I just haven't slept much in the last three days."

"Oh, right. I'm afraid I'm not much of a host. Ladies first—go ahead and choose a spot to sleep."

Before settling down in a corner for the night, I realized I had a slight problem. The issue wasn't that I was planning to sleep in an unstable, underground structure near a seventeen-year-old boy I'd just met. It was that I had to go to the bathroom. Bad.

"Umm, Johnathan?"

"Yeah?" He looked up from where he was spreading a thin blanket out on the floor.

"Where do you... uh," I dropped my gaze to the floor. "I need to use the bathroom."

When I brought my gaze back to his, his cheeks held a faint flush of pink.

"Well," he said, "there are toilets down here, but I haven't found one that works. I... uh... usually take care of business when I'm above ground, in a public restroom. But, when I have to down here, I use a bucket"—the pink of his face turned to a deep red—"I'll go find you one."

After all the embarrassing unpleasantness was taken care of, I settled myself in a corner away from Johnathan. I covered up as best I could with my jacket and rested my head on my arms. My last memory before falling into exhausted sleep was of Johnathan laying a blanket over me before going back to his corner of the room.

The sun was halfway to its peak when we ascended out of the depths of the Underground. The disorientation of not being able to tell if it was night or day until stepping out into the world above was going to take some getting used to.

Johnathan took me immediately to Pike's Market where there were public restrooms that you could use without being a paying customer. I washed my hair and cleaned up as best I could in the small sink. My clothes were a mess, but I had no others to change into.

There were few clouds in the sky and the warmth of the sun was addicting. Johnathan and I went to a park near the pier and lay on the grass, soaking up the rays while we could.

"What brought you here, Paige?" he asked, picking at the grass.

I told him about the boys and Sadie, about how freaked out I'd been—and still was—and about practicing to see what else I could do. I hesitated before telling him about my dad's reaction when he caught me using magic. The emotional wounds were still new; raw and painful.

One look into Johnathan's dark brown eyes revealed his deep

compassion. I trusted him and wanted to tell my story—to share my pain with him. I had a feeling he would understand completely.

We were both silent for several minutes after I finished. I looked down as I pulled at the grass and piled it up next to me. When I raised my gaze again, after I was sure I had control of my emotions, Johnathan watched me.

"Your turn now. Why are you here?" I asked.

His face became an emotionless mask. He sat up and bent his knees, resting his forearms there as he twirled a blade of grass between his fingers. He stared into the distance and started to say something before shaking his head and turning away from me.

"You don't have to tell me. It's okay."

"Sorry. I just… I can't talk about it." His voice was husky.

"It's okay," I repeated. "Let's go explore. Do you think I can find an extra set of clothes somewhere… for free?"

The homeless shelter Johnathan led me to was quiet at that time of day. The volunteer who greeted us didn't ask any questions, she just got me some pants, a shirt and some underthings from the shelves of donated items. At Johnathan's request, she also handed me a blanket.

Back in our Underground retreat, I changed clothes in the storage room. Johnathan showed me how he tapped into the water pipes in the ceiling for water to wash his clothes. While I hung my clothes over exposed boards to dry, Johnathan made a suggestion.

"I've been thinking that I should try to find out some information about this… magic. Now that there are two of us, I think it's even more important. What do you think?"

I sat next to him on the floor where he'd been watching me. "Where would we go to get information?"

He shrugged. "Well, I figure that since we're real… since our powers are real, maybe some other people really have certain powers, too."

"Like who?"

"Like psychics maybe. We should start with the psychics." He turned to me, a glimmer of excitement in his eyes.

I smiled. "Okay. Let's do it."

We set out to find a real psychic. After a couple of weeks and what seemed like a million imposters, we found one who was definitely legit.

Madame LaForte was a retired recluse who refused all visitors. But, even elderly paranormal women couldn't resist Johnathan's charms. He not only convinced her to invite us into her fortress of a house, but she even offered us stale cookies and a drink. There was a feeling about her that made me sure she was the real thing. There were moments during our conversation that I could see a glow surrounding her. As quick as it appeared, it was gone, only to reappear a few minutes later. Her touch felt different, too, like a small electric shock without the pain. I forgot all about the Madame for a minute as Johnathan's arm brushed mine and sent tingles flying up to my shoulder. My heart raced and I thought how glad I was that Madame LaForte only had a small loveseat for us to sit on. My heart rate continued to increase when he didn't move his arm away; he kept the contact with my bare skin. I lost track of the conversation for a minute. The elderly psychic's shaky, rough voice broke through my lapse of concentration.

".... are magical. I can feel it. I can feel your powers. You're strong, you two. Very strong." She stood and went to a dusty bookshelf where she removed an ancient looking white book. "I dreamed about you. There were more of you, but it was definitely you."

"More?" Johnathan asked. "How many more?"

She waved a wrinkled, knotted hand in front of her. "I don't remember. Three, maybe four. That isn't important. The important thing is this book." She handed it to Johnathan. "I was instructed in the dream to give it to you."

We thanked Madame LaForte and took the book back to our hiding spot. We poured over the information in the little white book. It contained information about creatures I thought were only in Fairy Tales, their strengths and weaknesses—how to remove them from the Earth. It talked a little about magic, but it looked like we'd have to figure most of that out on our own. One thing it talked about that I'd already figured out from my own practices was that magic wasn't without limitations. The more magic I did, the more exhausted it made me. We were both glad to read, though, that we could build endurance by practicing—like a marathon runner.

So, we started to practice and learn.

CHAPTER THREE

Channeling rods, we'd read in our little white instruction book, were used to channel spells—to make them go where they were aimed. I carved mine out of a dowel I'd pulled out of the back of a broken chair. Johnathan carved his out of a piece of the leg of the same chair. The book said we should individualize them, make them unique to us.

We'd been together for about a month. We hadn't run into much trouble in that time. An occasional homeless person wandered down into the Underground with us, but they were mostly harmless.

One night, when we were carving symbols into our channeling rods, Johnathan sat up from his slumped position and cocked his head to the side, listening.

"Wait here. I'll be right back."

"Okay," I said. I wanted to finish the symbol I was working on, so I didn't offer to go with him.

I will admit, I was a *little* annoyed when Johnathan returned with another teenage boy in tow. I kind of wanted to just keep Johnathan to myself.

"Paige, this is Alec. I found him wandering around down here... using a *star-bright* to light his way."

I really couldn't say I was surprised. Since visiting Madame LaForte, we'd kind of been expecting someone to show up.

"Hey, Paige." The boy with dirty blonde hair reached out for a fist bump. I obliged with a little reluctance. He saw our *star-brights* in the jar and added his to the collection before plopping down next to me. "What's that?" He pointed to my channeling rod.

"A channeling rod. Here." I tossed the white book at him. "Read all about it." I'm afraid I wasn't very good at keeping the annoyance out of my voice.

Alec paged through the book. Every time he turned the page, he made some sort of annoying exclamation. "Wow! Awesome! Where'd you guys get this?"

Johnathan joined us, handing Alec an open can of beans and a bottle of water we'd filled up that afternoon. "So, what's your story? What forced you Underground?" he asked Alec.

"I wasn't forced. It was a choice." He slurped a mouthful of beans out of the can. "The short version of the story is that I was in foster care and I didn't much care for the extracurricular activities of my latest foster parents."

"Oh?" I raised an eyebrow. "And what were these activities?"

"Chemistry. At least that's what the guy told me. But, I know a meth lab when I see one." His mouth turned up in a mischievous grin. "I made sure to blow their little chemistry set to smithereens right before I left, though."

"Why were you in foster care, if you don't mind my asking?" I said.

"I don't mind. My life's an open book." He set the now empty can on the floor and leaned back against the wall. "I don't have any

parents. Well, at least that I know of. All I know is that my mom abandoned me at the hospital right after I was born. I've lived in foster
homes all my life."

I had no idea what to say to that. So, I didn't say anything.

Alec fell right into the routine Johnathan and I had going. We
studied the white book and practiced spells for several hours every
day. We exercised every day, usually by running in various parks
around Seattle.

I didn't have much time to lament the loss of one-on-one time
with Johnathan. Not long after Alec joined us, we had our first run-in
with a Demon—and that was when I decided having Alec around
wasn't such a bad thing. If he hadn't been there, Johnathan and I
would likely be dead. Or worse. The thought of being possessed by a
Demon—having no control over my own actions, carrying out its
devastating orders—that was one of the scariest things I could
think of.

Demons were a mystery to me. I'd read that they were fallen
angels. Malevolent spirits. They were definitely malevolent. Whatever
they were, their main goal seemed to be to possess or just plain kill
humans. From what I'd read in the white book, Demons weren't
supposed to be roaming around our realm, outside of the Netherworld. The reason there were some running around, it stated, was
this: there were sorcerers and others who dabbled in the Dark Arts
but few were strong enough to summon a Demon. Even fewer were
strong enough to hold that Demon captive once summoned. Those
people all thought they were strong enough, though. These dabblers
in the Dark Arts would call up a Demon, thinking to force it to carry
out some unsavory deed for them, and they'd end up being too weak
to hold the thing inside their pentacle. Demons didn't really like to be
called up or summoned. Forced to adhere to another's will. So, they
broke out and killed whoever called them. And then they were free to
roam in our realm until someone sent them back to the Netherworld.

I know my dad believed in Demons, they're even mentioned in the Bible, but he refused to talk about them, afraid just doing so would evoke one's wrath or bring its evil upon us. Just the thought of them scared the crap out of me.

We sat in the lobby of an old hotel Underground. Johnathan and Alec were trying to convince me that Pentacles weren't dark magic. Alec drew an almost perfect circle. As he added the five point star to the middle, its points touching the circle, he said, "Pentacles aren't evil, Paige. They're just a tool that can be used for either good or evil purposes. We'll only be using them for good so relax and start practicing."

I reluctantly picked up a piece of chalk and touched it to the ground. I blew out an anxious breath. "I can't do it."

Jonathan dropped his chalk to the ground and scooted over next to me. I forgot to breathe when he put his hand over mine and started drawing the symbol with my chalk. The warmth of his strong but tender hand made me forget all about thoughts of evil. All I could think about was how good his touch felt. And, as he leaned over, his leg touching mine, I breathed in his smell.

"There," he said. He finished the pentacle but still rested his hand over mine. He raised his eyebrows and smiled a stunning half-smile. "Nothing bad happened. In fact, I'd say that felt pretty good." He squeezed my hand.

I nodded and Alec rolled his eyes.

"Now, draw one of your own." He slowly withdrew his hand from mine as he continued to hold my gaze.

I could feel the heat rising in my cheeks. I looked down and started drawing.

The circle drawn, I started on the star and then stopped and held the chalk up off the ground. "Shh. Be quiet for a second. I hear something."

The boys held still. Alec cocked his head like a dog, listening.

"*London Bridge is falling down...*" the British accent sang, louder as it drew closer.

A white ghost-shaped blob flew through our door. It stopped short when it saw us. The big nerd glasses it wore on its sheet-like face didn't even budge in spite of the fact that it had no ears or nose to hold them in place.

I glanced up at the books it carried. Physics, Human Biology, and Psychology.

Valedictorian wannabee. The laugh that was forming in my throat at that thought was stopped short as a million tiny spiders of terror crept up my spine.

"There you are," the Demon said with a slight British accent. "I knew I smelled something interesting." The thing dropped its books and opened its mouth w-i-d-e. Johnathan dove out of the way just as its protruding jaws and rows of terrifying shark-like teeth clamped shut with a loud chomp right where his head had just been.

Rolling to his knees, he reached for his channeling rod. Alec beat him to the draw and lifted his rod, yelling an unintelligible word as he aimed for the Demon. Blue flames burst from the tip of his rod and blasted into the Demon with the force of a cannon. The creature from another realm tumbled into the wall.

It righted itself with impossible speed, and with an inhuman roar, came at us.

"Paige, circle! Alec, fight!" Johnathan yelled, dodging the several new arms and jagged claws that had erupted from the Demon's form-less body.

I drew a pentacle with shaking hands while the boys fought. I concentrated on getting the star just right.

I raised my head when the pentacle was complete and froze in panic. The Demon had Johnathan in its grasp, pulling his head toward its many-toothed mouth. That unfroze me. I screamed something like "AAAHHHHH!!" as I aimed my channeling rod right at its glasses. I didn't take the time to form a particular spell in my mind—instinct just took over. A blast of hot air from my rod hit the Demon square in the glasses, pushed it up against the wall, and encircled it like a tornado.

The clawed arm that held Johnathan stuck out of the tornado until the wind finally whipped it around and around, faster and faster. Johnathan tucked and rolled as the Demon lost its grip on him.

The tornado didn't last long. I used up all my energy on that one spell and I sunk to the ground, exhausted. The Demon wobbled like a drunken sailor. Taking advantage of its temporary state of dizziness, Johnathan pointed his channeling rod at it and said, *"Blow."* A strong blast of air pushed the white blob toward the pentacle.

Alec joined, using the same spell. As soon as the Demon was within the boundaries of the circle, Alec aimed and growled, *"Bind."*

The Demon dropped to the floor, unable to move. Johnathan pricked his finger with the tip of his pocket knife and let fall a drop of blood onto the circle. I could sense the magic as he willed the circle closed, trapping the Demon inside.

The rage exhibited by the Demon when it realized it had been trapped was incredible.

"Wow," I exclaimed as I stared in disbelief. Rabies-like foam exploded from its mouth with every furious flip of its head. I could feel my face turning a dark shade of red at the disgusting language it screamed—even when it screamed in several different languages, I could tell the words were foul. It pushed against the pentacle barrier with a fury I'd never seen nor felt before.

"We need to combine power," Johnathan grunted with the effort of holding the circle together.

Alec stood next to him and concentrated on the circle. I pulled the little white book from Johnathan's backpack and flipped through the pages in search of a way to send the Demon back to the Netherworld.

"Thou doesn't need to know a Daemon's name when sending it back through the portal, that is only necessary when summoning," I read aloud.

"Just get to the *sending* part, Paige. Hurry!" I could hear the strain in Alec's voice.

The Demon realized we were going to send it back and it screamed furiously in protest. "Ye cannot send the magnificent Shalbriri back! Ye are just kids!"

My eyes widened, stunned that it had spoken its name to us. In its throes of fury, I guess it didn't realize what it was doing.

I shook off my surprise and found the spell below where I'd just read. I joined with the boys and felt the strength of the Demon pressing against the three of us, trying to overcome us. I read the words aloud, hoping the spell would still work even though my voice was high and shaking. *"Lacio expello locus exigo!"*

The void opened, and the Demon was sucked back into its own world.

Johnathan twisted toward me; his breathing was heavy and drops of sweat trickled down his brow. Dark eyes searching mine, he lifted a hand and pushed a strand of hair away from my face. He rested his hand on my cheek. His touch caused a wave of dizziness and I reached for his arm to steady myself.

"Are you okay?" he asked, his forehead creased with worry.

The muscles of his arm were tense, yet the touch of his hand on my face was so warm and gentle. I smiled a closed lip, shaky smile.

"I'm fine. You're the one that was nearly turned into Demon chow. Are you okay?"

He smiled, causing my stomach to do somersaults.

"I'm great," he said in a near whisper.

That night, the three of us decided to take our practicing more seriously. We focused the majority of our efforts on learning defense and fighting skills aimed at Demons and other Netherworld beings. After a little further studying on the matter, we figured that Mr. Ghost Demon was a lesser Demon and worried that others we might have to face would be much stronger and smarter than it was. I'm not exactly sure why, but I wrote the Demon's name in the White Book.

Another decision we made that night was that we should move our base camp around every couple of days and start using wards to keep unwanted guests out of our sleeping quarters.

That's how Seth joined our group. We heard something come in contact with one of the protective wards we'd placed around the entrance to our new digs, then a grunt as the ward worked as planned and threw the intruder a short distance away.

Alec disabled the ward, and the three of us went out to see what we'd stopped from entering our rubble strewn shelter. We found a burly blond kid with messy hair falling in his eyes. He scrambled to his feet and put his hands out in front of him, forming a ball of light between them.

"Whoa, dude. Relax the magic, there," Alec held a hand out and formed a *star-bright*. "You're one of us."

The boy dropped his hands and the light dissipated. His shoulders relaxed a little and one corner of his mouth twitched.

"I'm Johnathan, this is Alec and Paige. What's your name?"

"Seth." He looked at us each in turn. "Are you all... can you all, uhh, you know... do stuff?"

"Yeah, we can all do stuff," Johnathan half-smiled.

Seth's story was simple. Not long after he discovered his abilities, he realized they created a dangerous environment for his family. So he left.

He joined our practices and shared our living quarters as our supply of canned beans dwindled.

That same week, Johnathan returned from his search for where we would next shelter, with a small, filthy girl following closely behind him. She studied us with big green eyes—one of them peeking from behind a strand of shoulder length brown hair.

"Halli, this is Paige, Alec, and Seth." Johnathan pointed each of us out to her.

"Hi, guys." She stepped up and shook each of our hands with a strong grip. She wasn't as timid as she appeared.

"Halli's like us," Johnathan said, smiling down at her.

"Where'd you come from?" Alec asked.

Her face screwed up in concentration before she shook her head and stared down at the ground. "I don't remember."

Johnathan put a hand on her shoulder. "I found her curled up in a dark corner, shaking and confused. She only remembers her age and her name. Nothing else before waking up in that corner."

"Oh," I said, very near tears for the young girl. "That must have been terrifying. Are you hurt? Hungry?" I stepped up to her and wrapped my arms around her in a hug. The top of her head didn't even reach my chin.

She leaned into me for a minute before answering. "I'm not hurt, just dirty. And, yes, I'm starving."

Seth got her a can of beans. We were all a little surprised to find out she was thirteen years old, I would have guessed closer to nine or ten.

The addition of Seth and Halli strengthened our team, but the food situation was becoming dire. We were down to just a week's worth of beans.

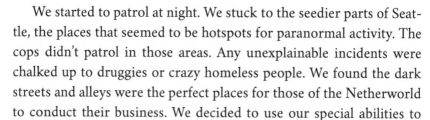

We started to patrol at night. We stuck to the seedier parts of Seattle, the places that seemed to be hotspots for paranormal activity. The cops didn't patrol in those areas. Any unexplainable incidents were chalked up to druggies or crazy homeless people. We found the dark streets and alleys were the perfect places for those of the Netherworld to conduct their business. We decided to use our special abilities to protect the poor and downtrodden people that lived or merely existed there.

We stayed out of human affairs and concentrated our efforts on the un-human. On dark forces like Demons and the evil men who summoned them. Or baby-stealing Faeries, flesh-eating Trolls, annoying Goblins, and other such nefarious creatures. My life as a pastor's daughter certainly hadn't prepared me for any of this—these weren't things he mentioned in his Sunday sermons.

With the protection of our fellow humans in mind, the five of us set out in an area we hadn't been before. We walked past a small grocery store and heard a terrified scream coming from inside. I was closest to the door, so I rushed in and I saw, with a small measure of excitement, a small group of Goblins. They were terrorizing the grocer and one of his customers. I shrunk back from the ugly little creatures that looked like chubby meth-heads. I didn't want to get any of the oozing yuck on me that was coming from the open sores that pocked their yellow-gray skin. They were all disgusting, but one in particular made me want to hurl when it stuck a short, fat finger in its bulbous nose and removed a slimy booger the size of a small rodent. It flicked the booger at the grocer. *At least it didn't eat it*, I thought with disgust.

A rope was wound around the grocer and the elderly customer. The Goblins were taunting them and throwing produce at them. The store was a mess.

"Hey! Perfect timing!" Alec yelled as he stepped to my side. "We just studied about Goblins."

I smiled.

It took us no time at all to dispatch the nasty creatures. I took aim and exploded my Goblin into a pile of green tar-like ichor.

Halli and Alec ganged up on one and it burst into flames before it was even aware we were there. Seth dropped a shelf full of canned goods on his, smashing it like a pancake. Johnathan cast a spell that made the Goblin's tongue swell up so big the creature turned purple and choked on it. He won the prize for the most creative kill of the night.

As creatures of the Fae, the Goblins' remains didn't stick around for long. They smoldered for a few minutes before evaporating back into the Netherworld where, we'd recently read, they would eventually reform. So killing them didn't really kill them, it just sent them away for a while.

Alec and Seth untied the grocer and his customer. The elderly woman hobbled away screaming from the store.

The grocer said, "Thank you, kids. My name's Joe and before you ask any questions, I don't want to talk about what just happened. I'd rather just pretend it was a bad dream."

Johnathan introduced us and asked, "Can we help you clean up this mess?"

"Oh, that would be great. Let me put out the 'closed' sign."

During the hour it took us to clean up the store, Joe skillfully turned the conversation in such a way as to coerce us into telling him we lived on our own. He didn't pry, or try to find out why or where we were staying.

Joe handed a bag full of non-refrigerator dependent groceries to each of the boys before he let us out the locked door. We started to walk away when he called, "Johnathan? Uhh, just so you know. I... uh, *throw out* the old stuff every Wednesday, you know, to make room for my Thursday morning shipment."

"Oka-a-y," Johnathan said.

Joe looked him straight in the eyes. "I always lock this *garbage* in a metal box out in the side alley... you know, so the dogs won't get into it." He slipped a key to the box into Johnathan's hand.

CHAPTER FOUR

P aige, you're with me tonight," Johnathan said. "Alec, you take
Seth and Halli and patrol around King Street. Paige and I will
go over a block and start there."

We were starting our nightly patrol. I was thrilled to be assigned as
Johnathan's partner for once. Usually he stuck me with Alec or Seth
while he went with the other one and Halli. This was a special occasion, and I hoped we wouldn't be interrupted by business. But, our
quiet time together, when I could just stare at his lovely face—okay,
not stare, but glance sideways at it often while we walked—was not to
be. Almost before we'd gone a half block, the chains around our necks
began to buzz.

We'd all started to wear the chains. Johnathan had placed a charm on them so we could communicate with one another when we were split up. The buzz meant Alec's group had spotted something. I snuck one last glance at Johnathan's dark chocolate brown eyes and sighed as we turned and headed back to King Street.

Halli met us at the corner. The camouflage spell she'd cast on herself flickered as she moved toward us. That's the only way I could tell where she was without tapping into my *sight*. A normal human, unaware of what to look for, wouldn't have noticed her at all. Demons and other Fae used similar spells when they wished to remain unnoticed by humans.

"We saw a Faerie trying to enter an apartment window," Halli whispered. "She's carrying something. Alec thinks it's a changeling!"

We weren't sure why Faeries brought changelings to our realm and exchanged them for healthy human babies, but I had my own ideas about it. The type of Faerie that typically did this was beautiful beyond words, but the changeling was a hideous creature with an ill temper. *I* think the changelings were really Faerie offspring that came out ugly. Maybe they were the offspring of a Faerie and a Troll or something, but Faeries hated anything that wasn't of great beauty—including their own children. I think they traded for a beautiful and healthy human baby so they could raise it as their own, and leave the hideous and annoying changeling for the humans to deal with. Like my totally irritating cousin. The one everyone hated to be around. His parents could often be heard saying to one another, "He gets it from *your* side of the family." It was quite possible my cousin was a Faerie changeling.

Quietly, we sneaked up the street to where Alec and Seth watched the window. The Faerie couldn't go completely into the dwelling without permission from someone inside, so unless the baby's crib was next to the window where she could just lean in and make the exchange, she would have to move on to another baby. She hovered near the open window, trying not to drop the wriggling bundle she held in her arms. Faeries ranged in size from the size of a hummingbird to petite human adult size; this one was about the same size as Halli. As she struggled with trying to open the window wider,

Johnathan signaled for Alec and Seth to move next to the building below either side of the window in case the Faerie finished the exchange before he and I could maneuver into place. The boys nodded and took out their channeling rods.

The window was two stories up in a three-story building. Johnathan and I slipped inside the building and stealthily ran up the stairs to the roof. The plan was to throw a binding spell on her *before* she made the exchange, because the binding spell would cause her to drop to the ground, and we didn't want to risk hurting the human baby. The changeling, however, we didn't care so much about risking. We hadn't left ourselves much time. She was just reaching through the window to lay the changeling in the crib when we peeked over the side of the roof. Johnathan and I pulled out our channeling rods and hit her with a double whammy.

"*Bind!*" Johnathan yelled.

"*Bindicus!*" I yelled.

We'd discovered the words we said weren't as important as visualizing in our minds what we wanted to happen. In fact, the words weren't even one hundred percent necessary. They just helped us to focus. Johnathan was pretty straightforward in his use of words. I preferred to make up my own words to sound more hocus-pocussy. Usually I did so by adding a Latin-sounding ending to a normal word. Johnathan laughed at my made-up words, but I didn't care. I thought it made them sound more mysterious and magic-y. Sometimes I even used real Latin words and they seemed to make my spells stronger.

Both spells hit her at the same time. Her face froze—eyes huge and mouth open—when her wings, arms, and legs snapped together as though we'd wrapped her up in an invisible tortilla. Gravity took over and she fell like a brick to the sidewalk below. Halli, bleeding heart that she was, cushioned her fall with a pillow of air.

"Crap!" grumbled Johnathan, whipping his head to move a strand of dark curly hair from his eyes.

"What? That was awesome! A double blast of binding—she doesn't know what hit her!" I did a celebratory fist pump in the air.

"Yeah, it was cool." He smiled at me, his dimples appearing all too briefly. "But, she dropped the changeling inside the window right before we hit her."

"Oh. I really hate when there's a 'but'."

That too-brief smile tugged at the corners of his mouth again, leaving me aching for more. "We have to go get it. Any ideas how?"

"Hmm. I don't suppose knocking on the door and asking the mom if we can just go get something we dropped in her baby's room will work?"

Johnathan rolled his eyes and shook his head.

I sighed. "I guess you're going to have to lower me down to the window so I can reach in and grab the little imp, then." I'd never much liked heights. Not that I was necessarily *scared* of heights, I just preferred to stay closer to the ground whenever possible.

None of us had yet perfected levitation, so Johnathan pulled a thin rope out of his backpack and fashioned it into a makeshift harness. He must have been a Boy Scout in his former life. I stuck my legs through the loops and tested the strength of his knots.

"Don't you trust me?" His eyes widened, eyebrows raised.

I smacked him on the shoulder. "Of course I trust you, or I wouldn't be about to put my life in your hands."

"Don't be so dramatic. A fall from this height wouldn't necessarily *kill* you. Just don't land on your head."

"You aren't exactly helping my jitters."

Just then, either the baby—or the changeling—let out a wail. Johnathan and I looked at each other, alarmed. He tied the end of the rope off on a pillar, then held tight to it right next to where the knot was tied at my waist. I concentrated on his broad shoulders and muscular arms as he helped me over the ledge. His momentary touch on my arm sent chills racing down it as he lowered me to the baby's window. I reached in and grabbed the bundle the Faerie had dropped, took a quick peek to make sure it was indeed the changeling, and signaled for Johnathan to pull me back up just as the door to the baby's room started to open.

Whew, I thought. *That was close.*

The blanket covering the changeling dropped open during the pull back to the roof. I peered down at the wiggling creature in my arms and shuddered as I wrapped it tight again, doing my best to avoid having my fingers bitten off by the hideous creature. Its face was that of a hairless dog, with a long muzzle and razor-sharp teeth. Slathering drool dripped from its pronounced overbite. Small, squinty eyes the color of a white T-shirt after it's been washed with a new, black towel, focused on my face. Its wrinkled skin had dark areas of rotting flesh. Of course, that was what the changeling really looked like. Only those with magical abilities could see through the camouflage placed by the Faeries. The human parents would have seen a passing replica of their kidnapped baby. I handed the bundle to Johnathan and wiped my hands on my pants.

We retraced our steps and met the other three on the sidewalk below. The baby's mother slammed the window shut.

The binding spell on the Faerie wouldn't last long without a continuous infusion of power—which was exhausting. So, our goal was to get her back to the Underground—to the pentacle—before the spell wore off. The boys bundled her into a large backpack and Alec carried her on his back. Johnathan handed the changeling back to me—lucky me—and we headed back toward the nearest boarded up stairway leading to the Underground. We knew where many of the stairways were. As we came upon new ones we would pry the boards away from the doorframes to gain entrance, but leave the boards on the doors so they looked undisturbed.

When we dropped to the floor of the Underground, I gave the Faerie an extra dose of the binding spell, just to ensure she wouldn't get loose before we arrived. There were few things as nasty as an irate Faerie. They were stronger than they looked and had some really powerful magic up their frilly sleeves.

We made it back to our hideout without incident. Alec and Seth removed the Faerie from the backpack and laid her in the pentacle we'd prepared beforehand.

"This one sure is a beauty," Alec said.

We'd discovered recently that he had a thing for Faeries, more so even than other sixteen year old, hormonal boys would have. They were beautiful creatures, and long known in folklore for their ability to draw men to them like cow manure draws flies. Alec ran his fingers through her silky yellow hair but stepped back out of the pentacle before Johnathan could yell at him. Another good reason to keep her bound until we could send her back to the Netherworld—Alec had almost been coerced into helping a Faerie escape a few days earlier. His will to combat her charms had been seriously weakened by her fluttering eyelashes and big alligator tears. He'd succumbed to her charm, and Seth and Halli had to hold him down while Johnathan and I sent her back and closed the gateway. Alec was totally embarrassed when the charm broke and he realized what had happened. Of course, we'd been reminding him about it on a regular basis since then.

The wriggling changeling I carried grew heavier by the second, and as I leaned over to set it beside the Faerie in the pentacle, the blanket caught in my gear belt made from a discarded fanny pack. The changeling unrolled from the blanket and, chittering incessantly, did a sort of lightning-fast monkey crawl out of the circle of the pentacle.

Standing beside me, Johnathan reached out to grab the horrid little creature before it skittered away. It clamped down on his hand like a needle-toothed vise.

Johnathan let out a horrendous, bellowing scream. It must have *really* hurt. I'd never heard him do more than grunt when in pain before.

I was locked in place, horror-stricken.

Whipping out her channeling rod, Halli aimed it toward the creature's clenched jaws, *"Release,"* she hissed.

As soon as Johnathan's hand was free, Halli followed her first spell with another.

"Bind!" she shouted, as the power of her spell sent orange sparks flying from the tip of her rod.

I dropped to the rubble-strewn floor next to where Johnathan lay writhing in pain, his injured hand grasped to his chest. "Johnathan! Oh, I'm so sorry! Let me see your hand."

"Send them back," Johnathan spat through gritted teeth. "Now!"

I scrambled to my feet. Seth grabbed the now-bound changeling and tossed it none too gently into the circle with the Faerie. I removed a stick pin from my belt and pricked my finger, drawing a drop of blood. I touched my finger to the circle's border and closed my eyes.

Sending my will into the circle, I muttered, *"Close."* I completely forgot to make it sound magic-y.

Nothing changed to the way the circle and its inhabitants looked, but I could feel the pressure of the force field surrounding them. I wondered briefly if I should remove the binding from the Faerie and ask her about the bite before sending her back, or at least try to get her name out of her so I could summon her again if I needed to. The twisted grimace on Johnathan's face was too much for me to handle, though, and the sight of it wiped away my previous thoughts.

I gestured for Seth, Alec, and Halli to gather around the circle. We held hands and concentrated on the sending spell we'd all learned by heart. I spoke the words, *"Lacio expello locus exigo!"*

A hole opened up inside the circle, and we caught a small, terrifying glimpse of the Netherworld as the Faerie and her changeling seeped into the void between our world and theirs.

As soon as the opening sealed shut, I broke the circle—which felt a lot like my ears popping—so it became just a drawing on the floor. I fell to my knees beside Johnathan once again and reached for his injured hand. I gasped at the sight. It was already swollen beyond recognition, red and mean-looking. The puncture wounds dripped with green pus and his whole hand was hot to the touch. The redness moved up his arm at an alarming rate.

"Johnathan, this looks horrible. What was that thing?" I asked. "Halli, get me some warm water and soap."

"I'm not sure what it was, but I have a feeling this isn't going to end well for me." He closed his eyes. "I can feel the pain traveling through all my blood vessels, all my organs, my skin, my hair..." He swallowed back a groan.

Halli rushed over with the soap and a bucket of water she'd warmed with a spell. I dumped about half the water over Johnathan's hand to wash away some of the green goop pouring from the wound. I slathered it with soap and poured more water over it. Johnathan had broken out into a sweat and his skin was a sickly color of gray. I sent Halli to refill the bucket with clean water, and I stroked Johnathan's forehead. Using the sleeve of my shirt, I mopped some of the perspiration from his face. His eyes were closed tight, his jaw clenched in pain.

When Halli brought the bucket back over, I decided the best way to clean out the wounds was to plop his whole hand in the water and just soak it for a while. While his hand soaked, I scooted over, laid his head on my lap and continued to stroke his forehead and run my fingers through his sweat-soaked hair.

I murmured softly to him, trying to soothe him and calm my own fears. "I'm so sorry. You're going to be fine. I won't let anything happen to you. It's gonna be okay, you have to be okay." I didn't realize I was crying until several tears slid from my cheeks onto Johnathan's face. He must have felt them land there as he forced his eyes open and tried a weak smile that was more of a grimace.

"Nothin' to be sorry about, Paige-girl. Not your fault... You're so beautiful, Paige... so beautiful. I think I might be in love with you... so-o beautiful..." His eyes closed again and his breathing returned to normal. The painful contortion of his face finally relaxed, and he fell asleep.

I, of course, was speechless. My mouth fell open, and I sat frozen in place. *Did he just say he loves me? The pain must be causing him to lose his mind—he usually acts like I'm just another one of the guys.* My frozen state was broken by Alec's laughter.

"Bahahahaha! You should see your face! I can't believe you didn't know he's got it for you—he stares at you all the time when he thinks no one's looking!" Alec sure got a big laugh out of my apparent naiveté.

I closed my mouth, cleared my throat and cast my eyes down to look upon Johnathan's glorious face.

"He's delirious," I said, without looking up, "He has no idea what he's saying." I touched his face again. "He's burning up."

"Whatever. His fever's just like a truth serum," Alec teased. *"John and Paige sittin' in a tree, k-i-s-s-i-n-g..."* the childish brat chanted.

I *really* wanted to be mad at him, but it was hard when it was all I could do not to smile. "Shut up, *Alice*." The new nickname didn't seem to bother him one bit. "Johnathan is really sick. We need to figure out what that thing was and what we need to do to make him better. That was no normal changeling."

I let Johnathan's hand soak for a good thirty minutes before I put antibiotic ointment on it and wrapped it in clean bandages with supplies we'd found in our last batch of food from Joe's *garbage*. I had Seth and Alec help me move Johnathan over to his sleeping bag, then I sat next to him.

I moved my gaze down to look at the pentacle drawn on the floor.

I shivered as the vision of the changeling biting Johnathan came to my mind. I gently touched his face and remembered his scream. I cursed myself for not questioning the Faerie before we sent her back to the Netherworld.

I stayed awake all night just to make sure Johnathan continued to breathe.

When he awoke the next afternoon, Johnathan seemed mostly normal except for a slightly swollen hand and a lingering low-grade fever. Either he didn't remember what he'd said to me in the throes of agony and brain-frying high temperature, or he was *pretending* like he didn't remember in order to save face. Either way, I was glad he didn't mention it because I had no idea what I'd say if he did. I'd loved him almost since day one, but I wasn't ready to reveal that to him. I'd already threatened to turn Alec into a toad if he said a word about Johnathan's sick-bed ramblings. There are some advantages to being magical.

We decided to forego our routine patrols until we were sure Johnathan was okay.

CHAPTER FIVE

Not a lot occurred during the week after the changeling incident. We patrolled as usual once we were sure Johnathan was okay. We did save a young girl, maybe eight years old, from a Troll that wouldn't let her cross a bridge. Yes, Trolls did sometimes live under bridges, just like in fairy tales. Most fairy tales *were* based on true events. And, even though most humans were unaware of the dark and evil things out there, they were there, lurking just beyond their awareness—the chill that ran down one's back, even in a warm room or on a hot summer day; the sudden feeling of fear after turning out the light that caused a person to run across the room and dive for the bed, for the safety of the covers; that strong sense of uneasiness that quickened one's step when walking home after dark. In those times, when that feeling of being watched just wouldn't go away—even in the safe confines of one's own home, darkness and evil lurked close by.

We'd begun perusing the local papers for anything that seemed out of sorts. Seth perked up, then waved a hand in the air as if signaling a teacher.

"I've got something, you guys. Listen to this." Seth cleared his throat. "'Suicide Rate at Edwards High School Skyrockets,'" he began. "'The Seattle School District reported today that there has been a sharp rise in suicides among adolescents attending Edwards High School. Edwards has a student body of just over 1,800 and is known for its strong academic focus and stellar sports programs. But, over the last three weeks, seven of its students, five boys and two girls, have killed themselves in violent manners, including gunshots to the head, jumping from an overpass, jumping in front of a train, and a wrist-slashing that was so deep it was almost an amputation of the hand.'"

"Oh, wow," Halli whispered.

Seth grimaced, then continued. "'Principal Brand Jorgenson is clueless as to what could have brought this horror to his school. He said in a comment to the press: 'The suicides of seven of our students is beyond tragic. We are all completely devastated. The school is taking this very seriously and the district has dispatched every available counselor to Edwards to speak with each student individually about the suicides and to assess each student for possible suicidal thoughts. We can find no connections between these seven students; they are of varying ages and our investigation has turned up nothing to link them to each other. Our thoughts and prayers are with the families and friends of the victims.'"

The rest of the article contained statistics on teen suicide, signs to watch for, and the numbers for local suicide prevention hotlines. We sat in stunned silence for a few minutes.

"There is definitely something going on there," Johnathan stated, breaking up our shared silence. "I think we should go take a look around that school."

"What are we going to look for?" I asked.

"I'm not sure. I just think we need to go there and check things out, see if we get any unusual feelings from the place. I think we should go now, but not all of us need to go."

"I'll go with you," I volunteered, then added, "why don't the rest of you stay here and get some sleep? We'll buzz you if we need help." I know the others were probably thinking I volunteered only so I could be alone with Johnathan, and they were partly right. Okay, mostly right. But, I also cared about whether or not they got enough sleep, and we had walked a long way on patrol that evening. It was close to three a.m.

Alec smirked knowingly, but before he could open his big mouth, Johnathan said, "That's a good idea. Halli's already asleep..."

"No 'm not," she mumbled from her curled-up position on top of her sleeping bag.

"Okay, sorry. Halli is *almost* asleep, and you two look like you're exhausted. Paige and I can handle this one. We won't be long. Like I said, I just want to get a feel for the place."

Alec just couldn't pass up this opportunity. "I know what you really want to get a *feel* for..." he said, a little under his breath. Then, he looked at me, smiled and winked.

I started to reach for my channeling rod. I thought, *toad*. A big, ugly, green toad with warts all over its body. I had no idea whether or not it was possible to change someone into a toad, but I was willing to test it out on Alec. Johnathan stepped between us, however, and gave Alec a light smack to the side of his head.

"Go to sleep, Alice. Put up the wards behind us. We'll take them down when we get back."

My heart fluttered when he turned to me with a cute smile, dimple creased cheeks and full lips pulled across his snow white, slightly crooked teeth.

Johnathan shook his head. "Let's go, Paige."

My heart nearly beat out of my chest when he put his hand on the small of my back as we turned to go out the broken-down doorway of the condemned shop we were staying in that night. His hand felt so warm... and so *right*. I leaned in a little, so our sides touched. I'd never dared act upon my feelings for him. I was never sure how he felt about me. He was always nice and gentle, but had never really made any advances toward me. Unless you counted his confession of love after the changeling bit him. I didn't think that counted, though. I still wasn't sure if the hand to my back was just him being nice, or if it meant he really had feelings for me. I was just happy to be alone with him.

We headed out toward Edwards High School, which was clear across the city from where we were. The walk would be very long, which made me smile. I almost cried when he moved his hand from my back to conjure up a *star-bright* so we could see our way to the nearest exit from the Underground.

Johnathan extinguished the light just before we sneaked through the abandoned building at street level. For the first time since we'd met, he reached to hold my hand. My pulse quickened and my palms broke out in instant sweat. I looked down at my feet to make sure they were still in contact with the ground—it sure felt like I was floating. I could not keep the smile off my face as we walked hand in hand, fingers entwined, through the lamp-lit streets of Seattle. Butterflies sprang to life in my stomach. Johnathan stopped and looked down at me.

"Is this okay? That I hold your hand?"

I swallowed. He bit at his bottom lip. Was he really so clueless as to think it might *not* be okay with me? I really did try to answer him verbally, but the words stuck in my throat, so I just smiled, nodded, and squeezed his hand tighter. He must have understood my voiceless reply because he let out a relieved breath and smiled back at me. Ooh. That smile did things to me. And the butterflies. His dimples were like a super-mega jolt of caffeine to those puppies.

The warmth of his hand and how perfectly mine fit with his made me forget about the ache in my feet during the long walk. We actually talked about things other than fighting Demons and stuff.

"What would you eat if you could have anything you wanted right now?" Johnathan asked.

"Steak, and crab legs, and garlic mashed potatoes. What about you? What would you eat?"

"Hmm… steak, definitely. I'm not so sure about crab legs, though. I'd have to go with fried shrimp, and a baked potato with tons of butter and sour cream."

We laughed about not being able to watch movies or use cell phones or other electronic gadgets because there was something about magical powers that seriously messed with newer technology.

Before I knew it, we were standing in front of Edwards High School. The darkness was thicker around the school—most of the outside lighting was turned off, or just wasn't working. Johnathan let go of my hand to fish his channeling rod out of his belt. I grabbed mine, too. We didn't necessarily *creep* toward the school, but we did step carefully. The closer we drew, the more uneasy I started to feel. My stomach dropped when I looked over at the school's marquee and saw a giant pile of flowers, posters, notes, and stuffed animals in a makeshift memorial to the students who had killed themselves.

We tried the front doors first. They were locked tight and we couldn't see any lights on inside the school. That seemed a little odd. Didn't they usually leave a couple of lights on even when no one was there? We made our way around the side of the school, trying each door as we went, and peering into windows for any signs of… I'm not sure what signs we were looking for, really. My main goal was to stay close to Johnathan.

We reached the back of the building, where there was a fenced-in area for the metal shop supplies. It looked more like a prison yard than a school, though. The chain-link fence was reinforced with barbed wire spiraling across the top; three chains with heavy-duty locks kept the large gates closed. Johnathan aimed his *star-bright* through the fence and gave it an extra dose of his will to make it shine further. Nothing there seemed out of place; all we saw were just the usual oxygen tanks for welding, scrap metal and sheets of metal, various tools, and half-finished projects.

Johnathan's light fell on a couple of metal tanks hooked together with coils and wires. It resembled something from a chemistry set—on a much larger scale. There were also some glass beakers attached to one side and some sort of carvings around the base of the entire contraption, carved into the metal there. Beneath it all, stood a couple of big propane tanks hooked up to some heavy-duty burners to heat whatever was in the metal tanks.

"Wow. What is it?" I turned my head sideways to observe it from a different angle. "I'm trying to picture what experiments you would do with beakers and Brunson burners that big. Imagine the damage an overzealous freshman could do with a lab gone terribly wrong."

"We need to get a closer look at that thing," Johnathan whispered. "It doesn't look like something that should be at a high school. And those carvings around the base look like runes. Did you ever master that unlocking spell?"

I looked at the locks and bit my lip. "I mastered it on the simple lock I practiced on. I'll give it a try."

I put my channeling rod back in my belt, placed my right hand on the first lock, and concentrated with all my might. The delicate spell involved telekinetically moving the inside locking mechanisms in the correct sequence to align them so the lock would open. It wasn't necessary to know the inner workings of the lock—that would make it impossible, since every lock was a little different than the last. I just needed to know what it felt like to have the mechanisms align.

So, I concentrated while Johnathan stood lookout. I was surprised to find that this lock wasn't as complicated as it'd looked. I felt the mechanisms slide into place after only a couple of minutes of intense focus, and the lock came open in my hand. One down and two to go.

The other two locks were just as simple. It was well worth my effort when Johnathan gave me a quick, celebratory hug before he pulled the chains free from the gate and pushed it open.

He knelt beside the odd contraption we'd spied from outside the fence. The carvings around the base were definitely runes of some sort. The tanks each had a large rune carved into the side that faced away from the gate. The thing had a definite feel of Dark Magic about it. And it made me nauseous.

My heart leapt into my throat when I heard the faint echo of footsteps coming from inside the building. Johnathan apparently heard them, too, because he turned to me and put his finger to his lips. He really didn't need to; I don't think my voice box was working at that moment anyway. The door leading out into the lot from the school creaked open, and a man's voice drifted out. Luckily, we stood on the opposite side of the contraption and our legs were mostly hidden by the propane tanks. There was no way we could have made a run for it without being seen, as the gate was directly across from the door where the voice was coming from. So, we just stood as still as statues, barely daring to breathe, straining to hear what was being said.

"I know we don't need the publicity, Mr. J., I'm not an idiot! We're working on tweaking the formula again… I know, Mr. J…. We will! As far as the media knows, there've been seven suicides and that's all they will ever know about. We'll take care of the other parents, don't worry." The man took a couple steps toward us. Johnathan reached for my hand and slid his channeling rod back out with the other.

"Now? Are you kidding me? I really need to check on this new formula. Okay, okay! I'm on my way." He hung up the phone and cursed before turning back into the school and slamming the door behind him.

I let out the breath I'd been holding. Johnathan squeezed my hand. We stood still for another minute just to make sure the coast was clear. After Johnathan chained and locked the gate as quietly as he could, we left the way we'd come.

The walk home was a somber one. Johnathan was lost deep in thought. He continued to hold my hand; this time he played with my fingers absently while he thought—no doubt planning our next move.

Dawn was breaking when we ducked into the abandoned stairwell that led back to our hideout. Johnathan stopped just before we reached the doorway behind which the others were most likely still sleeping. He turned to face me, then put his hands on my shoulders.

His gentle grip was warm and strong. I looked up into his dark eyes, so soft and tender as he looked into mine.

"Other than almost getting caught snooping around tonight, I really enjoyed being alone with you for once. I'd like to take you on a *real* date someday... soon, if that's okay with you?"

I smiled. I couldn't help it. I was definitely in love with him. I'd been waiting to hear something like this from him since the very beginning.

"That would be wonderful, John. Say the word, and I'm there."

When you'd waited this long for a boy to ask you out, you didn't waste time playing hard-to-get. And, we didn't exactly lead normal teenage lives. So something normal like a date sounded amazing.

Johnathan smiled and his eyes lit up. *Wow, he is SO hot!* His hands on my shoulders tightened. His smile faded slightly and he licked his lips, making me think—hope—that he was going to lean in for a kiss, but, he didn't. He smiled again instead, and then turned to take down the wards so we could safely go inside our home-of-the-week.

I fell to my sleeping bag, exhausted, and drifted to sleep with a smile on my face.

CHAPTER SIX

Seth reminded us that it was again time for a full moon. The supernatural world always seemed to kick it up a notch during a full moon. Thankfully, they came only once a month. Okay, twice a month, once in a while—that would be the *blue moon* so often talked about.

Johnathan and I slept only a few hours after our adventure to Edwards High; our three companions couldn't seem to keep quiet after they all woke up. It was late morning/early afternoon when I dragged myself out of my sleeping bag and showered in our makeshift bathroom. Seth was great at tinkering with things like water pipes. He almost always managed to tap into a functioning water pipe in the ceiling, below the main floor of the buildings on top of us, in order for us to have some sort of running water. It was easy enough to heat the pipe with a spell for a semi-warm shower.

I dressed in my clean set of clothes and carried the dirty ones out to my corner. It was a strict rule that everyone be fully clothed when in front of the others. That meant we undressed in the confines of the designated bathroom and carried our clean clothes in with us so we could re-dress before going back out. The rule was necessary, thanks to Alec. He used to love to parade around in his boxers. Johnathan put a stop to that when he saw how uncomfortable it made me.

I joined the others in a corner of the room where we could all sit on the floor with our backs against a wall. Johnathan had already briefed them on what we'd found and overheard.

"Well, there's something going on there for sure. What's our next step?" Alec asked.

"I've been thinking about it all morning," Johnathan said. "I think we need to go undercover for this one. Any ideas how we can get into high school without parents to sign for us?"

I thought Seth was going to choke on his own spit.

"You want us to go to school? Like, *students?*" he asked.

"Well… yeah. That *is* what I was thinking. Do you have a better idea of how we can find out what's going on there? We *are* teenagers, you know. We'll fit in."

"I know we're teenagers, Johnathan. It's just that… well… it's been a while since any of us were in school. I'm having flashbacks right now of the entire computer lab going up in smoke when I tried to turn a computer on. And lights flickering out anytime I got too near. The office could never make an announcement over the intercom when I was within ten feet of it." Seth shivered.

He was being a little dramatic, if you asked me.

"Yeah, I've thought about that, too," answered Johnathan. "We'll just have to be very careful about the classes we pick. No computer classes, obviously, or anything else that might include technology."

I joined in the conversation. "I see a couple of obstacles to this plan. You already mentioned the parent thing. Even if we could get around that, wouldn't we need our records from a previous school?"

47

"I don't think it would be too hard to get our hands on some records," Johnathan said. "We don't *all* have to do this, although it would be best if we did. We could spread out that way and maybe find out what's going on quicker. I'm going to spend a couple hours working on this. Alec, you come with me in case I need backup. Paige, you, Seth and Halli see if you can find us a new place for tonight. We've been here for a week now. It's time to move."

Yes, I was disappointed he didn't ask me to be his backup. We *did* need a new hideout, though, and I was usually in charge of that.

With that, our meeting abruptly ended. We got our stuff ready to move, something we were very good at because, one, we had very little stuff, and, two, we moved around so often.

We left our belongings there, no sense in carrying them around with us while we looked. Johnathan and Alec headed up to the ground level street. Seth, Halli and I followed a sidewalk in a direction I hadn't been before, deeper into the condemned area of the Underground. Most of the buildings here were dangerous-looking, with broken columns and bricks falling down. Seth crawled inside a broken doorway half-covered with debris.

"Seth! What are you doing? You're going to get squashed in there!" I yelled.

"It'll be fine." *He always says that.* "I just want to see what's in here."

I saw the faint glow of the *star-bright* he'd conjured up in his hand through the fallen boards and bricks.

I stood there with Halli, tapping my foot in frustration.

"He's such a pain," Halli said, rolling her eyes.

"Yes, he is. If he gets pinned under falling debris in there, I'm just going to leave him."

As if on cue, something crashed inside the room Seth was exploring. I bent down and peered through the small opening he'd crawled through.

"Seth? Are you okay?"

All I could see was a cloud of dust. I started to panic. I liked Seth. I would never *really* have left him in a pile of rubble.

"Seth! I'm coming in! Halli, stay here."

She started to protest, but I gave her *the look*—I learned that from my mom—and she folded her arms and leaned against a post with a huff of annoyance.

"This is awesome!" I heard Seth exclaim, much fainter than before. He sounded a mile away.

I breathed a sigh of relief. "What in the world are you doing? Are you okay?"

"I'm fine! I just found some stairs—accidentally. They were covered with some boards and I kinda fell through them. You've gotta come see this, Paige!"

I looked at Halli, unsure of what to do.

"Let's just both go see what he found," she said. And, with that, she ducked into the crumbling doorway.

"Ugh!" I followed behind Halli.

She'd already conjured a *star-bright* and held her hand out in front of her with the glowing star of blue light. "Seth? Where are you?" she asked.

"Come straight back from the entrance, but be careful. Watch for the floor to disappear," Seth answered.

We stepped carefully over broken chairs, fallen bricks, and other such garbage. Halli angled the light at the floor. She stopped abruptly and I almost ran into the back of her. I peeked over her head and saw why she'd stopped. There, in the floor, was a stairwell. I shook my head. I'd thought we were down as far as anything went in the city of Seattle without being under water. But there they were, a bunch of stairs.

Halli hesitated only a split second before starting down the stairs. I waited until she reached the bottom before following. I didn't want to risk too much weight on the rickety steps. I conjured up my own *star-bright*, hoping not to fall and break my neck.

But the stairs were quite sturdy, which was surprising, given the condition of the room above. I descended to the bottom and looked around, and, well… Seth was right. It was awesome.

My guess is the enormous room surrounding us was once an illegal gambling hall hidden beneath a legitimate business. Seth had likely fallen through what was left of the secret trap door. The room was in surprisingly good shape—the best of any of the buildings I'd seen in the Underground. There were plenty of usable chairs and tables that looked fine other than a huge layer of dust and rat droppings. It wasn't very often we found even one usable chair down there. On the far side of the room, a dirty, but probably beautiful, dark wood bar spanned at least twenty feet along one wall. The glass shelves behind the bar were all shattered, but part of a mirror was intact.

Reinforced with multiple support columns and huge ceiling beams, the building's frame gave me confidence in its structural soundness. There were small chandeliers with dangling crystals hanging from the ceiling, covered in dust and cobwebs, but otherwise fine. This was the perfect hideout for us. I'd been looking for a place like this, somewhere the five of us could stay more permanently. The entrance upstairs was so dilapidated that no one—except Seth—would even think about entering there. Plus, we would make it look like something besides an entrance anyway, with our wards.

I couldn't help myself. I hugged Seth. Hard.

A huge grin formed on Halli's freckled pixie face as the realization of what I was thinking dawned on her.

"We can stay here, can't we?" she asked.

We all acted like we didn't mind moving around so much, but everyone wants a secure place to stay, a place to call home. I was sure we'd found that.

"I think so, Hal. We'll have to run it by Alec and Johnathan first, but I think it's wonderful!"

"Good. Let's go get our stuff, then," Seth said, smiling from ear to ear.

A few hours later, after we'd hauled our meager belongings to our new hideout, I sent Seth back to wait for Johnathan and Alec, so he could show them where we were. Halli and I set to cleaning, which was something we usually didn't bother with when we moved. What was the point if we were just leaving in a few days? The most amazing thing was that we actually had running water! I guess an illegal gambling hall, hidden from the authorities, had just been hooked into someone else's water line and it had never been shut off. We found scraps of cloth and set to work straightening chairs and tables and cleaning all the dust off them. The worst part was cleaning up the rat droppings—and hearing the scuttling of the vile rodents in the walls.

It wasn't too long before we heard footsteps above. And then voices.

"Seth, what in the world could possibly be in *here* that you are so excited to show us?" Alec asked.

"Just wait. You won't believe this!"

"It really doesn't look safe," Johnathan said, his voice wary. "I thought you said the girls were here. Where are they?"

I heard the guys stop at the opening to the stairwell.

"Ta da! They're down there!" An image of Seth gesturing grandly down the stairs passed through my mind.

No one moved for a moment, and then Seth said, "I guess I'll go first... sissies."

He clopped down the steps as only boys can do. Halli and I stood a little ways from the base. I couldn't wait to see Johnathan's face at the sight of this place. Johnathan stepped down into the room after Seth. He stopped, eyes widening as he took it all in. Alec pushed him out of the way so he could step off the bottom step and come all the way in.

Never one for speechlessness, Alec said, "This place is too cool! Wow! Good job, Seth." He took off to inspect the bar.

"Well, what do you think, John?" I asked.

"It's amazing. Do you think it's safe?"

"It seems to be. The supports are stronger than any we've seen down here before. I think it was built to resist an earthquake! Oh, and the best thing, even better than having actual chairs to sit on? Wait for it... wait for it... *running water!*" I was unable to contain my excitement. The boys were great about rigging water pipes for our use. But, having a real sink with working pipes made it seem almost like a real home.

"Seriously?" He was awed by my proclamation.

I just smiled, grabbed his hand and led him over to the sink behind the bar where I turned the rusty faucet and, voilà! Running water!

He squeezed my hand and smiled down at me. "This is amazing. We might actually be able to stay here a while."

"That's what I was thinking," I said. "It's structurally safe, it's well hidden, it's huge. There's even a gas stove and a small ice box here behind the bar. Hey, wouldn't it be perfect if there was actually a flushing toilet, too?"

"Do you think... that's possible? Did you look for one?"

"No, not yet. It's been so long since I've had that luxury I didn't even think to look until now. Could you imagine? No more *buckets?*" I said dreamily.

Halli must've heard our conversation because she dropped her rag and ran to look for a bathroom. Johnathan and I stayed where we were. I was really enjoying his warm hand holding mine and he must have felt the same way because he made no move to let go.

The distinct sound of a toilet flushing preceded Halli's "Woo hoo!" from a doorway half the distance across the room from the bar.

Johnathan laughed. I laughed. Lost in relaxed laughter, and surrounded by the comfort of the first place we'd been able to call home in a long time, Johnathan's grip on my hand tightened and he pulled me to him. My breath caught in my throat as he wrapped his arms around my waist, then lifted me up and squeezed me tightly. His unrestrained joy and his arms wrapped around me so perfectly were my idea of heaven. He so rarely laughed, and we'd had so few moments of this kind of closeness.

I could have kissed Seth! On the cheek, of course. My first real kiss was saved for Johnathan. And every real kiss after that, too.

We spent the next couple of hours cleaning up, picking out our areas, and organizing our possessions. We checked out the stove and found that one of the burners still had gas piped to it. We discussed the plausibility of keeping the ice box supplied with enough ice to keep food cold, and decided it would be difficult at best. Halli came up with a brilliant solution. She gathered a few bricks, cast a freezing spell on them, and put them in the ice box. We wondered if they might actually stay cold in there for two or three days before we had to zap them again. Only time would tell.

Seth constructed a trap door over the stairs using broken boards from the room above. Meanwhile, Johnathan and Alec filled us in on what they'd found out on their information-gathering expedition.

"Some of us can register as siblings, stating we're homeless. They can't require past records that way," Johnathan explained. "But, I think it would be suspicious if we all did that. As homeless students, we don't even need a parent or guardian to sign for us. We asked a worker at a homeless shelter and she gave us a copy of the McKinney-Vento Act that says, basically, that schools have to register homeless kids even if they don't have a parent to sign for them, or past school records, or proof of immunizations.

"As for those of us who won't be registering as homeless, we talked to a couple of *document specialists* some thugs pointed us to. They said making fake school records wasn't a problem... the problem is their asking price for doing so."

"Yeah, I don't know where we would come up with that kind of money," Alec added. "They wanted like a hundred bucks per person!"

"I can probably get my real records," Seth said in a hushed voice.

We all looked at him.

Finally, I broke the silence. "How?"

"Well, don't be mad, 'kay? I sometimes contact my family." We all sat in stunned silence. "They understand why I had to leave and they'll do what they can to help us. I'll have my mom mail them to our grocer friend. I might even be able to have her send my sister's records for Paige."

"Okay. Perfect. Thank you, Seth," Johnathan said. I think we were all a little jealous that Seth's parents understood and supported him as best they could. "One more thing, though." Johnathan added as he turned to Halli. "You aren't going to be able to join us at the school, Hal. You're too young and look even younger than you are. But, we'll find something for you to do to help, don't worry."

Halli's face fell; some of the sparkle left her eyes. "I kind of figured

I wouldn't quite fit in as a high-schooler. I'll help however I can, though."

"Thanks, Hal. Okay, since Paige will hopefully be using Seth's sister's records, you guys'll need to act as siblings. We'll just need to find a parent to sign for you. Alec and I will be brothers. We won't need records if we play homeless... and we *are* homeless. They'll probably just test us for placement. I'll go talk to Joe tomorrow to see if he can play dad for Paige and Seth." Johnathan wiped at the sweat beading on his forehead. "I'm feeling kind of funny today."

"Funny how?" I asked.

"I'm not sure how to describe it. I feel a little shut-in, like I need to be outside. I'm just a little sick to my stomach, too. I'm sure it'll pass soon. It's nothing, really."

I wasn't reassured. For the first time in a couple of days, I thought about the bite he'd received.

"Let me see your hand, John," I demanded.

He bunched his eyebrows, surprised, as though he hadn't thought about his hand wound for a while either. He held his hand out to me. It looked the same as it had a couple of days ago. My concern deepened when his hand started shaking. He pulled it back quickly, probably hoping I hadn't noticed the tremors.

"See? It's fine, Paige." He smiled but his eyes showed worry.

"Johnathan, hold both hands out."

Eyes rolling, he held his hands out to me, palms down. They both shook. He closed them into fists and shrugged. "It's just because I haven't eaten today. Don't be such a worrywart."

"I *am* worried about you. I'm going to get you some food. You stay put." Yeah, I could be bossy at times.

I made him a peanut butter and jelly sandwich and brought him our last can of lemon-lime soda. He ate it all. He chewed each bite for too long and swallowed like he was forcing it down—like he had no appetite at all.

We cleaned up a little more. Halli and I focused on scrubbing the bathroom, while Seth looked for a way to rig up a shower in a back room that had probably been used for storage at one point.

Late in the afternoon, we all gathered at a table near the bar. Johnathan's face was pale, with small beads of sweat on his forehead.

"I really need to get out of here for a while," he said. "I didn't plan on patrolling tonight, but I'm thinking maybe Seth and I should go try to contact his family. The sooner we get those records, the sooner we can figure out what's happening at that school, and hopefully prevent any more so-called suicides."

"Johnny, you aren't looking so good, bud," Alec said. He was the only one that called him Johnny. Johnathan hated it.

"I'm fine, *Alice*," Johnathan said, a little defensively.

"Okay, whatever, man."

I knew I wouldn't be able to talk him out of going, so I just said, "I'm going with you. I could use an evening stroll."

Alec and Halli wanted to come, too, so we gathered our gear belts, set our wards, and headed for aboveground.

CHAPTER SEVEN

We walked the two or so miles to Frink Park, where Seth had found an old pay-phone with rotary dial—and he'd apparently been able to use it before without it going up in smoke and flames, although it had crackled a lot and cut him off before he was done.

He called his parents collect. He was able to convince his mom to send the records we needed. He didn't tell her exactly what we needed them for, but assured her it was for a good cause.

We decided to hang out at the park for a while before starting the walk back to our new home. This was one of our favorite parks. The seventeen acres gave us plenty of room to roam. It had a creek, wooded areas and hiking trails. We walked a little ways down a trail and stopped in a small clearing. In the center of the open space, a fire pit sat surrounded by a couple of benches made out of large logs. Johnathan stumbled up to a bench, and fell more than sat onto it. He was no longer pale; instead, his skin was flushed a dark red. He had rivulets of sweat pouring down his face and the hand tremors appeared to have extended to the rest of his body while intensifying tenfold.

I rushed over and sat next to him. I took one of his hands in mine; it was burning hot. I wiped the sweat from his brow, which was, unbelievably, hotter than his hands. "Johnathan! Oh my gosh, you're burning up! Are you okay?" Dumb question, since he was obviously *not* okay, but I was near panic.

"I don't know. I'm really dizzy and everything hurts. I feel like my skin is crawling. Something's not right, Paige." He looked at me with a desperation and fear I'd never seen before. Not from anyone, but especially not from my brave Johnathan. I was really scared.

The others gathered around us, concern written all over their faces, too. "What should we do?" Alec asked me.

"I... I don't know. We need to cool him off. See if you can find something to bring some water from the creek in." My voice shook. It was cool outside already and about to become even cooler since the sun was getting ready to set. Johnathan was shaking uncontrollably. "John, maybe you should lay down."

He gripped my hand with bone-crushing strength and I saw through the tears in my eyes that his other hand gripped the bench with equal intensity. His fevered eyes widened in terror. I could see his muscles *undulating* unnaturally beneath his skin.

"Paige... lock me in a circle. Do it now!"

"What...?" I hesitated.

"Now, Paige!"

I jumped up and looked for a place to draw a pentacle. The fire pit was surrounded by cement. I took out my chalk and drew a circle as big as I could in the limited space. I carefully and quickly drew the pentagram. As soon as my chalk made the last mark of the pentagram, Johnathan surged forward into the circle.

"Close it!" he choked out in a growling voice.

My heart raced and my hands shook uncontrollably. My mouth went dry as I tried to swallow. His eyes had turned a frightening yellow-gold color and his pupils dilated and constricted at a dizzying pace. I dug in my belt for a straight pin and almost dropped it before pricking my finger to draw a drop of blood to close the circle with. Halli stood nearby, and joined her power to mine to give the spell added strength.

The circle closed just as Alec and Seth came running down the trail.

"What are you doing?" Alec yelled, grabbing me by the arm.

"He wanted me to!" I yelled back, ripping my arm free and turning to face him.

"You guys, stop!" Halli yelled. "Look at Johnathan!"

We whirled toward him. Johnathan was in the throes of agony. His body doubled over, bent almost in half. And... he was *changing*. We stood watching, speechless, as Johnathan's humanlike screams turned to animalistic howls of pain and rage. His body contorted again, and he bent to all fours like a dog, except his arms were longer than his legs. His bones shifted shapes, stretching his skin taut to the point I thought he'd rip right through it. Black furry hair sprouted in thick patches over his body. His already large muscles grew to enormous proportions, ripping his T-shirt. Claws erupted from his hands and feet, ripping through his tennis shoes. His teeth lengthened and multiplied and his face elongated into the shape of a deformed wolf. He snarled and then looked up at the now-risen full moon and howled in rage and lustful yearning.

"Someone's gonna hear him. We need to put up some wards." Halli, always the voice of reason.

I couldn't move. The others set about putting wards up around our small clearing. I backed to the bench Johnathan and I had been sitting on just moments before and sat down hard. *This is my fault. The changeling did this to him.* Tears streamed down my face. I started to hyperventilate as the animal Johnathan had become screeched and howled and started to pound on the barrier that enclosed him. Each time a part of his body touched the invisible force field, a bolt of sheer blue power shot out from that spot.

Seth and Halli sat next to me, Seth's arm around my shoulders. Alec knelt in front of me.

"Paige, slow down your breathing, you're going to pass out," Halli said gently.

I tore my gaze from the awful sight before us and sought solace in Halli's eyes. She reached for my hands and squeezed them. "Breathe with me, Paige."

I followed her pattern of breathing slowly, in through my nose and out through my mouth. It helped stop the numbness that had started around my lips, but did nothing to slow the sobs that now escaped my throat.

We sat that way, huddled together in silence, for several minutes. We stared at our leader, now reduced to a howling, slobbering monster. He began to claw at his face. Streaks of blood spilled from each rip of his skin, but his claws relentlessly continued to dig.

"Johnathan, no!" I screamed. I ran to the circle and begged with the Johnathan-creature. "John, stop! You're hurting yourself! Please stop!" My hands clutched at my chest as the pressure built inside, ready to explode.

My pleading aroused his bestial instincts to a fever pitch. He redoubled his efforts to escape the circle. His yellow eyes watched me, unblinking, unwavering. He licked his lips. Drool dripped from his jowls. Fear shot through me like rivers of ice through my veins. Animal instinct kicked in, my fight or flight mechanism urging me to flee. I shuddered and retreated into the trees. I fell to the ground and screamed in anger and fear; my arms covering my head and ears.

Hours later, Halli coaxed me out of the woods. Arm in arm, we walked back to the clearing, where Seth had started a fire in the pit to keep us warm and give us some light. The creature that had been Johnathan didn't stop his screeching, or his howling attempts to escape until just before dawn. The moon fell in the sky and we could see the light of the sun as it started to light up the clouds to the east. He curled up on the ground into a fetal position and just rocked back and forth. A pathetic mewling sound escaped his throat.

Before the sun had fully risen, Johnathan transformed back into himself, his ripped clothing barely covering his body. He lay there, trembling, and my heart ached for him. For me. For us.

I broke the circle and laid my black pea coat over him. We all wore longer coats or jackets of some sort to hide our gear belts. I knelt next to him and reached to brush his hair out of his eyes. He flinched, closing his eyes tighter, then pulled my coat over his head.

I laid my hand on his shoulder. The trembling soon turned to sobs. After about five minutes of hearing his sobs and forcing myself not to cry, I pulled my coat back from his face.

"Look at me, Johnathan," I said, tender but stern.

He didn't try to pull the coat back over his face as I dabbed with my sleeve at his cheeks streaked with a combination of tears and blood. He kept his eyes closed.

"Johnathan, look at me," I repeated.

He drew in a breath, then exhaled sharply. He swallowed hard and opened his eyes, looking into mine. I almost couldn't stand the shame and sorrow I saw there.

"John," I pressed on, my voice surprisingly unwavering. "I will find a way to fix this, I promise. This is my fault. I'm so, so sorry. I *will* find a way to fix it."

Johnathan shook his head and sat up slowly. He took my hand in both of his and stared at them as he spoke. "This is *not* your fault. What... what *happened* last night? It's all a blur."

I didn't want to tell him, to remind him, about the last eight hours or so. But he'd asked. And, maybe, he would know some answers. "You... you... *changed,* John. You yelled for me to lock you in a circle, so I did, and then you changed into... *something.*"

"What?"

"I don't know. Like a half-man, half-wolf... *thing*. You were very angry and clawed at your face and arms in frustration. I... I think you would have hurt us... and others... if we'd let you out. I'm sorry, Johnathan." I'd been trying to hold back tears for his sake, but the memory of the creature full of rage tipped the scales and a few tears escaped and ran down my face.

"Please don't cry, Paige. You did exactly the right thing. I could never forgive myself if I hurt one of you, or anyone else for that matter. I don't know what's happening. I think I need to go see Madame LaForte. She might know what's going on and how to reverse it."

He stood, as if he meant to go visit the old psychic right that minute. "Johnathan," I said. "Let's get you home and cleaned up, first. Then, I'll go with you to see her."

He looked down at himself, seeing for the first time his torn and ravaged clothing, his bare feet, and the wicked, self-inflicted scratches. He was dirty and blood-streaked. "I can't walk through the city looking like this, can I?"

"No, you can't," Halli said. "Let's go to the creek and clean you up a little. You can wear Alec's jacket, but I have no idea what to do about shoes. Yours are torn to shreds."

"I'll just have to go barefoot." He stood up slowly, reminding me of an old man, and handed my coat back to me.

All five of us made our way to the creek, Johnathan stepping carefully in his bare feet. He stuck both hands in and splashed the cold water on his face and hair. He did the same to his arms, chest, and feet. Luckily, his pants had survived with only a few tears.

Alec's denim jacket was a little snug on the bigger Johnathan, but it didn't look too weird. The walk back to our Underground home was a quiet one and Johnathan's feet were raw by the time we reached it. He had an extra pair of shoes stashed away, shoes he'd found in a dumpster. They were bright blue and yellow high-tops. They looked ridiculous.

I tried to convince him to rest a little before going to see our psychic friend, but he was adamant that he was fine to go right then. He needed information. I understood. I wanted information, too, but, I was exhausted and I could only imagine how much more so he was. When I saw that I wouldn't be able to talk him into waiting, I insisted on going with him. The others wanted to go, too, but Johnathan told them all to stay, stating, "Stay here and get some rest. Madame LaForte will respond better if only two of us go."

There was no hand-holding or talk of dates on this outing. Johnathan barely spoke a word as we walked through the downtown lunchtime crowds to Madame LaForte's home. Johnathan knocked on the door and we heard a raspy voice yell, "Go away!"

"Madame LaForte, it's Johnathan and Paige. Could we please talk with you for just a moment?" Johnathan asked.

"Oh, *Johnathan*," she said in a softer tone. "Why didn't you say so? Just a minute, I'm coming."

The elderly psychic had a smile on her face when she opened the door. She *really* had a crush on Johnathan. "Come in, come in!" she said as she ushered us into the foyer. She shut and locked the door and then turned toward us. She laid her wrinkled hand on Johnathan's forearm to escort him into her sitting room... and she stiffened. She shrieked in disgust, *"You tricked me! You are not Johnathan! Get out! Get out! Get out!"*

Johnathan's face was a mask of shock, as I'm sure mine was. Madame LaForte backed away and held her pentacle necklace up in a defensive posture.

"Madame LaForte," I said. "What's wrong? This *is* Johnathan. We've done nothing to trick you."

She narrowed her eyes warily for a moment and then gestured me forward, "Come here, girl, slowly. *You* stay there," she shook an angry finger at Johnathan.

I went and stood in front of her. She gingerly touched my arm, and relaxed slightly. "Good," she said. "*You* are untainted... for now."

"What do you mean, *untainted?*" I asked. I wanted to add, *why are you being so weird?* But decided against it, since it was kind of a dumb question... she was always weird.

"He has been *turned*. I can feel the evil. He must leave my house. He cannot be here!" Her voice rose in pitch.

Johnathan held his hands up in a placating gesture and said, "Okay, Madame. I'll wait for Paige outside. Just, please, let her stay, we need some information."

"Fine. Leave."

It was up to me.

She turned to me when she was sure Johnathan was out of her house and said, "What happened to him? Tell me!"

I explained what happened with the changeling. Madame LaForte stood quietly and listened. As I described what had happened the night before, her eyes grew wide.

"Girl, I'm afraid your friend has been turned. Have ya heard of a *lycanthrope?*"

"No..."

"Very much like a Hollywood werewolf. His blood is tainted with evil."

"Okay. Then how do we fix it?" I asked. That was all I cared about.

She laughed a bitter laugh. "Fix it? You don't *fix it*," she said. "I know of no cure for this evil. If he's an honorable man, your friend will end his own life in order to spare the lives of his hundreds of potential victims. Including yourself."

I gasped at her harsh words. "He will do no such thing! I *will* find a cure if it's the last thing I do! There has to be a way!"

"Poor girl. If there is a way, no human knows it. Maybe the Fae people know of a way, but I doubt it. They would exact a harsh payment from you for any information anyway, harsher than most humans would be willing to pay. Death is his only cure, Paige. Death will bring peace for his tormented soul." She reached a comforting hand toward my arm. I jerked away, frustrated tears stinging my eyes.

"You're wrong." I said, and stormed from her house.

I didn't tell Johnathan about her suggestion for a *cure*. I did tell him the old woman didn't know of a cure but that she'd given me an idea of how to find one. When he pressed me for details, I said, "Just let me do this for you, John. You can't do it for yourself. Don't worry, I *will* find a way to help you."

The sky darkened as black clouds swept across it. The gloominess of the atmosphere matched that of my soul. We walked home in silence as rain poured down on us.

CHAPTER EIGHT

Johnathan went right to sleep as soon as we reached our new home. The night's activities had really worn him out. I, however, had a hard time falling asleep, even though I was exhausted. In my haste to find a cure and my subsequent anger at Madame LaForte's suggestion, I'd neglected to ask some important questions—like, how often will he change? And, when will he change again? Little things like that.

So, I tossed and turned for about an hour, then I gave up on sleeping for the day. I grabbed the white book and sat down at a table. I thumbed through the chapters on non-human beings, trying to remember the word Madame LaForte had used. *Likeand*-something. As I flipped quickly through the pages, a picture caught my eye. I backtracked, searching slower for the picture. I found it about five pages back—a drawing of a creature that looked very similar to how Johnathan had looked the night before. *Lycanthrope*, the caption read.

There was very little information. It basically said there were two ways to become a *lycanthrope*. One, it could be genetically handed down from father to son. Or two, a warlock is bitten by some form of *lycanthrope*—a warlock in the guise of a human, an Elf, or a Goblin. Even Giants weren't immune to the evil poison of a bite. The *change* took place only during a full moon. That was good; it meant I had a full month to find a cure. Oh, and there was no known cure. I latched onto the word *known* because that left the possibility there was a cure, but the people who wrote the book just didn't know what it was.

I laid my head on the table, cradled by my folded arms. I fell asleep thinking of what I should do.

I was awakened quite abruptly by a nightmare. It started out nicely. Johnathan and I were on a date at a fancy restaurant. I sat across the table from him and we held hands, lost in each other's eyes. The waiter brought our food and set mine in front of me—a perfectly cooked medium steak and an abundance of crab legs. Then he set Johnathan's plate down, and I gagged. Johnathan's steak was raw; fresh blood dripped off the plate. His nostrils flared, canine-like. He changed in an instant. He became the long-toothed *lycanthrope* and gulped down the raw meat in one mouthful, plate and all. Then he looked up at me with a wolfish gleam in his yellow-gold eyes. I awoke, screaming, as he lunged across the table at me.

More a startled yell, really. That wasn't even the embarrassing part; the embarrassing part was when I flung myself backward and tipped over in my chair. Alec laughed much longer than was necessary. Seth, bless his heart, tried not to laugh, but couldn't hold it in once he saw that I was okay. Halli was the only one that showed compassion. She ran over from where she'd been sweeping up some glass behind the bar and said, "Are you okay, Paige? Did you have a bad dream?"

"I'm fine, Hal," I said as I pulled myself up off the floor and put the chair back in its place. "And, yes, I did have a bad dream. I guess I shouldn't fall asleep sitting up." I punched the still-laughing Alec in the arm as I walked past him. I glanced over at Johnathan's sleeping bag. He hadn't even stirred at the commotion. Very unlike him. My stomach did a frightened little flip and I walked over to him. When I heard him snore, I let out the breath I'd been holding. I don't know what made me fear he wasn't breathing, but I was sure relieved to find that he was. I knelt beside him and placed a hand on his cheek. His temperature was normal.

He turned toward my touch and a soft *"Paige"* escaped his lips in a sigh. A little smile played at the corners of his mouth. My heart fluttered. Apparently, *he* wasn't dreaming about *me* turning into a monster.

He covered my hand with his—mine still pressed against his cheek—before he completely woke up. He opened his eyes and smiled, still half asleep. As soon as he was fully awake, he let go of my hand and sat up quickly, the smile leaving his face. He met my eyes for only a brief second before averting his gaze to the floor.

"Johnathan, your eyes," I started.

"What about my eyes?" He asked, looking up for the briefest of moments.

"They... uh... have flecks of gold in them. In the brown parts. That wasn't there before."

He jumped up and hurried over to the broken mirror behind the bar where he inspected his eyes. Still staring at his reflection, he said quietly and to no one in particular, "What color were my eyes when I... *turned?*"

I looked around at Alec, Seth, and Halli. They all looked at the floor.

"They were yellow, gold. No brown at all," I said, once it was clear that no one else would speak up.

He roared—roared like a *beast*—and punched the small sliver of mirror that remained on that portion of the wall. It fell to the floor in a crumble. We all stood in shocked silence. Johnathan *never* lost his temper. Even during a battle, he was cool and levelheaded.

I stepped toward him. He looked up at me, eyes blazing with...

rage? Hatred? Self-loathing? That look made me stop in my tracks and swallow the soothing words I'd been about to speak. Johnathan spun, catapulted himself over the bar and ran up the stairs and out into the Underground. Alec, Seth, Halli and I stared at each other, mouths open.

"He'll be back," Halli said. "He just needs to blow off some steam. What did you guys find out at the psychic's house?"

I told them what happened at Madame LaForte's house, leaving out the part about her suggestion that Johnathan kill himself, and continued with what I'd read in the white book.

"I'm going to go to the library and see what I can dig up there," I said. "Maybe one of you should go see Joe about finding someone to pose as a parent. I know Johnathan still wants to go ahead with the school thing." I buckled my belt around my waist and shrugged into my coat.

"I'll go see Joe," Alec volunteered. "Seth, why don't you come with me? Maybe we can finagle some beef jerky out of him."

"Okay. I wanted to grab another newspaper, anyway. And, I'm going to find a way to let Joe know we now have an ice box and stove—maybe our food supply will improve. I'm kind of tired of crackers and peanut butter." Seth said.

"Paige," Halli said, just as I started up the stairs. "Could I come with you? I want to help."

I really hadn't wanted any company. *But,* I thought, *it would be better to have two people looking through books for answers.* "Okay, I guess. It's going to be boring, though. I'm just going to look through a bunch of old books."

"That's fine. Let me get my stuff." She scampered over to her corner, put on her belt, and was still wrestling into her pink rain jacket when she reached me at the stairs.

We now had a double set of wards—one at the newly constructed trap-door entrance to our stairs, and one outside the dilapidated building where it was hidden. It took longer to leave or enter that way, but it was safer. Johnathan had taken them down when he stormed out, but didn't take the time to reset them. I waited until everyone was on the Underground sidewalk to reset the wards. At street level, we went our separate ways.

The Seattle Central Public Library was *enormous*. Eleven stories tall, and I figured easy to go unnoticed in. Luckily, you didn't need to have a library card to enter or to look through stuff. You only needed one if you wanted to borrow a book to take out. There weren't a lot of people there, but more than I would have thought for midday on a Thursday.

Since neither Halli nor I could use a computer without essentially blowing it up, I had to resort to asking someone where to start. That isn't an easy thing to do without looking awfully crazy or suspicious: *"Excuse me, but, do you mind helping me find a non-fiction book that might give me the cure for lycanthropy? My friend seems to have gotten himself turned into a werewolf."* So, I told a bit of a story to the nice lady at the helpdesk on the fifth floor.

"I have to do a paper for a 'myths and legends' class I'm taking. Could you help me find where to look for some nonfiction books about lycanthropes or werewolves?" I rolled my eyes derisively when I said *werewolves*, to let her know I believed in no such thing.

The accommodating librarian smiled and said, "Nonfiction, huh? I'm sure we can find something helpful." She typed on her computer for a minute, then said, "Hmm. My computer seems to have frozen. I'll have to shut it down and log into another one. I'm sorry. It'll take just a minute."

Halli and I smiled in understanding and took a couple of steps away from the computer when the lady turned her attention away. Being magical really had some drawbacks in today's electronic world.

A moment later, list in hand, we headed for the seventh floor.

Most of the books on the list were modern and not at all helpful. They were more or less children's books that pretended to know about werewolves. I needed to find something older, from a time when people believed the things they truly saw.

A moment later, we found a book called "The Werewolf in Lore and Legend" by Montague Summers, written in 1933. That was more like it. I started through it while Halli continued to look.

I found the table of contents and decided that what I was looking for would likely be in Chapter II, *The Werewolf: His Science and Practice.* I turned to page sixty-three and started to skim over the information. The book was a little hard to read; portions of it were written in un-translated French and Latin—I just skipped over those parts.

I cringed when I read, *"The distinctive features of the wolf are unbri-dled cruelty, bestial ferocity, and ravening hunger. His strength, his cunning, his speed were regarded as abnormal, almost eerie qualities, he had something of the demon, of hell."* I shuddered. I read on. There seemed to be a recurring theme in the writings of Summers.

"Lust, then, as well as blood is associated with the wolf."

"It is the devil or demons who change a man to a beast."

"It cannot, of course, take place without the exercise of black magic."

Hmm. An idea started to form on the edge of my consciousness.

Summers listed some of the theories that had circulated regarding lycanthropy and werewolf-ism. Things like, it was an illusion, and the human's body was laying inert somewhere else. One explanation: *"Evil spirits may mock and cheat our senses in 3 ways: (1) by exhibiting as present what is not really there; (2) by exhibiting what is there as other than it really is; and (3) by concealing what really is there so that it appears as if it were not."*

My idea began to take a more concrete form. This was caused by *evil spirits* and *black magic.* It could be an illusion or a trick of the mind. I wasn't sure of the connection, but my mind kept returning to a passage in the white book about *soul-gazing.* It was something that all wizards and witches could do. If you locked gazes with a witch or warlock long enough, several seconds, they could open up a conduit between your mind and theirs. Essentially, they could see into your soul and you could see into theirs. Even people with no magical abili-ties could get caught up in a *soul-gaze* with one of us.

I took notes. Because the thought kept returning to my mind, I wrote *soul-gaze* and underlined it three times. I looked up and saw Halli sitting nearby, looking through one of several books she'd pulled from the shelf. She also took notes. We would have to compare later.

I continued reading, but found nothing that talked about a cure.

Soon, I could no longer concentrate on the text because my eyes were blurry and my mind was fuzzy from exhaustion.

"Come on, Hal, let's go. I want to see if Johnathan made it home yet."

"Yeah, me too," she said.

We stopped for a minute on the fourth floor to gape at the *redness* of it—seriously, the *entire* place was red—floor, walls, ceiling, furniture.

"Wow," Halli said.

"Yeah," I agreed, the unaccustomed look of everything being of one color—and the same shade of that color—caused a moment of vertigo as my eyes adjusted.

"This library is too cool," Halli shook her head.

"That it is," I agreed. "Come on, let's head back."

She turned to look one more time as we reached the stairs.

The drizzling rain continued as we headed for home. I was a little jealous of Halli's raincoat; it was a smart choice here in Seattle. My pea coat and clothing were completely soaked through by the time we reached the shelter of the Underground. *I bet Seth's short cowboy duster kept him dry*, I thought with just a twinge of jealousy.

Seth and Alec were home, but no Johnathan. The sun was just hovering over the water, painting the clouds with colors of pink and orange; it would soon be dark out. "Maybe we should go look for him," I suggested.

"We thought about that," Alec said. "But, neither of us has any idea where he might have gone. Do you?"

"No, I have no idea."

"Maybe we can track him with a tracking spell," Seth suggested.

I thought about that. We had the necklaces set up so when one of us summoned the group using our connection, we could easily locate the summoner. It became somewhat more involved and difficult without being summoned.

"Okay, we'll give him until morning. I'm sure he's fine; he just needs some space right now." I sounded more confident than I felt. My stomach churned with worry.

There *was* some good news, thankfully. Alec and Seth had been able to convince Joe to help us sign up for school. He said he'd find someone to act as a parent; he couldn't do it himself because he was too recognizable. He told them to give him two days and he should have someone to play the part.

Our sleeping schedules were all messed up. None of us had had much sleep in the last couple of days. We all decided to try to get some now. Even though my body was desperate for sleep, my mind, once again, had other ideas. I couldn't turn it off. I kept going over the things I'd read at the library and the *soul-gaze* connection my subconscious mind insisted was there.

I finally gave up and dragged myself over to a table that was out of the way of everyone else's sleeping areas. I sat down with the white book and concentrated for a second to increase the brightness of the *star-bright* in my hand from a dim-light-to-keep-me-from-stepping-on-someone-or-something-or-walking-into-a-table-brightness, to a read-without-straining-my-eyes-too-bad-brightness.

I opened the book to the section on *soul-gazing*. I'd read this section at least a couple times before. None of us had tried it yet. I don't think any of us wanted the others to know what was in our souls. The book said that once you saw inside someone, you never forgot what you saw or learned. One passage caught my eye: *The soul-gaze was discovered and used in the beginning to cleanse the soul of one possessed by daemons. It is a dangerous process that requires a great amount of concentration —sometimes taking many hours of being locked together in the gaze. It is rarely —if ever —used in this manner anymore.*

I read the passage again. *That book at the library compared lycanthropy to being possessed by demons.* That was the connection. Maybe I could cure Johnathan with a *soul-gaze!* I slammed my fist on the table. *"Yes!"* I hissed. That had to be the answer.

I pulled out the paper with my notes from the library and started a list.

Find a way to practice soul-gazing
More info needed on method
Who can I ask???? Madame LaForte? Demon? Faerie?

When is best time?

I fell asleep at the table again. I was startled awake by Johnathan stomping down the stairs. I slammed closed the white book and my notebook. I didn't want him to see what I was thinking about doing. There was no way he would let me *soul-gaze* him—one, because it would be dangerous for me, and two, because there was something about his past he didn't want any of us to know.

Johnathan stumbled over to the table and sat across from me. He had to be utterly exhausted; he'd had little sleep in the last few days. I frowned at his bruised and battered face. These were new injuries, not the self-inflicted scratches from... *the day before yesterday?* I was having trouble remembering how many days or hours had passed since that awful night in the woods. He had crusted blood beneath his nose and smeared down the right side of his face from a cut somewhere around his eyebrow.

"Johnathan," I said, trying to sound gentle but allowing some of my anger and anxiety to break through, "You look like you've been in a fight. What happened to you?"

He grunted and laid his face in his hands, elbows propped on the table. I thought he was going to ignore my question. Worry, guilt and anger all fought for the top ranking position in my head. Worry won out. I touched his arm lightly. "Johnathan, look at me."

He drew a deep breath and then did as I'd asked.

"What happened?" I repeated.

He turned his head, but didn't hide his face again. "I got in a tangle with a... something."

Hmm. Evasiveness. I didn't like that one bit. "What kind of *something?*" I asked, working hard to keep my voice soft.

Johnathan glanced at my eyes then away again, down at the table. "A Devil-hound. It tried to attack a group of teenagers who were out partying."

"A *Devil-hound?*" I no longer tried to keep my voice down. "Are you crazy?"

That exclamation woke the others up. "What about a Devil-hound?" Alec asked, sitting up on his sleeping bag.

"Well, I couldn't just let it eat those kids! I was too far away for you guys to help, anyway." Johnathan insisted.

"Wait… you took on a Devil-hound… by yourself?" Seth chimed in.

The others joined us at the table. "Well, what're you waiting for? Tell us what happened," Seth said. Alec nodded in agreement.

Johnathan put his face in his hands again. "Fine. I'll tell you. But then I'm going to bed."

He raised his head, laid his hands on the table, and glanced at me. He bit at the corner of his mouth as he looked back down at his hands. "I was just wandering around… trying to get my head straight. It was after midnight and I ended up over by Edwards High School… I guess that's where my thoughts were taking me.

"The football field borders a small wooded area, and there was a group of kids in there, drinking and talking—maybe six of them. Anyway, I skirted around them, they didn't even know I was there, and I heard a rustling noise coming toward them from the side opposite me. I assumed it was just another kid joining them, but then the hair on the back of my neck stood up and I *felt* the presence of danger."

"Wait… what do you mean you *felt* danger?" Alec asked.

"I don't know," Johnathan answered, somewhat irritably. "I just felt it, my senses all intensified and my heart beat faster. I… I *swear* I could smell the thing."

He was silent for a moment as we all contemplated what that could mean. I'm not sure what the others were thinking, but my mind went immediately back to the creature Johnathan had morphed into, with the large muzzle and wolf-like features. I had no doubts he'd been able to smell the Devil-hound.

"Anyway, I snuck around to the side where the noise was coming from. The kids were all oblivious to the sound and the danger. As I crept closer, I could hear its heavy breathing. It was working hard not to let out a growl, but an occasional low one escaped its throat anyway. I saw it just as it came within sight of the group of kids. It saw them, but they hadn't seen it yet.

"The hound crouched to spring at the nearest one, a blonde girl. I could see the saliva dripping from its mouth. I was still too far away to get between it and the girl in time, so I distracted it by yelling 'Hey!' The hound turned its head toward me, still in a pounce-ready crouch. My attention was on it, not the kids, but the girl must have turned and seen it in the trees because she screamed.

"The hound decided pretty quickly that it wanted the girl and not me. It pounced for her just as she stood to run and it knocked her down just inches from the fire. I leapt at it and knocked it off of her. The hound and I rolled away from the fire—and the girl—and fought it out. The kids up and ran—all but one of them, who grabbed a branch and tried to help me. It's a good thing he did, because the hound ended up on top when we finished rolling and it took all of my strength to keep its jaws from clamping down on my face."

"Oh, Johnathan," was all I could say.

"The kid swung the branch like a baseball bat and hit the hound in the ribs," he continued. "It didn't knock it off me, but it weakened it enough briefly that I was able to push it off me and stand up. I yelled for the kid to go. He was reluctant to leave me alone with the hound, but I could tell he was scared spitless. He finally gave in to his fear and dropped the branch and ran." He stopped there and rubbed his face with both hands.

"So, what happened? How did you beat it?" Alec asked. His patience was next to nothing at this point; he wanted to hear the details of the fight. Boys!

Johnathan drew in a breath. "We fought; I won... that's about it."

"Johnathan! Give us the details, man! No one takes on a Devil-hound alone and beats it. Come on! Tell us how you did it," Alec practically yelled.

A Devil-hound was about twice as big as any breed of dog known to humans. Twice as big as a Bull Mastiff or a Great Dane. And they were all muscle, teeth, and claws. They were practically hairless and ugly as a baboon's butt. Their jaws were big enough to completely clamp around a person's head—and with one shake of its massive jowls it could easily decapitate a human from there. They could leap about fifteen yards in one jump. Yeah, formidable opponent.

"Okay, fine," Johnathan muttered. "The hound started to go after the boy that stayed to help. That gave me enough time to pull out my channeling rod. I blasted it with a fireball that basically just knocked it off its feet and rolling into the trees. That ticked the stupid beast off enough, though, that pursuit of the boy was forgotten. The hound jumped back to its feet and snarled loudly enough to shake the trees. I looked around, desperate for something to stop it with. As it crouched to leap at me I spotted the pile of wood the kids had been using for firewood. There were a bunch of old two-by-fours *full* of nails."

"Oh, yeah!" Seth yelled, pumping a fist, realizing that Devil-hounds came from the Fae... and the one thing the Fae could not tolerate was metal. Iron was the worst, burning their skin with just a touch.

Johnathan nodded at Seth. "I couldn't pull the nails alone, without the wood, so I just hoped enough of them were poking through the other side with their sharp points. I concentrated on the metal and levitated it. To my surprise, a bunch of nails came up from the fire where they'd burned free from the boards. So those nails, along with the boards and nails from the pile, whipped up into the air, and I sent them flying at the hound just as it made its leap. I must've had a butt-load of adrenaline rushing through me because some of the nails flew so hard they went straight through the hound.

"I wasn't fast enough to avoid the collision with the leaping monster, but I did start to tuck and roll. It hit me almost full force and knocked the wind out of me. I hit my head on a rock when I landed. The thing was thrashing around like crazy. I could smell its flesh burning where the nails were still embedded, boards and all in some places. They'd all hit on its right side and there was a board stuck to its head. It rolled off me and continued to thrash. I think I must have been a little dazed, because it didn't occur to me to move away from it until I'd been smacked in the face with the board/head combination a couple of times."

He touched his bruised face and shook his head. "I finally rolled away to a safe distance, but didn't dare stand up just yet. I was afraid I would black out if I did.

"The hound howled and yelped and even thrashed around in the fire. Sparks and ashes flew everywhere... I'm surprised the trees didn't go up in flames. Skin singed and smoldering, the whimpering hound finally crawled away in the direction it'd come. I was worried that the wounds weren't mortal, so I stood up slowly—and, yes, I was dizzy—and followed the beast. It was headed toward a large plastic culvert pipe sticking out of the ground at the edge of the trees. I was too weak to throw any big magic, so I concentrated on weakening the ground around the roots of a huge pine tree—I gave the tree a magical push until it toppled over on the wounded and slow-moving hound. It was crushed quite beautifully. All that was left was a big pile of smoldering ichor."

We were all silent for a moment. Johnathan eased his head down onto the table, resting it on his folded arms.

"Wow. Quick thinking with the nails, Johnny." Alec pounded him on the back.

Johnathan must have been extremely tired because he didn't retaliate when Alec called him Johnny. He just mumbled, or grunted, or something.

"Come on, John. Let me clean up your wounds before you fall asleep," I said. He grunted again.

Alec and Seth wandered off to find something to eat, talking excitedly about Johnathan's scuffle with the Devil-hound.

"I'll go get some water and cloths—and the first aid kit," Halli said.

"Thanks, Hal." I scooted my chair around so I was right next to Johnathan. I put my mouth next to his ear. "John, I know you're tired, but you need to let me clean you up a little. Now, sit up so I can see what new damage you've done to your gorgeous face."

That made him lift his head. I didn't often express my attraction to him. He looked me in the eyes, a small but sad smile playing about the corners of his mouth.

"Okay. But I'm going straight to bed as soon as you're done."

Halli brought the supplies over. We both dipped a cloth into the soapy water. Halli started cleaning the scratches on his arms and hands and I gently wiped the dried blood from his face. His left eye was nearly swollen shut and he had some abrasions to his cheek on that side as well.

The cut on his eyebrow started to bleed again as soon as the crusted blood was removed. I scrubbed the dirt out as best I could. Johnathan didn't even wince; he just sat there staring at nothing. The cut was deep and gaping and should have had stitches, but I taped the edges together with three butterfly bandages then squeezed some antibiotic ointment over it. Halli applied ointment to the deeper scratches on his arms and hands.

"Okay, John," I said. "That's good enough for now. Go get some sleep. But as soon as you wake up, you need to shower to get the rest of the dirt off you."

He gave me that sad smile again as he slowly stood up. He surprised me when he wrapped his arms around me in a fierce hug and whispered in my ear, "Thank you, Paige. I don't deserve your worry for me."

I was too startled to respond—this was the first time since his *changing* that he'd shown any affection toward me at all. He quickly let go and headed for his sleeping area, and was asleep within minutes. I stayed close by him all day and checked on him frequently, worried that his injuries might be more severe than they looked.

CHAPTER NINE

A couple of weeks went by before the school records for Seth and his sister made their way to us, via Joe's address. We didn't patrol every night during that time. On those nights when we didn't, it was usually because Johnathan would say, "I don't feel like going out tonight. Let's just get some sleep." But he wasn't sleeping much—if at all. I was worried about him—he seemed to be falling into a chasm of depression. And he refused to talk to any of us about it.

The records finally arrived, and Joe introduced Seth and me to our 'mom.' Getting signed up for school wasn't as easy as we hoped it would be for Johnathan and Alec. The admissions secretary at the school was surprisingly unaware of the loopholes regarding homeless students. It took her more than thirty minutes of phone calls to become educated on the subject. Finally, the district sent over a homeless liaison, and she had them signed up and ready to go in ten minutes. She left a copy of the McKinney-Vento Act for the clueless secretary to study, and gave Johnathan and Alec each a card with her contact information.

Seth and I showed up a couple hours later, with the mom Joe had found for us. Seth's records were missing the last six months or so, because that was when he'd left home, but the secretary didn't seem too concerned with it. We were in and out as fast as our mom could fill out and sign the paperwork. We were told to report to school in the morning and pick up our class schedules.

I was the only one in our group who couldn't use my real first *or* last name; I had to use Seth's sister's name. At school I would be known as Sasha Spurlock.

We left the office just as the bell to switch classes rang. A few students joked and laughed, but, overall, they appeared to be a downtrodden group. Another ten or fifteen had the dazed look of someone on a heavy dose of tranquilizers; one girl had silent, unnoticed tears streaming down both cheeks. She didn't even bother to wipe them away; her cheeks were red and chafed as if the salty droplets had been flowing for some time.

Seth walked our pseudo-mom outside; I told him I would meet him out there shortly. I wanted to observe my soon-to-be fellow students. Only one of the kids even looked my way. He was tall and thin, with neatly combed, short blond hair. His letterman's jacket was well worn, leading me to believe he'd had it for at least a couple of years. I was a bit surprised when he approached me, seeing the way the other students seemed oblivious to my presence.

He stopped a comfortable three feet away, smiled a smile that didn't come near to touching his eyes, and said, "Hi. I'm Brendon. Are you new here?"

I smiled back. "I am. I just signed up. I'll be starting tomorrow."

He wrinkled his brow and leaned in closer to whisper, "I don't want to scare you away or anything, but, if there's any way you can get into a different school, you should. This place isn't doing so good right now."

"Why? What's going on?" I asked, also whispering.

"I'm not really sure. I just know something's not normal. I'm sure you've heard about all the suicides? Well, that's just the beginning of the weirdness. Nobody's acting like themselves. Anyway, I need to get to class. Maybe I'll see ya tomorrow… but I kinda hope not, for your sake." He smiled his sad smile again, waved, and walked away.

Wow, the kids there really did need our help. I met up with Seth outside and told him what Brendon had said as we walked home.

"That's not a good sign, Paige," Seth said, shaking his head. "I wonder if we should take some extra precautions while we're here."

"Like what?" I asked, curious to hear his answer.

"I don't know exactly. How could the… bad guys, I guess… be getting to the students? That's what we need to figure out or hypothesize about first, before we can decide what precautions to take. Do you have any ideas?"

"Well," I began, "I guess my first *hypothesis*"—I smiled at his use of the word; always the scientific one, our Seth was—"would be the food. The tanks John and I saw looked like they could have held some kind of liquid, so I suppose they could be adding whatever it is to the food. Maybe that would explain why some kids aren't affected."

"Right. The food. That's exactly where my thoughts went. I think we need to expand that train of thought to include fluids—like the drinking fountains and soda machines and stuff," Seth added.

"Okay. But if it was in the drinking fountains, you'd think all the kids would be susceptible to whatever it is. I don't know of anyone that wouldn't use the drinking fountains. And what about the teachers and other adults? Don't they eat school lunch, too? Maybe we should focus on things that just the students do."

"Like what?"

"I don't know. I guess these are the things we'll have to figure out while we're there. Just to be safe, though, I think we should take our own lunches and drinks."

"I was afraid that was where this was headed… even though I was thinking the same thing. I was really looking forward to some good old deep-fried school burritos." Seth kicked a rock on the sidewalk to emphasize his disappointment.

"Well, maybe we'll figure out it isn't the food after all, and you can eat all the greasy burritos you want, ya big baby." I punched him lightly in the arm.

He grinned at me. Seth was always good for a grin.

"Let's go home so we can run this stuff by the rest of them," I said.

The others were somewhat anxiously awaiting our arrival.

"Did you have any trouble registering?" Johnathan asked.

"Not really, it actually went pretty smoothly," I answered. "I did have an interesting conversation with one of the students, though."

When I explained what the boy, Brendon, had said to me, and the way the other students were acting, Johnathan leaned forward. "I think it's time for a brainstorming session."

"Let me grab my notebook, I'll take notes." Halli ran to where her belongings lay and grabbed her notebook and a pen.

Seth brought up our idea about the food possibly being contaminated. "So, no school food. We'll have to pack our own lunches."

From the frown on his face, I could tell he was still thinking about those burritos.

"That's a good idea." Halli looked up from her writing. "But, won't it be a little weird for a couple of homeless boys to have food for sack lunches?"

"I wouldn't worry about it," I said. "They won't know Johnathan and Alec are supposed to be homeless. From the looks on most of their faces today, I don't think they notice much of anything anyway."

"Okay," Johnathan said. "So, we've decided the contamination could be from a food or drink source. What else could it be? Let's try to think about something only the students would be exposed to."

"Maybe the showers... in the gym?" Halli asked. "The teachers aren't supposed to use those."

"Good one, Halli. Write it down." Johnathan smiled at our young friend.

"I don't want to be a Downer Dan or anything, but what if, whatever it is, it's something the kids are willingly taking? Like a rave drug or something," Alec piped up. I was sure his experience with the foster system and certain foster parents and siblings had turned his mind to think of that as an option. And I couldn't dispute his idea. We had to consider it as a possibility.

Halli added drugs to our list.

"I think we're going to have to first decide which of the kids seem to be unaffected and then try to figure out what the difference is between them and the others," Johnathan said.

"I'm sure Brendon wasn't affected. I'll see if I can find him tomorrow and maybe get closer to him," I volunteered.

Johnathan frowned and his jaw tightened at the thought. But he swallowed down his jealousy and said, "That's a good idea, Paige. It would be a good idea for the rest of us to identify some students of both sides, affected and unaffected. We'll have to be subtle in questioning them. I don't want to scare them away or alert those who are leading this poisoning of minds. We could be in some serious danger if they find out we're there to stop them."

Our brainstorming meeting ended and we all pitched in to fix dinner. Johnathan handed out some meager school supplies: one notebook and one pencil for each of us, just enough to keep up the charade. We went to bed much earlier than we were used to that night. Seth wound up the alarm clock and set it for bright and early so we had time to get ready and walk the long distance to the school in the morning before the first bell.

Morning came all too soon for all of us night owls. We dragged ourselves out of bed. Halli was the only one to exhibit any signs of energy; she packed our lunches while the rest of us laid in our sleeping bags and groaned about the early hour. *Of course,* I thought to myself, *she can go right back to sleep when we leave.* But, I knew she probably wouldn't; she had plans to go back to the library to see if she could find anything useful to help me cure Johnathan.

We had to get creative when it came to our channeling rods. I'm sure they would seriously frown on us carrying them around the school on our belts. I ended up strapping mine to my lower leg, under my jeans. I just hoped they weren't planning on me taking P.E. The boys all figured out ways to carry theirs incognito, too. Then we threw on our jackets and headed for the streets above. Of course, it was raining—a slow, cold, drizzle that chilled the bones.

Alec and Seth both acted like they were actually *excited* about going to school. Not me. My stomach roiled like crazy. I thought I might even hurl up my breakfast at the beginning of our long trek. Watching the boys' horseplay helped settle my stomach faster than a can of ginger ale, though, and I was soon laughing along with them. Johnathan barely cracked a smile, however. I was really starting to worry about him. He was already showing signs of depression, and here we were on our way to a school full of depressed and obviously suicidal kids...

We split up when we were within two blocks of the school and came to the campus from different directions—me and Seth one way, and Alec and Johnathan another.

I pulled my hood down as we entered the building. There wasn't the usual noisy, before-school hustle and bustle going on. The students were mostly subdued and eerily quiet. We picked up our schedules; I breathed a sigh of relief when I saw that P.E. was not one of my classes. Seth and I compared our lists. We had only one class together, Geography. Apparently, his real sister hadn't taken it as a sophomore, as was the requirement here. *Great,* I thought, *I'll be the only junior in a classroom full of sophomores.*

Johnathan and Alec entered the office as we left. We did our best to ignore each other. I couldn't help but turn and watch Johnathan, though. I noticed I wasn't the only girl that did so; now it was my turn to feel a little bit of jealousy.

I decided to start right away with the mingling that was going to be necessary if we were to figure out what was going on. As Seth went his own way with the same idea in mind, I walked up to a girl that stood alone, staring down at a book in her hands, but obviously not reading it. Her eyes were glazed over and not moving back and forth like they would be if she was really reading.

"Um... excuse me? Could you help me find my locker? It's my first day here, and I'm afraid I'm not very good at reading maps or following directions." I smiled, threw in a little bit of self-deprecation, and shrugged my shoulders. Who said I couldn't act?

It took a minute before my words gnawed their way through the haze surrounding her mind. She raised her head slowly, her lips twisting into a grimace as she attempted to return my smile. Like it hurt to turn her lips up in that unnatural or forgotten curve. I was sure there was a pretty girl hiding under the messy hair and sullenness. She had dark circles under her eyes that stood out in severe contrast to her sickly pale skin.

After a long pause, she said, "Sure. What locker number do you have?" Her voice was rough and quiet, and her speech was slowed down a few notches below normal.

I told her my locker number, then waited for another lengthy pause while this sad girl slowly processed my words.

"Okay," she said. "That's close to my locker. It's this way."

I followed with a sinking feeling as we trudged on toward our section of lockers. There was a quiet desperation in these kids—quiet, yet screaming inside. It made me want to cry. And *blast* the person or people who were responsible. I watched for Brendon in the crowd. I wanted to make sure his worried but friendly face hadn't transformed into one of these half-zombies I was surrounded by.

We arrived at my locker. I opened it, stowed my jacket, and closed it, only to find that the girl was gone. I realized I hadn't even asked her name. I shrugged my shoulders and decided to find my first class with the ten or so minutes I had before the bell rang. I kept an eye out for Brendon as I roamed.

I was apparently reading the map upside down or something because it took me only three minutes to become completely turned around. As I stood there staring at the diagram of the school, turning it around in my hands, trying to figure out which way was up and where I was in relation to the stupid thing, someone stepped up beside me.

"Can I help you find something?"

I sighed in relief when I looked up into the smiling face of Brendon. He'd survived the night without being *taken* by whatever was plaguing most of his classmates.

I returned his smile with an exasperated sigh and said, "Please! I hate maps—they are a worse form of torment than a medieval maze! If you could maybe just steer me in the direction of my first class, I would be very grateful."

He studied my schedule and smiled again. "It looks like we have the same first hour. I think you'll like Mrs. C. She's pretty cool, even for an English teacher. I don't think you told me your name yesterday..."

"Oh, I'm sorry. It's P... Sasha." *Oops, I almost messed up already.*

If he noticed the slipup, he didn't show it. "Well, okay, Sasha, follow me."

I followed him to the opposite end of the school—yep, I'd been reading the map upside down—and into a classroom that boasted shelves full of paperback books and walls full of posters. There was even a reading area with a small couch and a bunch of big pillows to recline on. I think Brendon was right; I was going to like this teacher.

More kids began to trickle in and take their seats. Brendon sat next to me and gave me a running commentary about each new arrival. "The girl with red hair is Chari. She plays softball and is a riot to hang out with. She's still herself... for now."

I would have found that an odd thing for him to say under normal circumstances. But there, at the school of the damned, it wasn't so weird.

He continued. "That short kid is Cody. He used to be like the class clown or something. Now he's barely there. I worry that he's next."

"What do you mean?"

He sighed and frowned down at me, much as he had the day before when he warned me to change schools. "Something isn't right, here. Everyone is... I don't know... *changing*. They're either sad or stoned or... I don't know... oblivious to the world around them." He paused and rubbed his hands roughly over his face. "I told you to find a different school."

I looked at the fifteen or so students around me and then back at him.

"I *had* to come here."

I left it at that. I'd been almost ready to confide in him. And that was dangerous. For all I knew, he could be one of the bad guys, as Seth had put it.

The bell rang, and a few seconds later, an older lady with orange hair came rushing through the door. She dropped an armload of books on her cluttered desk. She moved things around, looking for something. She looked in the desk drawers, in her huge purse, even under her chair. She mumbled, "Hmm. Where could they be?"

"Uh... Mrs. C.?" said the now-grinning Brendon. "Your glasses are on top of your head."

"Oh... oh, thank you, Brandon. How did you know that's what I was looking for?"

He leaned over and whispered to me, "She always says my name wrong. And she loses her glasses several times during class... they're almost always on top of her head." In a louder voice he answered her, "Just a lucky guess, Mrs. C."

"Well... okay, then. Let's get started. *To Kill a Mockingbird* will be our next endeavor. Brandon, can you and..." She tapped her finger on her lips, trying to figure out if she was supposed to know me or not.

"Mrs. C. This is Sasha. Today is her first day at good ol' Edwards High."

Mrs. C. smiled. "Oh, well, welcome to my class, Sasha. Could you and Brandon help me hand out the books, please?"

I don't know what I'd expected, but the normalcy of her classroom activities kind of took me by surprise. Especially with the girl silently crying in the back row, the boy who looked like he hadn't washed his hair or bathed in days sitting across the room, and the other students in various catatonic states.

About fifteen minutes after handing out the books, the girl in the back—the one that was crying—stood up so fast that her desk scooted forward and bumped hard into the one in front of her. She started screaming and pulling at her hair. She turned as white as freshly fallen snow. Her eyes bugged out of her head, staring at the corner of the room, behind where Mrs. C. stood with a look of dread on her face. Her piercing screams tore at my eardrums until I thought they would burst.

"Ashley? What's..." That's all the teacher was able to get out. Ashley ran to the window with a shriek and started pounding on it. When that didn't have whatever effect it was she was after, she banged her head into it, hard. The glass cracked and she banged her head again, even harder. The glass shattered; huge shards fell to the floor. Brendon jumped from his chair and ran toward her. I followed. Everyone else, including the teacher, just stayed where they were. Most of the kids stared at her, but some of them were so lost in their own little world, I don't think they even registered that something awful was happening.

I choked back a cry when the girl reached down and grabbed a jagged piece of broken glass that was the size of a large butcher knife, and plunged it toward her stomach with an unearthly scream. Brendon reached her just in time and grabbed her wrists. Blood was dripping from her hands. I reached her a second after he did. Brendon looked at me with raised eyebrows, I don't think he expected anyone to help him. I grabbed the beanie off a boy's head who was sitting close by—he didn't even notice; he was one of the catatonic ones—and used it to shield my hand as I reached up to pry the glass from Ashley's hands. Her fingers loosened their grip easier than I expected. Her hands went limp, along with her whole body. I pulled the glass away from her and threw it to the ground. She collapsed into Brendon's chest, sobbing.

He looked at me over the top of her head. He was pale and shaking like a wet dog. I was afraid he'd pass out. I searched for something to wrap around the girl's still-bleeding hands. There was a role of paper towels on the teacher's desk.

"Mrs. C!" I yelled over the girl's sobs. "Please throw me those paper towels!"

She shook herself out of her shocked stupor and tossed the towels to me. I spoke in a soothing voice, for Ashley's and Brendon's benefit. His skin turned from pale to ashen and he swayed a little. I was afraid he was going to go down.

"Ashley," I coaxed, "give me your hands. Everything's going to be just fine. Ashley? Look at me." I held her hands in mine now. I pressed a wad of towels into her palms. In a sterner voice I said, "Hold these as tight as you can, to stop the bleeding." To Brendon I said, "You—sit down before you fall down."

He nodded shakily, backed up to a vacant desk, and sat hard.

"I'm going to take her to the office," I said, looking at Mrs. C. She nodded silently, relieved, I think, that someone besides her was there to take charge.

"Do... do you need any help?" I was a little surprised at the offer from the red-headed girl, the one Brendon had called Chari.

An escort would have been nice to make sure I didn't get lost, but I really wanted to spend at least a few moments alone with this bleeding girl.

"Thank you," I said sincerely. "But, I think I'll be fine. I wouldn't want both of us to miss learning about killing mockingbirds." I smiled.

She returned the smile and let out a breath, relieved, it seemed, that I'd turned her offer down.

Ashley looked toward the corner one more time and shuddered. I led her from the room, gently guiding her and whispering encouragement. We made it to the office with only a couple wrong turns. The secretary behind the desk was busy reading a magazine and didn't even bother to look up. "Excuse me," I said with obvious annoyance.

She glanced up with a sneer and looked like she was about to say something impolite, but the sight of Ashley's blood all over both of us stopped her short. "What happened?"

I scrunched my eyebrows together and shook my head. "She needs the school nurse." It took a lot of restraint not to add, *idiot* to the end of that.

"Oh, right." She opened the gate and pointed.

We entered the cramped nurse's room. I coaxed Ashley to the small cot against the wall and made her lay down. The nurse wasn't in there so I poked my head out of the room and told the secretary to find her. I probably should have *asked* instead of *told*, but I'd lived without any authority figures for too long and forgot the subservient manners expected of youth when dealing with adults. Even stupid, annoying adults. She narrowed her eyes slightly but then she paged the nurse to the office.

"Ashley," I said soothingly as I wrapped some gauze and tape around her wounds to try to stanch the bleeding. "What happened in there? What did you see?"

Her eyes met mine. *Hello...* there *was* someone home in there. The fear in her eyes was thick and heavy. Her lip quivered.

"What did you see?" I repeated.

She swallowed hard, almost choking on her own saliva. "I... saw... I saw... a monster." Her voice was hoarse. She looked away from me like she didn't expect me to believe her. But, I *did* believe her. I'd seen plenty of monsters in the little while since I'd left home. She didn't have to convince me they existed.

"I believe you, Ashley." I made my voice as soft and gentle as I could. "What did it look like?"

She closed her eyes tight and shook her head. I wasn't going to be the one to tell her she would never be able to remove that image completely.

"Ashley. I want to help you. Tell me what it looked like."

She opened her eyes and searched my face before finding whatever she was looking for there. "You're new here," she said.

"Yes. My name's Sasha. What did you see in there, Ashley?" I repeated.

She hesitated before deciding to trust me. "It was awful. At first it looked like my friend, Amanda. But, it couldn't have been her." She looked down and added, "She killed herself last week."

I waited.

"Then, she changed into a... a... *thing*. A thing with black scales and hand tipped wings. Like a... bat's. It had huge eyes and *teeth*, so many *teeth*. It *smiled* at me, like it wanted to eat me." She shuddered and closed her eyes again. Sweat beaded on her forehead. "It motioned me to come to it, then it shimmered and I could see Amanda again, but I could see through her. And... that *thing*... that *monster* reached out and held her... and touched her cheek... like it was her *boyfriend* or something.

"She smiled at me and motioned for me to join them. But... she's dead, so I knew it was a trick. Then the thing started chanting, *'kill yourself... join us... kill yourself... join us'* over and over in a creepy voice. I don't really know what happened then." She stared at her poorly bandaged hands.

"Ashley," I said, "What's happening here? What is..." I didn't finish. The nurse walked in. She looked from me to Ashley and frowned.

"You can go back to class now. I'll take care of her," the nurse said.

I reluctantly stood and headed for the door. I turned and looked at Ashley one more time before leaving. Her eyes were closed tight again.

I found my way back to English class just as the bell to dismiss rang. I waited outside the door for Brendon. He was still a little pale, but he smiled when he saw me. "So? How's Ashley? You didn't happen to run into Mr. Jorgenson, did you? He's the principal." The flash of terror in his eyes when he said *Mr. Jorgenson* sent up a red flag.

"The nurse is taking care of Ashley. No, I didn't see the principal, why?"

Brendon shrugged his shoulders offhandedly, but his body language showed instant relief. "Just wondering. He isn't in his office much lately."

I made a mental note to look into Mr. Jorgenson. I wondered if this could be the Mr. J. the guy that had almost caught Johnathan and me out by the giant chemistry set had been talking to on the phone. I pulled my class schedule out and studied it briefly. "I have History next... Mr. Grewa's class. Could you possibly head me in the right direction?"

"Sure, it's on the way to my next class. I'll walk with you."

I tried to pay close attention to the route we took so I would be able to navigate by myself the next day. It was difficult to concentrate, though, as I watched the kids passing me in the hallway. So many kids seemed in desperate need of help. We really needed to figure this thing out soon.

Brendon dropped me off at the door to Mr. Grewa's class and waved as he continued down the hall. "See ya later."

I stepped through the door and felt an instant sense of peace and comfort. The teacher was writing on the whiteboard, but looked toward me when I came through the door.

"Well, hello. You must be Sasha. Welcome to American History. I'm Mr. Grewa." He had a gentle voice and kind eyes that I imagined had twinkled before his students had turned into psychos. Now, though, those eyes reflected a deep sadness and worry that didn't match the smile he gave me.

"Yes, I'm Sasha. It's nice to meet you, Mr. Grewa."

"Well, Sasha, you can choose whichever seat you'd like, there is no assigned seating in my class. I'll get you a book and syllabus as soon as I'm finished writing today's assignment on the board."

I took a seat in the front row. I wasn't usually—well, okay, ever—a front row student. But the feeling of comfort was just so strong with this gentle man that I wanted to be close to him.

I'd barely begun to sit when a scratchy voice came over the intercom in the room and said, "Mr. Grewa? Could you please send Sasha Spurlock to the office?"

He glanced at me, his face drained of color, and paused before answering, "Okay. How long do you think she'll be?"

"Shouldn't be long. Mr. Jorgenson just wants to speak with her."

"Okay, I'll send her right up." He turned to me and asked, "Do you know your way to the office?"

I was more than a little concerned about the uneasiness in his voice.

"I think I'll be able to find it," I said with a confused smile. I left my stuff on the desk and slowly walked to the office. *Why would Mr. Grewa be worried about me going to the office?* His strange reaction coupled with Brendon's question about whether I'd seen the principal, raised an instant alarm. *Well, if two seemingly normal people are worried about me talking to Mr. Jorgenson, then it's important I talk to Mr. Jorgenson.* I picked up the pace and marched into the office with determination.

A few minutes later, I stood in the doorway to the principal's office until he looked up from his computer screen. He smiled. A chill went down my spine when my eyes met his. Not a good chill. It felt like all the air had been sucked out from around me. I briefly envisioned my body suspended over a vat of liquid nitrogen. With more than a little effort, I shifted my gaze from his and the creepy feeling subsided a little.

"You must be Sasha. Come in, have a seat."

I did as instructed.

"So, Sasha."

The way he said my fake name made me incredibly glad it wasn't my real name he was using.

"I heard there was a little... *incident...* in Mrs. Christensen's class this morning."

I nodded. I wasn't quite sure what response he expected, as he hadn't asked a question, so I stayed silent. It soon appeared that was the wrong way to respond.

I looked up at his face—not his eyes, never again at his eyes—and caught his aggravated, tight-lipped smile. I still didn't speak. If he wanted to know something, he could ask me a question.

Finally, he spoke again. Some of the forced softness had left his voice. "Well, tell me. What happened?" The pause between the two sentences was a little frightening.

"Okay. A girl—Ashley, I guess is her name—freaked out and broke a window. She cut her hands pretty bad and I brought her to the nurse's office."

"Yes, I already know that part"—that pursed lip smile again, the barely contained frustration. *What does this guy want me to tell him?* —"Did she *say* anything to you? About why she may have been 'freaking out,' as you so eloquently put it?"

Ah. I started to understand. He wanted to see if she'd told me anything incriminating. This guy had just gone from slightly suspicious and very creepy, to number-one suspect—and still very creepy. Well, I wasn't about to give him an inch.

"No, sir. She just cried. She didn't say a word to me."

"That's interesting," he said, "Nurse Paulson told me she heard you talking to the girl, Ashley, when she walked into her office."

He lowered his chin and raised an eyebrow. I really hated it when people looked at me like I was lying. Okay, so I *was* lying, but he didn't know that, and it still bugged me that he looked at me like that.

"You didn't ask me if I said anything to her. Your question was, and I quote, 'Did she *say* anything to you?'" I even emphasized the word *say* like he had.

That cracked his composure a little. His hands balled up into fists on top of his desk; he took a deep breath and blew it out noisily. "Sasha. I realize this is your first day here at Edward's High School, so I will forgive your insolence—one time. I want you to look me in the eyes and tell me what was said between you and Ashley."

I looked him in the forehead and said, "I can't remember exactly what I said. I was just trying to calm her down and reassure her until the nurse got there." I paused to think about what the nurse may have overheard. I stifled a groan as I remembered what I was asking her when the nurse walked in. "I think I asked her what happened. I was just trying to get her to talk to me, to focus on something besides the blood on her hands. I was afraid she was in shock or something. Was that the wrong thing for me to do?" I blinked my eyes innocently.

"No, no, I suppose not. You did just fine, Sasha." His switch from interrogator to comforter was extremely discomforting. But he switched right back to interrogator—a role to which he was much better suited. "I am going to ask you again, Sasha, what did Ashley say to you?"

I reigned in the sarcastic retort that was on the tip of my tongue. This guy was dangerous. I could feel it in the tingle of every nerve ending in my skin. I needed to watch myself.

"I don't recall her saying anything to me, sir." I did not want him to know what she told me about the monster and her friend, Amanda. I wondered if that was what he was digging for.

"You're sure? I only ask again because, as I'm sure you've heard, we've had some rather disturbing... tragedies... in our school recently. I just want to ensure we don't have another one."

I was positive that wasn't his reason for wanting to know. I was also sure that if he found out I knew *anything* about what was going on there, I would be in danger. So I stuck to my story.

"I'm sure. She only cried, no talking."

He sighed, cocked his head and raised that eyebrow again. I was bugged again. And, a little scared. Which bugged me even more. He apparently decided to try a different tactic. "Sasha, would you like to have a drink? I have soda here in my office fridge. Maybe a snack?" *Offering me food? That's interesting.*

"Um... no, thank you. I would just like to go back to class. I don't want to fall behind on my first day," I said with a sweet smile.

He wasn't ready to let me go and wasn't happy I'd refused his offer. "Water, then? Let me get you some water. You can return to class when I'm finished with you."

He really wanted me to eat or drink something. I remembered my talk with Seth the day before when we theorized that the problem here might be in the food or water.

"No. Thank you," I said sternly. "I don't want a drink. What else can I answer for you, Mr. Jorgenson?"

He stood abruptly and placed both hands flat on his desk as he leaned over, his face within two feet of mine. His face burned red as he lost his composure.

"You can tell me what that girl said to you!"

I stayed silent and stared him in the forehead.

He leaned closer, the muscles of his arms as tight as two coiled springs. The blood vessels on his arms and hands grew to the size of large earth worms. Just as I started to reach for my channeling rod, a brief knock came at the door. It swung open gently, and I turned to see the worried face of Mr. Grewa. "Mr. Jorgenson, I'm sorry to interrupt. I was wondering when you would be done with Sasha. I am outlining a big project today and it would make it difficult for her if she missed the instruction." I could tell he was scared of Mr. Jorgenson. It endeared me to him even more, that he would come and seek me even though he was scared.

Mr. Jorgenson stared at the teacher for a moment before looking away and returning to his chair. "I'm done with her. For now," he said.

I sat there, unsure if that meant I was excused. Mr. Grewa tapped me gently on the shoulder and nodded toward the door. I felt a moment of spite coming on. I didn't like bullies, and Mr. Jorgenson was the worst kind of bully. He was a bully that was a supposed authority figure for kids. It made me angry. I acted on that anger even though I knew I shouldn't. I leaned over a little bit extra as I stood and I ever so gently touched the back of Mr. Jorgenson's computer monitor. That's all it took to send it into cyberspasms. Mr. Jorgenson's head snapped up as the monitor made a sick sounding beep and then he swore. I'm sure his eyes were boring into my back at that point, but I was already walking out the door behind Mr. Grewa.

When we were safely in the hallway, he slowed his pace and tipped his head toward me so I could hear him speaking in a hushed voice.

"There are some frightening things going on in this school. Please be careful, Sasha. Remember when the storm rages around you and the waves are crashing down on you, find *something* to hold onto. I hold tight to my beliefs. Whatever it is that you value above all else, hold onto that. Don't ever give in to the storm, Sasha. Never give in to the storm."

I wasn't exactly sure what he meant, but I felt his concern and knew he was a good man. "Thank you, Mr. Grewa. Thank you for coming for me."

He squeezed my shoulder briefly and we walked the rest of the way back to his classroom in silence. This man was definitely an ally.

CHAPTER TEN

I found Seth in the crowded lunchroom and sat with him at a corner table. We saw Johnathan and Alec across the lunchroom at another table. My shoulders stiffened when two cheerleader-type girls sat down with them. I'm sure Alec was flirting up a storm. I just hoped that Johnathan wasn't. The thought made me sick to my stomach.

We pulled out our sack lunches and I told Seth about my morning.

"Be careful, Paige," he said quietly. "We can't be sure about anyone just yet. For all we know, Mr. Jorgenson is the ally and Mr. Grewa is a Demon loving spell-caster."

I shook my head. "I *know*. There was pure evil pouring off of our illustrious principal—I could feel it to my soul. And, just as sure as I am of his evil, I'm sure of Mr. Grewa's goodness. I could feel that, too. We can trust him."

"Okay. I trust your instincts."

"So, what about you? Has anything unusual happened in any of your classes yet?"

"Oh, you mean besides the catatonic classmates and teachers that continue on as if everything was perfectly normal? No, nothing unusual compared to your morning full of excitement. But, I have metal shop right after lunch. I'm crazy impatient to see this contraption you and Johnathan saw…"

"Be careful, Seth. I doubt they'll have it right out for just anyone to see. Don't go looking for it. That would be sort of suspicious, don't you think?"

"It was just out in the shop lot when you guys saw it. It doesn't seem like they were trying too hard to hide it," Seth said.

"Yes, it was just out in the lot, but it was the middle of the night. I'm sure they didn't expect anyone to be snooping around. Just be careful. Don't act suspicious."

"Okay, okay. I won't snoop. But, I still hope I can see it. Maybe I can figure out what it's for."

If any of us could figure that out, it'd been Seth. He was so into science and stuff.

I couldn't help myself. I glanced back over at Johnathan's table. He happened to be looking at me and he smiled. I, of course, smiled back. Until one of those blasted girls put her hand on his arm and said something to him. Something *flirty*, I was sure. He must have seen the murderous glare in my eyes because he shook his head at me and laughed before turning his attention to the perky blonde with her hand on his arm.

I was trying to decide which spell I was going to cast her way when Brendon sat down across from me, next to Seth.

"Hey, Sasha. How was History? Mr. Grewa's a pretty cool teacher," Brendon said.

"The part I went to was great," I answered.

"Hi, I'm Seth, Sasha's annoying little brother." Seth held out his fist for a fist bump. Brendon obliged.

"Oh, sorry. I'm Brendon. Do you play football?" He eyed Seth's muscular frame and big hands.

"I haven't played for a couple of years, but, yeah. I love football." And I could tell he meant it. His mouth was practically salivating with desire at the mere mention of the game.

"Well, our season isn't even halfway over yet. You should come to practice after school and see if the coach'll give you a chance for a spot... we've lost a few players in the last couple weeks. What position do you play?"

"Defensive line. I love to knock quarterbacks on their butts. What position do you play?" Seth asked.

"Hmm. . . quarterback. I guess you wouldn't be knocking me on my butt if we're on the same team, though, right?" Brendon answered with mock fear.

Seth laughed and said, "Naw, I'd hold back a little for a fellow teammate."

I assumed I'd been forgotten at that point. I started to clean up our lunch mess when the bell rang. That seemed to jog Brendon's memory of why he'd come over to our table. "What class do you have next, Sasha? I'll show you where it is and you can explain to me why you missed History."

"I didn't miss *all* of History," I argued. "I have pre-calc next... Mrs. Penrod's class."

"Ew, yuck. I hate math. Come on, we'd better get going, then. It's clear across the school."

On the way, I told Brendon about my encounter with Mr. Jorgenson. I didn't tell him everything. I still wasn't sure he wasn't a plant, there to gather information from me. I was pretty sure he wasn't, though, especially after the way he shuddered when I told him I'd been in Mr. Jorgenson's office.

There was no more excitement for the day. I couldn't wait until seventh hour, not because I loved Geography or anything, but because it was the class I had with Seth and I could find out how Metal Shop went.

I got to class before Seth did. He came through the door in an excited rush, stopping only long enough to find where I was sitting and lope over to me like an excited puppy. I was relieved to see the stupid grin on his face; I'd been worried his animated entrance was caused by anxiety.

"Sista! Guess what?" He plopped into the desk next to me and didn't wait for me to answer before going on. "Brendon stopped me in the hallway just now—he talked to the football coach and he said I can play. He said he'll just overlook the requirement for a physical and stuff. I can start practicing with them right after school today!"

I was happy for him. I hadn't seen Seth this enthusiastic about anything since the day he figured out how to throw magical flames. But we were there for a very specific purpose, and I wasn't sure football would fit into that. As much as I didn't want to deflate his enthusiasm, I had to bring him back to reality.

"That's great Seth. But, we really need to concentrate on why we're here. I'm just not sure football will help us figure out what's going on here."

He refused to let me ruin his high. "I think it *will* help, Pai... Sasha." He looked around quickly to make sure no one caught his slipup. "At least two of the suicides were on the football team, and Brendon said that over a third of the players have just stopped coming to practice. They are now *zombified*, as he put it. I think the team might be a target for whatever's going on."

"Okay... well, that's awesome, then, Seth. You might be onto something... and, you get to play your favorite sport while you investigate. Win-win, the way I see it." I couldn't help but smile at him. He was seriously stoked about this.

"Brendon said he's sure I'll be on the varsity team, too—as a *sophomore*. This is just so awesome!"

Before I could redirect our conversation to Metal Shop shenanigans, the Geography teacher walked in and shushed the class with a deep throated "ah-hem!" He dragged a TV on a rolling stand to the front and center of the room.

The teacher, a short and chubby man with a severely receding hairline and Harry Potter-esque glasses, looked as if he may have been quite jovial in times past. But, something had taken its toll on him. His eyes were bloodshot and his mouth was turned down in a perpetual frown. He didn't bother taking roll or even seem to notice his two new students. He just waited for the five or six of us who had been talking to quiet down and said, "We're going to watch a movie today about the Western Hemisphere. Take notes and try not to fall asleep." He turned out the lights and started the DVD player. It was a good thing Seth and I were sitting clear in the back. Even so, I was a little worried we would somehow negatively affect the electronics.

The teacher sat at his desk in the corner and just stared out the window. I leaned over to Seth and whispered, "So, how was Metal Shop? See anything suspicious?"

"Not really. Oh, I forgot to tell you, Johnathan's in that class with me. He looked out the big door to the lot when we were supposed to be cleaning up the shop. He said the tank thing wasn't where it'd been when you guys saw it."

I felt a rush of relief that Johnathan was in there with Seth. I knew he would use caution; I wasn't so sure Seth knew what caution was.

"What was the teacher like?"

"Grumpy, like all shop teachers, but he seemed okay. He didn't set off any warning signals. He didn't throw any wrenches at my head—I figure that's a good sign." He said that like it'd been a common occurrence in the past. I just shook my head; it really wasn't surprising to me, although, I would've thought that Alec would have had more wrenches thrown at his head than Seth. It wasn't a bad idea, really. *I wonder where I can get a wrench or two.*

I settled in to take notes like the teacher had instructed—just not notes on the movie. I wrote notes on the things I'd seen and learned that day. I drew a picture of the monster Ashley had described to me. I was definitely no police sketch artist, so it wasn't great, but it helped me to remember what she'd said about it. I figured the drawing could be passed off as just mindless doodling if the teacher happened to confiscate my notebook.

The DVD player and TV managed to evade our unintentional magical-force-of-destruction-of-all-things-technical until about ten minutes before the end of class. That was when the DVD player got stuck on a screen and then the TV sparked from behind and shut off. It took about thirty uncomfortable seconds for the teacher to even realize it. He stood and looked at his watch, then flipped the lights back on—the two banks of lights above Seth and I flickered. The teacher shrugged his shoulders.

"Class dismissed," he said in a monotone voice. "Quiz tomorrow."

The hallways were deserted except for us and our Geography classmates. Seth and I decided to wait by Johnathan and Alec's lockers. The chance was slim that anyone in this School of Doom would notice anything weird about us hanging out with the other new kids.

Johnathan didn't say anything about us waiting there for them. He must have gathered the same feelings as us about the abject indifference of most of the student body. As soon as Alec joined us, Seth excitedly explained about the football team and his hopeful place on it. I saw the excitement spread to the faces of the other two boys, too. I rolled my eyes.

"I'm going to practice, too," Alec chimed in. "I'm an awesome running back; they're gonna beg me to play after I show 'em my mad skills."

"How about you, Johnathan? Didn't you used to play on the line?" Seth asked.

"Yeah, I did," he said. The sparkle left his eyes abruptly and a troubled expression crossed his beautiful face. "I think I'll pass, though. You guys can get in with the jocks. I'll work some other angle."

I frowned. I knew he wanted to join them. What held him back? What was he worried about? I decided to call him on it. "John, I know you want to play. Why don't you just join them? I can work the fan angle. It'll be—"

"Paige! I don't want to, okay? Just drop it!"

He slammed his locker shut and walked away. My mouth dropped open. He'd never talked to me like that before. Tears stung the backs of my eyelids, but I refused to let them fall. I stood, face hot, and watched his retreating figure. Seth and Alec were just as stunned.

Seth was the first to compose himself. "Come on, sis. You can come watch me and Alec tear it up on the field." He couldn't hide the fact he was worried about Johnathan, too.

I shook myself out of my shock and forced a smile. "You guys go ahead. Have fun. I'm going to go home and see how Halli's day went."

"Okay," Seth said uncertainly. "See ya' in a couple hours."

"See ya'." I headed for the exit.

The lone walk home was a dreary one. Johnathan was nowhere in sight. I figured he'd decided to pull another disappearing act like he had the night he'd faced the Devil-hound. I spent the entire lonely walk home trying to decide what had caused him to act like that. He'd been excited about the prospect of playing football. That had been evident in his sparkling eyes and dimpled smile. What made him change from that to the sad and angry boy that had forgotten to use my undercover name and had yelled at me so vehemently? His mood swings were giving me whiplash lately. *Ever since he went all wolf on us that night.* That had to be it. He'd been steady as a rock up until then. Now, he was all over the place.

I shuddered as I recalled his uncontained rage inside the circle. He would've killed us all if I hadn't trapped him there. Maybe some of that rage still coursed through his body, even when the wolf was latent. Waiting for a full moon so it could make its next appearance.

I had to find a way to cure Johnathan before the next full moon. I had to.

Even though I knew the chances of him being home when I got there were slim, I was still disappointed when Halli confirmed that he wasn't.

"Where are the boys?" she asked. "Did you walk home by yourself?"

"Well, Alec and Seth have decided to infiltrate the football team, so they're at practice. I don't know where Johnathan is. He took off before I did."

I told her about his outburst. She wasn't as shocked as the rest of us had been. I thought maybe it was because she hadn't been there to see it. I tried to emphasize how un-Johnathan-like he'd acted.

"Halli, he *yelled* at me. *Yelled*. At *me*. Over nothing. It was... not right, definitely not right."

She shook her head. "That doesn't sound like our Johnathan at all. But, I found out some things today at the library that might explain it. One book said the blood of the wolf mixes with the human blood and is always circulating, even in between changings. Granted, it was just an educated guess on the author's part, but it makes sense. It said the wolf blood has high levels of pheromones and hormones and stuff and causes the human host to be quick to anger and more aggressive. It also said it gets worse with every changing and eventually, he guessed, would drive the person mad—especially someone who had been a 'kind and gentle spirit' before being changed."

I was speechless. This was not good news. "What was this book? What makes this guy such an expert about lycanthropes?" I spat out.

My anger didn't faze Halli—not a lot did faze her.

"It was an excerpt from a book written in the 1700s in England," she explained. "The author claims he was a werewolf—he was bitten when he was a young teen. He became a scientist and spent his life studying himself and others. He said he was afraid of his own aggression, afraid he would hurt the people he loved even when he was in human form. Because of the wolf blood and anger issues. I bet Johnathan feels the same thing. I think he's probably afraid of the way he's been reacting lately and he knows football would be a *very* bad idea for him. The wolf blood increases the human's strength and senses, too. If this guy was right, that means Johnathan could hurt someone very easily without even realizing what he was doing. That would devastate him with someone he doesn't know, and kill him with someone he loves."

I wanted the answer to be something else. I did not want to buy into what this supposed were-scientist thought. I felt Johnathan pulling away from me, and I was terrified to think it was going to get worse. The words of Madame LaForte kept invading my thoughts. *Death will bring peace to his tormented soul.* I picked up a chair and threw it with a grunt of rage. I slammed my fist into the table hard enough to bruise it. *I will not let this destroy him!*

Halli sat, quiet, while I calmed myself down. After a few minutes I sat, utterly defeated for the moment. I lowered my head into my non-injured hand. For a fleeting second an optimistic thought popped into my head.

"Hey, Hal," I said. "Did this science-werewolf say anything about a possible cure?"

She frowned and shook her head. "The book said he searched his whole life and couldn't figure one out. But, I don't think that should discourage you. He was looking only for a scientific or medical answer. He didn't venture into anything magical or even seem to know about the Fae... or Demons," she added quietly.

Had I mentioned to her my ideas about summoning a Faerie or Demon to help figure this out? I didn't think I had. I didn't want her, or anyone, to know about that possible plan. Because I knew it was foolish and dangerous. And I didn't want anyone to try to stop me from doing it anyway.

I chose to leave it alone. No talk about summoning. "You have a point there, Hal. This transformation can't be explained in human terms. Its basis is evil." *And evil is where I will have to go to rid Johnathan of it.*

"I'll continue my search tomorrow, but I'm afraid the answer isn't going to be in the public library. I've been thinking about going to that bookstore on Pike Street. Circle of Books, or something like that. We've walked past it a hundred times; it's the one with the pentagrams in the window. What do you think?"

"It can't hurt to try," I answered.

I was exhausted and my hand hurt. I went to my corner to lie down. I couldn't wait much longer to find an answer. If Halli struck out tomorrow at the bookstore, I had to start preparations to summon some help, soon, before the next full moon. I was having a hard time with the idea. What I was considering was something we'd spent months fighting against.

It scared me to realize I was leaning very heavily towards

summoning a Demon instead of a Faerie, too. They were both very dangerous beings, but Demons were pure evil whereas Faeries had more of a mischievous evil. I wasn't sure exactly what dangers lurked with the plan I was hatching.

But I was sure I'd do whatever it took to save Johnathan. No matter what the cost to my soul.

CHAPTER ELEVEN

Thankfully, Johnathan didn't pull another all-nighter. He showed up shortly before the football heroes. Halli and I were preparing dinner in the kitchen/bar area when he came moping down the stairs. I was too happy to see him safe and sound to be mad about the yelling incident, but I pretended to be mad anyway. He had to pay at least a little bit for his behavior, didn't he?

He shuffled to the bar and sat down across from where I stood. He looked me briefly in the eyes and then looked down at the bar before speaking.

"Paige," he began. "I'm sorry. I shouldn't have yelled at you. I don't know what's wrong with me lately. I get mad so easily. I feel like I'm on the verge of losing my mind most of the time."

I didn't say anything. I felt bad for him, of course. But he needed to suffer just a little bit longer.

He looked up at me again. The sadness in his eyes almost made me cave in, but I looked away, to the lettuce I was chopping. I knew I was acting a little bit like a brat, but I couldn't stop myself. He had *yelled* at me. And then he'd taken off. Again.

"Paige, please don't be mad. I didn't mean it. I'm so sorry." His hands twitched like he wanted to reach out and touch me. That did it.

I put the knife down and reached over and laid my hand on his. He hesitated and almost pulled away from my touch—ouch, that hurt right in the center of my chest. I gripped a little harder and said, "I forgive you. Just don't let it happen again, butthead." He released the breath he'd been holding and gave my hand a squeeze. He even smiled a little before he looked closer at it and frowned.

"What did you do to your hand, Paige?" he asked accusingly.

"Well, I… a… I hit the table." I couldn't think of a good story to tell him, so I just stuck with the truth, as embarrassing as it was.

He turned my hand to better view the damage. There was a bruise forming on the pinky side and the tender flesh there had started to swell a little. "Hmm," he said beneath his breath, "I guess I'm not the only one with anger issues." He surprised me then by lifting my hand to his mouth and gently kissing the injured side. His lips were so soft. My heart leapt to my throat and stayed there, pounding out an erratic rhythm.

His head whipped up. In his eyes I saw confusion and a little bit of fear. *Had he felt the change in the beat of my heart?* I remembered what Halli read about a werewolf's senses becoming stronger. My face flushed red. I didn't want him to know the effect his touch had on me, but I was reluctant to end the physical contact.

Johnathan's pupils dilated until they completely filled his irises. He inhaled sharply, his nostrils flaring, and jerked his hands away from mine.

"Can I help you two with anything?" he asked, his voice strained.

"No, I think we've just about got everything done," Halli said.

Johnathan sat and watched as we finished up. Alec and Seth's timing was perfect—they came bounding down the stairs just as we were dishing up the tacos we'd just made. They were completely *wired.* You would've thought two and a half hours of football practice and a lengthy walk home would have relaxed them a little. It didn't. They sat on either side of Johnathan and talked nonstop while they inhaled about five tacos each. It was pretty disgusting. Bits of half-chewed food flew everywhere.

"You shoulda' seen the two runs I made. It was awesome! They couldn't get me down," Alec spouted.

"*They* couldn't, but *I* did," Seth interjected. "I laid you flat on your butt!"

"Just once. The first run no one even came close. I have speed and skills you can't even touch, my friend. Speed and skills."

Seth rolled his eyes. "I would've had you then, too, if you hadn't been on the other side of the field."

I let them go on like this for another ten minutes before asking, "So... did either of you do any investigative work? As I recall, that *was* your excuse for doing this."

They looked at each other a little sheepishly. "Well," Alec began, "not *really.* You have to give us a chance to get to know some of the guys first, Paige."

"Yeah, we'll get on it tomorrow. There's a home game on Friday, and Coach said we can play even though we'll only have been to two practices! You guys *have* to come watch... so you can work the crowd angle, of course."

Halli and I smiled at each other. Johnathan tried to hide his unhappiness with a weak smile. He clapped Seth on the shoulder and said, "Of course we're gonna be there... and not *just* to 'work the crowd angle'."

"Okay, enough about football," I said. "Let's talk about what we learned today at the school. Who wants to start?"

I did want to talk about our observations on our first day, but I mostly wanted to steer the conversation away from football. It was causing too much distress for Johnathan.

"It seems as though you had the most interesting day," Seth said, "so you go first. Tell these guys what happened."

I filled them in. I told them about Mrs. C's fun-filled-classroom-of-horrors; about what the girl, Ashley, told me in the nurse's office; and—I saved the best for last—I told them all about the illustrious Mr. Jorgenson and our stimulating conversation. Johnathan was not very happy about the fact that I fried the evil-principal's computer, though. I just shrugged when he asked me what I was thinking.

"Paige! If he's as dripping with evil as you said, he probably knows all about magic and its effect on technology. You need to be sure to stay far away from him. Keep a low profile and stay out of trouble! Okay?" Johnathan fumed. His eyes flickered with a yellow hue.

I cringed.

"Okay, John. I'll try… but I have a feeling he's not going to leave me alone," I said quietly. I shouldn't have said that. Johnathan's eyes grew even more yellow and he clenched his fists on the bar. I could have sworn he almost *growled*. I had no idea what to say or do to calm him down. Halli came to the rescue.

"Alec, your turn. Tell us how your day went," she said, all cool and calm. As everyone turned their attention to Alec, I chanced a peak at Johnathan. He was taking deep breaths with his eyes closed, and his fists slowly unclenched. When he opened his eyes again, they were back to his normal dark chocolate color, except for the specks of yellow that had appeared a couple of weeks ago.

"My day was boring compared to Paige's," Alec said dejectedly. "The only thing that even came close to being exciting—besides football practice—was when a boy in my French class fell asleep and woke up screaming. He didn't even act embarrassed, he just stared into space and cried for the rest of class. The teacher completely ignored him. Acted like nothing unusual had happened. It was weird."

Seth and Johnathan didn't have much to add. Johnathan had been able to become a little friendly with a boy in his geometry class. And, of course, the cheerleaders at lunch. *Grrr.*

The hour was late and we all had to be up early in the morning. I hated the early-morning thing already, and for that one reason more than any other, I wanted to figure things out. Soon.

The next day at school passed without much excitement. I was able to avoid Mr. Jorgenson and was pretty excited to find Johnathan waiting for me at my locker after school so we could walk home together. He kept a frustrating distance between us, though. I was afraid he wouldn't try to hold my hand again until after I found a way to cure the lycanthropy tainting his mind and body. His near loss of control at the racing of my heart the night before had obviously scared both of us. I, however, was still willing to take a chance—even if it meant death by gorgeous-werewolf-boy for me. I sidestepped closer to him and shrugged my shoulder into his arm. What I really wanted to do was grab his hand, but I was too chicken—not because of fear of how he might react, but because… well, just because. Being in love was a new experience for me, and the idea of making a romantic gesture made my palms sweat and my heart race.

He smiled down at me. That made my heart skip a few beats. I decided to try something a little bolder. His smile was worth it. I put my arm through his, like a Victorian lady might do when walking with a gentleman friend who was courting her. That did it. His muscles tightened. His bicep squeezed my hand next to his ribcage. I heard his sharp intake of breath and before I knew what was happening he swung his body in front of mine, grabbed my upper arms with his hands, and spun me into a small alleyway between two buildings. He pushed me against the brick wall of one of those buildings.

Johnathan's eyes dilated again, pools of darkness looking down into mine. His skin was warm and flushed and his nostrils flared with each quick breath. He leaned his head down until his forehead touched mine. He shook; his grip on my arms tightened.

"Johnathan." My voice squeaked, embarrassing. "You're scaring me a little."

That did something to partially transport him back to reality. He loosened his grip on my arms and closed his eyes. His breath came in quick little pants. He stayed in that position for an eternal minute before pulling his head away from mine. The dilation of his pupils was no longer a complete takeover of his irises, but his eyes flashed yellow-gold where they should have been dark brown. He stared at the triangular spot where my neck and collar bone met. I'm sure he could see my heartbeat, strong and fast, in whatever vein lies close to the surface there. He squeezed his eyes shut again and refused to take the breath his lungs hungered for. He released his grip on my arms and slowly backed away from me until his backside smacked into the wall opposite the one I leaned on. In slow motion, he slid down the wall until he was in a sitting-fetal position, his arms wrapped around his bent legs and his head bowed into his knees.

I took a step toward him.

"Don't!" he snapped without looking up. "Don't come near me." He must have heard the strangled gasp that escaped my spasming throat, because he added, a little less gruffly, "Not right now. Just give me a minute, 'kay?"

I stood in stunned silence. I knew I should just leave him to collect himself, but I wanted to try to understand. I couldn't just walk away from him, even if that's what he wanted. So I just stood there like an idiot.

He mumbled something. I stayed where I was, scared to invoke another hotheaded carnal canine response from him. But I tapped into my magic just a little to enhance my hearing. I wanted to hear what he was mumbling. I didn't think of it as eavesdropping. He knew I was standing there. I could hear my dad's gentle voice saying, *if you have to rationalize your actions, then you're probably doing something you shouldn't be doing.* I did it anyway.

"I can't hurt someone I love again. I can't. Not again. Never again."

I felt his despair in the pit of my stomach. He had some extreme deep-rooted secrets, I already knew that, and I wondered in desperation who he'd hurt before, what had happened. My guilt got the better of me and I allowed my hearing to return to normal.

After several minutes, Johnathan took in a great lungful of air and raised his head. He wouldn't—or couldn't—look at me. "Sit down a minute... please. Over there," he added, pointing to the other side of the small alley.

I did as he asked.

He still wouldn't look me in the eyes. "I am so, so sorry. I don't know what's happening to me. Please, forgive me."

His voice broke, and it felt like something inside me broke along with it. I held it together, though. My instincts told me Johnathan needed me to be strong. So that's exactly what I did. No tears, just strength.

"It's okay, I'm okay. No harm, no foul, right?" I was proud my voice shook only a little.

"No, it isn't okay! I'm turning into an animal! I can't control my feelings or my impulses. I *swear* I can hear and feel when your heart speeds up. I can *smell* your excitement and your... fear. And... it makes me want to... do things." He rubbed his eyes as if trying to rid them of some vile sight.

I sat there in silence. I'd been waiting for him to tell me what was going on inside him, but I realized I wasn't ready to hear what he was telling me.

"We have to stay away from each other. You have no idea how hard it is for me to say that, but we have to. You can't touch me. Your touch lights fires... I would *die* if I did something to hurt you. You have to understand, *please*."

I had to answer him. I couldn't just sit there like the sorrowful statue of a jilted woman. I tried to speak, but my throat was full of mucous and barely contained tears. I coughed to clear it enough to whisper, "I understand. And it's me that should be apologizing to you. I'm sorry I touched you when it was obvious that it was the last thing on earth you wanted." I didn't mean that in a pouty, poor me, you don't care about me way. But I'm afraid that's how it sounded to him.

"No, Paige, you're wrong. You have no idea how I want... how I *need...* your touch; how I have to stop myself a hundred times a day from reaching out to take your hand or touch your face. It's torture. I'm dangerous. I know you see it in me. I can smell the fear that's still rising from your pores, so don't try to deny it. Just promise me you'll keep your distance from me. I should just be a man and leave... go far away so I can't hurt you or the others. I will... leave... if I have to, to protect you."

Now I was scared. He couldn't leave. He couldn't. "Don't even think that! You can't leave. I promise I'll stay away from you, okay? Just promise me you won't leave."

He finally looked in my eyes. His had returned to their new normal color of brown with yellow flecks. "I promise not to leave unless it becomes necessary. That's the best I can do."

We walked in silence the rest of the way home, making sure to keep a safe distance between us at all times. Too far for an errant swing of the arm to accidentally touch his.

Keeping my promise was going to be really hard.

CHAPTER TWELVE

As soon as Johnathan and I reached the bottom of the stairs to our new home, he asked—in a demanding tone—that Halli and I make our sleeping areas in a room separate from the boys. Up until then, we'd all just claimed a corner or area of the common room, where all the tables and chairs were. He insisted Halli and I move into the large room across from the bathroom that had most likely been an office or storage room once upon a time. His excuse—for Halli's sake—was that it just wasn't right to have teenage boys and girls sleeping in the same room now that we had a choice. Oh, and, "girls need more privacy than boys do."

Halli inhaled and opened her mouth like she was going to argue the point with him until I caught her eye and shook my head in warning. She clamped her mouth shut on whatever she'd been preparing to say and just shrugged.

"It'll be great, Hal," I said. "We can even decorate without the boys raggin' on us about stuff being too *girly*. It'll be fun."

She narrowed her eyes and raised one eyebrow in my direction, but she didn't say anything. I sighed in relief that my little friend was so in tune to the body language of others.

We cleaned up our new room before moving in our meager belongings. I'll admit it was kind of nice to have our own space; the door even had a lock on it—I could go back to sleeping in just a t-shirt and underwear.

While we arranged our stuff, I told Halli what happened in the alley to provoke this separation of the genders' thing.

"The part of me that knows Johnathan wants to intensely deny what you just told me," Halli said. "But I've seen this coming. And everything I've read has just confirmed my hunches. The one thing that's really bothering me, though, is that his personality is changing at such a rapid pace. According to that book I read at the library yesterday, it took the author years to start losing his humanity."

"Halli! He isn't *losing his humanity*. He's just having trouble dealing with the changes. He'll be fine. He's going to get a handle on this. It doesn't really matter, anyway, because I am going to figure out how to rid him of this... problem."

The look of pity she gave me only made me more determined in my quest. I would do whatever it took to see him untainted again. Whatever. It. Took.

After a few minutes of silence, I spoke. "Did you find anything helpful at the bookstore today?"

"Oh, yeah, maybe. They weren't real happy with me just reading the books in the store and taking notes. I forgot I was in an actual store that wants to *sell* things. I did my best before they realized I wasn't going to buy anything and showed me the door. Anyway, I did find an obscure, leather-bound book in a dusty corner that gave some clues. Let me grab my notes."

She rummaged around in her newly deposited pile of junk until she pulled out her gear belt and removed a small notebook from the zipped pocket. She flipped the pages until she found the one she was looking for.

"Ah, here it is," she said. She read from her scribblings. "Only the Daemons know the way of the Daemons. I suppose that there are only two ways to rid myself of this blasted curse—one, to kill myself before the next harvest moon appears in the night-sky; or, two, to summon a Daemon and barter with it for the answer. I'm afraid that there is still too much Christianity left in my bedeviled soul to allow me to do either of the aforementioned heinous acts. Thus, I will be forever needful of the loathsome cage my father had the Mage Rothfuss build for my confinement during these dreadful nights whilst I am possessed of the Wolf."

My stomach lurched. I tucked my head to my knees to keep from vomiting. My visit with Madame LaForte replayed in my mind for the hundredth time. Once again, I refused to see Johnathan's death as an option. That left the other suggestion. Despite the fact I'd already entertained the idea that I might need help from the Fae or a Demon, hearing it stated so definitively caused the contents of my stomach to try a rather aggressive escape by way of my esophagus. I won the battle of anti-regurgitation for only a moment. As soon as I made the terrifying decision that I'd been toying with over the last three weeks—and knew it would be with a Demon, not the Fae—all systems were go for the vomit volcano that exploded forth. What a disgusting way to christen our new room.

"Paige, what's wrong?" Halli asked.

I shook my head and continued to dry-heave.

"I'll go get some water... and towels," she said.

I took some slow, deep breaths and finally stopped my rebellious stomach from further launchings. I'd broken out in a cold sweat and had to wrap my blanket around my shoulders to keep from shivering.

I am going to summon a Demon. The decision was firm in my mind, despite the obvious dread it caused me. I had no choice. And this time, I was not rationalizing. I really had no choice. *I will commit this vile sin for Johnathan's sake.*

I didn't want to drag Halli any further into this, so I evaded her questions about my sudden illness while we cleaned up the mess. I was on my own with this one. I needed to do some further research on the summoning of Demons before I attempted it. Many a magically powered being had attempted before me, and stronger magic users than I had failed to be able to contain the Demon they'd summoned. I might have a slight advantage in that I'd helped send a few Demons back to where they'd come from. Still, I resolved that Johnathan may have to go through another changing before I was ready. A full moon was quickly approaching. If I failed, it meant not only a sure and fiery death for me, but a life of torment for Johnathan. I could not fail.

We finished cleaning up just before Alec and Seth came clomping down the stairs. Johnathan had been busy cooking hamburgers for dinner. I stayed a good distance away from him while we prepared and ate our burgers—not only because of our deal, but also because I was sure his increased sense of smell would pick up on my recent fear-vomit episode. I was pretty sure it already had, but he chose to be a gentleman and not bring it up.

News from football practice brought a possible break in our self-assigned case.

"A couple of guys on the team invited us to a party after the game tomorrow. They hinted that there would be something more than the usual party fare," Alec said.

Seth chimed in, "Yeah, I asked Brendon about it. He told me not to do it, said he's heard about what goes on at those parties and it isn't something I should get mixed up in. And, listen to this, most of the suicides were kids that had attended at least one of these parties. I asked him how he avoided them, the parties, because these guys were pretty insistent that we come."

"What did he say?" Alec asked.

"He has to work at his parents' diner or something. He told me to just think of an excuse and not to go no matter what."

"So," Alec said. "That means we really have to go."

I was afraid Alec was right on that point. We had to go check it out. I was also more than a little relieved Brendon had found a way out of it and was smart enough to know something wasn't right.

We stayed up late strategizing about how to stay safe at the party and what information we needed to gather. Once again, poor Halli was left out. She would come to the game with us, but would be home, safe and sound while the rest of us went on to the party.

It was a great distraction for me. A distraction from other plans I had to make.

The next day was a rough one. I tried really hard to avoid Mr. Jorgenson, but he *was* the principal, after all. He had access to every area of the school *and* my class schedule. He called me out of Mrs. C.'s class first thing. Brendon and Chari both looked at me like I was headed to the chopping block.

During the long, slow walk to his office, I thought about what his excuse for pulling me out of class would be this time. I hadn't been involved with any more freak-outs or anything. I reminded myself not to look into his eyes, and I told myself to be cool—no more computer-crashing antics or other such rebellious acts that might alert him to my magical nature.

Head held high and shoulders squared, I entered the office with an air of indifference. The snotty school secretary sneered as she let me behind the counter.

"Mr. Jorgenson is waiting for you in his office."

I thanked her with all the fake sincerity I could muster and headed boldly for the Evil-meister's office. I was determined to both show no fear and to feign respectfulness in hopes I could get myself off his radar.

I stopped in the doorway to his office.

"Sasha, come in and have a seat," he gestured to the chair he had positioned directly in front of his desk—and conspicuously out of arms' reach from his new computer monitor. *Hmm. So much for getting off his radar.*

119

I sat. I focused my eyes on the top of his desk. He was silent for a very uncomfortable amount of time, so I looked up, intending to bypass his eyes and look at the spot of skin between his eyebrows. He apparently anticipated that, because he expertly moved his head just enough that I found myself staring, transfixed, into his emotionless eyes. A feeling of intense coldness started on top of my head and flooded over me, quickly reaching my toes. I shivered. I knew I needed to shift my gaze from his, I just couldn't remember why or how. Vertigo threatened to take over my senses. I was *falling* into... his... eyes.

The peculiar words Mr. Grewa had spoken to me two days before suddenly popped into my mind. *Remember when the storm rages around you and the waves are crashing down on you, find* something *to hold onto.*

Johnathan's face appeared in my mind, blocking the powerful effects of Mr. Jorgenson's *soul-gaze.* I was able to pull away then. I blinked and kept my eyes shut for a few seconds, fighting the shudder that threatened to expose my fear. When I once again opened my eyes, I was determined not to show him how scared I was. I looked him in the eyes. Not the smartest thing to do, but like I've said before, I hate bullies. I couldn't let him win. Besides, I figured I knew how to break his *gaze* now anyway. So, with a vision of Johnathan planted firmly in my mind, I looked Mr. Jorgenson in the eye—for a second. Or less. Maybe. I shifted my gaze to his forehead and was a little bit satisfied that the skin there had turned an angry shade of red.

"Miss Spurlock."

I waited for him to continue, which he didn't. "Uhh... yes, Mr. Jorgenson?" I really did try to keep the sarcastic tone out of my voice.

I must have been unsuccessful, however, because his hands curled into tight fists atop his desk before they disappeared under it.

"I wanted to see if you remembered anything else Ashley might have said to you the other day. She hasn't been back to school and I'm worried about her. Also, I want to assure you that you are safe here. The events you witnessed on your first day here must have been more than a little disconcerting for you."

It was obvious to me he was making this up as he went along. He hadn't thought of a Plan B in case the *soul-gaze* didn't work. I felt a small sense of pride prickling my chest. He'd underestimated me. The sense dissipated as I realized that made me an even bigger target—and also put Seth, my *brother*, in the danger zone.

I decided to try my hand at damage control. Which meant I had to act weak, and I hated acting weak. "It was very scary, Mr. Jorgenson. I haven't slept well the last two nights. Every time I close my eyes I see Ashley freaking out and the blood dripping from her hands." *It would be perfect if I could muster up a tear or two.*

I couldn't.

"Yes, well, I can only imagine. Would you like to talk with a counselor? I can set that up for today if you want."

"No, sir. I think I'll be okay. I'll let you know if I change my mind, though."

He repositioned himself in his chair. I was sure he'd noticed my failure to respond to his first question, but he couldn't seem to figure out how to get back to it while he was acting as the concerned principal.

I took advantage of his lack of planning ahead. "I would like to get back to class, Mr. Jorgenson, if there isn't anything else, that is."

Jorgenson made one last attempt to lock me in a *soul-gaze*. I pictured Johnathan firmly in my mind and boldly looked him in the eye. So much for acting the intimidated young girl. A half-formed smile froze on his lips when he realized his *gaze* wasn't working. His composure cracked.

"What the... *how* are you doing that?"

I batted my eyelashes—the picture of innocence. "Doing what, Mr. Jorgenson?"

He narrowed his eyes at me. "Nothing. Go back to class, Miss Spurlock."

I rose from the chair and turned toward the door to the office. Before I could reach it, he added, "I will be watching you very closely, Sasha. *Very* closely."

The chill that ran down my spine was insuppressible. I just kept walking though. The bell to change classes rang just as I reached Mrs.

C.'s room. Brendon came rushing out and almost smashed into me. His relief at seeing me was evident as he released a held breath.

"Sasha, what did the old creep want?"

I shrugged. "Apparently he's worried about my well-being after the incident the other day. He offered me counseling."

Brendon shook his head. "Well, I'm glad I caught you before your next class. I wanted to talk to you about something."

"Okay... talk away."

"Okay. Did Seth say anything to you about the party tonight after the game?"

"Yes, he mentioned it," I said.

"Well, don't let him go. Those parties are bad news. I'm not sure what goes on there, but people don't come back from them the same way they were before. Why don't you guys come to my family's diner after the game? I'll score you some free food—maybe even a shake."

"That sounds great. I'll have to run it by our parents, but I'm sure it'll be fine. Thanks, Brendon." I smiled and waved as we headed to our separate classes.

Of course, we *had* to go to the party, but he didn't need to know that. Maybe we could stop by the diner first. A shake sounded awfully good; I couldn't remember the last time I'd had one.

CHAPTER THIRTEEN

M r. Grewa's class was awesome. He loved history and it
showed in his teaching. Even the zombie-kids seemed to
pay more attention in his class.

He excused the class as soon as the bell rang, but stopped me
before I went out the door. "How are you doing, Sasha? Any more
trips to the principal's office?" No tiptoeing around his concerns, and
it was obvious he was concerned. I really loved his straightfor-
wardness.

"Actually, yeah, I was called there during first hour today."

He didn't even try to hide his alarm. He lowered his head to search my eyes.

"Mr. Grewa, I'm fine, really. I'm a lot tougher than I look."

"Yes, yes, I can see that." He nodded and furrowed his brow in confusion.

I decided to see if I could get some information out of him. I instinctually trusted him. Not enough to spill my guts completely, but enough to let him see I wasn't exactly just another high school student. "Mr. Grewa, what did you expect to see when you looked in my eyes just now? What were you afraid Mr. Jorgenson had done to me?"

The gentle teacher raised his index finger in the universal *Wait just a minute* sign and stepped over to close the door.

"Sasha, I don't know what's going on at this school and I don't want to scare you, but every other student that's been called into his office after having shown any amount of backbone during one of the odd occurrences that have happened here lately, has come out of there a changed person. *Every* other student."

"What do you mean, *changed?*"

"They either act like their brains have been scrambled somehow, or they become a member of his entourage... or, more accurately, his lackeys. Or, they just disappear..." He looked up at the clock. "You should get going to your next class, but we should definitely talk when there is a little more time. Be safe, Sasha."

He ushered me out of his classroom with a strange, hopeful look on his face. I was thinking—distracted—or I might have noticed the three rather large boys closing in on me as I hurried down the hall. Before I knew what was happening, one of them had knocked my books out of my hand and the other two crowded me up against a row of lockers.

The biggest of the three grabbed my face with one of his giant hands and forced me to look up at him. "We got our eyes on you, *Miss Spurlock*. Mind your own business or you'll be sorry, real sorry." Disgusting spittle flew from his puffy lips, reminding me of a Troll.

"But, *we'll* enjoy it, won't we, Bubba. We'll enjoy it *real* good," said the zit-faced boy pressing up against me.

"Shut up, idiot! I'm the only one who talks," said Bubba Big Lips. Zitface cringed a little. The other boy snickered.

I'd had more than enough at this point. I knew I couldn't just zap them right there in the hallway. It wouldn't be smart to show my hand this early in the game. So instead of magic, I employed some of the Ninja Turtle moves Halli had been teaching us. Did I mention Halli was an incredible martial arts expert? She doesn't remember how she learned it or even what discipline exactly she was trained in, but she was good, *real* good, as Zitface would say, grammar be damned. She was like a mini Jackie Chan. Except female. And not Chinese.

They stood so close to me that I wasn't able to use my arms. I needed to clear some space. I stomped on Snicker's instep with bone-crunching force, which caused him to back away with a yelp. I raised my arms and slammed them down hard and fast on Big Lips' forearms to break the grip he had on my face. He wasn't expecting that. An elbow to Zitface's nose and a knee to Big Lips' groin was enough to allow me the space to escape. I glanced back as I walked away and was satisfied to see blood dripping from Zitface's hands as he held them to his nose; a somewhat green-skinned Big Lips doubled over, clutching his groin; and Snicker hopping around on one foot.

It had turned out to be a very eventful day indeed. I couldn't wait until lunch to compare notes with Seth. I refused to look over my shoulder to see if they were following me. If they wanted to continue the fight, *bring it on*, I thought. I was in the mood for a good throw-down. I figured those three must be some of the lackeys Mr. Grewa had mentioned. It sure hadn't taken long for Mr. Jorgenson to sic them on me.

I slipped into my next class just as the final bell rang.

I saw Snicker in the hall on my way to lunch. I noted, much to my satisfaction, that he was still limping. I smiled my sweetest serves-you-right-smile at him and continued to the lunchroom. I was glad to see that Seth was sitting at the same table as Alec and Johnathan. Seth and Alec now knew each other from football, so it didn't give anything away if we all sat together.

I sat down and Seth said, "*Now* can I tell you guys?"

"Tell us what?" I asked.

"Yeah," Johnathan said. "But hurry up. Looks like Brendon's headed this way."

"Okay. These three punks cornered me in the locker room after gym class and started asking questions about 'my sister.'" He looked at me.

"Wait," I said. "What did these punks look like?"

"They were big, but not as big as Johnathan—except one that was fatter, with big lips." He described the three thugs that had pushed me up against the locker.

"Was one of them limping?" I asked with a small measure of smugness.

"Yeah, and one of them looked like he was getting two black eyes—wait, how did you know one was limping?"

"Well, I had an encounter with them, too. They kinda annoyed me."

Brendon sidled up to the table before we could finish our stories.

"Mind if I sit with you guys?" he asked.

"Not at all. Have a seat, *Brendonna*." It didn't surprise me at all that Alec already had an annoying nickname for Brendon.

He sat between Johnathan and me. I'd left the empty seat between us on purpose; I didn't want there to be any chance that we might bump arms or brush legs.

"So, Sasha, I heard you had a little run-in with some of the school bullies earlier—and that they came out on the losing end. So, what's the deal? Spill your guts, girl."

"That explains a lot," Seth said.

"What do you mean? What did they say to you?" Brendon asked.

I turned to Brendon and explained. "Seth was just telling us he had a 'run-in' with the same crew in the locker room."

"Well, as I was saying, they cornered me after class. They didn't even care that the locker room was full. Not that it mattered. No one came to help or even see what was going on. They all just scattered as quickly as possible," Seth said. "Anyway, they surrounded me and started asking questions, mostly about you," he nodded toward me.

"First, the kid with the black eyes"—*Zitface*—"asked, 'Do you know karate like your sister?' I was a little confused and wondered if you'd had anything to do with the darkening circles under his eyes. I said, 'Yeah, I do' and kind of jerked toward him and raised my hands like this"—Seth raised his hands like a gangsta-rapper, totally making me laugh—"he jumped three feet! It was awesome."

"What else did they ask?" I said.

"They all kind of backed up a little then and started asking questions. It sounded like they'd memorized a list. 'Where did you move from? Does your sister have any other *talents*?' The question that bothered me the most, though..." He hesitated and glanced at Brendon before finishing, "was, 'Do you know what a *soul-gaze* is?' I was like 'What the crap are you talkin' about? You guys tryin' to flirt with me or somethin'? I'm not your type—douchebags just don't do it for me.' Then I just shoved past them and left the locker room."

Seth had a way with words.

"What's a *soul-gaze*?" Brendon asked.

As if on cue, we all shrugged in the I-don't-have-a-clue fashion.

Brendon turned to me. "It's your turn. Tell us what happened after second hour."

I recounted my encounter with the bad boys. Brendon was in awe of my hand-to-hand combat skills and brazen disregard for the bully code—in that I didn't bow down and get pee-my-pants scared and hand over my lunch money. Johnathan was irate. His eyes started to change color and I knew he needed to calm down before he lost control. I kicked Seth under the table and discreetly nodded at Johnathan, then pointed at my eyes with my back turned to Brendon. Seth immediately understood.

"Johnathan, let's go check out the ice cream bars. I'm in the mood for some frozen deliciousness." Seth stood and gestured to Johnathan to follow him. Johnathan drew in a shaky breath and closed his eyes for a few seconds before standing.

"Hey! I want one, too. Wait for me!" Alec said, almost falling in his hurry to get up from the table.

"So... karate, huh? What color belt do you have?" Brendon said.

"Yeah, well, not officially or anything. We just watch a lot of *Ninja Turtles*. Michaelangelo is my favorite, so I guess you could say I'm an orange belt."

The fact that he understood the reference—and laughed—moved Brendon up a notch in my book.

The boys made it back to the table with their ice cream. Johnathan was a little calmer, but he still continued to look around for the bullies. I hoped they were far from the cafeteria, not because I was worried for them—they deserved what they deserved—but because I was worried Johnathan would lose himself to the Wolf and go on a beating, killing frenzy. We needed to get him out of there.

"Come on, guys, let's go get some fresh air," I said.

I headed for the front doors of the school, hoping the bullies wouldn't cross our path. We made it safely outside and Alec was able to distract Johnathan by talking about the football game that night.

I didn't see the Bad Boys again that day. After school, Halli met us with dinner at a nearby park. We hung out until just before the boys were supposed to be at the field to prepare for the game, then walked there together. The plan was to pass Halli off as my cousin. Alec and Seth headed to the locker room while Johnathan, Halli and I started for the football field. The game didn't start for another hour but there were plenty of students milling about, so we milled about with them and tried to listen in on conversations. We wandered over by the fenced-in shop area where Johnathan and I had gone our first night there, where we'd seen the tank contraption. We peered through the locked gate, but didn't see anything unusual—not that we expected to.

"We really need to figure out where they're hiding that thing. I'd like to take a closer look at it and get a sample of what's inside those tanks," Johnathan said.

"Maybe we should make another late night visit, since that's when we saw it here before," I suggested.

He squirmed a little and frowned at that suggestion. I doubted it was the thought of returning at night, but the thought of being alone with me that bothered him.

"All five of us could come. That way we could spread out a little and have back-up if needed," I said. The twitching muscle in his jaw instantly relaxed. It broke my heart, the idea he was afraid to be alone with me.

As the football stadium filled up, we made our way to the student section. I looked around at the sparse crowd. The visiting team bleachers had more spectators. There were only four cheerleaders on our side. I assumed there'd been many more before their school had been invaded by weirdness and suicide. The crowd was equal parts subdued and over-the-top zealous. I could guess by watching them which students had started the party a little early and which students had some brain-fry going on from past parties. I wondered, as I looked around, which were Jorgenson's followers. How many more were there?

As the teams ran out onto the field to warm up, it was obvious that the Edwards Falcons were undermanned. The visiting team had at least twice as many players.

The announcer came on the speakers: "Please stand for the National Anthem. Directly following the National Anthem, Principal Jorgenson wishes to say a few words."

My stomach flipped just a little. I'd really been hoping he wouldn't be here, that he'd be holed up in his Evil Lair somewhere, plotting his revenge on the Girl Who Dared Defy His Gaze.

Even though I knew it was coming, a chill still ran down my neck when his voice came over the loudspeaker. "Parents and students, welcome to Friday Night Lights at Edwards High School! It's great to see the support for our football team and our school after a very rough and tragic few weeks. I want to assure you all that we are deeply concerned with the well-being of our students and are doing all within our power to keep them safe. Your support is a wonderful step in the healing process. We would like to dedicate this game to the memory of those we've recently lost. I would like to welcome the Garfield Bulldogs to our field tonight and wish our Falcons good luck! Let's get it started!"

Really, I thought. *Let's get it started? Isn't that a song or something?* What a lame-o. A lame-o that made my skin crawl. I had to force myself not to slink down and hide. The announcer's box was right above and to the right of where we sat, and I could almost feel his creepy eyes scanning the crowd for me.

I forgot all about Mr. Jorgenson once the game started. I'd almost forgotten how much I loved football. Alec had not been exaggerating when he said he had mad skills as a running back. He must have run up almost two hundred yards and he scored two of the three Falcon touchdowns. I knew he could run fast, but his ability to sense holes in the defense was equally impressive. Seth was also awesome. He had five sacks and was still a force to be reckoned with when they started to double up on blocking him.

We ended up winning by two points when Seth outmaneuvered his blockers and tackled the Bulldog punter in the end zone for a safety. It was awesome. The adrenaline of a tight game is infectious. Even some of the zombie kids perked up a little.

We waited by the outside entrance to the locker rooms for our triumphant friends. They were totally stoked, chest-bumping with each other, then Johnathan. They even hugged me and Halli. I was glad they'd taken the time to shower before coming out.

They talked excitedly about the game as if we hadn't just witnessed it for ourselves: "Did you see when I vaulted over that kid's head for a touchdown?" and "Did you see the third time I sacked the QB and he had to be helped off the field?" And a million other "Did you sees."

"That was an awesome game!" a passing teammate called. "You guys are MVPs. Are you comin' to the party? You *have* to come to the party, it's gonna be epic!"

"Yeah, we'll be there," Seth answered.

"Bring your hot sister, too." He leered at me. I wanted to tell him to go suck a raw egg, but I smiled instead, like it was a privilege to be called "hot" by one of such obvious greatness. I glanced over at Johnathan, but he seemed to be handling himself okay.

We waited a few more minutes for Brendon to exit the building. The plan was for us to go to his family's diner and take him up on his offer of free food while pacifying his fear of us attending the party. Then, we would go to the party.

"You guys ready to taste the best burgers and fries you've ever had?" he asked.

"And shakes?" Seth asked, hopefully.

Brendon laughed. "Yeah, and shakes. You guys deserve shakes for sure after that game. That's the first game we've won since... well, since the beginning of the season."

Lucky's Diner was decorated with green shamrocks, rabbit's feet, horseshoes and other supposedly lucky memorabilia. I looked around at the booths and tables packed with customers—a good indication of the quality of the food. Brendon's parents had saved us a booth close to the kitchen, and his sister brought us drinks while Brendon went in the back to change into his work clothes: a green t-shirt with *Lucky's* on the front, a pair of Levis, and a white apron.

It was, by far, the best food I'd eaten in at least a year and a half. The burgers dripped with grease. I had a bacon cheeseburger that took up more than half the plate. He brought us a huge basket of fries to share and refilled it at least twice that I know of. I soon had a little brain-drain going on, as all my circulating blood was shunted to my guts to help digest the cholesterol-laden feast. Johnathan ate his burger, probably two baskets of fries and the half of Halli's burger she couldn't finish.

I didn't think any of us could possibly eat another mouthful. I was wrong. Brendon brought out six huge chocolate shakes in tall glasses and sat down to drink his with us.

"Hey, Sasha," Brendon grinned. "What did the blonde say when she saw the Cheerios box?"

I pursed my lips and raised an eyebrow at him. "Blonde jokes? Really?"

"She said," he continued as if I hadn't even spoken, "awesome, donut seeds!"

Johnathan spit chocolate shake across the table. I smiled as his laughter mixed with the other boys'—even though it was at my and my fellow blonde's expense.

I rolled my eyes as Seth and Alec tried to top the other's jokes.

"See what you started," I smiled and pointed at Brendon.

The diner became busier as it got later, so Brendon had to leave us to go help in the kitchen. We thanked him, and then headed for the party we told him we weren't going to. Halli reluctantly started for home, after one more attempt to persuade us to take her, too.

CHAPTER FOURTEEN

The party was held at the home of one of the football players—with no parents in sight, of course. The home was just a little bigger than average but the backyard was large and bordered on a thick forest of trees. A fire blazed in a fire pit on the huge covered patio, which also housed two enormous barbeque grills, granite countertops, a stainless steel fridge and sink, plush patio furniture, and a granite-topped bar that seated twelve. Much nicer than most indoor kitchens I'd seen.

By the time we arrived, the party was going full blast. There had to be over a hundred kids there. We'd all vowed not to partake of *any* food or beverages offered—not that any of us, except for maybe Johnathan, could have forced one more bite into our mouths. In order to not look conspicuous, Alec and Seth picked up a drink and pretended to sip from it occasionally, careful not to let the contents so much as touch their skin.

I was more than shocked when I spotted Ashley, the window-breaking girl, over by a big canopy-tent set up in the corner of the yard. I'd been sure I would never see her again—sure that she was either locked up in a special home for the insane somewhere, or at least that her parents had the common sense to remove her from the psycho school, and all things related to it. Yet, there she stood, as zombie-like as ever, a drink pressed desperately to her lips.

I walked over to her, stopping a few feet away.

"Hey, Ashley," I said. "How have you been? I haven't seen you at school this week."

Three long seconds passed before she brought her gaze to mine. Her eyelids remained half closed, over unfocused red eyes. She tilted her head to the side, as if trying to place me.

"Hey… you. What's up?" she slurred.

"Just got here, ready to party. What're you drinking?"

Another long pause. Ashley's gaze focused on the cup in her bandaged hand, then her eyes widened like she was surprised by its presence there.

"Oh… umm… not sure… exactly. I think… a… I got it from there."

The liquid sloshed over the sides of her cup as she gestured to the canopy-tent. She turned pale, wavered back and forth, eyes closed. I carefully took the cup from her, led her to a chair, and helped her sit.

I made my way around the corner of the three-sided tent, then stopped dead in my tracks. The chemistry-set-on-steroids contraption Johnathan and I had seen at the school that night sat right there in the middle of the tent, right in the middle of this packed party. Standing on either side of it, coiled hoses in hand, were Big Lips, Zitface, and Snicker. They filled cups with the blue-tinted liquid that came through the hoses from the large tanks. It smelled like a dark combination of charcoal and watermelon. I stepped back around the side of the tent, out of their line of vision, and listened.

"What's this stuff supposed to do? Why's it any better than the beer over there?" a boy asked.

"Are you kidding me? *Sentience* is way better than beer." That was Big Lips talking. "For one thing, it works a lot faster. Just one small cup and you're on your way to la-la land."

"Ya, and plus it gives you *special powers*," said Zitface.

"Shut up, Scott! I do the talking," Big Lips said.

"What's he mean by 'special powers'?" the now curious kid asked.

"No more questions, do you want some or not? Believe me, you're missing out if you don't try it at least once." He sounded like a used car salesman.

"Ya, dude, I'll try some—if you're sure it's better than beer," the kid said.

Big Lips laughed. "There is no comparison, dude. No comparison."

I didn't know what to do. Should I try to stop the kid from drinking it? Should I go tell Johnathan I found what we were looking for?

The kid came out of the tent with the cup. I remembered a little spell I'd perfected by performing it frequently on Alec.

"*Tangle pedicus,*" I whispered.

The boy tripped, sending his cup, with the liquid inside it, flying. He swore quite proficiently as he went down, and a group of jocks near him laughed like only half-buzzed teenagers could.

I didn't wait around to see if he got back in line for another drink. I needed to find Johnathan. After a few minutes of searching, I couldn't find him anywhere. He shouldn't have been hard to spot—he was one of the taller guys there and was without doubt the best-looking one. I figured he'd be surrounded by girls. I found Alec and Seth with several football players, re-telling game stories. I tapped Seth on the shoulder. "Have you seen Johnathan?"

He shook his head. The kid standing next to him said, "That big kid you guys walked in with? I saw him leaving a few minutes ago. The cheerleaders had him surrounded, all of them flirting like crazy—he looked *über* uncomfortable, like he was ready to bolt. And, that's pretty much what he did—bolted right out into the trees."

"Ugh. Seth, can I talk to you for a second?" I said through clenched teeth.

"Uh, yeah, sure."

We walked a few steps away. As loud as the music and raucousness was, I didn't think we'd be overheard.

"What's up, sis?" Seth said.

"What's up is that I found the device we've been looking for. It's here, it's making the drug, and they're handing it out like candy on Halloween. We need to figure out a plan before more kids get poisoned. Now is not a good time for Johnathan to pull one of his disappearing acts."

"By device I assume you mean the chemistry lab thing you and Johnathan saw outside the high school?"

"Exactly."

"Let's spread out and look for him, I guess. Todd said he went into the woods, he's probably just in there chillin'. I don't want to make a move unless we all discuss it first," Seth said.

"I agree. Find Alec and meet me over behind the canopy-tent."

I waited a long two or three minutes for Alec and Seth.

"Okay, guys," I said, once we were all together. "I'll take this end. Seth, you enter the trees at about the center of the yard, and Alec, you take the far end. Meet back here in fifteen minutes whether you find him or not. If not, we'll have to make our plan without him."

I entered the trees at a spot that looked like it could be a trail, but it was too dark to know for sure. The trees and vegetation were thick, making for difficult progress. I stumbled every few steps because I couldn't see where I was going, and I swore I would throttle Johnathan when I found him. I tried to think of this from his point of view—he was probably overwhelmed by the scents of the hormonal teenagers surrounding him, plus all the noise, alcohol, and other substances that were being passed around. It quite possibly could have caused him to go over the edge, so he left before that happened. I was still mad, even though I figured I knew why he'd left without telling any of us. We needed him now, and he really needed to figure this thing out, gain some control of himself. I still felt too worried and angry to be understanding.

If I hadn't been preoccupied with my thoughts, I might have noticed I was being followed. By the time it finally registered that I heard noises behind me, it was too late to do anything about it.

"Johnathan?" I whispered.

Big Lips and his stooges burst through the trees behind me.

Before I could utter a sound, Big Lips clamped one hand over my mouth while the other hand encircled the back of my head—his two hands pressed together like he was trying to squeeze my teeth out through my eye sockets. For a moment, I panicked, forgetting I could still breathe through my nose when my mouth was no longer an option. I started to fight him, but they knew my tricks this time and his two buddies stepped up close, grabbed my arms and swept my feet out from under me with perfectly synchronized kicks to my legs.

I landed so hard on my tailbone it rattled my teeth. A sharp pain shot up my spine and exploded in the back of my head. Big Lips was able to follow me down without letting up hardly any pressure from the grip he had on my mouth. I lay on my back, my head pushed up tight against a tree. My legs were tangled in the lower branches of a pine tree, the right one twisted at such an angle I was sure it would snap. I was close to being bent in half at the waist. Pain became secondary to fear as Big Lips straddled my torso, Zitface held both my arms pinned against the tree my head was pressed against, and Snicker sat on my legs, pushing them and the branches they were twisted in down a couple of feet. I twisted and bucked my hips, trying to throw Big Lips off me.

They're going to rape me. Terror raced through my veins and I tried to scream, only to have the hand over my mouth clamp down tighter. A tear escaped and rolled down my temple into my hair.

Breathing became difficult through my nose as I tried to gulp in more air to fuel my struggle. I couldn't inhale enough through the narrow passages, I was suffocating. I stopped resisting, my nostrils flaring with the rapid intake of breath.

"Not much of fighter now, are you?" Big Lips sneered. "Someone evidently thinks you're *special*. I personally don't see it, but I'll enjoy carrying out my orders anyways. Now, I'm gonna take my hand off your mouth, but if you make any noise I'll use my fist to knock all your teeth down your throat. I hope you do decide to make noise, because I'd love to see you choke to death on your own teeth and blood."

He removed his hand and I took a deep breath through my mouth. What I really wanted to do was to spit in his face, but I determined that to be an unwise decision, based on the situation. So, I swallowed down my defiance borne of fear and anger, and kept quiet when he removed his hand.

"Hand me the stuff, TJ," he said, holding his hand out to the thug that sat on my legs.

TJ dug a small plastic bottle from his jacket pocket and handed it to Big Lips. "Here ya go, Bubba," he said.

Bubba twisted the top off and the smell—charcoal and watermelon—instantly hit my nostrils. Only, this was much stronger than the odor that had come from the tent.

"This is a super-dose of *Sentience*, Miss Spurlock." Bubba's big lips twisted into a demented smile. "It oughta mess ya up real good."

A fresh wave of panic flooded through me, sending my heart rate soaring higher. A collage of zombie-like teenagers flashed through my head. I forgot all about staying silent.

"No!" I screamed and then clamped my mouth shut tight as he brought the bottle close to my face. I bucked my hips and twisted my head side to side.

Bubba clamped his free hand around my jaw and squeezed, forcing my mouth open. He was so strong.

"Away!" I yelled.

All the helplessness, anger, fear, and disgust inside me, came roaring out in a tangible force.

A strangled yell escaped Bubba's mouth as he took flight. The small bottle he held fell to the ground beside my head, and several drops of the liquid it contained splashed into my open mouth. I swallowed by reflex.

My attack had been so focused on the thug trying to pour poison down my throat that it hadn't affected the other two at all. They looked from me up to where their leader was flying through the air, eyes wide and mouths open. They still held onto my arms and legs.

I drew in a breath to form another attack, but before I could unleash the magic an enraged roar pierced the night. I turned my head just in time to see Johnathan emerge from the trees.

At the same time, I felt my brain disconnect. I wanted to call out to Johnathan, but the words became lost somewhere on the way from my brain to my mouth. My throat worked frantically to speak, but nothing came out.

Johnathan grabbed both boys by the front of their shirts and lifted them into the air before slamming them into each other face-first. I watched as the teeth that were knocked free of their bloody gums flew in slow motion, and before they had a chance to hit the ground, they turned into soaring cockroaches that disappeared into the air.

I blinked with eyelids that weighed ten pounds.

"John... what..." My mouth betrayed me still. The screams inside my head were stuck there.

Johnathan released his grip and the two boys slumped to the ground. Zitface tried to crawl away.

An angry animal growl issued from Johnathan's throat right before he slammed his fist into the back of the whimpering kid's head and knocked him out cold.

In slow motion, I willed my eyes to look at Johnathan's face. For the flash of an instant I saw my John. I found my voice and screamed as his face morphed into an unrecognizable mask of fury. He stared back at me, eyes blazing red, with the face of a wolf demon. I turned my head to avoid the smoldering venom dripping from his canine teeth. I tried to scoot away as maggots fell from his matted fur. A hole gaped in his chest and where his heart should have been was an empty cavity of darkness that went on for infinity.

I screamed, the horror was enough to break the barrier between my brain and throat. I squeezed my eyes closed to shut out the monster Johnathan had morphed into. He was still there, in my mind, even with my eyes closed. My eyelids flew open and my blurred vision landed on Bubba, entangled in the branches of a tree. The branches turned to snakes and wound themselves around him, crawling in and out of his mouth as he opened it to scream. The maggot infested beast noticed him at about the same time as I did. He jumped an impossible distance and grabbed Bubba by one dangling arm. Bubba's terrified eyes bulged from their sockets as he fell to meet the pounding fists of the Johnathan Wolf-Demon.

I closed my eyes for a second and when I opened them, Bubba had changed into an Ogre—a mewling, pitiful Ogre that cried like a newborn kitten and begged Johnathan to leave him alone. He didn't. He was in a rage.

I shook my head to try to clear it. Something wasn't right. I looked back up at the big-lipped Ogre. He had blood streaming from his bulbous, gray nose and from a large cut to the left side of his furry uni-brow. The wolf was now holding him up by the throat and snarling viciously, snapping its teeth.

I should stop Johnathan. No, that isn't Johnathan. He doesn't have maggots in his hair.

In my periphery I saw Alec and Seth running toward us.

"Johnathan! Stop, you're gonna' kill him!" Seth yelled.

I watched as each of them grabbed a huge, hairy arm and tried to pull the wolf away from the Ogre. I was relieved to see that Alec and Seth looked normal. Except for the little Faeries flying around their heads.

The tree where my legs were still entangled drew my attention. I shrieked when the bark of the trunk started to morph into an angry face, and the tree limbs started to move around my legs like sinuous arms—entangling me even tighter. I kicked and tried to sit up and scoot backwards. Then *all* of the trees grew faces and arms that grabbed at me. The trees pulled my arms and legs until they ripped from my body; the pain and pressure so strong, I blacked out for a few merciful seconds. Awareness returned as my limbless head and torso lay there helplessly screaming, a detached portion of my mind watched as the trees took my amputated extremities and attached them to their trunks to make new, grotesque branches. I continued to scream.

I screamed for hours. For days. For years. For an eternity.

Then, Johnathan was beside me. *My* Johnathan, not the Wolf. He touched my face with his gentle hands, searching my eyes, murmuring softly. "Paige, it's okay. Look at me, look at me. You're okay, everything's okay."

I stopped screaming. I started trembling. Ferocious tears sprung to my eyes and flowed down my face. I wrapped my still-attached arms around Johnathan's neck and sobbed. I closed my eyes—that was a mistake, the gore returned, replaying on the backs of my eyelids like some sadistic movie caught in an eternal loop of terror. I whimpered—no, I'm not proud of that, whimpering is against my code of honor and dignity. But, I didn't scream, and that's what I really *wanted* to do—I was afraid if I started again, I would never stop. I would just keep screaming until there was no air left to breathe.

I opened my eyes, afraid to close them for more than a blink, but seriously afraid to look at the trees. I buried my face in Johnathan's neck. He wrapped his arms tightly around me, his face pressed close to my ear, whispering, "Shhh. It's okay. I'm here. You're safe. Shhh."

He rocked me back and forth, soothing and gentle. I continued to sob.

I twitched when Seth spoke; I'd forgotten he was there. "Johnathan, what happened? What's wrong with her?"

Johnathan's arms tightened around me. He moved his mouth away from my ear long enough to answer. "I'm not sure. Just give her a minute. You guys make sure no one's coming this way. And, keep an eye on our unconscious *friends*."

I heard Seth and Alec move a small distance away. Johnathan's mouth moved next to my ear again, his warm breath a soothing distraction. "Paige, you're okay. You need to slow down your breathing. You need to slow down your breathing, Paige. Breathe with me."

He took a slow, deep breath in, and then slowly let it out. In and out, over and over, until my respirations fell into sync with his. I stopped sobbing and took only an occasional shuddering breath. I became aware of Johnathan's scent, strong and musky. My thoughts turned from monstrous trees and Demon eyes to other, much more pleasant things. Like Johnathan's lips. That's when I remembered my promise to him.

I pulled away. Well, I tried to pull away, but his encircling arms held me tight. "John," I said.

He loosened his embrace just a little, enough for me to look up into his eyes. I fully expected to see the predatory, golden-eyed Johnathan I'd seen in the alley that day. I was more than a little relieved to see just a really worried Johnathan staring back at me.

"John," my voice rasped, almost gone from the extensive screaming I'd put it through. "I'm sorry, I'm so sorry. You can let go of me now." There was nothing in the world I wanted more than to stay wrapped up in the safety of his arms—but, I'd already broken my promise to him and I couldn't continue to compromise his mental well-being. His words from the alley came back to me: *I will leave, if I have to, to protect you.*

He narrowed his eyes and tilted his head. "Why are you sorr..." Understanding dawned on his face. I prepared for him to let go of me and push me away. Instead, he shocked me completely by crushing my head to his chest. I felt his warm lips pressed to the top of my head—all my resistance vanished and I melted into him again, relishing the warmth of his body pressed to mine and the feel of his hot breath in my hair.

The faint sounds of music drifted to my ears from the party in the distance. I closed my eyes, exhausted from the night's events, and shuddered as a picture of maggots and wolf hair invaded my mind. I quickly opened my eyes.

"We should get you home. Are you hurt anywhere? Will you be able to walk okay?" Johnathan spoke quietly, almost in a whisper.

"I... don't know if I'm hurt. I think I'm okay... physically anyway," I said.

He sighed and loosened his hold. "Okay, let me help you up. Move slowly, in case you *are* hurt."

Johnathan crouched next to me, placed one strong arm around my back and offered me his other hand as a way to pull myself up. First, I had to untangle my legs from the tree branches—which triggered a flashback and a bout of terror that caused me to clamp down hard on Johnathan's hand with both of mine.

"What's wrong? Are you hurt?" he asked.

Not hurt, just terrified, I thought. My throat was too constricted to speak so I just shook my head.

"Hey, guys, come give us a hand here. Help Paige get her legs untangled," Johnathan said just loud enough for Seth and Alec to hear.

They hurried over and pulled my legs from the branches. I exhaled the breath I'd been holding and Johnathan helped me stand. I clung to him as a wave of dizziness swept over me and I felt his strong arm tighten around my waist. We stood for a few minutes until I was sure the dizziness had passed. Alec and Seth had deep frowns on their faces as they watched me closely.

"What happened, Paige?" Alec asked. "What's going on with you?"

"Let her recover a little before you start giving her the third degree, Alice," Johnathan said.

"It's okay." I looked at Alec and answered, "They had some of that liquid stuff that was at the party, in the tanks—only Big Lips over there said it was a special, extra-strong dose just for me. When I blew him off me with a spell, he dropped it and some of it spilled into my mouth. I can't imagine how bad it would have been if they'd made me drink the whole thing." I shuddered.

Seth bent down and picked up the plastic container where it had fallen. A small bit of liquid remained inside. He secured the lid and placed the bottle in his pocket. He looked up to see us all staring at him and said with a shrug, "Maybe I can figure out what's in this stuff."

"Just be super cautious with it. It's horrible," I said.

"So, what did it do to you?" Alec asked. "Why were you screaming your brains out?"

I looked at him and flinched when I saw a small Faerie still flying near his head. I'd hoped the effects had worn completely off—but seeing that Faerie caused me to think they probably hadn't.

"What?" Alec asked as he searched the area above his head to see what had caught my attention.

"You don't see anything?" I asked, hopeful that maybe there really *was* a Faerie circling his head and it wasn't the *Sentience* at all.

Alec looked at me through squinted eyes, his head tilted sideways. "Nooo... do *you* see something?"

I shook my head and squeezed my eyes shut, but only for a couple of seconds. The monsters were still there when I closed my eyes. I couldn't stop the tears from falling, again—at least this time I had the sobs somewhat under control with just a small hitch every few breaths. My throat hurt. I was exhausted. I was scared. And, I was drugged. This had not been a good night. Even having Johnathan there next to me, holding me, wasn't enough to erase the horrors.

Alec looked anxiously from me to Johnathan. "Maybe I see something... maybe I just looked in the wrong place. What am I looking for? I'll look again."

I laughed as I continued to cry.

"Let's get you home," Johnathan said.

We set off in a direction that would skirt far around the party-house. My legs felt all wobbly and I was glad for Johnathan's support. I worried about being so close to him and the strong possibility it would cause another animalistic response from him. I kept expecting him to push me away after the shock of the fight wore off. But he didn't. He held me close and lent me his strength.

The drug continued to play with my mind on the long walk home. I saw things everywhere. A homeless man hunched in the threshold of a building turned into a praying mantis with hundreds of red eyes. It lunged for me and I let out a nearly silent scream that would have burst some eardrums if my vocal cords hadn't been pushed past their limits. A short burst of psychotic-sounding, wheezing laughter came as a purple fish wearing a top hat and carrying a tiny cane floated past. I flinched and let out a squeak as a star exploded in front of my face. This barrage continued as we walked.

After each sighting I had, Alec would ask, "What's wrong, Paige? What do you see?" And, every time he asked, I would just shake my head, unable to speak.

Finally, Johnathan and Seth yelled at him to shut up and stop asking.

The Underground was the worst by far. Except for the limb-stealing trees, that is. As soon as we descended below, the monsters came out in force to torment my flimsy mind. Seth went down the stairs first, and when he turned to look up at us, his face twisted into a mask of horror. Millions of spiders spewed from his mouth, eyes, ears and nostrils. The spiders headed straight for me, growing larger as they approached. I ripped out of Johnathan's grip and turned to run, screaming silently. My rubbery legs couldn't keep up with the terror-adrenaline racing through my body and I tripped on the step that led out to the city above. I smacked my head hard when I went down, but not hard enough to knock me out, unfortunately. I rolled down the three or four steps to where Johnathan was just turning to follow me. He stopped my descent, grabbed me around the middle and lifted me up. I looked into his face, still hysterical, and saw the Wolf-demon again—worse this time because it was staring at me with its hungry predator eyes.

To my drug-ravaged mind it was real and it wasn't my Johnathan. I fought for my life, scratching at its face. It roared as my fingernails hit home and sunk into the soft skin around its eyes. I swear I could feel its teeth sink into the center of my neck as I continued to scream my sickening silent scream.

Someone wrapped their hands around my arms and I fought those, too. They dragged me off the steps and down to the more stable footing of the Underground sidewalk.

"Just hold her down for a minute... until she calms down. We'll never get her home like this—not without serious injury to her and us," the Wolf-demon growled.

Seth held my right arm. A lone spider jumped from his face

directly at my eyes. I shook my head with frantic, exaggerated movements. I caught sight of Alec, holding my left arm. His mouth was twisted up into a demented smile, rimmed with grotesque clown makeup made of blood and pus. His eyes spun like a top and his throat was slit from ear to ear, leaking black, tar-like liquid.

They held me up against a brick wall. My strength was waning. I closed my eyes and slumped to the ground, led there gently by their hands. *Wait, that doesn't make sense. Why would these monsters be gentle?* Nothing made sense. Exhaustion took over. I lowered my head and continued to take rapid, shallow breaths.

Then, he was there, kneeling in front of me. He stroked my face and spoke gently, like he was trying to calm a frightened bird. "Paige, you're okay, you're safe. Nothing's going to hurt you." My Johnathan. The spell broke when I heard his voice quiver and my heart ached at the sound.

I looked in his eyes and was relieved to see they were, indeed, *his* eyes. I tried to reach for him, but Alec and Seth still held my arms. "John? What's happening to me?"

"Let her go, guys," he never took his eyes from mine. "I don't know exactly what's happening, Paige, but I know it'll be all right. We'll figure this out and the drug'll wear off. I want you to let me carry you the rest of the way. Just hide your eyes and think good thoughts. We'll be home soon."

I nodded. He didn't give me a chance to stand up, just scooped me up in his arms and stood. I barely had enough energy to wrap my arms around his neck. I buried my face in his shoulder and thought of the first time he'd held my hand. I fantasized about what our first date would be like. I breathed in his scent. And... I refused to close my eyes or look at anything but Johnathan's shirt.

The only sounds on the way home were those of the boys' feet on the ground and Johnathan's breathing. By the time we reached our Underground haven, I felt like my mind was on the mend. For the time being. Who knew what the long-term effects would be.

Halli met us at the bottom of the stairs where Johnathan lowered me to the ground.

"Hal," Johnathan said, "Paige has had a rough night. Will you go help her get ready for bed, please? We'll fill you in once she's settled."

"Of course. Come on, Paige. You look awful," she took my arm and walked with me to our shared room.

I fell unconscious as soon as I lay down.

CHAPTER FIFTEEN

My head hurt where I'd whacked it against the stairs the night before. I was surprised I felt no obvious ill effects of the drug—like in a hung-over, hugging-the-toilet kind of way.

The last one to wake, I emerged from the bathroom to three apprehensive stares and one mostly curious one—the curious one being Halli, as she hadn't been witness to my multiple displays of insanity.

Johnathan wouldn't meet my gaze. "How're you feeling?" he asked, looking down at the dishes he was drying.

"Um... okay, I guess. My throat feels like I swallowed a cactus, but other than that..." I shrugged. I really didn't feel like talking; it was difficult to force air through my ravaged vocal cords and my voice came out in a squeaky whisper.

"Are you hungry? We saved you some lunch." Halli slid a covered plate across the bar to where I stood.

I really wasn't hungry. I removed the aluminum foil from the plate and picked up a fork. Then set it back down, shaking my head.

"You really should try to eat something, Paige," Johnathan continued to avoid my eyes. "At least drink something." He set a tall glass of water in front of me. I was more than a little devastated that Johnathan had reverted back to the antisocial, scared-to-look-at-me version of his new self.

"Are you gonna tell us what you saw last night?" Alec asked.

"Give her a break, *Alice*, she just woke up and has no voice," Johnathan said.

"Come on, Johnny, you know you want to know what that stuff made her see, too. I've never heard anyone scream like that before in my life! It must have been horrible to make *Paige* scream like that."

"Alec…" The glass Johnathan held in his hand shattered. We all stared at him in silence as he dropped the remaining glass shards to the floor and wiped the blood from his hand onto his pants. The cool, calm, and collected Johnathan from the previous night had vanished, replaced by the high-strung, on-edge, ready to explode Johnathan we'd been seeing the last few weeks. Gold flecks glinted in his brown eyes.

He walked from behind the bar and toward the stairs.

I stood to follow him, calling out to him to wait for me, but my voice only produced a small squeak. He must have heard the sound, because he stopped walking long enough for me to catch up. We silently climbed the stairs; he stayed a few steps above me. He took down the wards when we reached the exit of the ruined room above our home and I followed him out onto the Underground sidewalk. The darkness and the smell of mold, though familiar, seemed worse than usual.

He walked a few paces, then stopped, his back to me.

I waited.

"Paige," he finally said. "I don't… last night…" He slammed his fist into the wall he faced. Small pieces of brick flew around him. He lowered his head and breathed heavily.

"John," I whisper-croaked. "I'm pretty sure I know what you want to say. Our deal isn't broken just because you were able to control yourself last night. You still want me to stay away from you." I know I could have worded that differently so it didn't sound like I was blaming him, but it hurt me that he couldn't tolerate me near him. And my childish side wanted to make sure he knew it.

His hands tightened into fists and it took him a moment to respond. "You know I don't *want* you to stay away. I *need* you to—for your own safety." He turned to face me, looking me in the eyes for the first time that day.

"Last night, I think I used up all the hormones or adrenaline or whatever makes me act like a rabid animal." He paused and drew a deep, shaky breath before continuing in a slightly less angry tone. "I used it all up on those scumbags that were hurting you. Then, you were so freaked out, screaming… your eyes were *crazy*. I was afraid… so afraid, that you were lost… that I would never see *you* again… just those crazy eyes darting back and forth… looking at things that weren't there. I was so scared your mind was blown like all those kids at the school."

He sat on the remains of the centuries-old sidewalk and lowered his head to his arms, folded on bent knees.

I wanted to go to him, to comfort him as he had me the night before. But I sat a safe distance away and waited for him to collect himself.

Finally, he looked up, but not at me this time. He stared at the dilapidated building across the street and started chucking pieces of broken stone at it. "Anyway, I could handle being close to you last night. The fight, the fear, all the adrenaline spent—it all made me forget about the… the *beast* I've become… and, I could handle it. I could be close to you and help you, and comfort you…"

He was suffering. More so than I was. I felt like a real jerk for having played the guilt card.

"It's okay. I understand. It was a one-time thing and I'm forever grateful to you. I wouldn't have survived without your help and strength. I'll keep my distance, like I promised. Don't worry," I said. *And I will find a way to fix this. Soon.*

"I don't know how much longer I can go on like this," Johnathan whispered, almost to himself. He threw a rock hard enough to break a large piece of brick off of the opposing wall. "I want to be near you, Paige. I hope you know that. I want that more than almost anything. But I won't compromise your safety for my own wishes. I can't. It has to be this way for your safety. Maybe I should just leave..."

"Don't say that ever again. Ever. You aren't going anywhere. We'll find a way to fix this, John, I promise." I wanted to tell him I was close to figuring out a way, but I didn't want him to start asking questions about how. There was no way he would be okay with what I was planning. No way.

"I'm just being realistic, Paige. There is no way to *fix* this. If it gets any worse... if I even come close to losing control again... I *will* leave. I have to."

Oh, he infuriated me! The fact that I had no voice was probably a good thing because I would've let him have it—loudly. However, because my voice was nothing but a whisper of sound, I picked up a broken brick and chucked it at him instead. Not hard, just hard enough to get his attention.

"No, Johnathan. It won't come to that. You will not leave me." With that, I walked back into our hidden home and left him to brood in the dark, damp street.

Alec and Halli still sat at the bar and Seth had just finished cleaning up the broken glass Johnathan had crushed in his hand.

I sat at one of the tables and laid my head on my arms. The pounding headache I'd expected upon awakening had finally arrived. It could have been triggered by stress, from falling on the stairs, or from ingesting a horrible drug, or possibly from all three.

Seth spoke quietly, like he didn't want me to hear what he said, "We need to tell her. It's coming up fast and we need to plan for it this time. Halli, why don't you go tell her?"

151

"I'll tell her," Alec didn't try to keep me from hearing him.

"Let's all go talk to her. It isn't like it's a surprise or anything. She knows it's coming, too," Halli said. She jumped down from the bar stool and came over to the table where I sat. Alec and Seth followed her.

I lifted my head and wheezed, "You guys aren't very good at whispering. What do you need to tell me?"

Alec and Seth both looked at Halli. "It's nothing you don't already know, we're just reminding you so we can plan ahead."

"Reminding me of what?"

"Well, there's another full moon tomorrow night..."

A distressed choking sound escaped my throat and I buried my face in my arms. "I *know* there's a full moon tomorrow night. Do you think I haven't been keeping track of when Johnathan would change into a monster again?" I *had* been keeping track, all the while hoping a cure would present itself. One hadn't.

The others were silent for a minute.

"So..." Alec broke the silence. "We should figure out what the plan is... you know, for Johnathan... so he doesn't go on a killing rampage."

"Alec, seriously. Do you have to be such a jerk?" Seth snapped.

"I'm not being a jerk, I'm just being realistic."

"We all know why we need a plan, Alec. You didn't need to spell it out for us. You're so insensitive sometimes." Halli said, then placed her hand on my arm in support.

I sat up straight. No time for further wallowing. "Thanks for reminding me. You're right. We do need a plan. I think we should go back to the park we were at last time. The place was pretty secluded and was easy for us to ward. What time do you think we should go? Early enough that we can prepare the circle in plenty of time." I was out of breath by the end of that short speech. I used up a lot of extra energy to force air through my battered vocal chords.

"I think we should go early in the evening," Seth proposed. "At least a couple of hours before the moon is set to rise. That should give us enough time to prepare."

"What time is it supposed to rise?" I asked.

"According to the almanac, at 8:18."

"So, we should plan on being in place at the park by five or six," I concluded.

The others nodded.

"We should roast marshmallows or make s'mores or something... you know, *before* we have to lock Johnny in the circle." Alec looked around at the rest of us. "It doesn't have to be such a downer this time, now that we know what to expect."

I just rolled my eyes at him. Leave it to Alec to bring food into any situation. "I think we should figure out a way to prevent John from scratching up his face this time," I said, remembering the horrible gouges from the Wolf's enormous claws.

"I was thinking the same thing," Halli agreed. "Any ideas?"

"Duct tape," Seth suggested. "Duct tape is the miracle invention of the century. We can tape his hands together before we close the circle. That would make it harder for him to tear at his face."

"That's an idea... but will duct tape be strong enough? He's strong already, but when he *changes*, I'm pretty sure his strength increases like a hundredfold," I said.

Alec tapped a finger on the table. "Maybe a combination of duct tape and a binding spell to keep the tape intact and in place..."

I thought about that for a second. "Good idea, Alec. Do you know a binding spell that'll work?"

"I just happen to," he smirked. "I found it necessary to experiment with duct tape and binding spells once... or twice, maybe."

I raised an eyebrow at him. "I don't think I want to know the details of your *experimentation*."

"No, no! It was nothing weird. Just a broken frame on a bike that I desperately needed."

"Uh-huh."

"Seriously, Paige, that's all it was... well... and maybe I used it again to win a bet. And, it's a good thing I did, because *that's* how I know it'll work on skin without ripping it off when all is done."

"What kind of a bet... never mind, I don't want to know." I shook my head. "We'll give it a try as long as it's okay with Johnathan."

"Speaking of Johnathan, where is he?" Seth asked.

My stomach did a little flip as the thought occurred to me that he may have played another disappearing act. Things would not turn out well if he *turned* without us there to lock him up. "He was just outside on the sidewalk. Will you go see if he's still there, Seth?" My energy was running low, plus I didn't want to be the one to discover him missing if he wasn't there.

"Sure," Seth jumped up and headed for the stairs.

"I'm gonna go practice that binding spell, it's been a while since I used it." Alec stood and walked to the back room where we stored stuff.

"Hal, can you bring me some water and ibuprofen? My head is killing me," I whispered.

"Of course, you should really try to eat something, too," she said as she stood.

"I don't think that's such a good idea right now." My voice was almost completely gone and just came out as a wheeze of air.

Halli was gone only a short time. She placed a glass of water, two ibuprofens, and a package of crackers on the table in front of me. I choked the pills down. The thought of eating the crackers caused my stomach to rebel. I pushed them away and willed the medicine to stay down. I wasn't necessarily sick to my stomach. It was more of an anxiety reaction. The thought of eating made my stomach irritable; I didn't feel sick as long as I didn't think about or look at food.

"Paige, when you're ready to talk about last night, I'll be here," Halli said.

"I know you will, Hal," I paused then shook my head as the images tried to return. "It was horrible and I don't *want* to relive it, but I think I need to get it out. Maybe when my voice comes back a little, 'kay?"

The door at the top of the stairs opened and I held my breath until I saw two sets of feet descending. Johnathan was still there.

Seth brought him over to where we sat. Johnathan sat as far from me as he could while remaining at the same table.

"Seth said you guys need to talk to me," Johnathan stated without looking up from his hands.

I gestured for Seth to speak; I didn't think I could squeak one more word out.

Seth swallowed before beginning, "Well, John... tomorrow night is... well, it's time for... for another full moon." He paused and looked at Johnathan expectantly.

"I knew it was getting close," Johnathan said, still not looking up. It killed me to see him so broken down. His cheeks blushed red. He was angry and embarrassed. I guess it would be embarrassing for a boy to turn into a monster once a month. We girls were used to it...

Seth looked at me and I nodded for him to continue. "So, we were thinking it would be a good idea to go back to the park. To the same place as... as before. If that's okay with you, I mean."

"That's a good idea. We should go early to be safe."

"Yeah, that's what we were thinking. The moon rises around eight."

"Sounds like you guys have it all figured out, then. Just let me know when you're ready to leave." There was more than a touch of bitterness to his voice. I guess he didn't appreciate other people making plans for him—without him.

Johnathan started to stand from the table. Halli reached out to stop him and he reflexively threw her hand away from his.

"Sorry, Johnathan," she said, surprised at his reaction. "There's just one more thing we should talk about."

As if on cue, Alec came traipsing out from the storage room with a ring of duct tape wrapped around one of his arms, the other end of which was stuck to a piece of metal pipe. "I remembered it!"

"Remembered what?" Johnathan eyed the tape suspiciously.

"Oh, hey Johnny. I was just seeing if I could remember this spell. Did they tell you our plan?"

Seth jumped in before he could answer. "We told him most of it. We haven't talked about his hands yet."

"My hands? What about them?"

I tapped Halli on the arm. He would hopefully take it better coming from her.

"Well, Johnathan, we were trying to think of a way to protect your face, you know, from your... the, uh, claws. Seth suggested duct tape, and Alec knows a binding spell that'll make it stronger and unbreakable until he releases it."

Johnathan was silent. His hands curled into tight fists and he turned a deeper shade of red. He was close to losing it.

I tried to speak his name, but nothing came out but a weak whoosh of air. Without thinking about what I was doing, I reached across the table and touched his hands to get his attention. He jerked away like I'd touched him with a branding iron. I had his attention, though. His eyes flickered with gold.

I mouthed *sorry* and pointed to my throat to explain that my voice was now completely gone. A spark of tenderness flashed across his face as he fought to gain control of his demon. Several deep breaths later, he was able to unclench his hands. He looked at Halli. "My face will be fine. I don't need your binding."

I slapped my open hand on the table—a little harder than I'd planned. The noise echoed off the walls. I tried to talk again—to no avail. I looked at the others, frustrated and desperate. I needed them to talk him into this. I couldn't stand the thought of him gouging his face again. What if he damaged his eyes?

"Don't be such a martyr, Johnny. Your girlfriend over there doesn't want your pretty face all scratched up and we think we have a way to prevent it. Relax, man." Leave it to Alec to be blunt where delicacy was needed.

Johnathan looked at me then back at Alec. "She isn't my girlfriend," he said with a hint of sorrow amongst the anger. "Scratches heal."

I balled my hands into fists. I wanted him to look at me, but he avoided my eyes like the plague. So, I stood up and leaned over the table until our eyes met. *Let us do this,* I mouthed, then added, *please.*

"Paige... it really doesn't matter, does it? So what if I scratch my face? Maybe we'll all get lucky and I'll slice my jugular this time." Boy, did he know what to say to make me furious.

I slapped him. Hard. Right across that gorgeous face that was the subject of such contention at that moment. Not the smartest thing I'd ever done. About as smart as it would be to rattle a nest full of hornets that were already enraged, or to reach into a den full of irate rattle snakes.

Johnathan growled, placed both hands flat on the table and stood so swiftly I was surprised the whole table didn't tip over. He towered over me; his eyes were almost all gold now, very little of the lovely brown left around the edge of the irises.

"Uh, guys? I think you should both step back and settle down for a minute," Seth said. "Paige? Seriously, step back."

The strain in his voice prompted me to do as he asked. Johnathan's entire body shook. *I'm such an idiot. I just promised him I would stay away from him so as not to provoke him—and what do I do? I slap him. Awesome move, Paige.*

I walked away—keeping a wide berth around where he still stood shaking—and went into my and Halli's room. I shut and locked the door behind me before slamming my fist into it. I stomped my feet a few times like a two-year-old because of the pain that shot through my hand and up my arm.

I spent at least an hour just laying on my sleeping bag, eyes open, thinking about the events of the past twenty-four hours or so. Once I calmed down, I decided I really owed Johnathan an apology and a better explanation—I still had to convince him to let us bind his hands the next day. The fact that I had no voice was probably a good thing. I don't think he would have let me near enough to talk anyway. So I sat up and pulled a notebook and pen from my backpack.

Johnathan,

First I would like to apologize for my behavior. I didn't mean to lose control. Slapping you was stupid on so many levels and there is really no excuse for it. Please forgive me. I wanted to argue one more point as to why you should let us bind your hands tomorrow night. Yes, I worry about your face being wounded, but more important than that, I worry about your EYES being wounded. Lost eyesight is not something you can get back. You were very lucky last time that the injuries you got didn't include your eyes—many of the scratches and gouges came too close. Please consider this danger, John. And, please accept my apology for my irrational behavior. It's been a really stressful couple of days.

Love, Paige

I folded it and wrote his name on the front.

I stealthily opened the door. I walked into the large dining area and over to the bar where Halli was heating some soup for dinner. The boys were nowhere in sight.

Halli noticed me and came over to where I sat on a stool. I showed her Johnathan's name on the folded letter as a way of asking where he was.

"Johnathan needed some fresh air. Alec and Seth thought it would be a good idea to go with him." She left it at that. No explanation needed.

I nodded and walked over to Johnathan's sleeping corner. I laid the note on his pillow then went back to the bar.

"He came very close to losing it, you know," Halli said, still stirring.

I nodded and looked down at the countertop.

"After you left the room, it took him a good fifteen minutes to stop shaking and for his eyes to go brown again. You really need to be more careful, Paige. Remember me telling you about the werewolf guy that wrote that book? About how he said as it got closer to the full moon each month, he became more and more irrational and out of control of his anger?"

I did remember, now that she brought it up again. I wished I'd remembered a few hours earlier, maybe I would've thought about my actions a little more. Probably not though, I was having some trouble with my own emotions since the *Sentience* incident.

Her voice softened just a little in response to the sadness on my face. "Just try to remember that from now on. I know you've had a rough couple of days, but Johnathan needs us all to be understanding of his mood swings, even if it's hard. When you're feeling better, we need to get back to searching for a cure. I worry he's going to get worse with each cycle."

I nodded in agreement. I was further along in the cure business than she knew—but I wasn't going to tell her that, or anyone else.

CHAPTER SIXTEEN

The boys came back long after Halli and I had gone to bed. I heard them come down the stairs as I lay wide awake. I also heard the wonderful sound of Johnathan laughing at something Alec said. That sound came to my ears far too infrequently these days. I closed my eyes and wished for better times.

A few silent minutes passed and I heard a gentle knock on my door followed by his soft voice.

"Paige, are you awake?"

My heart sped up. I went to the door and opened it just a crack.

"You didn't need to apologize," he whispered. "I'm the one who should be apologizing to you. I'm sorry I lost control and wouldn't listen to reason. You're right to be worried about my eyes being damaged. I'll let Alec and Seth bind my hands this time. I'm sorry." He raised a hand like he was going to touch my face, but dropped it before it reached me.

I mouthed, *I'm sorry. You're forgiven.*

He smiled and shook his head. "No need to say you're sorry, but if it makes you feel better, you're forgiven, too."

I smiled back and mouthed, *Thank you.*

"I'm going to bed now. Try to get some sleep."

I nodded and closed the door when he turned to go.

I was finally able to fall asleep knowing he forgave me and he was going to let us better protect him.

Once again, I was the last one to wake up. I would have woken up screaming if my voice hadn't been gone. I dreamt about the trees, their bark-faces laughing at me as I lay screaming, blood pouring out of the holes where my arms and legs had been ripped from my body. My voice still worked in my dream and I awoke with the echoes of my own screams bouncing around in my head. The worst part came right before waking up. Johnathan stood over me, his nostrils flaring with the scent of my blood, drool slipping down his chin as his teeth grew and sharpened…

I clamped my hands over my mouth and breathed heavily through my nose until I calmed down. I took my clothes to the bathroom where I showered and dressed in record time. I did not want to be alone with my thoughts.

Halli had a special treat waiting for me at the bar. She'd risen early and gone to Joe's to get the ingredients. She heated some water and squeezed lemon juice in it, then stirred in a teaspoon of honey.

She handed me the steaming cup and said, "Here, this is supposed to help with your throat. And you should try not to talk for most of the day and maybe by tonight you'll have a little bit of a voice."

I smiled my appreciation and took a sip of the warm liquid. It felt wonderful going down my damaged throat.

"How does it feel, Paige?" Seth asked.

I nodded and smiled.

"I don't know guys, it's been kinda nice having Paige as a mute. Do we really want to hurry the process of her getting her voice back?" Alec teased.

I slugged him in the arm.

Seth and Halli laughed; Johnathan's mouth twitched a little like he wanted to smile but couldn't quite remember how. I watched his reflection in the remnants of the mirror behind the bar. He eyes were filled with sadness, the sparkle gone from them. Just beneath the layer of sadness there was fear. I realized I'd been so wrapped up in how this lycanthropy-thing was seriously interfering with my relationship goals that I hadn't thought enough about how Johnathan must be feeling.

He'd lost all control of his body and emotions—that must be such a horrible thing for a strong, independent leader-type boy. He was scared. I could see it clearly now. And, knowing Johnathan as I did, I was sure he wasn't scared for himself. He was terrified he would hurt someone—I imagined the thought of hurting anyone was bad, but the thought of hurting one of us was almost more than he could bear. Hitting me with the force of a hurricane, I finally understood that he was serious about leaving. That he was thinking about it right now. *The only thing that's keeping him here is the knowledge that we can lock him in a circle and keep him from going wild on the city of Seattle. If he could figure out a way to lock himself up during the full moon, he would be gone in a heartbeat.*

The thought of him leaving was so much more terrifying than anything else, including limb-amputating killer trees, that I knew I would summon a Demon. I would do it soon. No more pussyfooting around. No more *research*. Tonight had to be the last time Johnathan *turned*. My focus shifted then and there from Mr. Jorgenson and his designer drug, to curing Johnathan. I still planned on doing what I could to stop the *soul-gazing*, evil principal, but that cause would come second.

Johnathan looked up into the mirror and caught my determined stare. I didn't look away. I wanted to convey to him my determination—and my faith in him. He got a quizzical look on his face and tilted his head to the side. I just smiled at him. A smile, I'm sure, that didn't reach my eyes. A smile that said, *You aren't going anywhere, and I will make sure of that.*

He shook his head in confusion and broke the gaze first.

We gathered our supplies—Alec made sure to include marshmallows—and headed for Frink Park around four that afternoon.

Thanks to Alec and Seth, the walk to the park wasn't as glum as it could have been. They spent most of the time trying to burn each other with insults. Even Johnathan couldn't help but laugh a couple of times.

It all started when Alec said, "A thought just crossed my mind..."

He was promptly interrupted by Seth. "A thought crossed your mind? That must have been a long and lonely journey."

"Keep talking, Seth; someday you'll say something intelligent."

"Do you ever wonder what life would be like if you'd had enough oxygen at birth, Alec?"

"Hey, Seth, by the way, the zoo called, the baboons want their butts back, so you'll have to find another face."

"Wow, really, Alec? I could eat a bowl of alphabet soup and poop a better insult than that."

"Johnathan, speaking of faces, ya' know what I like about your face?" Alec asked.

Johnathan shook his head.

"Yah, me neither."

"Alec, I'm not gonna get into a battle of wits with you, I never attack anyone who's *unarmed*," Johnathan retorted.

That cracked me up—in a silent, wheezing sort of way.

"Ah, Johnny, I was just kiddin'. You're lucky to have been born beautiful, unlike me, who was born to be a big liar."

Johnathan rolled his eyes. He did have a half smile on his worried face—for which I was grateful to Alec and Seth, even though they were both dorks.

"I don't ever think I could learn to like you, Alec," Seth said.

"Except maybe on a deserted island—with no other provisions in sight."

"Seth, I really admire you 'cause it's been said that what you don't know, can't hurt you—and that means *you're* invincible!" Alec laughed hard at his own wit. The rest of us laughed at him laughing at himself.

The two of them traded barbs the rest of the way to Frink Park. I stopped keeping track of their awesome mental powers when I became lost in thought; making seriously scary plans for the next week.

There were a few people milling around the park. Luckily this wasn't a very popular park. I think few people even knew about it. We went back to the fire-pit area where we'd been last time and began setting up wards of silence and concealment. This took some time; we'd hurried it last time out of necessity and probably weren't as protected as we should've been.

We had about an hour and a half before sunset. Alec started a fire in the pit while I drew the containment circle with chalk on the cement. The atmosphere was subdued as we sat around the fire and roasted marshmallows on small limbs Seth cut from surrounding trees. Even the two barbsters couldn't improve the mood. We mostly sat in silence and burned more marshmallows than we ate.

Johnathan became agitated as the moonrise-sunset approached. He couldn't sit still; he paced back and forth in front of the fire. When he started to make little growling noises under his breath I said, "I think it's time, John. Let's bind your hands and then I'll close you in the circle."

For just an instant his eyes flashed yellow and his muscles tensed like he was going to bolt—Johnathan and The Wolf were battling for control. Johnathan won out—this time—because he stepped over to where Seth held the roll of duct tape and submitted his hands to him.

"I think we should tape them with your palms together, prayer style. Any other way and I'm afraid when your... when the... the claws pop out they might do some damage to your hands," Seth said. He was having trouble looking his friend and leader in the eyes.

"Whatever," Johnathan mumbled.

Seth wrapped Johnathan's hands together from fingertips to halfway up his forearms with several layers of duct tape. Alec—surprisingly silent—stepped up and touched the tape that encircled Johnathan's hands. He looked up at Johnathan for a second before closing his eyes and bowing his head in concentration. He muttered some words I couldn't quite make out while Johnathan stared up into the cloudy sky.

Nothing noticeable changed about the tape. Alec tested it by finding the end and pulling softly at first, and then with much of his considerable strength. The binding didn't budge. Alec smiled as he stepped back. "You test it now, Johnny," he said.

Johnathan tried to pull his hands apart, they stuck fast.

Halli and I stood. We were cutting it a little closer than I'd wanted to and his agitation was increasing by the minute. I could see the muscles under his skin rippling. "Step into the circle, Johnathan," I whispered. He slipped his shoes off, not wanting to walk home barefooted again.

He gazed longingly at the open trail leading into the woods. He shook his head, squared his shoulders, and stepped into the circle. Halli joined me on the opposite side of the circle from where I stood. I pricked my finger and wiped the drop of blood that formed there onto the circle at my feet. Halli and I sent our will into it, urging the circle closed… but it didn't close.

The sun disappeared and a small rim of white peeked up over the tree line, and Johnathan let out a half-howl, half-scream as he started to double over. He stepped outside the circle, then his hungry, golden eyes found mine, locking me in place.

I flashed back to the party… the wolf's dripping fangs… the trees. I couldn't move. Luckily, Seth could. He whipped out his channeling rod and pointed it at Johnathan.

"*Immobile!*" Seth shouted.

Johnathan became still as stone and fell to his back. I snapped out of my petrification and helped Seth and Alec drag his transforming body back into the circle. As we laid his writhing body on the ground I noticed that a stray clump of melted marshmallow had landed on one line of the circle—the flow of magic had been interrupted. I kicked at the marshmallow and redrew the circle quickly, knowing the immobile curse Seth had used wouldn't last long. I re-pricked my finger, dripped more of my blood onto the circle and Halli and I joined forces to will it closed. The familiar *snap* resonated in the clearing, and Johnathan was trapped.

I never would have thought it possible, but this changing was worse than the first time, for me and for Johnathan. Me, because I kept flashing back to the drug-induced hallucinations I'd had just two nights prior. Johnathan, because the Wolf was even angrier this time. Binding his hands did prevent him from gouging himself, but it also made him freak out in a far more intense way.

He tore at the tape with his two-inch-long teeth, sometimes missing the tape and tearing into the skin of his forearms. Alec was surprised and more than a little proud of himself to find that not only did his binding spell keep the tape intact and Johnathan's hands together, it also turned out to be impenetrable—even by werewolf teeth.

The werewolf slammed his head, shoulders, and body into the invisible barrier surrounding him; and pushed, pulled, bit, and stepped on his bound hands, trying to free them. A couple of hours into this nonstop aggression, a large cut opened on his left eyebrow after a particularly hard smack against the barrier. I'd been cowering as far from the circle as I could and still be within our protective wards, rocking back and forth with my arms wrapped around my knees, trying not to think about the horror of this night combined with the horror of the *Sentience* after-effects.

I was unable, however, to tear my eyes away from the wolf's face, dripping with blood—part of me was able to process that somewhere inside the terrible monster was Johnathan. *And I love Johnathan.* So when the blood started pouring down the matted fur of his muzzled face, I was transfixed. Even more so when I noticed the wound was rapidly healing, as if an invisible surgeon was knitting the skin back together. Within a matter of minutes, where the gaping laceration had been, was just a pink line of newly healed skin partially obscured by clumps of bloody fur.

The night dragged on. I couldn't bear to watch, yet my gaze kept returning to the torture within the circle. Halli tried her best to distract me, to get me to rest. I couldn't. She gave up after a while and just sat beside me, offering her silent support. I'm sure she and the others were feeling anguish, too—just not as strong as me. After all, he was the boy I loved... and I still blamed myself for what had happened to him. I forced my thoughts away from the scene playing out before me.

I silently made plans for how and when I would summon a Demon. I knew exactly which one I would summon. The only one whose name I knew. If only I'd questioned the Faerie that brought the monster-changeling into our midst before I'd sent her back to the Netherworld. I should have been summoning her. Or, trying to summon—I had no idea if I was strong enough. I pushed those thoughts from my mind.

I will admit, the thought of what I had to do was terrifying. If there was any other way I could think of to get the information I needed, I would do it. The fact was, I was running out of time—I would not let Johnathan suffer through this again.

I worried about what the Demon would ask in return for answers I was seeking—all the time knowing I would give him whatever he asked. I worried about being unable to contain him in a circle—thus, allowing him to roam free on our plane, wreaking havoc on any humans he was to come in contact with. I also worried that Johnathan or I would not survive the attempt to remove the curse. If so, I self-ishly hoped it was me and not him that didn't survive.

Those were the thoughts that went through my mind all during the dismal night; Johnathan's howls and the sound of his body slamming into the circle made for the perfect horror background noise to play along with the scenarios and dread that floated through my head.

Just as I began lamenting about this seemingly endless night, I looked to the east and saw just an inkling of yellow shining through the trees. I looked back at the Wolf and held my breath as he appeared to calm a tad. Then, a tad bit more. By the time the sun—still not above the tree line—brightened enough to scare away the moon, the Wolf was transforming back into Johnathan. The process looked and sounded extremely painful. I heard his bones and joints snapping in and out of place; watched his muscles and skin stretch far beyond what should have been possible without breaking. I covered my ears so I couldn't hear his bones cracking or the sounds of his groans.

But I kept watching. I couldn't tear my eyes away from the transformation. The changing was awful, horrible and nearly mind-destroying to watch. But I couldn't stop.

Soon, it was over. Johnathan lay trembling inside the circle, shirt ripped to shreds, basketball shorts thankfully intact.

"Let's go let him out," I whispered to Halli.

With a surge of will from us, the circle was broken. I knelt close to him, and as much as I wanted to reach out and touch him, to comfort him, I knew that was a monumentally bad idea. He lifted his head in slow motion. He avoided my gaze and that of our friends; shame and embarrassment apparent on his face.

"Come on, Johnathan. Let's get that tape off your hands," Alec said, all the teasing of the evening before gone from his voice.

Johnathan held his hands out in Alec's direction, resting his elbows on his knees, head bowed to rest on his arms. Alec removed the binding spell, then unwound the tape from his friend's hands and arms with more gentleness than could be expected from any teenage boy in this universe or any other. I must admit my perception of Alec changed just a little in that moment—I felt a warmth in my heart for him much stronger than the friendship we'd built on a foundation of amusement and battling of foes together. I would never tell him that, though.

"Okay, Johnny Boy, all done," he said with teasing gentleness.

Johnathan sat there for a few minutes, his forehead still resting on his arms, his exhausted limbs trembling. When he lifted his head with a look of weariness I'd never seen before, I found the thin, pink scar cutting through the tail-end of his left eyebrow where a deep gash had been just hours before. His beautiful, dark, curly hair was a mass of dried blood and sweat. His normally tan skin was flushed red—I felt heat radiating off him even though I kept a safe distance of two or three feet from him.

Oh, man, it was hard to keep from reaching out to touch him. I rocked back and forth on my knees, the anxiety taking over. Johnathan looked at me, finally, and surprised me by reaching over and touching my face. He'd reached over to wipe the tears from my cheek. Tears I hadn't even realized were there.

I brushed at my face with both hands and felt a small rush of anger that while *he* could touch me whenever he wanted, *I* had to deny my instincts to comfort him. Irrational, I know, but nonetheless there.

"Paige, I'm sorry..." he started to say.

"Not. Your. Fault." I said in a harsh whisper. *This is* my *fault, not yours.* I wiped at my face again.

"We should start for home before all the morning commuters come out," Seth said, handing Johnathan his shoes.

Johnathan slipped them on and stood slowly, bones crackling. He pulled off his tattered, bloody shirt and replaced it with one Halli handed him.

The trek home was long, our feet splashed in puddles becoming larger by the minute thanks to the downpour that had started shortly after we left. We were all ready to collapse from our second night out of three with little or no sleep—and Johnathan more than the rest of us. His muscles continued to spasm every so often, and, even though he tried hard to hide it, I saw a painful grimace on his face each time.

Halli came up beside me. "Won't it be suspicious that all four of you miss school today?"

I just shrugged. It didn't matter. I doubted anyone would notice. Well, maybe Brendon and Mr. Grewa would. And Mr. Jorgenson. He seemed to notice a lot when it came to me. It still didn't matter; there was no way any of us could go. It would be stupid to try—if something crazy was going to break loose, we would all be too tired to deal with it anyway.

The warmth of our dark Underground haven was a welcome thing. Seth led the way, his channeling rod shining with a *luminosity* spell—the same spell we used to light the old lamps with down in our living quarters. The glow it emitted was a little bit blue-tinged, but otherwise looked almost like fluorescent lighting.

My bed was a welcome sight. I took only enough time to change into dry clothes before I crawled into my sleeping bag and fell asleep.

CHAPTER SEVENTEEN

None of us stirred the entire day. We all awoke in the late afternoon to noises in the room above us. It sounded like footsteps, only... louder. Like a dinosaur had been resurrected and was not happy about it, and was taking it out on the building above us.

We congregated at once in the common area. The huge rafters that had seemed so sturdy when we moved there were creaking like the planks of a ship caught in a gigantic whirlpool. Plaster chips fell from the ceiling. Small at first, and then larger. One the size of an open history book fell onto a table in the center of the room.

"What the he... heck is up there?" Alec asked.

"I'm afraid we're going to find out one way or another real soon," Johnathan said. "I'm thinking we'd better go up and see before whatever it is ends up down here with us." As if to accentuate his point, a massive foot broke through the plaster on the other side of the room, across from the stairs. This foot was the size of a couch—a big one that, like, four people could sit on. It was bare except for a mass of hair and years of dirt and grime buildup.

We looked at each other, but no one moved for a full three seconds, then we all ran for our belts and channeling rods. The boys were quicker because their stuff was closer; mine was back in our room, as was Halli's. By the time we reached the bottom of the stairs, they were at the top, disarming the wards and unlocking the padlocks. We caught up to them just as they opened the door.

The owner of the giant foot was still trying to wrangle said foot from the floor/ceiling, and not being quiet about the process. The stench that poured off the filthy, sweaty creature was a truly disgusting aroma reminiscent of rotting flesh and chicken poop.

Back to us, deep roars of frustration escaped its throat.

"What is that thing?" Halli whispered.

"I believe it's an Ogre," Seth whispered back.

"Hmm. Doesn't look *anything* like Shrek," Alec sounded so disappointed.

The Ogre's biggest problem was that it was so *tall*. If it could have stood up straight, it would've had better leverage for a bigger tug. Frustration took over and it started to pound on the floor with a crudely made club as big as Halli, maybe bigger. We sneaked closer while it was still occupied and unaware of our presence. That didn't last long. The giant foot popped free with the breaking of a board or two and the Ogre slammed the club down with a triumphant roar.

That's when it saw Halli off to the side. Good thing she could move somewhere between the speed of sound and the speed of light. The Ogre whipped the club around, amazingly fast for its size, and was denied the pleasure of cracking open her skull by the width of a few hairs. She somersaulted away, landing on her feet a couple yards out of the club's reach.

The five of us spread out equal distances apart, far enough away that it couldn't hit any of us without taking a step. Rotating in a slow circle, the monster looked at each of us in turn. I got the feeling that Ogres weren't very smart—the slack-jawed look, drooling spittle, and inarticulate grunting were clues. Apparently deciding Johnathan was the biggest threat, it raised the massive club and took a hunched step toward him. Bent almost ninety degrees at the waist, its back dragged on the ceiling.

"Argh, shtoopud hooman childs!" the Ogre roared.

Johnathan dodged the blow with little effort, and while the Ogre was occupied with him, the rest of us went into motion.

"Giant formation!" I yelled. This was a tactic we'd practiced many times since barely surviving our first contact with a large and ugly Troll. Trolls were faster and smarter than Ogres, which was becoming more and more apparent, so I figured we could easily out-maneuver this dumb Ogre—especially in such a confined space.

Halli and I moved behind the monster, with Alec and Seth on either side. Its focus remained on Johnathan, who kept it occupied with quick little attacks at its feet.

I watched closely, as did Halli, for the Ogre's next move forward. Johnathan, seeing we were in position, provoked the monster by shooting a searing blue flame at a bare big toe. The Ogre let out a deep, angry yowl, smacked its head on the ceiling, and started to take a huge shuffling step toward Johnathan. That was the cue for Halli and me to attack. We simultaneously pointed our channeling rods at the enormous ankles and yelled, "Tangle pedicus." The plan worked great—all except for one thing. The massive Ogre did, indeed, trip over our spell—which was exactly our intent. But as it tripped, the arm that wasn't holding the club stretched out and pinned Johnathan beneath giant fingers.

We all started toward him, but I motioned for Alec and Seth to stay put. They had a job to do. While they wove a lashing spell around the legs of our attacker, Halli and I ran to where Johnathan was splayed beneath the giant outstretched hand. He struggled, trying to push himself out from under it with no success. The veins in his neck and face bulged with the effort, ready to burst; his face was bright red. I freaked out when the Ogre started to close its hand around him, only Johntathan's head and shoulders visible above the encircling fingers. I heard bones cracking.

I didn't know the Latin phrase for *Let go, you big, stupid Ogre,* so I just improvised by envisioning what I wanted and sending my will blasting at the hand that was crushing Johnathan.

"Open!" I yelled, in case my visualization wasn't enough to let the spell know what the plan was.

A split second later, I heard Halli yell, "Loose!" unleashing a spell of her own.

With a spasm that shook the room, the Ogre's fingers flew open and Johnathan was free. The Ogre let out a surprised grunt and moved the disobeying hand in front of its eyes to examine it. Johnathan wasn't moving away very fast, which meant he was either hurt or in shock.

We each hooked an arm under his armpits, hauling him backwards several yards before the Ogre could notice and react. The boys must have successfully completed their lashing spell, because the giant beast tried to rise up to its knees but couldn't because its legs were stuck together from crotch to feet and its knees wouldn't bend. It flipped onto its back with astounding agility and swung the club in a wide circle in an attempt to take out Alec and Seth. They dove out of the way.

In a flash, the Ogre flipped back over and reached for Johnathan again, as if suddenly remembering he was the prize it wanted. Halli and I gave one last Herculean effort and tugged Johnathan far enough away that the tips of its fingers just grazed his feet. We'd both fallen to our butts with our last pull and Johnathan still wasn't reacting as he should.

"Halli, cover us," I directed.

She nodded and turned to face the giant Ogre. The contrast in their sizes was almost comical. But Halli was a formidable opponent.

There was never a time I wasn't glad we were on the same team. It was like having our own little magical Tasmanian Devil when she unleashed on something.

And that's exactly what she did. The Ogre never had a chance, really. I turned my attention to Johnathan and in the next moment the Ogre was nothing but a *huge* pile of super-smelly, green ichor splattered everywhere—all over the dilapidated room and all over us—especially Halli, who'd been standing right in the center of the splash zone. It was a really good thing that stuff wasn't toxic.

I wanted to know what attack she'd used, but I decided I could find out later. I needed to see why Johnathan was still not responding appropriately. This whole interaction—from the time we pulled Johnathan away from the furniture-sized fingers to the Ogre-explosionfest—was less than thirty seconds.

When I finally got a good look at Johnathan, shining *star-bright* right down on him, I gasped. His lips had turned an awful blue color and I could see the cords in his neck straining with each attempt to pull air into his lungs.

I used my super-human, adrenaline-powered strength to rip his shirt down the middle. "Oh," I croaked.

The whole left side of his torso was misshapen and bruising at an incredible rate. Almost every rib on that side appeared to be broken, and while the right side of his chest rose and fell with each grueling breath, the left side didn't move. That meant, I realized, he had a collapsed lung. The pressure was building on the collapsed side, which crowded the right side, making it more and more difficult for him to suck in any air at all. Recognizing the problem was a start. But I had no idea what to do about it.

My slime-splattered companions raced over and knelt beside Johnathan and me.

"What's wrong with him?" Alec asked.

"Collapsed lung," I said.

"He doesn't look so good," Seth said. "What should we do?"

I hated that they all turned to me for an answer. The only thing I could think of to do was call an ambulance—and we couldn't do that.

First of all, we had no phone. We also had no parents or guardians, and that would be a huge problem if the authorities found out. Foster care was not somewhere any of us wanted to end up. Also, the whole technology-ruining thing was a big problem in a hospital. Not that any of these reasons would have stopped me from calling, had a phone been available.

I didn't have an answer. Something tickled the edges of my memory. Something about *decompression*. I remembered a lecture in an advanced first aid class I'd taken, but it hadn't really been part of the class. The paramedic instructor was just trying to impress us with his feats of medical heroism. Andy, that was his name, I remembered—amazing the things you think of in times of great crisis. I concentrated hard, trying to remember exactly what he'd said. *Needle decompression, between the second and third ribs in line with the middle of the collarbone on the affected side,* the voice of the cocky but cute instructor came back to me.

Johnathan's whole face was turning blue now. I didn't have a needle, but I rummaged in my fanny pack for something—anything—that I might be able to use.

"What are you looking for, Paige?" Seth asked. Then, with more urgency, "What are you doing? Johnathan's dying!"

"A tube... I need a small tube of some sort." I pulled a pen out of my pack and removed the ends and the ink. I held it up to examine it. "Too big. It's too big around." I set the pen down and dumped the contents of the pack on the floor, frantic.

Seth unzipped his pack and pulled out the most wonderful thing in the world—a blowgun that was small in circumference and made out of Black Ironwood. I vaguely remembered him taking it from an Imp we banished back to the Netherworld. Too small for a human to use as a weapon, he'd kept it as a novelty item.

I grabbed the blowgun out of his hands and pulled a pocketknife out of my pocket, glad Johnathan always insisted we keep them razor sharp. I was scared to use the metal blade on Johnathan—I'd read a lot about silver being detrimental to werewolves. Even though my knife was not made from silver, I still had reservations about using it. I'd seen firsthand the damage steel and iron did to the Fae, burning their skin away like an attack from a million microscopic piranhas. And the *thing* that bit Johnathan was likely related to the Fae. I didn't want to take a chance. So I used the knife to cut off a three-inch length of Seth's blowgun, cutting at a sharp angle to make a pointy edge that would puncture Johnathan's body.

I turned my attention to Johnathan. His efforts to breathe were almost nil at this point. I wasted no time on thinking, because if I allowed myself to think about what I was about to do, I knew I would probably chicken out. With my left hand, I found what I hoped was his second rib, and with my right hand, I stabbed the modified blowgun in at a forty-five-degree angle, slipping it under the third rib. It slid in smoothly and I knew when I'd gone in far enough because a *whoosh* of air escaped through the tube—and continued escaping as the previously entrapped air finally had an exit.

I examined Johnathan's face, sure his skin would be turning pink again. It wasn't. His efforts to breathe had ceased completely while I'd been busy puncturing his chest.

"Halli, mouth-to-mouth! Hurry!" I said. I was afraid to move; afraid the tube I'd just placed would shift and become of no use if I didn't continue to hold it in place. I watched as Halli tipped Johnathan's head back, plugged his nose, and placed her mouth over his. She breathed into his mouth, pausing in-between breaths to allow the air exchange to take place.

"Should I start chest compressions?" Seth asked.

"No. I can still feel his heart beating. He just needs oxygen," I answered, my left hand lying over Johnathan's heart.

He took a shuddering breath on his own. I don't think I've ever been as relieved as I was when Johnathan opened his eyes. He blinked at Halli, still leaning over him, then looked at Alec and Seth. When his eyes landed on mine, they stayed locked in place.

"Paige," he groaned. "Chest... hurts."

I smiled, and breathed for the first time in several long seconds. "I know, John. I'm sorry. You've broken some ribs and collapsed a lung, but everything's gonna be fine. You're going to be fine."

He placed his hand on top of mine that rested on his chest over his heart. My other hand still held the tube firmly in place; air whooshed out with each breath he took. His hand on mine was cool at first, but grew warmer and warmer. He closed his eyes and squeezed my hand. His grip was stronger than I thought would be possible after what had just happened.

The adrenaline rush subsided in an abrupt fashion—I hit a brick wall. My body shook like I was freezing and a bout of weakness overtook my limbs. I became dizzy and a little nauseated. *Shock,* I thought, referring again to the first aid class I'd taken so long ago, before my world was full of monsters. *I'm in shock. Johnathan should be in shock.*

I looked at his face again. His color returned and his breaths came easier. He opened his eyes like he felt me staring at him. He removed the hand that held mine and raised it to my face. His touch was like an ember—was it because I was so cold? Or, had he gotten that warm, that fast?

He snaked his hand around the back of my head and pulled me down. He laid a gentle kiss on my forehead. His hand dropped back to the rubble-strewn ground as I sat up straight again. My skin tingled where his warm lips had touched.

Seth, always the thinker, wiped the blood from around the tube in Johnathan's chest and said, "Move your hand, Paige. I'll tape it down so you don't have to hold it."

Johnathan closed his eyes again, grimacing. I scooted around so I could lay his head on my lap, hoping to make him more comfortable. Alec, Seth and Halli huddled close. We were all silent, allowing him some recovery time.

Johnathan's eyes flew open; he jumped a little and grimaced at the pain the movement caused. "I heard something," he said. "I think there's someone out there." He pointed in the direction of the demolished entrance, out toward the Underground street.

Halli stood. "I'll go check it out."

Without saying a word, Seth followed her.

I examined Johnathan's left side again... and thought I was losing my mind. The bruising was already changing from new bruise purple-red to old bruise yellow-brown. And I could *see* his ribs reshaping, moving ever so slowly under his skin back to their original positions. I watched, transfixed, my eyes glued to the miraculous healing. I remembered the cut above his eye the night before, and how fast it had healed.

"Alec," I whispered, "Look."

Alec's eyes widened. "Wow. That must be a Wolf thing."

I laid my hand on Johnathan's cheek. He was *so* warm. I stroked his cheek, his forehead, his hair. His eyes were closed again. Less air was leaking from the tube in his chest, which I hoped was a good sign.

Seth and Halli came bounding back into the building. "Did you see anything?" I whispered.

Halli shrugged. "I thought I might have seen someone turning the corner, but if there was anyone there, they were gone by the time we reached it."

"Wow," Seth said, looking at Johnathan. "He's healing fast. Just like the cut on his forehead last night. I wondered if that was only something that happened when he was in Wolf form—I guess I have an answer to that mystery now."

"We should probably try to get him downstairs. We're kind of unprotected up here. Someone knocked out our wards at this entrance," Halli said.

That wasn't good. I didn't think the Ogre had been capable of disarming magical wards—which meant his appearance here hadn't been accidental. Someone sent him. Someone who knew where our hideout was.

"Okay," I said. I leaned down close to Johnathan's face and said in a quiet voice, "Johnathan? Do you think you can move yet? We can carry you if not."

I felt the exhale of his warm breath on my face; smelled the scent of it. His nostrils flared and his eyes opened so fast it made me jump. They weren't *his* eyes staring up at me, but the golden eyes of the Wolf. He clamped his hand around mine that was still pressed against his face, and squeezed. His eyes rolled back a little and a small growl escaped his throat. He still held tight to my hand, crushing my fingers against each other. He closed his eyes and breathed in and out a few times before his grip relaxed. Without opening his eyes, he said, "Move. Away." He released my hand with a shove.

I scooted my legs out from under his head, letting it hit the floor with a thud. I stood and took several steps away.

Seth and Alec were stunned silent for a second; I had to assume they didn't know about my and Johnathan's deal, or his struggles with staying in control around me. I'd talked to Halli about it late at night, when sleep evaded us both, so she knew, but this was the first time she'd witnessed the harshness behind these incidents.

"Johnathan," Alec said, "what the heck, bro? She just saved your life."

Johnathan responded with a growl. His fists were clenched so tight at his sides that they shook.

"It's okay, Alec," I said. "I'll explain later. He didn't mean to be a jerk, he can't help it." I tried to speak with an understanding tone, or at least a neutral one, but the words came out with a little bit of bitterness nonetheless. The hurt stabbed into my heart every time he rejected me like that, even though I knew why he did it.

"It's seriously *not* okay, but whatever," Alec mumbled.

"Come on, guys, we can talk about this after we're safely downstairs behind warded and locked doors." Halli looked around. Her eyes lingered on the destroyed wall where the Ogre had entered.

"Johnathan? Do you need help? Should Alec and I make you a stretcher?" Seth asked.

Johnathan inhaled slowly, then opened his eyes. "I think I can do it myself."

"Good thing, 'cause I wasn't going to help you." I never knew Alec could be so protective. You'd have thought I was his sister or something.

"Alec, he really does have a good reason what for he just did," I tried to explain.

"No. Alec's right to be mad at me. I don't deserve any of your help. You should have just let me…"

"Don't you dare finish that sentence." I turned and stormed down the stairs.

The others followed, Johnathan and Halli taking up the rear. Johnathan grimaced a little as he plodded down the stairs, but he made it on his own. Halli stayed at the top to set the wards and relock the padlocks.

Johnathan went to his sleeping bag and sat, using the wall as a brace to slide down and then rest against when his butt hit the floor. He was breathing heavier than normal, but doing well considering what he'd just been through.

The rest of us took turns using the bathroom to wash at least some of the goo off from the Ogre-explosion. I went last, keeping a close eye on Johnathan's condition from across the room.

When I came back out to the common area, Halli turned to me. "Johnathan thinks he's healed enough to take the tube out. He doesn't want the skin to heal too much around it and make it hard to pull out."

"Okay..." I said. "I think we should test it first, to make sure no more air is leaking from his damaged lung."

"How do we do that?" Alec asked.

"I don't know... plug it off for a few minutes, I guess. See if it's harder for him to breathe. Why am I all of a sudden the medical expert?"

"Because you're the one who stabbed him to save him," Alec said. "You are the MVP today. . . and the only expert we have."

"I agree with Paige. We should plug it off first to make sure you're okay," Seth said.

"Fine, should I just hold my finger over the hole, or what?" Johnathan asked.

"I guess," I said. "Just do it tight, so no air can escape."

He did fine when the tube was plugged. No increased trouble breathing. "Okay. I'm fine. Now will someone please take it out?"

I started toward him and then stopped at the distressed frown on his face. "One of you guys'll have to do it," I said. *Keep your distance, Paige—please,* I could almost hear him pleading with his eyes.

"Oh, for crying out loud, this is ridiculous. What is going on with you two?" Alec looked back and forth between us.

"Someone come take this out and then I'll explain," Johnathan said.

"I'll do it," Halli volunteered. "Just tell me what to do, Paige."

I sighed. I guess I was going to remain the expert, whether I wanted to or not. "I guess just peel the tape off carefully then slide the tube out. You should cover the hole with something that won't let any air leak out, I think."

She grabbed the roll of duct tape from Seth and knelt down beside Johnathan. Halli pulled the tube out quickly; he didn't even flinch. She fastened a couple strips of duct tape in an X over the hole.

"Okay, tough guy, tell us why it's okay for you to be such a jerk to Paige," Alec demanded.

I didn't bother sticking up for Johnathan this time. My heart was still stinging and my body too exhausted from the huge adrenaline rush and subsequent crash to be understanding and supportive at that moment. *Let him explain this to them.*

Without going into any details about our encounter in the alley, he explained as best he could the danger he believed he posed to my well-being. He used words like *lust, uncontrollable,* and *animal.* And phrases like *never forgive myself, rather die,* and *I should just leave.*

The way they all looked at me, even Halli, all full of pity, was more than I could take. I stood, knocking my chair over backwards, and walked with carefully controlled steps—determined not to let myself run like I wanted to—to my room. Once there, I slammed the door like an angry five-year-old.

I didn't cry behind that closed door. The day had been too hard and my emotions were all spent. I just sat, arms around knees, and rocked back and forth until fatigue overtook me.

CHAPTER EIGHTEEN

We thought it would be a good idea for Johnathan to stay home from school for a couple of days, in order for him to fully recover. He argued that he was fine, but his body had been through quite a shock, even for a fast-healing lycanthrope. Alec, Seth and I went to school the day after the mutant-Shrek attack, and Johnathan reluctantly stayed home with Halli so he could continue to heal. He wouldn't admit it, but I could tell by the way he moved that his ribs still hurt.

Our collective goal for the week was to locate the *Sentience*-maker and to find proof that Mr. Jorgenson was behind its manufacture. We not only needed to destroy the contraption, we needed to do something to ensure it wasn't remade. My goal was to find out who—or what—Mr. Jorgenson truly was. And his motive for manufacturing the horrible drug. It didn't appear to be for money, because I'd never heard anyone mention selling it. They always just gave it away. I was sure it was made with some kind of dark magic, and that's never a good thing.

Brendon was waiting next to my locker when I arrived. Relief washed over his face and he smiled when he spotted me coming toward him through the crowd. "Sasha! Where were you yesterday? I was a little worried that you guys decided to ignore my advice and go to that party anyway."

"Oh... uh, Seth and I both got like this twenty-four-hour flu or something, so our mom kept us home."

We walked to our first class.

"Well, I'm glad you're okay. Do you remember Ashley? The girl from Mrs. C's class that... broke the window?"

I nodded. There was no way to forget.

"I guess she was at the party. The next day she ran out into the traffic on the Pacific Highway and was hit by a truck. She... uh... didn't make it." He glanced over at me, eyebrows creased with a worried frown.

He was right to worry, but not for the reason he thought. I stopped in the middle of the hallway so abruptly the boy walking behind me ran into me. I clenched my teeth to keep from screaming out a four-letter word or two. I thought back to the party, and to Ashley standing next to the drug-dispensing tent with a cup in her hands. My fists shook with anger. *This has to stop*, I thought. My mind *tripped* back to the scene in the forest behind the party house. The hallucinations that had been lurking at the edges of my conscious-ness since that night strained at the walls I'd constructed to keep them at bay. One broke through—*the trees ripped at my arms and legs, their cruel faces laughing*—I dropped my books and barely kept from screaming.

"Sasha? Sasha! Are you okay?" Brendon stood in front of me, holding on to my upper arms.

I blinked rapidly to try to clear away the visions writhing in my head. My eyes wouldn't focus; Brendon was all blurry standing in front of me.

"Sasha, you're making me nervous. Snap out of it or I'm taking you to the nurse's office."

The mention of the office cleared things up for me. It would not have been a good time for me to run into Mr. Jorgenson—I probably would have killed him, or died in the process. I was angry about the drug and what it had done to so many of these kids. More than that, though, I was mad at myself for not stopping the madness sooner—for at least not trying harder to help Ashley that night. I felt immense guilt as I remembered my vow to put everything else on the back burner until I could figure out a cure for Johnathan. *At least Johnathan is still alive, still breathing, still has a chance to recover from his demons.*

I shook my head. "I'm fine, Bren. It's just so sad. It made me remember some things I'd rather forget."

"Okay, wow, I'm sorry. I shouldn't have broken the news to you like that, I guess."

The bell rang before I could respond, which was good because I didn't know what to say to him. Anger caused a deep, burning pressure that felt like an elephant with hemorrhoids made of flaming emergency flares sitting on my chest. Maybe the hemorrhoids were guilt…

I stomped off to class, leaving Brendon hurrying to catch up to me. I sat in my usual spot; Brendon plopped down one desk over. Chari, the petite redhead who'd tried to help with Ashley that day, wandered in and sat in the desk in front of me. She turned and said, "Hi, Sasha. I guess you heard about Ashley." Her voice broke. Her eyes were red-rimmed and moist. "I can't believe this is happening again."

I was always terrible in situations like this; I never knew what to say and usually ended up saying something stupid or sounding insensitive. I ran through several options of how to respond before settling on one that seemed safe, and might result in some needed information. "Were you friends with her? Did you know her well?"

She shrugged. "We used to be friends… before she started losing her mind. She used to be so fun to hang out with. I *hate* this school! I *hate* what's happening here and that no one seems to be doing anything about it."

More kids trickled in to class as the tardy bell rang. Mrs. C. wasn't there yet. I scooted my desk up so it touched the back of Chari's chair. I leaned forward and whispered, "I'm going to make an assumption here, so please forgive me if I'm way off base. I assume Ashley started to 'lose her mind' after using *Sentience*. Is that right?"

She didn't seem to be insulted by my words. "Yes. She went to one of those parties about a month ago, even though I thought I'd talked her out of it. She was never the same after that weekend. I tried to help her, but she was just so far gone. She would be fine and act almost normal one minute—and then she would *see* things the next and freak out. The worst time was in this class, on your first day."

"Do you know if she just used the drug that one time, or did she continue to use it?" I knew the answer, of course, but asked this for two reasons: one, I wanted to know if Chari knew where to get *Sentience* other than at the parties; and two, I wanted to know if Ashley continued to *see things* after just one encounter with the drug.

"I don't think she used it again for at least a week. I don't know if it took that long to wear off, or what. Her eyes got all weird, sunken-like and… I don't know… dull, I guess. She wouldn't eat, and she had these big, dark circles under her eyes. That was when she confided in me about drinking *Sentience* at the party. She was hysterical and begged me to help her find more. She said she thought she would die if she didn't get more. I refused to help her. She didn't need my help, though, she found it on her own."

"Why haven't the parents of these kids or the police done something about this? They have to see what's happening here."

"That's a good question. It's like they're all in denial or something. I tried to tell my mom about it and she just brushed me off. She said, 'It's probably just hormones. Teenagers are dramatic, Chari.' Ashley's mom came in after the window breaking incident to talk to Mr. Jorgenson. I saw her in the office. She said he called her to come in. I waited around until she left. She looked unnaturally…

content, I guess, when she left. Like everything was right in the world."

Of course Mr. Jorgenson was involved with the parents, too. "Do you know if he's talked to the other parents? Of the kids who've hurt themselves or the ones who are walking around like zombies?"

"I don't know about all of them. But a lot of them, yeah. I saw Bryson's parents—he's the one who stepped in front of a train—they came in the day after he died. His mom was sobbing and his dad just looked like he was still in shock. I was TA-ing in the office that day so I saw them leave. They both looked happy as can be when they left. It was weird."

Weird indeed. He must be using mind control or hypnosis on them. That would explain the lack of action from the parents and police.

I needed to word this next question carefully, so she didn't think I was a drug-seeker myself. "Do you have any idea who Ashley might have gotten the *Sentience* from, at school? My dad knows someone on the Seattle Drug Task Force. I could turn them in." I had no idea if Seattle even had such a task force.

Chari looked around the classroom, nervous, she leaned closer to me so our heads almost touched. She whispered, "I saw her talking to Bubba Peterson." *Big Lips.* "And he took her to Mr. Davis's room. I followed them."

"Who's Mr. Davis?"

"He's the Psychology teacher with the creepy eyes; he's new this year. I peeked through the window on his classroom door, but lost sight of them when he led her through a door in the back of his room. His class is the only one with an extra door like that, that I know of. Anyway, when I saw her later, her eyes were all glossy and she was *staring* at things—on the walls and ceiling, following with her eyes things that weren't there. She would let out a terrified squeal or laugh randomly. It was just like with Amanda, before she killed herself."

I remembered Ashley saying something about her dead friend, Amanda, when she told me about her hallucination in Mrs. C.'s classroom. I opened my mouth to ask another question, but I didn't get the chance. Mrs. C. finally entered the room and shushed us all. We spent what was left of the class talking about our feelings over the passing of another student. There wasn't much talking from the students; they were all zombied out. Mostly, Mrs. C. talked and cried.

I observed the other students closely. Obviously, many of them had partaken of the drink, but not all of them appeared to be having hallucination issues. Some did, but others were just zoned out. I decided from this that not everyone reacted the same way to *Sentience.* Or they were high on something else entirely.

Mr. Grewa's class turned out to be anything but boring. At least for me—the other kids may have been bored. He was busy writing on the whiteboard when I walked in but turned to look at me as soon as he heard my books hit the desk.

"Sasha, I'm so relieved to see you here today."

I believed him. His expression held such genuine concern as he looked into my eyes, assessing my level of *thereness,* I assumed.

"I was worried when you didn't show up yesterday."

"Oh, well, I had a touch of the flu or something, but I'm as good as new today."

"To be honest with you, I was a little worried you'd decided to go check out one of those parties that have been occurring all too frequently as of late. My students have not been returning whole from them—they seem to leave something of themselves behind after participating in the festivities. I'm very worried about the future of this school and my beloved students." He stared at the wall with a far-off gaze.

He shook his head sadly and returned his gaze to mine. "I'm sorry for blithering on like that, Sasha. I know you can see there's something wrong here—I can see it in the way you analyze the other students and you're so aware of your surroundings."

I decided right then to trust this great man with at least part of my secret. An inside ally was a good thing to have—and some advice from an adult perspective might be helpful, too.

"Mr. Grewa," I walked over to where he stood and lowered my voice as more students trickled in, "can we talk privately for a minute?"

"Of course, Sasha, just let me get the class started on an assignment and then we'll go out into the hallway to talk."

I nodded and left the room to wait for him just outside his door.

I sat on the cold tile floor and rested my back and head against the dingy wall adjacent to his classroom and waited. I closed my eyes and tried to think of what I was going to tell him and what questions to ask him. I was deep in thought when he sat down next to me on the dirty floor. I tipped my head up and sat straighter, a little surprised he would sit on the floor—but not really, because he was just that kind of down-to-earth, cool teacher.

"What did you want to talk about, Sasha?"

"I'm not quite sure where to begin..."

"At the beginning, I suppose, is the best place. Start with what brought you to *this* particular school," he said.

"Well... I can't tell you everything, and I'm going to trust that what I *do* tell you will be kept in strict confidence," I paused and looked at him.

"Of course, and I trust you will do the same with what I tell you."

I nodded. "Okay, well, I'll start at the beginning. We—there are four of us that came here, and one more that's too young for high school, so she's working some outside angles—we came here for the sole purpose of finding out what's going on. We read about the unbelievable number of recent suicides and decided we had to investigate."

"Who *are* you? I mean, why *you*? You're a teenager, and I assume the others are as well, but I sense something different about you... an ancient aura, a deeper knowledge of the world that surrounds us, the ability to *see* what the rest of us can't. Who are you, Sasha?"

I cleared my throat and looked down at my worn jeans. I had no idea how to answer that question. I was the daughter of a preacher and his pretty, softhearted wife... but that wasn't what he was asking, and I didn't know the answer to what he *was* asking. "I don't know," I whispered.

Mr. Grewa didn't try to push me to answer; he didn't get angry or annoyed or call BS. He just sat next to me and waited for me to collect my thoughts.

"I'm... *we,* are more than just teenagers, Mr. Grewa. We have special... *abilities* we use to help people. There are things of nightmares in this world, and people are unaware of the danger that constantly surrounds them. We protect as best we can, but we're all new at this and we're kind of making it up as we go along." I suddenly became afraid he wouldn't believe me, or worse, he'd think I was crazy.

Softly he said, "Such a large burden to be placed on those so young. Have you been able to learn anything? What can I do to help you? I've felt so helpless this last month and a half, I'll help in any way I can."

His sincerity was palpable and sent a crushing pain through my chest. "We're so close to figuring it out. I just need information. The drug that's causing this is being manufactured in a big tank thing—and I think it's being kept somewhere on the school property. I'm a hundred percent positive Mr. Jorgenson is behind it, but I have no idea what he gains from turning kids into hallucinating zombies. Mr. Grewa, this is no ordinary drug he's making—it's made with *Dark Magic.*" I waited for him to laugh at me and tell me there was no such thing as magic. He didn't.

"Magic... I've never really been a believer of magic, yet I can't disprove its existence. I've realized, more so of late, that dark machinations abound in this world—and there seems to be a large concentration of them gathering at *my* school and destroying *my* beautiful students. Sasha, these special abilities you spoke of, are they *magical* abilities?"

I was afraid to answer that. The last grownup to find out about my abilities tried to confine me to a *treatment center.* So I said: "I'm not really ready to talk about that."

"Okay, you don't have to tell me anything you don't want to. Just know that I trust in you and you can trust me. What else do you know about this drug?"

"It causes horrible hallucinations. They have it at all these parties and hand the drug out for free in the form of a drink. I'm pretty sure Mr. Davis, the Psychology teacher, is in on it. Someone told me he supplied some to… a student… here at the school after she'd had some at a party. What do you know about Mr. Davis?"

He glanced up at the ceiling for a few seconds before responding. "I don't know much. Miss Lloyd was the Psychology teacher for the last fifteen years and had every intention of returning to teach this year, but when we got here the first day, she was gone and he was here—no explanation. He doesn't associate with the other teachers. In fact, I've only spoken with him a handful of times. He is quite often with Mr. Jorgenson."

"Tell me about his eyes. And his classroom."

A shiver made its way down his neck and shoulders. "His eyes, now that you mention it, are odd. His pupils aren't round, they are more like slits—like a cat's. It's so disconcerting that I can't even tell you what color they are. I've never been in his classroom. I've been teaching here for seven years and I never even knew that hallway existed. In fact, if it wasn't impossible, I'd say it hadn't existed until August of this year."

"It isn't impossible," I said to myself. "What about Mr. Jorgenson? Is he new this year, too?"

"No, not this year. He came halfway through last school year when Mrs. Hendricks, our former principal, suddenly died. Had a heart attack in her office one night when she was here late. The janitor found her when he went in to empty her garbage. She was only fifty-one. It was tragic."

I was out of questions that he could answer.

"Sasha? Is there anything else I can answer for you? What's your next step?"

I sighed. "My next step is to take all the information I've gathered today and present it to my friends. Then we have to make a plan to end this—soon, before anyone else is hurt."

Mr. Grewa stood and offered his hand to help me up. It was warm and callused. I briefly wondered what had callused this gentle man's hands.

"We'd best get back," he nodded to his classroom. "Heaven only knows what's going on in there without supervision."

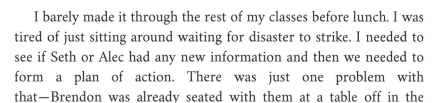

I barely made it through the rest of my classes before lunch. I was tired of just sitting around waiting for disaster to strike. I needed to see if Seth or Alec had any new information and then we needed to form a plan of action. There was just one problem with that—Brendon was already seated with them at a table off in the corner, and we couldn't talk openly with him there.

I sat next to Seth and plopped my homemade lunch on the table. I scanned the lunchroom for the three thugs. I hadn't seen them that morning and I was curious to see if they'd survived the wrath of Johnathan. The students were even more subdued than usual; even the girls at the cheerleader table were sullen. One of them perked up as I watched, she smiled and pointed to one of the entrances. Her fellow cheerleaders followed her pointing finger and they all smiled, too. I looked as well, then sucked in a breath as my eyes fell on Johnathan.

He'd stopped at the entrance and looked around the lunchroom. He spotted the waving cheerleaders, smiled shyly and waved back. The worried crease in his handsome face softened when he spotted us and he wasted no time getting to our table.

"What are you doing here?" I asked, remembering too late that I wasn't supposed to know him very well; we'd just met recently as far as Brendon knew. I covered, lamely, with, "Your fan club is over there and obviously disappointed that you shunned them." I nodded toward the cheerleader table.

He glanced their way and blushed when he saw they were all looking at him, at least one with an angry pout. "I prefer the company at this table."

"I thought you were instructed to stay home and recover from the *accident* you had yesterday," Alec said.

"I'm fine. I have an important assignment to do and it was just a waste of time to sit home when there's nothing wrong with me."

"What kind of accident were you in yesterday?" Brendon asked.

Before he could answer, though, Chari stepped up to our table and dropped her lunch tray next to my unopened sack lunch.

"Sasha, why do you sit here with all these boys? I feel like it's my duty as a fellow female to sit with you and even things out a little—although, two girls to four boys is probably overkill. We *way* outnumber them in brain cells."

I laughed and Brendon threw a French fry at her.

"You interrupted," Brendon chided. "Johnathan was just about to tell us what happened to him yesterday."

Johnathan made up some story about falling down a flight of stairs. I really wanted to continue the conversation Chari and I had started in first period, but I didn't know how to bring it back to that subject without causing a major downward spiral in the mood at our happy little table.

I saw we had only five more minutes of lunch left. During a short lull in the conversation—centered around football, what else?—I looked at Chari and said, "You mentioned a new Psychology teacher this morning, a Mr. Davis? What's he like? Where's his classroom?" I admit, I could never be a news reporter; I suck at segues.

As I'd feared, Chari's mood darkened, but she answered me anyway. "He gives me the creeps. I was in his class at the beginning of the year, but I checked out after the first day. His eyes are weird, like his pupils are elongated or something, not round. He spent the entire hour the first day just taking turns staring into our eyes without saying anything. It was too über-creepy for me. I'll show you where his classroom is when you're done eating if you want."

Elongated pupils struck a chord; Mr. Grewa had mentioned the same thing. That detail was significant; the Fae people always had something different with their eyes—be it no pupils, all pupils, no white, funny-shaped pupils—they all had eyes that deviated from the human norm. I wasn't sure what elongated pupils meant, but I needed to find out.

"Yeah, I'm ready whenever you are. I'm not very hungry today." I tossed my unopened paper sack at Seth. "You can have that."

I followed Chari down a dim hallway I hadn't known existed. It was tucked between the boys' locker room and the weight training room—two areas where I'd never had the need or desire to explore before. We reached Mr. Davis' door just as the bell rang. I tried the knob; it was locked, of course. Sometime since Chari had watched Ashley disappear into the inner sanctum of his classroom, Mr. Davis had covered the window of his door with thick black paper, so I couldn't even look inside.

"We'd better get to class," Chari said. "This whole area gives me the heebie-jeebies. I don't remember this hallway or room even being here before this year, and I'm pretty sure there was no construction going on this summer."

What I really wanted to do was *unlock* the door and go exploring. I couldn't do that in front of Chari, though, so I settled for a quick ward-check. I placed the palm of my right hand on the door and opened my senses. I instantly felt the magical ward that protected the door. I was shocked to find I could actually *see* the ward, too. That was not something I'd ever been able to do before. The intricate weave was made up of hundreds of different-colored blood vessels, still pulsing with life and blood. I slammed shut my senses with a shudder. The ward was made with Dark Magic that made my skin crawl.

Chari and I walked back to our lockers together. We talked along the way, mostly about Brendon. "Do you think Brendon likes me? I wish he'd ask me out," she said.

"What's not to like?" I asked. "I can suggest to him that he ask you out."

Her eyes lit up. "Would you? Maybe we can double—me and Brendon and you and *Johnathan*."

I stopped. "Uh... Johnathan, huh? Why do you suggest Johnathan?"

"Oh, come on. Any idiot can see the way he looks at you, like you're the most amazing thing he's ever seen. Like you're a full-course Thanksgiving dinner and he's a starving animal that hasn't eaten in a week. *And*, you watch him with about the same intensity when he isn't looking."

I didn't realize my infatuation was so obvious. She had no idea how close she was to the reality of the situation when she compared me to food and him to a starving animal. All I could do was laugh and say, "Okay, I'll see what I can do about setting you up with Brendon."

The laugh ended when a chill ran down my spine and a strong feeling of foreboding invaded my senses. My eyes were drawn across the hallway. Mr. Jorgenson stood there, watching us. His face was partially hidden in shadow; giving it an even stronger look of evil. He didn't turn away or even try to pretend he wasn't staring at Chari and me; he just smiled a disturbing smile and nodded his head like he'd just had the greatest idea since iPod.

That man made me furious. I wanted to wipe that vicious grin off his face, but right there, in the middle of a hallway full of students, wasn't the right time to do it. So, I just gave him the universal I'm-watching-you sign—I pointed to my eyes with two fingers and then turned them slowly to point at him. I didn't even try to hide the look of disgust and fury on my face. I did succeed in wiping the grin off *his* face—and I didn't even have to cause chaos to do it.

His brows drew into an angry scowl and I could almost hear his teeth grinding together from clear across the hall. He took one step toward me—yes, I still stared him down—and then turned sharply and fled the scene.

I huffed out a small, mirthless laugh and caught up to Chari. "See ya later," I said when she turned into the doorway of her class. We were both late; the bell had rung during my stare-off contest with the principal.

"See ya, Sasha. Don't forget to talk to Brendon." She smiled, her cheeks a little flushed.

I really had a hard time concentrating in Pre-Calc. I just wanted to get back home and start making some real plans. I had some information I hoped would help us end this madness and I wanted to get on with it.

Mrs. Penrod asked me to answer a question I didn't even hear, so I just answered, "Pi-R-Squared?"

She shook her head in exasperation and called on someone else.

Finally Geography, my last class of the day, and the one class I had with Seth. I slumped into a seat and waited for him. In the hallway, between classes, I found myself looking over my shoulder to see if Mr. Evil was lurking somewhere, ready to turn me into a toad. Paranoia—even when it's justified—is exhausting to the body and soul.

In a hushed voice, I gave Seth the rundown on my earlier encounter with Mr. Jorgenson. He shook his head and said, "You probably shouldn't have done that, Paige. None of the rest of us are even on his radar—well, maybe I am, because I'm your *brother*—but you've been on his radar since day one. You'd think you'd try to get off it, but you just keep making even bigger *bleeps* on his screen."

"He infuriates me. I just want to blast him off the face of the earth." The lights in the room flickered and then went out.

"Settle down before you start shooting lightning bolts from your fingertips."

I looked down at my hands and saw that I *was* building up power in my fingertips. They let off little blue sparks of energy—not a good thing in a dimly lit room. I closed my hands into fists and placed them on my lap under the desk while I concentrated on shutting down the magic. *I used to have such good control,* I thought as I took slow, deep breaths to calm down.

The teacher opened the blinds on the windows in the room and started class as if nothing had happened. One of the students had noticed my sparking hands; he stared at me, open-mouthed, and then asked if he could be excused.

For the rest of the class period, my right leg bounced up and down at the speed of a jackhammer. Seth kept watching me like he thought I would spontaneously combust.

After the final bell, I told Seth I was going to grab my jacket out of my locker and I would meet them near the front of the school. I saw no signs of Mr. Jorgenson nearby. I grabbed my jacket and started walking. Chari came up beside me.

"Hey, Sasha. What are your plans this afternoon?"

I couldn't tell her my plan was to go to the Underground home I shared with four other teenagers and plot the downfall of the evil school principal. That just sounded crazy. So I improvised, like I do so well.

"Umm… no plans… really, I guess."

"Do you want to hang out and watch football practice with me?"

"Yeah, sure. That sounds like fun." *Dang it!* I'd forgotten all about football practice—my strategizing session would have to wait because I knew there was no way Alec and Seth would give up one more day of their masculine male-bonding activities, especially with the knowledge it would soon be over anyway. I tried to look on the positive side; Chari seemed really fun to be around *and* maybe I could get some more helpful information from her.

I felt a little guilty that Halli had been alone for most of the day and would be alone even longer. I even considered contacting her through our necklace link, but decided against it. I didn't want her to come blazing in thinking the battle had begun. Sometimes I was envious of all the cell phone junkies surrounding me.

At the front entrance, right next to the office, I felt that same cold chill I'd felt earlier—*he* was somewhere nearby, watching us. I walked slower and turned my head toward the office; I turned my body and walked backwards a few steps. As I continued the slow circle, I spotted him leaning against the wall opposite the office, next to the vending machines. He stared right at me. I stopped walking when his attention turned with obvious purpose to Chari. She continued a few steps before realizing I'd stopped, still talking about the football team—and Brendon, of course.

I watched Mr. Jorgenson. Even took a step toward him. The look in his eyes as he watched Chari was one of a predator who had just spotted its next kill. He actually licked his lips as he turned his gaze back to me, grinning like a psychotic clown from an insane asylum circus. He nodded again like he had in the hallway before pre-calc. I closed my hands into fists as I felt the power trying to exit through my fingertips.

"Hey, Sasha… what's wrong?" Chari finally noticed I'd stopped walking.

Deep breath, in. And. Out. "Nothing… I'm just looking for the boys. We were supposed to meet around here somewhere."

"Oh, well, maybe they're waiting outside."

"Yeah, maybe." I continued to meet Mr. Jorgenson's gaze until my view of him was blocked by a group of kids. I jumped when someone came up behind me and put hands on my shoulders.

"Whoa, a little jumpy there, Sasha." It was Brendon. "What are you two doing?"

"Oh, hi," I said. "We're just looking for Seth and the guys... thinking about watching your practice." I looked over at Chari, whose cheeks flamed red.

"That's a great idea. Don't worry, I won't tell the other guys you're only coming to watch my stellar skills and gaze longingly at my posterior in tight football pants." He turned to Chari and smiled. "Maybe we can go to the diner and get shakes after practice, my treat."

"Um..." Chari's face turned even redder. She must have been even newer at this crush thing than I was. "That'd be great. I love shakes."

I rolled my eyes. "Yeah, maybe. Let's go see if my brother's waiting outside." I took one more glance in the direction of the vending machines, sure my stalker would be gone. He wasn't. He was there, leaning against the wall. Now he looked at Brendon with the same predatory look he'd been using on Chari a minute before. *What is going through his maniacal mind?*

Alec, Seth and Johnathan were waiting out in front of the school, next to the electronic marquee flashing the date and time of the next home football game. They must have been standing a little too close because the LED lights kept flickering off and on. Chari and Brendon walked a few steps ahead of me.

A cold gust of wind whisked my jacket from where I'd slung it on my shoulder and blew it behind me onto the grass. I walked over to pick it up. When I stood and turned back toward the others, Mr. Jorgenson blocked my way.

Anger and fear prickled my insides. I opened my mouth to ask him what he wanted and he pressed a cold, long, thin finger to my lips. "Shhh, *Sasha*. I just wanted to ask you how you enjoyed the party on Friday night. I heard you had quite a *screaming* time. Be sure to let me know when you *need* more."

He smiled, and spiders crawled out from between his teeth and out of his nose... eyes... ears. I closed my eyes and tried not to scream. I was mostly successful, letting only a small hoarse cry escape my throat. I don't think anyone but Jorgenson and Johnathan—with his hyper-sensitive ears—heard it. I felt Mr. Jorgenson's finger abruptly leave my lips, and when I opened my eyes, Johnathan was there between us. I couldn't see what his eyes looked like, but they must have been terrifying because Mr. Bully Principal was backing up, and his spider-infested grin had been replaced by a grimace.

CHAPTER NINETEEN

After football practice, at which Johnathan stayed within two feet of me at all times, watching for Mr. Jorgenson to reappear, we all graciously declined Brendon's invitation to his diner to get shakes and sent him and Chari off on their own. Chari was... well... giddy is the only word I can think of. And, Brendon was totally into her, too. As we parted ways, he reached down and held her hand. She turned to look at me with the world's hugest smile on her freckled face. I smiled back and waved goodbye.

We returned home just around dusk; the setting sun had turned the clouds into a prism of pastel colors. I took one last, long look at the beautiful sunset before descending into the darkness.

Halli was just taking off her jacket when we reached the bottom of the stairs into our home. "Where have you been?" I asked.

"At Joe's store. I was tired of sitting around by myself, and I figured when no one was home by four-thirty or so that you'd all stayed at the school for practice. So, I went to see Joe, since he's really the only person I know here besides you guys."

I felt guilty again for leaving her by herself all day. "Sorry, Hal. I found out some good information today and I think we need to sit down and make a plan."

"It's no big deal," she said. "I understand. I just wish I could be more help."

"Just be ready to come to the rescue when we call for you," Seth said. "I don't like the idea of being in a firefight without you there."

Halli's lips twitched up just a little at the edges. "I'll be there as fast as I can run. Maybe faster," she added cryptically.

"What do you mean by that?" I asked.

"Nothing. Joe gave me a pan of homemade enchiladas. I'm going to go warm them up, and then you can tell us about your information-gathering."

The enchiladas were wonderful and almost made up for missing another shake at Lucky's. I told them what I'd learned that day from Chari and Mr. Grewa. Alec added some information he'd learned from one of the kids in his Spanish class—there were more than just the three lackeys that knew where to get *Sentience* outside of the parties. He'd gotten a boy to tell him the names of two other boys with connections.

I listened with a jealous twinge as Johnathan told us that one of his cheerleaders had seen Mr. Davis enter the door in the back of his classroom with one of those boys and only Mr. Davis came back out. She swore the kid came back later through the front classroom door, sweaty like he'd been running.

"So, what's our next step?" I asked. "We need to end this before anyone else dies."

"Agreed," Johnathan said. "I think our goal should be to find out more about Mr. Davis and the door in his classroom. We do that tomorrow. I have a feeling that's where we'll find the drug. Then we destroy it."

"And, Mr. Jorgenson and Davis along with it," I said.

"Are you sure they're the ones responsible for all this?" Halli asked.

"There is not a doubt in my mind that Jorgenson is the one spearheading this operation. And, I'm almost as sure Davis is in on it with him—after tomorrow, I intend to be a hundred percent sure."

"How can you be so sure, Paige?" Seth asked, not in an argumentative way, but with concern. I'm sure he was thinking he didn't want to *destroy* anyone, but if he did, he wanted to know it was truly a bad guy.

"She's sure and so am I." Johnathan's face wrinkled. "He *smells* wrong... like darkness and rot."

I nodded. "I've *soul-gazed* with him, remember, Seth?"

He nodded. "Okay, so what's our plan for tomorrow?"

No one spoke up. Finally, Alec said what we were probably all thinking. "I think we're gonna have to use Paige's unfortunate *ingestion* to our advantage." He turned to face me more fully. "You're gonna have to solicit one of his thugs for more of the drug. Like you're really *needing* it. Hopefully he'll take you to the secret door in Mr. Davis's classroom and you can see what's in there. Just don't drink anymore of that stuff, 'kay?"

"I'd rather die," I whispered.

"Don't say that," Johnathan snapped.

Silence fell over the large room—you could have heard the proverbial pin drop. I was looking down at the table thinking he was a bit of a hypocrite. Hadn't he just tried to tell me yesterday that I should have just let *him* die?

Halli broke the silence. "Do you really need to ask for more of that horrible stuff? Why don't you just wait until no one's there, *unlock* the doors and explore on your own?"

"I thought of that," I answered. "But the outer door, the one to just get into the classroom, is heavily warded. I'd be willing to bet that the inside door is even worse. I'm afraid I'll need an escort."

"You aren't planning on going in by yourself, are you?"

"Well... I'm not sure how anyone else can go with me. Carrying out a drug deal isn't something you usually share with friends and family."

"I really think one of us should go with you," Seth said. "We can think of a plausible excuse."

I shook my head. "I don't think that's a good idea. I'll go by myself and *one* of you guys can follow at a safe distance. I'll activate the necklaces if I get into trouble."

"I don't like this," Alec said.

"I don't either," Johnathan agreed. "But, whether we like it or not, Paige is the one they slipped the stuff to, so she's the one they'll expect to want more... to *need* more. It has to be her. And *I* will be the one that follows her."

The other two boys protested, but Johnathan stopped them with an even look. "I have extra-sensitive hearing. I will probably be able to hear any trouble before she can summon us with the necklaces." No one could argue with his reasoning.

"Okay. So, tomorrow I'll approach one of the flunkies and tell him I need some more *Sentience* with the hope that he'll take me to Davis' classroom and into his secret lair. Johnathan will follow... at a safe distance. I'll find out if the tank-thing is in there and look around for anything else that might be of use to us. I'll get the drug and come back and report to you guys. *Then* we plan to take these monsters out."

"That about sums it up," Johnathan said, though he didn't look at all happy about it.

"Okay, well, since that's settled, I'm going for a walk." I stood and grabbed my jacket.

"Wait, isn't it kind of late for you to be going out by yourself?" Alec asked.

"I think I can take care of myself, *Alice*."

"Well, at least take your gear belt," he said.

"I'll go with you, Paige. I need some fresh air," Halli volunteered.

I really wanted to go by myself. My objective was to go to the occult bookstore and find some info on summoning Demons. Halli knew I was searching for a way to cure Johnathan, but she *didn't* know that search included a plan to summon evil from the depths of hell in order to find the answers. And I didn't want her, or anyone else, to know about it. But I didn't want to further raise suspicion by trying to talk her out of coming with me. It might have become a habit of Johnathan's to disappear by himself, but it wasn't mine. I would just have to be sneaky about what I was researching.

We both grabbed our belts, as Alec had insisted, and headed for the stairs. Outside, where I could be sure we were out of earshot of Johnathan, I turned to Halli.

"My real objective is to go do some research at that bookstore you went to. Hopefully they'll let us browse long enough to find some information."

"Okay, it's up by Pike Place Market. I wanted to look at that book some more, too. I hope it's still there."

We walked in silence. My mind flipped from one thought to another—from the plan for school tomorrow, back to the horrible night at the party, forward to the wickedness I was planning on calling forth—hoping with all my heart I was strong enough to contain it and send it back to the Netherworld after bargaining for the information I needed. I thought about Johnathan and my fervent desire that he not have to endure one more *changing*. I thought about the possibilities of what the Demon would ask of me in return for information. I had no idea what to expect. My contemplations were interrupted when we reached the bookstore.

The clerk behind the counter looked up as the chimes on the door announced our entrance. She had jet-black hair—dyed, I'm sure—all except her long, stringy bangs, which were dyed neon green. I counted at least ten piercings in her face—eyebrows, lips, nose, cheeks—and more than that in her ears. She was dressed all in black, which was fitting for her place of hire. She wore a large pentacle pendant that hung down between her breasts and about a gazillion bracelets on each arm. She was pretty much status quo for a place that sold occult books and paraphernalia, I figured.

She rolled her eyes and looked purposefully at her watch. "We close in fifteen minutes." She returned her gaze to the grunge magazine that was lying open on the counter.

Halli and I shared a smile as we walked deeper into the store.

"This is perfect," I whispered. "That girl isn't going to pay any attention to what we're doing."

Halli walked straight to the back of the store where the Werewolf book had been before. While she looked for it, I searched a nearby shelf labeled *Rituals*. My eyes fell on an old book with a broken spine. The title was faded to the point it was barely readable—*Daemonic Rituals*. I looked to make sure Halli was occupied. My hand shook as I pulled the book from the shelf.

I'm sure it was just my nerves acting up that caused me to think the book's cover was made from human skin—that was just insane... there had to be other types of animal hide that looked similar to the heavily pored skin of humans, right? My instincts all screamed at me to drop it—and I almost did. My hand continued to shake and become sticky with sweat.

I took a determined breath and opened the book to the chapter listing. It looked to be handwritten in old English script. I ran my finger down the chapter listings and stopped at *Daemonic Summoning*. My heart beat heavily in my chest; I closed my eyes, the guilt of what I was planning almost too much to bear. I forced my thoughts to Johnathan, to the anguish he suffered every second of every day, to the changes in his personality... to the very real danger he posed to me with the end result being that we couldn't be together. I opened my eyes and turned to Chapter Thirteen.

I had the information I needed. Now I just needed to get rid of Halli. I'd decided I had to complete the *summoning* that very night—while the steps and incantations were still fresh in my mind. I hadn't written anything down for fear of being found out. Halli had seen me sliding the book back onto the shelf but didn't say anything.

There was another reason I wanted to do it tonight; I had an important mission to accomplish the next day and I didn't want the distraction of a pending *summoning* to cloud my concentration.

"Did you find out any new information from that book?" I asked Halli.

"Not really. Just stuff we've already read or seen for ourselves. What about you? Did you find anything useful? Why were you over in the *Rituals* section?"

Crap! She'd noticed. "Well... I was just looking to see if maybe there was a ritual that would help us rid Johnathan of the lycanthropy. Something that maybe Madame LaForte doesn't know about... or that she doesn't approve of and doesn't want us to attempt or something. I didn't find anything useful either." The lies came out pretty smoothly.

"Hal... if you don't mind, I'd like to take a little walk by myself, to clear my head. I'm just a little bit freaked out about tomorrow and just need some alone time. I won't be gone long. You should head back home. Just tell the others I'll be back in an hour or so."

She frowned. "Paige... I don't think that's a very good idea. I understand wanting to be alone, though. As long as that's your only reason for ditching me." She looked into my eyes.

I decided to be straight with her. Well, mostly straight. "The truth is I need to do something I'm not very proud of and I don't want you or anyone else to be involved. Please just go home. I'll be right behind you as soon as I get this taken care of."

Again, the frown. "Paige..."

I didn't let her finish. "Halli, just go—I don't want your help with this. I'll be fine. Go. Home."

"Okay, I'll go. I just want you to remember I've been with you on this from the very beginning. You can trust me. *I* want to help Johnathan, too. He found me... and saved me. Without him I would be dead and I'd do anything to repay him. You all are the only family I have... I have no remembrance of the time before he found me huddled in the darkness and scared out of my mind. You guys are my past, present, and future. And... you're my best friend," she added quietly.

Ugh. She had to play the guilt card. It wouldn't have affected me so much had she made a habit out of it—but she'd never played the guilt card with any of us, as far as I knew. I *really* didn't want her to see what I was going to do, but I felt like I needed to throw her some sort of bone.

I took a deep breath and released it. "Okay, you can come with me. But, you have to stop where I tell you to and stay there until I come get you. No arguing."

She smiled. "I won't argue. Paige, what exactly are you going to do?"

We started walking again. I headed for a nearby abandoned building. "I'm going to get some information from someone—someone I shouldn't be dealing with. That's why I need you to stay back, because I don't want you to be associated in any way with my bad decisions."

"Just how dangerous is this?"

"Um… I'm not exactly sure. It'll be worth the danger if I can get the answer I'm seeking, though. Totally worth it."

I turned into the alcove of the empty building I planned to use. The door was chained and locked with a heavy-duty keyed master lock. There were no windows—none were needed in the old warehouse. I took the lock in my hands, closed my eyes, and reached out with my mind to *feel* the lock's mechanisms. I concentrated for only a few seconds before feeling the mechanisms slide into alignment; I pulled on the lock and it opened in my hand. I was getting really good at the lock thing.

We entered the warehouse and closed the door behind us. I turned to Halli. "Stay right here by the door. That way you can make an escape if you need to."

She tilted her head and raised an eyebrow, but she didn't argue.

I walked across the concrete floor, my footsteps echoing in the nearly empty building. Bile rose in my throat at the thought of what I was about to invoke. I walked to where I was partially hidden behind a large, empty shelving unit, about fifty yards from where Halli stood.

I closed my eyes and breathed deep to calm the increasing edginess that had crept up on me. I rehearsed the words of the incantation in my head… once… twice… three times. The time had come. I pulled the chalk out of my gear belt and drew a careful and concise pentacle. I pulled several hairs from my head and placed them in the middle of the pentacle. This was the part that scared me the most; the Fae could cast some pretty nasty spells when they got their hands on your hair. But, it was necessary. The book had called it an *offering of trust*—my guess was this *trust* was really just insurance that the Demon would be able to find me when the time came to pay up.

I pricked my finger with a needle, not even feeling it as it penetrated the skin. The blood welled into a nice-sized drop, and I bent and smeared it on the line of the circle where one tip of the pentagram touched it. I repeated the act with each of the remaining four sites where the star touched the circle. When the last drop was in place, I willed the pentacle closed. I felt the familiar *snap*, the change in the atmosphere between our realm and another, and knew it was sealed.

"*Cieo ciere civi citum, accio envoco precari. Cieo ciere civi citum, accio envoco precari. Cieo ciere civi citum, accio envoco precari. Shalbriri. Shalbriri. Shalbriri envoco,*" I chanted.

I opened my eyes. For a few seconds, nothing happened. Then, the circle began filling with blue smoke that stayed within the confines of the chalk lines I'd drawn. I felt a moment of hysteria when the idea popped into my head that a chalk drawing was the only thing keeping me from being devoured by a soul-eating Demon.

With a roar of protest that nearly broke my eardrums, the familiar form of the first Demon I'd ever fought—alongside Alec and Johnathan—erupted into the center of the pentacle. It grabbed the strands of my hair with an ethereal appendage that could have resembled an arm if it hadn't been so... well... *ethereal*. The Demon *Shalbriri* still wore the nerd glasses that just hung in midair due to the fact that the wraithlike Demon had no nose or ears. It turned to face me and said in an eerily quiet voice, "*Who dares to summon me?*"

"I do. I want to bargain with you for some information." The book had said not to show weakness but also not to act superior. In other words, treat the Demon like you were on equal ground—even though, if I wasn't able to hold him in the circle, he had the power to wreak apocalyptic havoc throughout the entire Pacific Northwest.

"And, who are you to invoke this summons? A Human girl-child can't possibly hold me to this realm." It actually smirked. And laughed, as it looked me up and down like I was a prized horse it was considering for purchase.

"I am seeking information. And I *am* strong enough to keep you contained within the pentacle. Are you willing to bargain with me, or should I send you back to where you came from?"

The Demon showed me a grotesque mouthful of razor-sharp teeth in the semblance of a smile. It pushed against my will that held the invisible prison erect. I stumbled backwards into the empty shelves.

"No!" I yelled, forcing all of my will into the circle. The Demon pushed harder. I felt like my eyeballs would squeeze right out of my head from the pressure of its attempted escape. I was going to lose. The Demon would be loosed on the unsuspecting people of the world and it would be my fault. My only comfort was I would probably be dead and wouldn't see the results of my futile attempt to make right the wrong I'd caused to Johnathan.

The pressure was too much. I was going to implode. That was when Halli decided to ignore my order to stay put. She stepped around the shelves and stood by my side, adding her considerable will to mine. The pressure in my head instantly receded and with our combined force, the furious Demon was brought to submission.

It bellowed in frustrated rage. I stayed silent as it continued its tirade for a few long minutes. When it finally quieted down I said, "Are you ready to bargain now?"

"I will bargain with you, Human, as you leave me little choice. However, you may not like the price I ask. You had best weigh the importance of your need." It spoke with a slight English accent that sounded funny coming from a blob wearing glasses.

"The importance is mine to determine—and I've already determined it. I would not have summoned you had I not been willing to pay the price."

"Fine. What is it you seek?" It plopped down in the center of the

pentagram and played with the strands of hair it held. It reminded me of a pouting preschooler that hadn't gotten his way.

I wanted desperately to look at Halli to see her reaction. Was she upset? Angry? Scared? But, I also *didn't* want to see her reaction—what if she was staring at me with anguish or, worse, *pity*? I had to concentrate on keeping the circle intact and on bargaining with a being that had thousands of years of practice at making such deals lean heavily its way.

"Answers. I seek answers. My... *our*... friend was bitten by some sort of Fae changeling..."

The Demon interrupted with gales of laughter. It literally rolled around on the floor within the confines of the circle. My anger was piqued, to say the least. And I have yet to learn to control my actions well when I'm angry.

I started toward the circle, intent on inflicting pain on the laughing Demon. Halli grabbed my arm and pulled me back, "What are you doing? Are you completely crazy? Are you just going to walk right in there and—what?—*zap* him? Not to mention, break the circle and *release* him!"

I shook her hand off my arm and glared at the Demon. Halli was right, of course, it would be suicide to break the circle now. Not to mention homicide and a few other unforgivable sins.

"What has it done to your precious friend? Is he turning into a rotting Troll? Or, mayhap a Revenant of some sort? Do tell, into what sort of beast has he turned?"

"A Werewolf," I yelled. "He is cursed with lycanthropy."

"Ahh. . . I see. I suppose you want me to tell you how to reverse such a curse."

"I think I know a way. I just need confirmation... and some direction... before I proceed. I think I can *soul-gaze* with him, lock him in a *gaze* and then... well, it's the *then* I'm needing help with. How do I extract the curse from his body?"

"You have the right idea, girl. And I know the answer to your query. Before I answer, we must strike a deal. What are you willing to give in return for your answer?"

Anything, I thought. "What do you ask of me?" I said.

Shalbriri paced back and forth as it thought. It even removed its glasses at one point and hocked a big glob of slime onto them then wiped them off on its flowing, sheet-like body before placing them back on its face. *"I, Shalbriri, ask in return for my knowledge..."*

CHAPTER TWENTY

The hour was late when Halli and I returned home. I had difficulty sleeping for what remained of the night. I rehashed over and over the conversation with the Demon Shalbriri, committing to memory the steps of the exorcism it had explained. Before Halli fell asleep I asked if I could practice a *soul-gaze* on her—it was something we all knew about but had always been reluctant to do, not wanting our innermost secrets revealed even to each other. I hated to ask her now, but I needed to be sure I could do it. The only *gaze* I'd been involved with was the involuntary one with Mr. Jorgenson that, I'm sure, seared a big globule of my brain cells.

Soul-gazing with Halli was probably not my best idea. When we first locked *gazes* I saw and felt something of her life since joining our group. That went by in an eternal flash—I know, that really didn't make sense, eternal was long, flash was short. What I meant is I knew and could feel that those memories took only a short time to experience, but it seemed like forever. Really, truly, forever... like I'd always been in her mind and always would be. It was hard to explain.

The reason it wasn't a good idea to choose Halli for this foray into the *soul-gazing* abyss, was that her mind and her past were mysteries even to her. Her memories ended with an abrupt jolt. I hit a wall so hard that my head erupted in pain. Beyond the time Halli showed up in the Underground, there was nothing. Not *nothing* exactly—there *was* something there, I just couldn't get to it. I pushed a little harder, which succeeded only in causing more pain to both of us. Whatever her past, she'd built a fortress around it.

I broke the *gaze*. "Sorry, Hal. I didn't mean to cause pain. I didn't think about your amnesia inhibiting the process. Thanks for letting me practice on you. At least I know I can lock *gazes*, and that's all I really needed to find out."

She rubbed her temples, eyes closed. "The mind is such an amazing mystery. To be honest, I thought about the amnesia aspect. I was kind of hoping you'd be able to break through and see into my past."

"Well, it's obvious there is something there your mind doesn't think you can handle. Maybe it's best we just let it do its job of protecting you from whatever that is." I lay down and covered my eyes with my forearm. "Thanks, Hal. You're the best—really and truly the best."

She climbed into her sleeping bag. It rustled as she moved to a comfortable position. "Night, Paige. See you in the morning." She started snoring so quickly, I had to stifle a laugh.

The pale girl in the mirror stared at me with dark circles under her sunken eyes. I splashed cold water on my face. It didn't help. I still looked like the walking dead.

I wandered out into the common area of our home and plopped down into a chair next to Alec.

"You look terrible," he said.

I stuck my tongue out at him.

"Hey, look at the bright side, at least you'll look the part of the drug-seeking waif in withdrawals today when you ask for more drugs."

"Great," I muttered. I slumped down in my chair and rested my head against the back of it. "That's the look every girl dreams of achieving—drug-seeking waif."

"Who's a drug-seeking waif?" Seth asked as he and Johnathan joined us.

"Apparently, I resemble one this morning," I said with a yawn.

"Not true, Paige," Johnathan slapped Alec on the back of his head. "You look a little tired, is all. And still beautiful… always beautiful." He reached out a hand like he was going to caress my face, and then dropped it to his side before the gesture was complete.

"I'm going to go grab some breakfast. What do you want, I'll get it for you," Johnathan said, looking at me.

"Oh, I really don't feel like eating this morning. Thanks anyway, Johnathan."

"Are you sick?"

"No, I'm just tired—not enough sleep last night." The truth was I felt pretty yucky, and the yuckiness increased as the morning wore on. "I'm gonna go grab my stuff. Everyone make sure you have your channeling rods today—we may need them."

I barely made it to the bathroom before I started vomiting and then dry-heaving into the toilet. *This is really not a good day to be sick,* I thought. I rinsed my face and brushed my teeth again and actually felt a little better.

The others were waiting when I returned to the common room. Halli had our lunches ready to go as had become her habit since we started going to school. She handed mine to me and hugged me, saying, "Please be careful, Paige. Call if you need me—I don't want to miss the big fight."

"Don't worry, Hal, not a single one of us wants to be in a big fight without you there. You're one tough little imp."

"Shut up. I'm not an imp." She tried to scowl. But it wasn't very scowl-ish.

On the way to school, the boys made me go over the plan three more times just to make sure we were all on the same page. Johnathan would be nearby. Alec and Seth would be out of sight but in close range, so they could be there quickly if needed.

"I really don't know why you guys are so worried. Everything's going to go just as planned. They are fully expecting me to come for more—everyone does once they've tried it, right?"

We went to our first hour classes as usual. Seth had learned that Mr. Davis's free hour was during third period, so that's when I was going to find someone to take me to his room. We didn't want other students to be around just in case something went wrong.

Brendon and Chari were already sitting in desks next to each other. I sat in the desk in front of Chari and turned to face them. "How's it going, you two? How were the shakes last night?"

They looked at each other and smiled. Brendon said, "It's going good and the shakes at Lucky's are always stellar, duh."

Chari laughed. "They were awesome. There are not many things better than having your own milkshake expert catering to you. I have never had so many peanut butter cups in a shake before."

The bell rang and Mrs. C. shushed the class. We were well into *To Kill a Mockingbird* and we had a quiz that day to get ready for the big test she would be giving in the next week. The quiz took up most of the class time because it was open book—and those always took longer as everyone flipped through the pages to find the answers.

Just before the end of class, before the bell rang to dismiss, the school secretary came on the intercom and said, "Mrs. Christensen? Please send Chari Larsen and Brendon Becker to the office. Mr. Jorgenson wishes to see them."

The rustling of pages and whispering students gave way to dead silence as everyone turned to look at Brendon and Chari like they were about to take the long walk down Death Row. They looked at each other, Chari with big, round, frightened eyes. Brendon tried to act unconcerned as he shrugged his shoulders. They stood and walked to the door; Brendon grabbed Chari's hand as they left.

I stood to follow them, sat back down, then stood again. I didn't know what to do. I flashed back to the way Mr. Jorgenson had acted yesterday. I had to do something. I ran from the room and all the way to Mr. Grewa's class. If he would intervene, maybe I could forestall the inevitable clash between me and the principal. I'd rather confront him with only myself and my four friends around to see it.

I slid to a stop at his desk, where he was talking with another student, and I waited impatiently for him to finish. When the student finally took his seat, I whispered, "Mr. Grewa, Mr. Jorgenson called Chari and Brendon out of class a few minutes ago. I'm really worried about his intentions—he was acting especially off-balance yesterday and he saw me with both of them. Could you go check on them? Please?"

He dropped the pen he'd been holding and swallowed. "Of course, Sasha. You stay here, though—I'll be right back."

The hands on the clock slowed to a near stop while he was gone. I sat at my desk and bounced my leg up and down so fast I'm sure it was a blur to anyone who looked at it. My stomach churned again—whether from whatever had caused my vomit-fest that morning, or from anxiety, I wasn't sure—but I was sure glad I'd skipped breakfast.

Mr. Grewa finally came stumbling through the door, "Sasha, let's talk in the hallway." He was out of breath and grunting.

As I followed him into the hallway, I noticed the blazer he wore was smoking and singed. The anxiety I'd felt a moment before turned nearer to panic. "What happened?"

"He... um... *zapped* me. I went to his office and before I could even say anything, he... he told me to sit. Chari and Brendon were in his office. They looked shaken up and Brendon's nose was bleeding. I

215

refused to sit and he... *forced* me down into a chair... somehow. Without touching me.

"I started to ask him what was going on, but he pointed his finger at my mouth and uttered something—and then I couldn't speak. He said, 'You tell *Sasha* that I have her friends. I'm going to do something *very* special with them just for her. Tell her she should keep her nose out of my business or her brother is next.' Then he *zapped* me... like electricity... all over..."

My panic morphed into anger. "Stay here," I commanded. "Keep the other students in the classroom."

I stormed down the hall toward the office. The anger continued to build with each step I took—along with the anger, my magic was building up inside me, fighting for release. My fingertips started to emit flashes of blue energy; my waist-length blond hair stood on end, spreading out behind me. The lights in the ceiling flickered and then burst as I walked beneath them. As the anger and magic continued to build, the lights in front of me began to burst; then the lights further down the hall. I heard things exploding, and people screaming inside the classrooms I passed.

I saw two people coming toward me down the hall, and realized it was Johnathan and Alec just in time to hold back on the blast I'd been about to release in their direction. Seth came out of a classroom on my right at the same time Johnathan and Alec reached me.

"Paige! What is going on?" Johnathan asked.

"Jorgenson—he has Brendon and Chari. I'm going to get them." I kept moving.

"Paige, wait," Seth said from beside me. "You're going the wrong way. I just saw them pass my class and turn down the weight room hall."

I wanted to scream in frustration. That meant they were headed for Mr. Davis's room—and whatever lay beyond the secret door. I made an abrupt about-face and sprinted back to the hallway where Seth had seen them go.

Seth, Alec and Johnathan proved in that moment what great friends they truly were. Not one of them tried to stop me or even slow me down; they didn't say a word about needing a plan. They all just reached for their channeling rods and spread out beside me like a formidable advancing army.

I reached the classroom door first and slammed it open. It wasn't locked this time. There were about ten students in the room, all huddled in a corner, as far away from the mysterious door as they could get.

"Get out," Johnathan snarled.

All but a few obeyed instantly—those few that hesitated were pulled along by one of the boys that played football with Alec and Seth. As he slipped past us he said to Seth, "I wouldn't go in there if I were you—Jorgenson and Davis dragged Brendon and some girl in there. There's been a lot of screaming coming from behind that door."

I didn't think I could get any angrier or magically keyed-up, but I was wrong.

Chari's scream pierced my ears..

"Leave her alone, you psycho!" Brendon yelled.

I paused at the closed door and placed one sparking hand on the frame. The heavy wards reacted to my touch and sent a blast of electricity down my arm as my hand was pushed away. There were only two ways I knew of to get rid of a ward. One was to take the time to magically unravel it—which could take minutes or days and could result in a sudden explosion if one wrong move was made. The second was to blast through it and hope you—and those on the other side of the door that you *didn't* want to hurt—were standing far enough away to avoid most of the blast and resulting shrapnel. This one would take considerable magical power to blast through. I didn't think that would be a problem with the way I was glowing and sparking, with every hair on my head standing at attention.

The problem with blasting a ward was some wards contained a death-curse element. Meaning, the person that tried to blast it died instantly when the magic combined. I counted on my intuition being right—the intuition that told me Jorgenson wanted me alive—and I would find no death-curse woven into the ward. That and the fact I hadn't felt one. And I was almost sure I would have.

I reached for my channeling rod and backed up, along with the boys, to the back of the room, as far from the door as we could get. "On three," I said, aiming my rod at the door. "One... two... three!"

We shot enough power at the door to demolish the Empire State Building. When the smoke cleared, the door was still shut tight. Jorgenson laughed from the other side.

I strode to the door and pounded on it. "Jorgenson! Come out and face me instead of cowering behind your dark-magic wards!"

"Oh, I think not, child. We're going to take your little friends and *portal* on out of here. Good luck finding them before they're permanently *altered*." One would expect an evil laugh after an exclamation like that—but all that came out of his depraved mouth next was a surprised "*Umph*."

Someone tried to open the door from the other side. I realized it was Brendon when he said my name, "Sasha! Get help! He's crazy, he's..." I felt the familiar *zip* of a magical spell being cast and heard Brendon's body crash into the door, then slide to the floor. Chari's sobs sounded in my ears.

There were a few seconds of scrambling and then a *whoosh* and a *pop*—the opening and closing of the portal, I assumed. I threw my channeling rod across the room and into a wall, leaving a big hole in the drywall where it hit. I pounded on the door again, then stopped—the wards were down. I opened my *senses* and felt for the ward again—not there. I looked with my *sight* opened to see if I could see anything like I had the time before—I saw the broken remnants of the ward, like severed blood vessels, spilling dark sticky blood where they lay. I closed my *sight* with a shudder and reached for the doorknob. It rattled in my hand, still locked the normal, human way, but the lock was an easy one for me and took me less than a second to pick.

The boys followed me inside. There was the giant chemistry set, as we'd suspected. Alec drummed on the tanks and they sounded full to the top. "Paige, we'll work on getting rid of this while you try to figure out where he took them."

I nodded. I heard police and fire sirens close by. That meant we needed to hurry; they would probably evacuate the school and I'm sure some of the kids would talk about my crazy electronics display. Unfortunately, none of us had yet been able to successfully form a portal, and really had no idea how they worked. So we'd have to figure out where we thought he'd taken them and get there the old-fashioned, non-magical human way.

I found two clues as to where they'd gone. One was a wet clump of leaves that had possibly blown through the portal as the captors and their captives were whooshed through. The other was a stack of bones with meat still hanging off them. They were huge bones, like the size of a buffalo's thigh bone.

"Okay, Paige. We're going to destroy this thing and evaporate what's inside. Stand back," Seth said.

I watched as Alec and Seth cast an implosion spell. As soon as the tanks were sucked in upon themselves—before the liquid could spill to the ground—Johnathan threw an evaporation spell at it. The liquid disappeared in a cloud of quickly dissipating steam.

It must not have dissipated completely, because the watermelon-charcoal smell wafted through the air and caused a strange sensation in my throat. I was shocked the smell didn't make me want to puke, or run and hide or something. Instead, the smell caused an almost unbearable craving for more of the awful stuff that'd caused me so much terror. My body shook with tremors. A feeling of burning hunger started in my stomach and spread—up my throat, into my watering mouth, my nose, my head. Instant vertigo almost knocked me to my knees as the desire for the drug reached my brain. A prickling sensation touched every inch of my skin. It was insane to *need* something so strongly—to think I would die without it—and that *something* was a substance I despised with all the hatred my soul could muster. It was a supremely disorienting feeling. And it made me *furious.*

I let out a scream of rage so loud it could probably be heard in Tacoma. I ran out into the far side of the classroom and slumped to the floor before I could pass out. The room spun around me and the feeling didn't subside when I closed my eyes. I wrapped my arms around my head as tight as I could, and still the room spun. The *need* tore at me like a rabid beast. My whole body began to shake. Ice ran through my veins.

Someone touched my shoulders. I lifted my head and opened my eyes. Seth was the one holding my shoulders; Alec knelt next to him. I peered beyond them and saw Johnathan pacing frantically, slinging desks out of his way. He stopped and looked into my eyes and I saw his fury—his irises were yellow-gold and appeared to glow. But that part could have been the creation of my fractured state of mind.

"Paige? What's wrong? Are you okay?" Seth asked.

I tried to explain in stuttering gasps. "The smell... the drug, it... it... I *hate* it... but, I *want* it. The room... everything's spinning. Seth, make it stop."

He sat next to me and wrapped his arms around me. I buried my face in his strong chest and started to sob. I could feel Alec on my other side; he patted my back, trying so hard to comfort me. Still, Johnathan paced. I wanted *him* to comfort me, but even in the wrecked state I was in, I knew why he didn't. He was so close to losing control. Low growls escaped his throat as he tossed the desks around.

When the odor dissipated, my desire eased. Though not entirely—if someone had handed me a cup of *Sentience* at that moment, I would have poured it down my throat while at the same time wanting to throw it across the room.

The room finally stopped spinning and the shakiness resolved. I raised my head from Seth's shoulder so fast I almost whacked him in the chin. During my breakdown, I'd forgotten what we were doing there. "Holy crap! How long was I like that? We need to go find Chari and Brendon!" Alec and Seth jumped out of my way as I leaped up.

"Just for a few minutes. But you're right, we need to get out of here before they lock this place down," Seth stood.

"Okay, let's go, then. I have an idea about where he might have taken them. Let's get outside and I'll tell you." I searched the ground for my channeling rod.

"Here," Jonathan handed the specially carved rod to me. His eyes were almost back to their usual dark brown with gold flecks. My hand brushed his as I took it from him; he closed his eyes and jerked his hand away.

Through grinding teeth I said, "Let's go."

The explosion that had sent the *Sentience*-making contraption to the evil-magical-devices graveyard had caused the barely contained panic in the school to erupt into full-blown hysteria. There was no exit to the outside from Mr. Davis's room and one look out into the hallway was enough to show us we weren't leaving easily through there. Alec solved the problem by blasting a hole through the outside wall. I would have preferred he use a quieter spell under the circumstances, but it worked for our purposes.

We exited on the opposite side of the gym from the parking lot. The football field was down a small hill to our right and the edge of a small forest was fifty yards to our left. We followed Johnathan in the direction of the trees. When we were sufficiently hidden, he turned to me. "What did you find in there? Where do you think he's taken them?"

I told them about the leaves and the bones. They all looked at me with blank faces, so I explained.

"The bones made me think, what use would they be? Some medieval dark spell? A biology project? To eat? That led me to think about what animal would possibly be able to eat bones that big. Any guesses?"

They were all silent for a few seconds, then Johnathan snapped his fingers. "I knew I recognized that smell from somewhere! The Devil-hound I fought—its breath smelled like those rotting bones."

I nodded. "Show us where that culvert is, John. I bet you breakfast in bed for life that's where the portal took them."

"Wait," Seth said, "we need to summon Halli. She'll lop all our heads off if we let her miss this."

I felt terrible I'd forgotten about Halli in all the events of the last twenty minutes or so. I touched my necklace and sent the spell out. She'd be able to track where we were now that the lines were open between us. "We don't have time to wait for her. She'll have to catch up with us when she gets here."

Johnathan took off at a lope and we followed him into the trees. He led us down a path to the small clearing where the kids had been partying the night of his run-in with the Devil-hound. You could see where the fire had been burning and there was still a pile of discarded boards lying near the fire pit. The kids hadn't been back to their secluded party spot.

Johnathan continued without pausing, through the clearing and into the trees on the other side. There wasn't even the semblance of a trail there. He pushed his way through the thick trees and bushes, breaking branches that barred his way. We followed at a safe distance so flying tree limbs didn't whack us in the face.

The culvert wasn't far from the fire pit area. It would be a tight fit for the boys, especially Johnathan, and I didn't want to be stuck behind their slow-moving crawls. I jumped in front of Johnathan as he slowed in front of the opening and I dove into the culvert head-first. The angle of the large plastic pipe was slight, at first, as it descended into the ground. I heard Johnathan growl at me when I dove into the dark tunnel—not the wolf-growl I'd heard so often as of late, but just a typical boy growl. Like an, "Ugh! Stupid girl" growl.

"Paige, what are you doing? Get out of there and let me go first!"

"Not gonna happen, John. Are you guys coming or what?" I continued the forward descent.

"Seriously, are you trying to make the vessels in my head explode?" Johnathan muttered.

I smiled and kept crawling. The descent grew steeper the farther in I crawled. My channeling rod, held before me, glowed with a blue *luminosity* spell. After about fifty yards, I no longer had to crawl—the angle steepened and I began to slide in the slimy muck that covered the bottom and sides of the culvert. I started wishing I'd gone in feet first. The pipe was too small to sit up or change positions, and trying to slow down using only my hands and arms was not at all effective.

I held onto the channeling rod with all my strength and closed my eyes and mouth tight to keep the muddy, slimy goo from splashing up into them. I was thankful for the head start the boys' slow progress for the first fifty yards had given me—at least I didn't have to worry about Johnathan plowing into me from behind.

At that point, when I realized I had no control over the speed of which I would go barreling into whatever or wherever the culvert ended, that I started to get scared. The anger I'd felt ever since Mr. Grewa's class had melted away—you can hold onto the burning fire of anger for only so long before it either burns itself out or your internal organs ignite and your entire spirit is consumed in the flames. I guess I was lucky my rage just burned out. I was still plenty angry; it just wasn't taking over my thoughts anymore. Anger had moved to the middle portion of my brain and apprehension of what lie ahead was quickly moving to the forefront.

The boys had reached the steeper section; I heard them barreling down behind me. I have no idea how long we raced toward our unknown destination—I wasn't good with estimating distance under the best of circumstances, and this was for certain not the best of circumstances. I could tell Johnathan was gaining on me and hoped that the end of the tunnel wasn't a *dead* end. It occurred to me as the boys slid closer that some culverts ended in a grate; the thought of being smashed against one by three large, fast-moving boys was not a pleasant thought at all.

I didn't have much time to imagine the results of such a gruesome ending. The end came with a sudden change from a sharp angle to straight up and down. I flew headfirst out of the tunnel, fell five or six feet, and landed in about a foot of rancid water... and other stuff I'd rather not think about. I rolled to the side and stood. Miraculously, I still held the lighted channeling rod in my hand and I watched in the dim light as Johnathan splash-landed where I'd been just a second before.

He rolled just as I had—our hours of training were paying off—and I had to leap out of his way before he bowled right into me. That leap resulted in Johnathan missing me with his roll; however, I landed on something beneath the water and twisted my right ankle. I tried to stay upright, flailing my arms to keep my balance, but I fell anyway in what seemed like slow motion, and landed with my outstretched arms right on Johnathan's gut. His breath came out in a whoosh of air. I scrambled off him as he sat up and tried to take a breath. The pain in my ankle burst into my foot and up my leg. Tendrils of burning embers attacked every nerve ending with pulsating flames. I breathed through the pain until it started to ebb.

Meanwhile, Seth and then Alec came shooting out of the tube above. Seth landed with a grunt and thankfully rolled the opposite direction from Johnathan and me. Alec sat up where he'd landed and, after realizing he'd lost his channeling rod in the fall, started crawling around in the water to try to find it.

"Are you okay, Paige?" Johnathan said as soon as he was able to breathe again.

"I twisted my ankle."

"I'm so sorry. I should have rolled the other way." He offered me his hand, then pulled me up.

I balanced on my good foot, not quite ready to test out the injured ankle. "There is nothing to apologize for, John. You had no way of knowing which direction I was. If anything, it's my fault for not moving farther out of the way."

His hand touching mine felt good, and I left it there for as long as he would let me—which wasn't very long.

"Try putting some weight on it now," he whispered, probably afraid we'd be heard by our enemies.

I was hoping for an element of surprise to help us when we found them, but I wasn't counting on it as I was sure they would have alert spells set up around their hideout. They probably already knew we were there.

I lowered my right foot to the ground and put a tentative amount of weight on it. Pain shot up my leg and down into my foot and I hoped Johnathan couldn't see me wince in the dim light. But, of course, he saw it. He had the eyesight of a night creature and he looked right at my face to gauge my reaction.

"Paige..." he began.

"It's fine. I just need to *walk it off*, as you athletes are always saying."

The first few steps were painful, but after a sloshing lap around the cavern, the pain subsided enough that I could walk at a normal pace with only a small limp.

"See?" I asked. "I'm fine. Now let's get going."

Johnathan narrowed his eyes with doubt. "What happens if we have to run?"

"I don't plan on running from them... from *him*. I'll stay and fight."

Johnathan started to protest but I stopped him with a raised hand. "I will not stay behind, Johnathan. We're wasting precious time talking about a moot point." I limped toward the only tunnel.

He and the others had no choice but to follow. Alec found his channeling rod after he crawled around in the disgusting water and finally remembered he could *call* it to his hand—something we'd practiced almost daily.

The tunnel was tall enough for all of us to stand upright in, although Johnathan's head nearly touched the cement ceiling. The water on the tunnel floor slowly decreased until there was only a trickle that ran down the very center. The fusty smell of mold and decay receded the further along we went. I wasn't allowed to be in the lead for long; I'd taken only a few steps when Johnathan nudged his way past me and put himself on point.

"Hey, guys, stop for a second," Seth whispered.

Johnathan halted and we all turned to face Seth, who brought up the rear.

"Shouldn't we put a noise suppression spell at least on our feet? So they don't hear us coming?"

"Good idea, Seth," Alec and Johnathan said. I nodded agreement.

We probably should have already thought of that, but we'd never been on the offensive side of monster hunting. Always before we'd found ourselves reacting to a situation we'd stumbled upon—even those situations that occurred because of our now-suspended nightly rounds about Seattle and its neighboring communities.

We all took a moment to cast the spell about our feet. It was a peculiar thing to know we were walking and yet were unable to hear our own footfalls. Johnathan stopped abruptly a few yards later. We all came to a halt behind him. He put a finger to his mouth and then cupped an ear to tell us he heard something.

Soon, the rest of us were able to hear muffled voices echoing down the cement walls. We weren't able to make out what was being said until we'd gone another fifty yards or so. Up until that point, we'd seen nothing but the tunnel walls surrounding us.

Johnathan looked back at us and pointed to his right. There was a windowless door there. The sound came from up ahead, though, so we walked past without investigating. We passed several more of the doors on our left and right before the tunnel split into a Y. Johnathan listened at each of the tunnels before proceeding down the one to his left. We could see to the end of it where there was another door. This one was slightly ajar, and faint light poured from the opening.

We stopped and listened. Now we could hear the conversation that was taking place. I opened my *sight* for a few seconds to check for any wards—I saw only a quickly constructed alarm ward that we would trip as we came close to the door. I closed the window to my *sight* and listened to the exchange beyond the partially opened door.

"I'll drink it, I'll drink it! Just don't hurt him anymore, please!" It was Chari. She sobbed, near hysteria.

The anger I thought had burned itself out? Apparently there was still an ember of it inside me and it flamed up into a full-fledged bonfire at the sound of Chari's desperate plea.

"No Chari, don't," Brendon choked out.

"Shut up Mr. Becker. Your little girlfriend has made a wise choice." Jorgenson's voice drifted down the tunnel.

"I'll drink it... but first I want to know why? What do you get from this, Mr. Jorgenson? What's your purpose here?" Chari asked.

Jorgenson laughed. "You are in no position, young lady, to make any demands. However... as it appears that your *friends* have failed to come to your rescue, I will answer your questions just so you and your boyfriend know what fate might possibly be in store for you.

"Mr. Davis and I *invented* this amazing liquid with a specific need in mind. You see, dear girl, I am a Warlock and Mr. Davis over there is my apprentice—among other things. I have worked alone for more than a hundred years and have decided that my goals will be better met if I am able to form a dark coven—with me as the leader, of course.

"I don't want just *anyone* to be in my coven, however, and that is where our ingenious potion comes into play. Its main purpose is to *weed out*, if you will, the weak. We've discovered a most helpful side effect, too—we've been able to detect those with even the slightest penchant for magic. When the monsters induced by the potion present to the partaker, if the partaker has any magical abilities, they tend to use them in defense.

"Granted, I've found very few of those, but that was just a lucky side effect. The *weeding-out* process is very simple—either you survive your initial dose with your mind intact. Or, you don't."

"I'm guessing that those who survive are *recruited* into your little *coven*, then?" Brendon spat.

We stayed still out in the tunnel. This was good information, and Chari and Brendon seemed to be safe as long as Jorgenson was busy gloating.

"You say you're a Warlock. Shouldn't you be using a cauldron or something to brew your special potions, instead of that *thing*?" Chari asked with derision.

"Oh, my dear, cauldrons are *so* nineteenth-century. Only those who don't care about oppression choose to keep to the old ways.

"To answer your question, Brendon, yes, the survivors are *asked* to join me. Those who choose to are taken under my protection and tutelage… those who choose not to still end up serving me, just not in the same capacity. See Lucifer over there? He used to be a student at your school, a strong one, a defiant one. Now he serves me as a witless Devil-hound—all brawn, no brains—and no agency to make his own choices."

"And, you care nothing about those whose minds you've destroyed. Those whose lives have ended." Chari wasn't asking a question, just stating an obvious fact. I had a feeling she was employing the same tactic I'd seen her employ in Mrs. C.'s class, where she would get her talking about a favorite subject until, before we knew it, class was over and a quiz was averted. In other words, she was stalling.

"Unfortunate collateral damage, I'm afraid it can't be helped," his voice dripped with mock concern. "Now, shall we get on with it? I have a feeling that you, at least, will be a strong one. Your boyfriend… well, we'll see about him."

I tensed my muscles, ready to spring, as did the boys.

"Wait, you still didn't answer my question. Why? Why do you need to build a coven?" Chari asked.

"I suppose we can tell her, huh Mr. Davis? Since she will shortly be joining our forces?"

The man that had nearly caught Johnathan and I the first night we came to explore the school spoke. "Yes, Master Brone, I suppose we can."

Brone? I thought Jorgenson's name was Brand. Obviously an alias.

Johnathan stiffened beside me. I thought maybe the name Brone had touched a nerve somehow, but then he turned to look down the tunnel behind us. He cupped his hand around his ear again and pointed to Alec and Seth, pointed to his eyes then pointed down the tunnel back the way we'd come. They nodded and took off at a quick but silent pace.

I missed the first part of Brone's explanation. "… an army of sorts. I'm tired of being considered a second-class Fae. They won't even allow Warlocks to live among them in the Netherworld. We will conquer the Fae and become rulers over them. And then… we'll have enough strength to conquer mankind. I will rule both realms. Isn't that a wonderful opportunity for you two to be part of? A new order where the Fae and humans live in the same realm, ruled by me. Of course, humans will become the servants of the superior Magical Folk—as they should be."

"I don't even know what 'fay' are, why would I want to help conquer them? So I can become a *servant* to more *creatures* like you?" Chari asked. "Yeah, no thanks."

"Oh, don't you worry. I'll teach you everything you need to know if you prove to be as strong as I think you are. You will even have the rare opportunity to learn and practice the art of dark magic. That is why I can recruit only the strongest young humans. Not just anyone can survive the initiations and training involved in becoming a Warlock. And, it takes time. Not to worry, though, once you're a full-fledged Warlock you can live indefinitely and you won't be a human any longer, really. You'll be one of the strong.

"Now, no more questions. Let's get on with this. After Brendon sees you drink willingly, maybe he will as well. Although, I don't mind being forceful... in fact, I rather enjoy it." I heard footsteps and then a liquid being poured.

I nudged Johnathan and mouthed *Now*. He turned to look back down the tunnel where Alec and Seth had gone. I turned as well, just as they appeared at the far end. Accompanied by none other than Mr. Grewa.

I must say I was *not* expecting that. I was hoping it would be Halli. They reached us and Seth put up a soundproof bubble around our group. "He followed us. He wants to help."

I shook my head. "Mr. Grewa, it's too dangerous. We have to go in now. You stay here."

He nodded, eyes wide with determined fear.

Johnathan threw back the door and the four of us entered and spread out. The weak alarm ward sounded. I scanned the room, assessing where the biggest dangers lay. My gaze fell on Chari—her feet and one hand tied to the chair where she sat—just as she tipped the small cup to her lips with her free hand. "Chari, no!" I yelled.

Our eyes met and she thrust the cup away from her lips and dropped it to the ground. For an instant, I thought the smell of the liquid would cause me to have another episode like the one at the school. I fought it down, concentrating on my anger and the dangerous situation we were in. The smell wasn't nearly as strong as it'd been earlier; I'm sure that helped.

The mayhem began with the Devil-hound, *Lucifer*, lunging toward Johnathan. I turned my attention to Jorgenson, who leered at me with a vicious smile on his face.

"*Sasha*, so glad you could make it," he said. "And, you brought friends." He reached inside his jacket pocket and pulled out a green sphere the size of a golf ball. He launched it at me and I brought my channeling rod up just in time to shoot it out of the air with a crackling bolt of blue fire.

I smiled at the Warlock, Brone. On each side of me, the battle raged. Johnathan had dropped his channeling rod and had the Devilhound in a wrestler's grip. Alec faced who I assumed to be Mr. Davis, while Seth warded off an attack by a group of apparent recruits—including the three losers who had attacked me at the party.

Chari and Brendon were helpless, each tied to a chair across the room from each other. Brendon, bruised and bloody, struggled to free himself.

I took this all in in a quick glance before turning my full attention back to Brone. He raised his hands, palms out toward me, and spoke the words of a spell. As he spoke, a blazing white sphere formed between his hands. I took advantage of the length of time his spell was taking and pointed my channeling rod at the forming sphere.

"*Explodus,*" I yelled. Another one of my made up Latin words.

This time, orange flames burst from my rod, hitting the sphere just as he released it. Instead of exploding as I'd intended, his sphere *engulfed* my orange-flamed bolt of magical attack—swallowed it like an oyster—and continued toward me. I didn't have time to think about how to react, much less time to form a defensive ward to block the sphere. *I'm dead*, I thought. I took one step back on my injured ankle, toward the entrance, and ducked. A form flew from the tunnel and leaped in front of me, taking the full brunt of the dark magic sphere right in the chest.

I dropped to my knees beside Mr. Grewa.

"No! Mr. Grewa, *no!*" The effect of the sphere wasn't anything I'd been expecting. It didn't burn or explode or instantly kill. It *seeped* into his chest and spread tendrils of charged energy coursing over his body, encapsulating him in a cocoon of sparking cords. He looked into my eyes and struggled to speak. Nothing came out except drool. His eyes bulged and his veins swelled and burst beneath the surface. Purple splotches appeared all over his exposed skin. His eyes popped.

Their fluid splattered my face. Frothy blood escaped his open mouth, then his nose and ears.

Then Brone made a big mistake. He laughed. "Grewa was a weakling—a non-talented weakling."

"You'll never understand the strength in kindness, *Brone,*" I said, quiet and deadly.

I left my channeling rod on the floor next to what was left of my beloved teacher and friend. I stood and faced Brone, electricity-like magic coursing through my enraged body, flying from my fingertips, standing my hair on end. I no longer felt pain in my ankle. The smugness on Brone's face turned to fear—the blood drained from his face as he watched my advance. He reached in his jacket again and produced another glowing orb, this one green like the first. He threw it, not at me as I'd anticipated, but at Chari, still tied helplessly to the chair.

"No!" Brendon yelled.

I had to take my attention off Brone long enough to free-throw a bolt of energy at the flying sphere headed toward Chari's face. There was a big chance I'd hit both the sphere and Chari, frying them both, without the channeling of the rod. I had to take that chance though because the alternative left her dead for sure.

My bolt struck the orb dead center and a small explosion ensued in front of Chari's turned head. The left side of her face took the full brunt of the blast. Her skin was reddened and her hair singed, but otherwise, she looked okay.

I continued to advance on Brone, who had started to back toward a smaller version of the contraption the boys had destroyed at the school. I couldn't let him reach it. I let blasts of energy fly at him with both hands—the biggest beams of energy I'd ever created. With a wave of his arm he diverted the blasts away from him and they flew past him and into the cement wall behind him. *I need to learn that trick,* I thought.

He crept closer to the device. I let loose with a barrage of power—a continuous flow rather than a short burst. He raised his hand in front of him; a shimmering defense shield blossomed from a bracelet that hung from his wrist. My barrage pushed him backwards, but did him no harm as the blasts ricocheted off his shield.

The smug grin reappeared on his face as he reached his goal. I decided on a different tactic. *"Paralyze!"* My hope that his shield wouldn't defend a nervous system attack was correct; it just hit him a nanosecond too late.

He reached out and flipped a switch on the device just before my spell hit him. He fell to the ground like a severed tree branch, unable to move even an eyelid.

My satisfaction at seeing him fall was short-lived. I froze in horror as the runes carved around the bottom of the tank started glowing neon orange. When the glowing reached the single, larger rune carved on the tank, the liquid inside began to aerosolize and spew out of small nozzles around it. The smell hit me like a tornado. An angry and terrorized scream ripped from my throat as I turned away from the mist.

I pulled my shirt up over my nose and mouth, but it was futile. The smell and the need permeated my soul. I turned and saw Johnathan, bloodstained and sweating, standing over a dead and quickly dissolving Devil-hound. Alec and Seth had the thugs tied with duct tape. They worked at untying the cords that held Brendon to a chair. They all pulled their shirts over their mouth and nose when they saw me do it.

I was borderline freaking out and frozen in place, not knowing what to do, the *need* overcoming me where I stood.

"Sasha! Help me, get me untied," Chari broke the trance, at least temporarily.

I knelt beside her chair and worked on the knots around her ankles. She'd worked the one on her hand almost loose. I was able to free one leg before the need for the drug took over. I curled into a ball at her feet. *I have to fight this.* The drug pulled at me—and I fought it. I fought the unbearable desire. I fought the hallucinations that crept in on my consciousness. I fought the ice in my veins and the sick in my stomach.

I felt someone kneel down beside me. "Paige, are you okay? What's wrong?" Halli. She'd made it to the fight. Her anxious voice helped distance me from the torment of the drug.

"Hal, glad you could make it. It's the drug... it's spraying... breathing it," I choked out.

She stood to her full four feet eight inches and aimed her channeling rod at the offending device. She blew it up so efficiently that all that fluttered down from the blast was ash. Damage had already been done, though.

Chari screamed and started yelling. "Get them off of me... get them off... get them off!!" over and over.

"What the *crap*..." Brendon shrieked as he scrambled backwards and fell over the chair he'd just been freed from.

I was shocked when my eyes fell on a newcomer to the melee. He was talking in a soothing voice to Alec and Seth, whose eyes were wide with fear. The man's profile seemed familiar but I didn't recognize him until he turned to face me. It was Joe, the grocer. *I must be hallucinating. Why on earth would Joe be here?*

"Halli, we need to get these guys out of here, out into the open where they can breathe some fresh air. Help me gather them together over here." He sure *sounded* like Joe the grocer.

Halli finished untying Chari's foot and hand and led us over to Joe and the boys.

"Okay, we all need to be touching. I'm going to portal us out of here... I hope," Joe said.

I'm forgetting something. Something important. Something dangerous. Think, Paige, think. A noise came from the other side of the room just then, followed by a grunt of rage and flying debris.

"No! Joseph! It can't be! You're all dead. I saw it with my own eyes!" Brone was beyond furious.

"*Brone.*" Joe narrowed his eyes.

"Now I know who these kids are, why they embody such strong forces. They must *die!* The *Quinae Praesidia* must be abolished!" From the amount of spittle flying from his deranged mouth, I think he meant it.

He aimed his hands at us and roared a spell. It produced a vortex of spinning flame that sucked the air out of the room. Brone's hair whipped around his head; his clothing wound around his body. The sparse furniture in the room moved toward the tornado he created. The vacuum effect pulled us toward the vortex, now infused with crackling light. Almost as one, Alec, Seth, Johnathan, Halli, and I yelled, *"Fiero!"* and blasted him and his mini-black hole with an impressive amount of firepower. The entire back half of the lair erupted in a ball of flame that seared our hair and skin.

"Hold on to each other!" Joe yelled over the roar of fire.

We all grabbed the hand of the person next to us.

"Now, lend me your power!" Joe yelled.

I wasn't exactly sure what he meant, so I just did what Halli and I did when we closed circles together. It must have worked. I had enough time to look in the direction of where Brone had stood. He was still alive, moving toward us, engulfed in flames, screaming profanities.

Then we were sucked away. I don't know of a better way to explain what happened. We were pulled into another dimension or something, surrounded by impenetrable and palpable darkness. I couldn't breathe. The suffocation lasted for ten or so very long seconds. The darkness lifted, and my feet were on solid ground again. I opened my eyes and was relieved beyond measure to see the familiar surroundings of the Seattle street outside the entrance to our Underground.

CHAPTER TWENTY-ONE

Breathe deeply, in and out, in and out," Joe instructed as he herded us beneath the overhang of a nearby building. "Get that junk out of your systems. Keep breathing." His voice had a calming influence and I found myself absorbed in his soft-spoken words instead of the horrors of the drug-induced hallucinations that threatened to start.

The terror in Chari's eyes slowly faded, and a semblance of sanity returned to her face as she turned her gaze to mine.

Alec bent over, hands on knees, breathing too fast.

"Slow down, Alec, you're going to hyperventilate," I said.

He raised his head to meet my gaze. He was really pale; his pupils were constricted with fear. He winced, closed his eyes, and appeared to listen to Joe's voice as his breathing slowed.

Johnathan leaned against the building, seemingly unaffected by the drug. He was worried, but his worry was for the rest of us; his gaze swept from one to the other of us as we battled our own demons.

My mind was clearing quicker than I thought it would. For that, I was thankful.

"Okay, guys. We need to get off the street and out of sight. Are you all able to move now?" Joe asked.

I nodded. Seth started to reply but all that came out of his mouth was a strangled sound followed by an enormous amount of projectile vomit. It splashed on the sidewalk and up onto our feet and jeans. Disgusting—I really didn't need to see what he'd eaten for breakfast.

"Sorry... I do feel better now, though." Seth spit a few times then wiped his mouth with his sleeve.

Joe looked at the mess on his shoes—his nose wrinkled in disgust—then up at each of us in turn. "Ready to move?"

Everyone nodded this time.

"Let's go then, down to the Underground. Johnathan, you lead the way."

Johnathan pushed himself off the wall and started down the dark stairs.

"Isn't this place condemned?" Brendon asked, his voice shaky.

"Yep," Johnathan answered.

Brendon shrugged and entered behind Johnathan, whose channeling rod was now glowing with blue *luminosity*. Brendon shook his head in disbelief.

All we heard as we progressed to our home were the sounds of our weary footsteps. I had a million questions floating around in my head, as I'm sure we all did... except maybe Joe... he seemed to know what was going on. He'd sure fooled us with the whole *I'm-so-scared-of-the-Goblin-attack-that-I-can't-ever-talk-about-it* act. And Halli? He'd come with her, faster than she would have been able to walk by herself, for certain—she'd known about him and hadn't told us. I was sure.

We reached our warded stairway beneath the crumbling room that had been recently destroyed even further by the giant Ogre. Johnathan paused and looked at me first and then the others.

"We've never let anyone else into our home. Do we trust these three with our secret?"

"I already know about your secret, Johnathan," Joe said in a soothing voice. "And, I don't think you need to worry about these two kids talking about it. We can always do a *mind-sweep* before we take them home... if you're worried."

Johnathan's eyes narrowed and flickered yellow a couple of times before he gained control. "If it's okay with my companions..." he looked at each of us before continuing. "We'll go down. And, *you* will answer some questions, Joseph."

Joe nodded. There was no irritation in his actions, only concern.

"Guys? What do you all say?" Johnathan asked.

"Trust them," I said.

"Let them go in," Seth agreed.

"It's fine," Alec added.

"We can trust Joe," Halli chimed in. "I don't know your friends, but I feel like they can be trusted, too."

Johnathan turned to the trap door and cleared the rubbish away before removing the wards we'd placed there that morning. We followed him down the stairs and into our home. Brendon and Chari remained shell-shocked and quiet.

Johnathan dropped his channeling rod on the nearest table. "Everyone sit down... please."

We pulled two tables together since our numbers had grown from five to eight.

I started the conversation by saying, "Brendon and Chari... I'm so sorry you two got dragged into this mess. Are you okay?"

"I'm okay... I think," Brendon answered. He reached for Chari's hand resting on the table. "How about you, Char? You okay?"

She looked down at their hands. "I think I am. My face is a little burned. I don't know if I'll ever be able to sleep again... but, I think I'm okay."

"What *are* you guys?" Brendon asked.

None of us jumped to answer. After several seconds of silence, Halli looked at Joe.

"We aren't sure..." she said. "None of *us* really knows. But, I think Joe knows what we are, don't you, Joe?"

All eyes turned to him. He cleared his throat and appeared to be weighing his words before he spoke. "I can see that you're upset"—he looked at Johnathan—"I'm assuming that's because you feel deceived by me—and I have been a bit deceiving—but only because I had to be."

"Tell us what we *are* and then you can pander for our forgiveness," Johnathan stated.

"You are the *Quinae Praesidia*—roughly translated, it means Five Protectors. There are only five of you on earth at any given time. Your job while you're here is to protect Earth—and the humans that inhabit it—from beings that would destroy humankind and have this earthly realm for themselves. Your existence is all that stops them."

"Wait, so there are only five?" Seth asked. "Mr. Jorgensen said he'd found other kids that had magical abilities. What does that make *them?*"

"There are some with an inclination toward the magical arts—but they must be taught to use their abilities—and they must rely mostly on Dark Magic to perform. It's always best, for them and those around them, that they never learn of their abilities."

"So, what's different about us?" I questioned. "We've had to learn—to teach ourselves—how to use our magic; how do we know we aren't tapping into Dark Magic?"

"My dear Paige, some very evil devices must be utilized when invoking Dark Magic—things like blood sacrifices, calling upon Demons, *pairing* with Demons and Dark Fae. You haven't used these types of practices while teaching yourselves, have you?" His gaze stopped on me for a split second before turning to the others.

Does he know about the Summoning? *How could he know? Quit being so paranoid.*

"Of course we haven't, Joe. What kind of people do you think we are?" Johnathan said.

I avoided Halli's gaze. She knew my secret shame—shame I would endure again in a heartbeat if it meant saving Johnathan.

"Okay, so we're *Quinae Praesidia* and we're here to protect. What does that really mean?" Alec asked.

Halli asked no questions—I had a feeling she'd already heard most of this.

"Like I said, there are only five of you on Earth at one time—there is one exception to that, though. When only one is left, he or she becomes the trainer of the next Five. So, I guess, officially, there are six here right now, but the *trainer's* abilities diminish as the Five grow stronger. That's a blessing and a curse. A curse because... well... because magic is cool, obviously, but a blessing because when you're no longer a threat, the monsters stop coming for you, and you can live out the rest of your life in relative peace."

"What do you mean, *when only one of you is left?*" Johnathan asked.

Joe sighed. Sadness filled his green eyes. "It's a dangerous calling, Johnathan. More so now than ever before."

We sat in silence for several minutes; lost in our own imaginings of losing our friends... of being the last one left.

"Joe, I may be stating the obvious here, but, you're the last one—the trainer—aren't you?" I asked.

He nodded. "The last of my quintet died around the time Halli was born."

"Why did you wait to tell us? You've known about us for months," Johnathan said.

"I waited to make sure—and to watch you. As you may have already figured out, the Goblins in my store were a test. You passed. Since then, I've been watching you, waiting for your talents to grow, watching to see how you handled yourselves."

"It was Joe that was outside the night of the Ogre attack," Halli offered.

"Yes, I was here. You all handled that situation quite well. Johnathan's injury was unfortunate, and I apologize for putting you in that kind of danger. I had to know if you were ready."

"*You're* the reason the Ogre came for us? How it knew where to find us? The reason Johnathan almost *died?*" I stood and placed my shaking hands on the table.

"Yes."

"That's all you have to say? *Yes*? Johnathan almost died!" I shouted.

Halli touched my arm. "Paige, John's fine, though. That's what we need to remember."

I shook my head at her, incredulous. "He almost *died*, Hal." I sat, exhausted, and rubbed my hands over my face, trying to erase the memory of Johnathan lying pale and breathless.

"Sasha, why does everyone keep calling you Paige?" Brendon asked.

"Well, my name is really Paige. I had to use Seth's sister's school records to sign up for school… and her name is Sasha."

"You guys came to Edwards on purpose, then. Why? If you knew what was going on… why?" Brendon asked.

"Because that's what we do," I answered. "We help people when they can't help themselves—when they have no idea what they're up against. We read an article in the newspaper—well, Seth read it—about all the suicides happening at your school and we knew something wasn't right. So we put ourselves in a position to help."

"This is *exactly* why I know you're ready to officially train. You're already doing the work you were meant to do—and doing an amazing job of it for as little as you know. You need training now so you won't put yourselves in such danger next time, though," Joe said.

We were silent once more. This was a lot to take in for five teenagers that had been on their own for so long; learning as much as we could from a single book and trial and error. It was a lot to take in for two normal teenagers who'd discovered the world they live in is much more dangerous than they'd ever imagined.

"So… what now?" Surprisingly, it was Brendon who asked.

"Well, young man, we need to get you and your girlfriend home. After all the chaos erupting at the school today, I'm sure your parents are frantic," Joe answered.

"Well, yeah, but what about these guys?"

"These guys are in great danger and we have much to talk about.

How about we get you two home and out of danger, then the six of us will make some plans," Joe said.

"What if we want to help?" Chari stared at her hands atop the table.

"The best way for you to help is to stay safe—and to keep this secret to your graves."

"No worries about that," Brendon said. "It's not like anyone would believe us anyway."

After Brendon and Chari got their stories straight—what they were going to tell their parents about their disappearance from school—Joe escorted them to their homes. They both protested and begged us to keep them in the loop. We promised we would—knowing full well it was a promise we'd break. Their lives would be much safer without us in them.

While Joe was gone, we had a lengthy discussion. "How long have you known about Joe?" I asked Halli.

"Not long," she said. "I started going to his store the last couple of weeks while you guys were at school—I was bored and trying to stay out of trouble."

"I understand why you went there, Hal. I just don't know why you didn't tell us as soon as you found out who he was—what he was. And what we are." I said.

She shrugged. "He asked me not to." From anyone else, that might have come across as indifferent. Coming from Halli, I knew it came from her innate goodness and trust in people. It wasn't even a question for her—she trusted Joe, so she did as he asked.

"He didn't tell me everything, anyway. He figured out there was something bad going down at the school as soon as you guys asked for his help getting signed up. He asked me to let him know when the real fight started. He told me he had ways to get us—him and me—there quickly, so as soon as you contacted me he portalled us to the football field. He couldn't portal us right into where you were because it wasn't somewhere he'd been before. We followed your trail from there."

"I'm starving." Alec rubbed his stomach. "We should eat while we discuss."

None of us could stay mad at Halli, if we'd even been mad to begin with. We fixed and ate lunch. Joe returned just as we were cleaning up.

"Gather around, Five. We have some things to discuss," he said.

That didn't go over so well.

"Don't think you can just come in here and start ordering us around, Joe. We need your help to learn, I get that. But don't try to boss us," Johnathan snapped. "We've done fine on our own so far and we can do fine without your help if we have to."

"I apologize for sounding bossy. We have much to cover and no time to waste. You can't even begin to understand the amount of information you don't yet know. You've been surviving without training, but by no means have you been thriving. Without me, you could all very well be dead now, with no hope for the future of mankind. Your purpose is more important than you as individuals—the sooner you understand that, the better this will go. I will 'boss' you, Johnathan, because I have to. And, you will listen to me, because the world is counting on you. Now, please, sit down so we can talk."

"We will not—"

"Yes, we will. Just sit down, John. He's right, we do need his help and he did save our butts today." I averted my eyes from his so as not to see his anger.

He sat. So did the rest of us.

"First thing I want to put out there is that we can't just assume Brone is dead. In fact, chances are he's not. He may have been severely injured—most likely he was—but you can never count a Warlock with *his* strength out. We have to prepare for the likelihood that he'll be back. Now that he knows the Five are back, he will not rest until you're all dead... or he is," explained Joe.

"I have a question. What, exactly, is a Warlock?" Alec asked.

"We really do need to start with the basics, here, I guess. A Warlock is also known as an 'oath breaker'. He is one who once belonged to a coven of wizards—or minor mages. These wizards aren't nearly as strong as the Five or most of the Fae. They're the soothsayers, potion masters, those who can commune with the dead. They almost always have just one of the powers but they know about the others. They stay as far away from the Fae as they can and don't involve themselves in anything un-human."

I thought of Madame La Forte.

"So, a Warlock is a former member of a coven, who broke his oaths with them—usually by betraying the trust of the coven. Warlocks turn to Demons to call up dark power; they reject the reverence of Mother Nature; they fight against humankind in their lust for more power. Warlocks usually work alone, but have been known to form Dark Covens to increase their power. Brone is a very old Warlock with a huge desire for power. It's like a drug to him. The more he gets, the more he wants.

"I've thought him dead before. In fact, before today, I was sure he was dead. I saw him die with my own eyes... by my own hand."

"How will we know if he survived?" I asked.

"He'll come for you."

That silenced our questions for a minute.

Joe went on to explain how Brone could easily track us by our magical spells—which leave a trail of sorts.

"Let him track us down. We defeated him today, we can do it again." Alec sat up straighter.

"Don't underestimate his power. He didn't know he was dealing with the powers of the Five and he was caught off guard. That won't happen again. We need to prepare to leave at a moment's notice; you aren't ready to fight him by a long shot."

"We're just going to let him scare us away from our home? That's your plan?" Johnathan asked, disgusted.

"That is the plan if you want to live to fight another day. Prepare your belongings, only those things that can fit in your backpacks. Keep them near at hand at all times. I don't plan on moving you out just yet; you're as safe here as anywhere else in the city. Let's prepare to set up some stronger wards. Training begins now."

I glared at Johnathan with narrowed eyes, willing him to keep his mouth shut and do as he was asked. He squirmed under the intense gaze I'd learned so well from my mom. He clamped his mouth shut and ground his teeth until I thought they'd break. But, he stayed quiet.

I fell into my bed well after midnight. We were exhausted. Joe had not only started right in on teaching us the *proper* way to cast spells, but he also started teaching us physical combat. He was surprised at how much we'd learned from Halli. His observation of her skills brought the first genuine smile to his face I'd seen all through the rigorous day.

We were all awakened a short two hours after we'd been dismissed.

"Five! To me... assemble!" Joe said. At first I thought he'd said it out loud but then I realized the words were inside my head. I'll admit—it freaked me out a little.

Halli and I jumped up at the same time—I was glad to see she'd heard Joe, too. It was a relief that it wasn't just more insanity taking over my brain; I'd had enough of that lately.

We grabbed our backpacks, threw on our shoes, and sprinted to the main room. Joe had instructed us to sleep fully clothed in case we needed to make a quick exit. The boys were already there, since it's where they slept anyway.

We stood in front of Joe.

"That was a practice run. Next time will be the real deal. Good job. Now go back to bed," he said.

He didn't have to tell me twice; my pillow was calling me. As we turned to go I heard Alec mutter, "*Seriously?*"

I looked back at Joe. He was standing closer to Alec than I was, so I know he heard him. I was relieved that he chose to ignore it. He turned and walked to a table on the far side of the room, slumped down into a chair and laid his weary head on his arms.

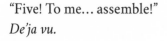

"Five! To me... assemble!"
De'ja vu.

I awoke to Joe's voice in my head again a few hours later.

I started to put my shoes on a little sluggishly, and then remembered what he'd said. *Next time will be the real deal.* That put more speed into my shoe application process. Halli and I were up and out the door, backpacks in tow, shoes and gear belts on, faster than the first time by a hair.

"This better be the real thing," Alec wiped the sleep from his eyes.

As if in answer to his comment, the trap door at the top of the stairs exploded up into the room above us as the wards were set to do when they were tampered with. Joe stood in front of us and commanded, "Hold hands!"

We scrambled to find and grasp each other's hands. It seemed to take endless seconds as Joe made sure we were all connected. Looking at the stairs, a wave of fear and revulsion coursed down my spine.

"Brone," I gasped.

The Warlock nearly fell in his rush to get to us. He wore the same clothes he'd been wearing in his lair and at school earlier that day—only they were burned to his charred skin. The whole left side of his face was a mixture of open wounds, dripping with pus, and blackened flesh that looked like it would turn to ash if touched. His eyeball on that side was nothing but a shriveled raisin hanging from a thin strip of ligament. His injuries were a grotesque representation of what happens when a ball of flame erupts in your face. It was definitely something I could have gone without seeing in my lifetime—something I could never erase from my memory.

He leaped from the top of the stairs to the bottom.

My grip on Johnathan and Halli's hands tightened with anxiety. I felt the tug of the portal Joe created and my last glimpse before being swept away was of the grotesque Brone, lunging toward us, his deformed mouth forming around a scream of rage.

CHAPTER TWENTY-TWO

T he landing this time was way more disorienting than last time. Probably because it was still dark, the sun was not yet peaking over the western horizon, and because I had no idea where we were. If I had to guess from the looming shapes and lack of trees around us, I would have guessed the surface of Mars.

As it turns out, I was several hundred million miles off on my guess.

Alec created a *star-bright* in his hand, illuminating a dreary landscape of mostly rocks and sagebrush. We were in a shallow canyon, with walls of rock on each side, twenty yards or so apart from what I could tell in the dim blue light.

"Where are we?" Alec pulled his jacket closed around him.

"This is Cowiche Canyon, just outside Yakima," Joe answered.

"Yakima? You portalled us all the way to Yakima?" Seth's mouth hung open in shock.

"Yes, and it wasn't easy. I'm afraid it sapped what little was left of my strength."

"Well, it's freezing out here and I don't see much in the way of shelter, so what now?" Johnathan said.

"We should be close to some shelter. Find a rock formation next to the trail that looks kinda like the Easter Island statues. Let me know when you find it. I'm going to sit here and rest up a little," Joe slumped to the hard, cold ground.

We each lit up our channeling rods and spread out to search the canyon walls. It didn't take long.

"Found it," Seth yelled from a short distance away.

I was closest to Joe so I jogged back to him and helped him up. He tottered a bit as he stood; I steadied him with an arm around the waist and a grip on his arm. He shuffle-stepped to where the others were gathered in front of a large rock that truly resembled the faces at Easter Island.

"Now what? There's no shelter here, either." Johnathan hadn't let go of his attitude yet.

"What is visible with your eyes isn't always the true picture," Joe said. "Look with your *sight* open."

I concentrated on opening my *sight*. I drew in a sharp breath as the true picture presented itself before me—the rock wall that seemed, a second before, to butt up next to the Easter Island rock was actually a few feet to the side and rear of it. I let go of Joe and stepped into the space that hadn't been there a moment before.

A short and narrow entrance opened up into a large cavern after several yards. I was busy inspecting the apparent caches of supplies there when Halli came through.

Alec and Seth were next, followed by Johnathan, who helped Joe amble in.

"Whoa, this is awesome," Alec said. "Paige, it was so cool when you went through, I didn't have my *sight* open yet—you're incredibly fast at that, you know—and it looked like you just sort of *melted* into the rock wall. Freaky cool."

I smiled. The scary situation we were in was just another adventure to him. A *freaky cool* adventure.

"What is this place? Who left all these supplies in here?" Halli asked.

"It's a refuge. They can be found in various places around the world—they're all marked with a natural replication of something else. There's one in Arches National Park in Utah that looks like an elephant... a ginormous elephant. That one has a huge cache of supplies." Joe's eyes closed with exhaustion.

"So, like Halli asked," Jonathan interjected. "Who put the supplies here?"

"I don't know—I just know they were always there when we needed them. My trainer said there are forces out there that are on our side, humans that are somehow aware of our mission. Some of those wizards and minor mages we talked about last night. She even thought that maybe the archangels had a hand in assisting us."

"What about the Demons and the Fae... and Brone? Don't they know these exist?" I gestured around the cave.

Joe sighed. "They've accidentally stumbled across one here or there. They can't see or enter them, but when they suspect a refuge somewhere, they just destroy the whole area. Like Mt. St. Helens... that was a great refuge. Mia was in there when Brone blew it up..." He drifted off, the exhaustion finally overtaking him.

We let him rest, moving away from him to explore our new digs. "*Brone* was responsible for Mt. St. Helens?" Seth said. "Was Joe serious? I've seen pictures of that disaster—he must've had some major bad Demon mojo helping him."

"Yeah, no joke," said Halli. "I wonder who Mia was."

"Had to be one of the Five with Joe," I said. Silence ensued as we all thought about losing anyone from our group. It made my stomach do massive flips.

Johnathan broke the silence of our morose thoughts. "I hear water flowing. It's coming from the tunnel to the left." He stood and started toward the tunnel of which he spoke—there were only two, I supposed we'd explore the other one later.

Ten or so yards into it, the rest of us could hear the water. The floor of the tunnel slanted downward at a gentle angle. After about a hundred yards, it opened into an underground cave, with a small stream running through its center. The openings on either end of the stream were too small for even Halli to fit through, but big enough for the stream. The cave itself wasn't big; the five of us could barely fit. And that was with Alec standing in the middle of the stream. Johnathan had to duck his head to fit inside. The water was frigid. I had no idea how Alec could bear to stand in it. We filled the water bottles in our packs then trudged back to the main cavern where Joe slept.

It had to be daylight outside by now, but none of us were up for exploring just yet. We found five warm blankets in the supplies. Halli draped hers over the sleeping Joe then climbed under mine—two bodies created more heat than one anyway. Inside, the cave was warmer than it had been outside on the trail, but it was far from cozy.

"Paige... you awake?" Halli whispered.

"I am now," I said.

"Sorry. I couldn't sleep anymore and I really need to go outside and get some fresh air. You'd think after living in the Underground for months, I'd be okay with a cave, but it's kinda making me claustrophobic. And I need to pee."

"Okay, let's go explore our new surroundings a little." I threw the blanket off us.

We attempted, unsuccessfully, to sneak past Joe. "Where are you two headed?"

"I just need some fresh air, Joe. We'll stay close, I promise," Halli said with such a sweet smile that Attila the Hun couldn't have refused her.

"Okay, but be on full alert and don't be gone long. We have some training to do today," he closed his eyes again.

I smiled to myself. Joe's training the night before had been grueling but exhilarating—I'd learned so much in just one short session that my desire for more lent to an excitement I hadn't felt in years.

The sun was shining and we had to shade our eyes as they adjusted to the unaccustomed brightness. Seattle was rarely this bright. Some of my excitement ebbed when I was finally able to see my surroundings. Cowiche Canyon was desolate, especially when compared to the greenery of Seattle and its surrounding communities.

Halli and I walked down the trail that lay outside our hidden refuge. The scenery consisted of rocks and bare hills—okay, maybe not completely bare, there was a lot of sagebrush and a scattering of white and yellow wildflowers that were quickly fading as autumn approached. I saw some pine trees here and there, but they were sparse. The trail was lined with rocky dirt and dried grass. The trail followed a winding creek with some bigger trees growing near it along with tall, green grass along its edges.

We climbed a nearby hill and saw nothing but the same terrain for miles—it was odd to be able to see for miles, to not have trees block your line of vision in every direction. We didn't explore for long, as we found each new bend in the trail or each new hilltop presented us with the same bleak terrain.

The others had started to stir when we returned to the refuge, our eyes adjusting to the dim lighting provided by several rocks Alec had infused with illumination spells.

Joe was awake, sitting with his back against the wall of the cave and drinking water from his eco-friendly aluminum bottle. "Glad you're back. What do you think of Cowiche Canyon, girls?"

"It's very… wide open," Halli said.

"Yeah, it's hard to believe we're still in the same state. Lots of rocks and sagebrush, very few trees," I added.

"Lesson number one for the day—Warlocks, including Brone, have a *very* hard time transporting, or portalling, into places with sparse vegetation. It also makes it most difficult for him to trace our use of magic. Because we have a more pure magic, we don't have to rely on things of the earth or Dark Magic to perform a spell. When Brone, or one like him, makes a portal, he uses the roots of the trees to channel the magic—like a telegraph from one to the next. If there's a large gap between the roots, the magic is cut off and the portal ends where the telegraphing stops.

"Remember how I mentioned last night that Warlocks are no respecters of Mother Nature? The use of living vegetation to magnify the Dark Magic drains the life out of the source plants—if the same group of roots or plants is used more than once or twice, the entire chain will die. Brone often draws power from the living plants of the earth to add strength to his spells, thus killing the plants."

"I understand why you brought us here, then," I said. "He won't be able to portal here or track us easily. If he does show up, his magic won't be as strong because there isn't a lot of plant life for him to draw from."

"That's right, Paige. I worry a little about the growth along the creek edges, so we all need to stay clear of there—especially when we're practicing magic. It's likely that even though he doesn't know for sure where we are, he may come looking here, as it is one of the closest areas with this terrain."

"Does he know about the refuge here?" Seth asked. The worry in his voice made me think about the violent demise of the Mt. St. Helen's refuge.

"No, I'm almost positive he doesn't. We only used this one once and it was when Brone was wreaking havoc over in Hawaii."

"How long can we safely stay here?" Johnathan asked.

"Not long, I'm afraid. Even though I doubt Brone will come after us again this soon, it's better to be safe. His previous actions, and his grievous injuries, would indicate that he'll spend some time recovering and regaining his strength. He'll probably start recruiting a bit more heavily now that he knows the *Quinae Praesidia* are back in action, too. My guess is we'll be free from his harassment for at least a few months, but, like I said, it's better to be safe. We'll spend a few days here training and preparing—regaining our strength. We won't be portalling out this time. It took too much out of me and I grow weaker magically by the day. We'll have to hoof it to our next destination."

"Why can't you just teach us how to portal?" Seth asked.

"Oh, I plan to do just that. However, portalling is tricky, and if not done correctly, can have disastrous results. Like being trapped in the darkness between realms… forever." He shuddered. "It must be practiced and perfected before attempting it, and we don't have the time for that."

"Okay… but, can't we take a train or something?" Alec asked.

"Ahh, if only we could. That used to be an option, but today's trains are packed with electronics and run by computers. Six of us on a train would blow the system apart before it got up to full speed. I'm afraid we're stuck walking until one or all of you become proficient in portalling."

"Well, let's get on with the training, then. I really don't like the idea of trekking to… where is it we're going next?" Alec asked.

"I have a few ideas, we can discuss them and decide as a group before we set out," Joe said.

"How do we know where we *should* go? I mean, you said we're here to protect people. How do we know who needs us the most?"

Joe smiled. "Good question, Halli. I asked my trainer the same thing. Her answer? There are forces involved that are much greater than we are. Wherever circumstances took us, wherever we ended up on what seemed like a whim, wherever our decisions took us—that's where we ended up being needed. It's like the Five are drawn to places where dark forces are strong at work. Wherever the five of you decide to go is where you'll need to be."

"That's a lot of responsibility. What if we're wrong?" Halli asked.

"You won't be. It's part of being who you are. *Quinae Praesidia.*"

"So, what you seem to be saying is that we'll travel a lot. No settling down anywhere," Johnathan said.

"That's right, Johnathan." He let that settle in our minds for several seconds before changing the subject. "Is everyone ready to get to work?"

We spent the rest of the day outside the confines of the cave, practicing and training. Joe was right; we had no idea how much we didn't know. Cowiche Canyon was not a deserted place; apparently, it was a semi-popular trail to hike. Joe avoided the hikers by leading us in an endurance run that took us away from the popular trail and off into the unused back country. We rested briefly and drained half the water from our bottles before setting wards and beginning practice.

Joe explained that although we could all do all the spells he was going to teach, each of the Five has a different strength. He set out this day to begin discovering ours. He already knew Halli's was hand-to-hand combat; he said he'd put her in the octagon with any UFC fighter out there and apologize to the guy later for ending his career. He was certain my strength was in channeling attack spells—the fact that I could hit a small target with killer accuracy without the use of my channeling rod was an unusual and valuable strength. We tested my accuracy against the others for a good two hours. I never missed a target no matter the size. And I didn't use my channeling rod once.

During this session we were able to discover Johnathan's strength. Basically, his strength was… *strength*. The strength of his spells, that is, although his physical strength is nothing to ignore, either. He can throw a spell with more oomph than any of us. More than Joe or the other four in his group could back in the day, too. Joe said he was ninety-eight-percent sure that Johnathan's spells were stronger than Brone's Demon-fueled spells. This revelation made Joe almost giddy.

After lunch, the wind kicked up, blowing dirt and rocks all over us. Miniature tornados—Alec called them *dust-devils*—sprung up around us, throwing aforementioned dirt and rocks into us like missiles. The experience wasn't very pleasant. I suggested we move off the top of the hill we were training on, but Joe had other ideas.

"Now would be a great time to test your defensive spells," he yelled above the howling winds. "Let's see who can block the wind from reaching us. Use a shielding spell."

We'd practiced a little bit with this, shielding spells came in handy when someone was throwing stuff or shooting at you. They could be used to block magic spells like those Brone had used on me in his lair, but they took too long to produce—I would have been fried like a piece of bacon before I could even begin to produce one. We hadn't been able to discover a quick way to conjure a defense spell on our own; I hoped Joe was going to show us one.

I was still trying to picture in my head what results I wanted from the spell before I even attempted to construct it with my will. The dirt clods and shards of rock hitting me in the head were distracting.

Before I could even begin to form the spell, the wind stopped—I no longer felt the pelting of objects.

I closed my eyes, trying to concentrate, but as soon as I realized the wind had stopped, I opened them. My jaw dropped when I realized the wind hadn't actually *stopped*—it just wasn't hitting us. Dirt and twigs still whipped around us as if we were covered in a dome of impenetrable glass. I looked around to try to figure out who was responsible for our sudden peace and comfort, convinced it had to be Joe. I was wrong, but it was easy to see who'd done it.

Joe gaped at Seth, who had a smug little grin plastered on his face.

"Seth? How did you do that so quick?" I asked.

"I don't know. Something just clicked in my brain. I bet I can do it faster next time."

"Okay, let's test that theory," Joe said. "Drop the shield, and when I say 'go' we'll see how fast you can erect it again."

The shield around us dropped; the pelting began again with a vengeance.

"Go!" Joe yelled.

Less than a second. Wow. That was unbelievable.

"Well, it looks like we've found your strength, Seth." Joe smiled.

"Awesome! I *love* my strength," Seth pumped his fist in the air.

"It still isn't fast enough to defend against a magic fireball, or an everyday bullet—but there are ways to make it faster. Probably the greatest thing about your talent is you can share it with your colleagues here," Joe said.

"Yeah, I know, I already did. See?" Seth gestured to the dome of protection surrounding us.

Joe shook his head. "There's another way you can share it, Seth. We can make shield bracelets that are infused with your shields and your friends can wear the bracelets and tap into them to construct shields of their own, almost as quickly as you can. It's an invaluable tool and will invariably save the lives of you and your friends."

"That's so cool. When can we make the bracelets?" Seth asked.

"Tonight. The materials should be available in the refuge."

"Okay, okay," Alec said. "It's a cool talent. Let's figure out mine now."

"We may not be able to figure it out tonight, Alec. But no worries, we'll know in time what your special strength is."

"What's your strength, Joe?" Halli asked.

"My strength... *was*... wards. My wards were impenetrable by even the most diligent and nasty of enemies. My illusion wards fooled even myself sometimes." He shook his head. "But, my strength is a strength no more. Let's get on with this. We still have a couple hours of daylight. We'd best make good use of it."

"Well, what other strengths are there? I mean, can't we just try them all until we find mine?" Alec was determined to know his strength right then and there.

Joe laughed. "Alec, Alec, Alec... show some patience, my boy. There are innumerable talents. Let's just continue on with my lesson plans and we'll come across it eventually."

"Ugh," Alec groaned.

I stole a glance at Johnathan. We stood close together in the confines of Seth's shield. Johnathan's muscles were tense, his jaw worked back and forth as he ground his teeth. "Drop it, Seth." He growled through clenched teeth and turned away from Seth. Joe caught a glimpse of his yellowing eyes and frowned.

"Huh?" Seth scrunched his eyebrows together.

Johnathan's nostrils flared in and out and he closed his eyes.

"The shield," I said quietly. "Drop the shield. Johnathan needs some air."

"Oh, yeah, right." Seth stole a glance at Joe and dropped the shield.

Once again pelted by wind and dirt, I turned to Joe and said, "He's just a bit claustrophobic."

Joe watched with brows furrowed, his mouth turned down in a frown, as Johnathan jogged a short distance away. "Okay, let's take a break."

After a short time-out we learned and practiced various spells like levitation, paralyzing spells, reflecting spells, and even an invisibility spell that didn't really make us invisible. It just made us blend in with our surroundings. We hadn't come across Alec's strength by the time Joe announced it was time to head back to the refuge.

Alec's disappointment showed in his sour mood. We jogged back to our new temporary home—Joe insisted we exercise our bodies as well as our minds and magic, and increase our endurance along the way. Alec took off from the rest of us and sprinted most of the way. I bet he had the world's biggest side ache before he reached the cave. The quick-paced run had at least one good side effect—it made Alec too tired to be ornery.

***

Joe woke us early the next morning and we headed off in a different direction than the day before—jogging, of course. Alec was in much better spirits, sure that his special powers would be revealed today. He made it sound like he was a budding superhero.

"What's our plan for the day, Oh Captain, My Captain?" Alec asked Joe when we'd finished our run.

Joe raised an eyebrow at him. "Today, you're going to *begin* to learn how to portal. This spell takes time and practice to learn and *no one* is to even *think* about attempting it with themselves or another person until I am completely convinced that they're ready. Do you all understand?" He looked at Alec.

"What? I know... I won't try it without your prior authorization, Sensei. I promise." He crossed his heart just to prove it.

Joe shook his head with a sigh. "Just remember, the consequences of a portal-gone-wrong are both horrifying and permanent." He looked each of us in the eye to make sure we understood the gravity of his statement.

He proceeded to explain that you could only portal, *safely*, to somewhere where you'd been before. That statement, of course, brought on a round of questions, starting with Alec.

"So… it *is* possible to portal somewhere you *haven't* been… it's just not as safe?"

Joe's exasperated sigh actually echoed across the canyon. "Alec… it is possible. But highly dangerous. It's just too hard for your mind to form the correct picture for the spell to build upon. And while I'm thinking about it, don't *ever* try to portal somewhere make-believe—like, say, Willy Wonka's chocolate river or Alice's Wonder-land. That's one of those mistakes that'll land you eternally in *between.*"

"*Between?*" Halli asked.

"Yeah, *between.* As in between here and there—floating endlessly in nothingness, neither *here* nor *there.* Not a fate I would wish on anyone… well, almost anyone.

"We'll start by portalling small objects and go from there." Joe began pulling small twigs from a dead bush.

We practiced moving the twigs by picturing them in the place we wanted to open a portal to—which, in this case, was down the hill by a lone pine tree we'd paused at on our way up there. It was a difficult spell to master, that was for sure. I would have the picture planted firmly in my head. But when I would go to open the portal, infusing the spell with my will, the picture would crumble and I'd have to start all over again. There were more than a few twigs, I'm afraid, that ended up in the *between* because of me.

We all struggled with this new skill—all except Alec. It seemed he'd found his strength. While the rest of us continued to work on moving lightweight twigs, Alec was moving rocks the size of Halli. Joe was astonished at the speed of which he caught on to this most difficult spell.

Joe caught a lizard and had Alec portal it to the tree. He did it without a problem. The rest of us were pretty much on our own at this point; Joe was fascinated by Alec's strength in portalling.

"Now, try moving the rock further, like to the creek we crossed a mile or so away," Joe instructed Alec.

"No problema, Coach." Alec concentrated for only a few seconds before the rock disappeared. We all ran the mile back to the creek to see if it had arrived there safely—and there it was.

This went on into the afternoon. The rest of us were able to move our twigs and even some small rocks to the pine tree. Johnathan was able to move larger objects, but didn't even come close to the accuracy of Alec. Alec didn't lose an object in the *between* even one time. Even so, I was still shocked when he asked Joe, "Hey, Chief, how about you let me portal myself back to the cave when we're done?"

Joe studied him in silence for a minute or two. I couldn't believe he was actually considering it. "Well, it *is* your strength. What do you guys think?"

"No way," I said. "It's too big of a risk."

Halli agreed with me.

"Paige, he hasn't screwed it up all day, not once. I think he'll be fine," Seth said.

I shook my head and looked to Johnathan to be the voice of reason.

I should have known the boys would stick together on this. They lived for danger. Johnathan half smiled at me apologetically before saying, "I think we should let him. Seth's right, he's been spot-on all day."

"Joe, you can't seriously be considering this!" I argued.

"Actually, Paige, I am. If Alec wants to take the risk, knowing the consequences if he messes up, I say he should. He is amazing at this."

"Whatever... just don't come crying to me when you're stuck in the *between* forever, Alec," I said with a huff.

Alec took extra time constructing his portal. He closed his eyes and then... *poof*... he was gone.

We all ran back double time. I was sure we'd find Alec, lounging and gloating, waiting for us in the cave.

Johnathan reached the entrance first and we all came huffing and puffing in behind him. I searched the inside of the dim cave for any signs of Alec. He wasn't there.

"Alec?" Johnathan said.

I glared at Joe.

"Alec, come on, this isn't funny," I said.

Still nothing. I started picturing him floating in a sea of nothingness; my heart pounded in my ears and I thought I was going to throw up. I crouched down and put my head between my knees, trying not to hyperventilate.

Laughter came from the unexplored tunnel next to the *bathroom* tunnel—Alec's annoying laughter. I'd never heard a more wonderful or infuriating sound before in my life.

"Not funny, Alec," I said when his maddening face peaked out from the darker shadows of the tunnel.

Johnathan's eyes flashed yellow-gold and he let out a deep growl as he spun around and stomped to the entrance of the cave. He pulled deep gulps of air into his lungs as he worked to calm down.

I glared at Alec. He shrugged his shoulders and raised his hands in a gesture of innocence.

That night, as we ate dinner from the cached supplies, we decided on where we wanted to go. We would start out for Moab, Utah the next morning—a place where vegetation is sparse and hiding places abundant.

CHAPTER TWENTY-THREE

W e divvied up the freeze-dried packages of food, filled our water bottles, and started out on our long trip early the next morning. I don't think we could even officially call it morning, as the sun hadn't yet begun to peek over the eastern horizon.

We were all unhappy with the fact we would have to trek the entire way to southern Utah, but Joe had good reasons. None of us, including the amazing Alec, were strong enough to portal that great a distance—not to mention the fact that Joe was the only one who'd ever even been there before, and his powers were weakening by the minute. There was also the worry that Brone would be able to easier track us if we used powerful magic, even in a semi-desolate place.

Joe thought it would be good for us anyway; we could train as we traveled and maybe even thwart some new forms of evil along the way.

Johnathan kept his distance, not only from me, but from everyone. If I hadn't already been absolutely sure about risking everything to cure him, I was now—after seeing his depression deepen as the anger inside him took over. His eyes flared yellow-gold over little, insignificant things. I could see it was becoming harder and harder for him to control his wild emotions.

I wanted so badly to go to him and comfort him somehow—knowing my comfort would only make things worse was hard to take. So, I stayed as far away from him as our situation would allow. I watched in misery as the others distanced themselves from him, too.

Joe couldn't help but notice the changing atmosphere. He pulled me aside one day when we'd been on the move for about a week.

"What's going on with Johnathan, really? And don't tell me it's just claustrophobia."

We all knew we'd have to tell Joe sooner or later about Johnathan's affliction—sooner, now, because it was almost time for a full moon.

I refused to look at him as I explained. "He was bitten by a changeling and he now turns into a lycanthropic beast with every full moon."

Joe's silence caused me to look up at him. His face had turned gray as ash. He swallowed.

"How—how has he not killed you all?" Joe's voice came out as a near squeak. "Please tell me he hasn't tasted human blood, please."

"No, he hasn't tasted human blood. We've locked him in a pentacle each time."

"I should have guessed," Joe whispered. "His eyes—the yellow when he's angry. It makes sense now."

I didn't tell him how the next time would be different. How it would be the last.

As the time of the full moon drew nearer, we walked on eggshells around Johnathan. Maybe the volatility of his emotions was worse this time because he couldn't take off on one of his solo clear-the-head, nighttime treks like he had when we were in Seattle. Or, maybe the beast inside was just becoming stronger, fighting for release, furious it hadn't been able to sate its lust for human flesh, its need for violence, its desire to cause mayhem and sorrow. The tension was unbearable. I couldn't wait for the full moon to rise and for this torment to end one way or another.

Johnathan surprised me one day as we traversed across the Nevada border from southern Idaho. I was walking, lost in my own thoughts, and was startled when someone grabbed my arm. I started to jerk it away as I turned to see who it was. My eyes met Johnathan's. His face was flushed and he breathed heavily.

"Can we talk for a minute?" he pleaded.

My heart leapt into my throat and my pulse quickened. The desperation in his eyes broke my heart. "Sure."

He kept his hand on my arm and led me back away from the others. We were in a desolate area with low-rising mountains flecked with occasional juniper trees. The temperatures were starting to dip, especially at night when I was thankful for the warmth of a good old-fashioned fire or a magically warmed stone next to my rocky bed. We dropped back from the group, and he removed his hand from my arm.

"I think I'm going crazy. I can't sleep, and when I do, I dream of ripping the flesh off of... off of... people." His hesitation led me to believe his dreams were of me, Halli, Seth and Alec. "I feel like the *wolf* is taking over—or trying to, at least. Paige, I don't know what to do. I think I need to leave, so I don't hurt someone."

Panic reared its head and I stopped walking. I grabbed his arm this time and he wheeled around so fast I took a step back.

"No, you can't go. You can't, because then you *will* hurt someone. You have to stay where we can lock you in the pentacle. You know you can't leave. You can fight this, please, just hang on for one more time. Things will get better, I promise!" I was desperate to convince him to stay.

His eyes downcast, he shook his head sadly. "How can you promise that? Things have only gotten worse. The desires are stronger than ever. I can hardly stand to be anywhere near you. When I see you sleeping, the urge to... to... *take* you, to *kiss* you... and... and... *more*... is so strong that I can't bear it. It scares me, Paige. Sometimes the urges are to just hurt you or someone else... like I need to see... to taste... blood and flesh. To feel bones breaking between my jaws, flesh ripping in my teeth."

His eyes flashed the terrifying yellow-gold. His pupils constricted, nearly disappearing in the yellow.

I swallowed hard. I had to force myself not to back away from him. I was scared, but I didn't want him to see that. "I *know* it will get better. You have to trust me." I couldn't tell him my plan; he would leave for sure if he knew the danger I was planning to put myself in.

"I want to trust you." His nostrils flared. "I can smell your fear. I can hear your heart racing, pushing the blood through your veins faster, stronger—readying your body to flee from the danger I am. The flush of your skin as the blood pumps faster... all of these things turn me on... turn the monster on." He reached for me, and I let him.

He won't hurt me. There's enough of my Johnathan left in him that he won't hurt me.

He grabbed my upper arms and pulled me close to him, our chests touching, our hips touching. I held my breath and lowered my eyes from his. His hands left my arms and traveled to my face with impossible speed. The heat of his hands on my cheeks gave the feeling of standing in the middle of a flame. He lowered his head until his forehead touched mine; he was scorching hot. My pulse quickened to an unbelievable rate, my chest felt ready to explode. Oh, how I hoped he would kiss me—and oh, how I prayed he wouldn't, not like this, not when he wasn't entirely himself. I didn't think he could stop at a kiss, and I knew I didn't want anything more than a kiss.

His breaths came in quick little bursts of heat on my face. His hands trembled, the muscles in his arms twitched.

"Paige." A tortured whisper.

"I know you're strong enough to fight this. Just hold on, please. Trust me," I whispered back. I brought my hands up to his forearms and rested them there, not trying to pull his hands away from my face, just giving him support with my touch.

He took a shuddering breath in just as I exhaled. His hands tightened on my face and he tilted my head up, our noses smashed together now. A desperate growl sounded deep in his throat. Our lips were mere millimeters apart.

"Johnathan, stop."

His long, beautiful eyelashes brushed against my skin as he closed his eyes. His hands tightened once more, his forehead pressed harder to mine for just a second before he gained control and released me. I stayed where I was, afraid to move, afraid any action on my part would provoke the beast. Johnathan stepped slowly away, and then he started running—away from me, away from our friends—into the surrounding hills.

The others saw or heard him take off and stopped walking. Halli came toward me as I stood, shaking, willing the tears not to fall.

"What happened?" she asked, her face full of concern.

"He… almost lost control. He has to come back… he has to. I can fix this if he comes back," my voice rose with a note of hysteria.

"He'll come back. He just needs to cool off. Don't worry; he'll come back, Paige."

Joe heard her words as he walked toward us. "She's right. The Five are connected in ways no one understands. He'll be back soon. The connection is stronger than the monster he's fighting. We'll stop here for the night; my bet is he'll be back by morning."

He was almost right. We broke camp after a somber breakfast. Johnathan joined us again just before lunch. He didn't say a word to any of us, and he stayed at least twenty yards behind us. I was just overjoyed that he was there. Only a couple more days remained until the full moon according to Seth's calculations—and his calculations were always right. Two more days.

The night the full moon was set to rise, we made camp early, then ate a nervous and quiet dinner around the warmth-giving campfire. We were far enough from civilization that we couldn't even see the flickering of lights. The only indication that we were still on the same planet as other people was the occasional lights of an airplane passing far over our heads.

Halli and I shared more than one meaningful look as we prepared the pentacle for Johnathan. She knew most of my plan for this night and she gave me her full support. We finished drawing the pentacle in the dirt and watched as Alec and Seth prepared Johnathan's hands with the spell-bound duct tape. No one spoke. Not even Alec.

Johnathan's eyes were downcast as he walked slowly to the circle. He entered it earlier this time, to avoid the fiasco that ensued last time, when we were almost too late in closing it. Halli and I gave each other one last look before each of us pricked a finger. As Halli leaned down to touch her blood to the circle I stepped inside with Johnathan, bent and touched the circle at the same time as Halli and we willed it closed before anyone could stop us.

"Paige! What are you doing?" yelled... well... everyone except Halli.

"I know what I'm doing. Everyone relax."

An eerie calmness came over me.

"Halli, break the circle now," Joe ordered.

"No, Joe. I won't. I can't anyway; we both closed it and it'll take us both to break it."

Joe, Alec and Seth continued to plead. I had to yell to be heard. "Everyone stop talking! I know how to help Johnathan. I need you all to be quiet so I can concentrate. There is no way you're talking me out of this, so you might as well just sit down and relax—it's going to be a long night."

Joe turned and stomped away. His hands were clenched into tight fists, held stiff at his sides.

I realized then that Johnathan hadn't said anything. I looked up into his eyes. They were filled with terror and hurt.

"It's okay," I said.

"How could you do this? Please, I'm begging you, get out. I'll kill you and you know it. How could I possibly live with that? You're killing both of us…"

"Do you trust me?" My voice was steadier than I ever imagined possible in all the times I pictured this moment.

"I do trust you, Paige. Please…"

I touched a finger to his quivering lips. "I'm going to fix this. I know what I'm doing. Please trust me and do as I say."

He closed his eyes and nodded.

The time neared. I could see the ripples begin under Johnathan's skin just before the sun was to fall below the horizon.

"Put your arms around my waist."

He lifted his bound hands over my head and let them fall. I tuned out all else around us. Only Johnathan and I existed in this world. I felt his trembling mass of duct tape and hands on the small of my back.

"Paige, this is too dangerous. I could never forgive myself if I hurt you."

"Trust me," I said.

I turned within the circle of his arms so my back was against his chest. I spoke a word and gestured at the tape that bound his hands and wrists—the tape fell away.

"Paige, no!" His entire body shook.

"Trust me," I repeated.

He took a deep breath and nodded as I turned back to face him.

I placed my hands on his face. "I'm going to lock gazes with you now—a *soul-gaze*. Don't break that gaze no matter what. Wait for me to break it—no matter what. Do you understand?"

He nodded, his face flushed and sweaty with the effort of not killing me.

I looked into his brown-golden-yellow eyes, and locked gazes with him as the sun dropped beneath the horizon.

Dizziness and disorientation threatened to break my concentration. I felt his arms tighten around my waist as the gaze caught hold.

Time meant nothing while locked in the gaze. At first, I was lost in Johnathan's memories—those things he never talked about, never told any of us about, the reason he'd left his family and hid in the Underground. The scenes played like a movie in my mind, but more real. I felt simultaneously like it was happening in front of me and *to* me. Like I was both Paige and Johnathan at the same time.

The sun was high. The warm air felt like spring. There were blossoms on the trees in the large backyard. A middle-aged woman, John's mom, was digging in a garden, smiling and humming as she worked. Two young girls, his sisters, played on a swing-set and ran in and out of the playhouse connected to it.

"Johnathan, come swing us!" the younger of the two yelled—Emma was her name. She was four. I rode along in Johnathan's mind, a passenger along for the ride as his deepest secrets were sliced open.

"Okay, Emma-bug, hang on tight!" The voice was Johnathan's, but seemed to come from all around me—from me.

He/we pushed the two girls high into the air. Their giggles made John laugh.

"Wanna see something cool I can do?" John whispered to his sisters with a glance at his mom to make sure she was still busy in the garden.

"Yes!" came the enthusiastic reply accompanied by clapping hands.

"Okay, watch this rock." John placed a golf-ball-sized rock in the palm of his hand. He concentrated on it, his back to his mom. The rock started to levitate and spin. His sisters oohed and ahhed. "Keep watching, it gets better," he said.

The levitating spinning rock began to glow with blue light.

Then two things happened almost at once. John's mom screamed, "Johnathan! What on earth..." and Johnathan lost his deep concentration. A burst of magic erupted from his hand, and the rock, along with a fiery bolt of yellow flame, soared into his sisters. The girls flew backwards, stopping only when their fragile bodies slammed into the shed.

Johnathan raced to them, his mother right behind him. But it was too late. They were dead. Emma and Linzee lay in a heap at John's feet. He threw himself to the ground next to their burned and broken bodies. The anguish that erupted from him was more than I could bear—it was a visceral, real pain that knocked the breath out of him. His, and my, chest tightened and we couldn't breathe. It was physical and emotional and psychological, paralyzing in its intensity.

I almost broke the *gaze*, but I managed to gain control and force us in another direction at the last second.

The disorientation subsided. I knew I needed to find the Demon-tainted area of Johnathan's mind, so I began sifting through his memories and his feelings to find it. I couldn't help but linger in spots that showed his feelings for me. His love for me was deep and strong—it looked like a thick cord woven of shiny silver that connected his soul to mine. The warmth that flooded over me came from him and his feelings for me. I knew he could feel my love as well. Nothing was hidden in a *soul-gaze.*

I continued my search for the foul contamination that gave the beast its presence in Johnathan's soul. I knew when I'd found it. An area of penetrating darkness surrounded the center of his being. It reached out from his core with black tentacles, growing to touch every other part of him. It touched every recent memory of which I was a part with thick tendrils that pulsed with lust and violence. I felt guilt at all the petty remarks I'd made and the many breaks in my promises to stay away from him. I now knew the strength it had taken for him to control himself and what a precarious cliff that control was balanced upon. I pulled myself away from those thoughts so I could concentrate on the task at hand. Destroying the darkness.

Okay, this is where the information from Shalbriri comes in. I sure hope the Demon knew what it was talking about.

I wasted no time because I had no idea how much time I had. I'd read that time had little meaning when trapped in a *soul-gaze;* a second felt like an eternity and an eternity could seem like less than a second.

I used the words provided me by the Demon. "*Lupinus inficio* I command that you come to me to battle for the soul of this human you inhabit. This command I make with the authority of a mage, more powerful than the likes of you."

Shalbriri said this would challenge the entity leaching Johnathan's soul. Like a dare to a sixth-grade boy, it wouldn't be able to resist.

He was right. The specter of evil formed itself into a wolf-head shape, and snarled—a ghastly sound that had the ring of many voices calling out as one. I could feel how much it wanted to tear into me. The tentacles that were wrapped around Johnathan's feelings for me snapped free and came for me, having been denied for so long. It's hard to explain what was going on. I knew my body was safe for the time being and that all these things were happening on another plane. My brain convinced itself that my body was there, battling against the evil—so what was really a battle of mind and soul seemed like a physical battle.

I was ready. I severed the tentacle with a flick of my wrist and a word. Magic was a lot stronger when you used the right words, we'd all discovered that since our real training had begun. I felt strong, ready to end Johnathan's torment. I raised my arms to invoke the spell I was sure would end it... and something slithered across my line of vision. It looked like smoke, only more solid. It was something different than the darkness I was fighting. A new enemy had entered the fray.

The smoky image hovered above my head. My hands dropped. *What on earth am I thinking? I can't do this. I'm not strong enough—I'm nothing but a weakling. I'm going to die and so is Johnathan.*

Paige! Johnathan yelled in my mind. *What's wrong? Don't give up! Kill it!*

A thought slowly floated into my head—something the Demon had said. *What was it? A shadow? Yes, a shadow! The Shadow of Doubt!* The Demon had warned me about this. All I had to do to defeat it was banish the doubts. That's all, just banish the doubts...

The shadow loomed as thoughts of inadequacy overwhelmed me. I could see the other tentacles of Johnathan's demon pulling free from their positions and banding together to come after me. *I can't do this.*

Paige, I love you, and I trust you, came the soothing thoughts from Johnathan.

The shadow above me was sucked away into the void as I let out a mental battle cry and raised my hands once again; the enormous single cord of blackness that now connected to the wolf's head reached me just as I brought my hands down with a powerful thrust of will and a word of magic that I didn't know I even knew.

"*Contorqueo-tortum!*"

The tentacle twisted violently, then exploded into a million tiny pieces that withered and crumbled to ash as they fell. The wolf's head snarled furiously and came at me with the tremendous speed of a sheet on the winds of a hurricane; its features a blur as it hurtled toward my face. I held up the shield bracelet Seth had made for me and invoked the magic it contained. The shadowy Demon slammed into the shield with such force that my teeth rattled. I wasted no time as the Darkness regrouped; I dropped the shield and blasted the lycan with a strength made up of my love for Johnathan and the outrage I felt at what it had done to him.

The evil that had held Johnathan hostage for months now started swirling like water down a flushed toilet. I opened a portal to the Netherworld, and there was Shalbriri waiting, as we'd agreed. The Demon reached through the portal and snagged the swirling remains of the lycanthrope curse and dragged it down—hissing and snarling—to the Netherworld from where it had come. The portal closed.

All was silent.

I broke the *gaze* just as the first rays of sun peaked in the east. We'd been standing in each other's arms, locked in the *gaze* the entire night. I smiled at Johnathan, and then slumped in his arms, exhausted beyond compare. He lowered me gently to the ground, tears streaming down his face. He sat beside me, and pulled me into his lap.

"You did it," he said in a hoarse, unbelieving whisper.

"I told you to trust m—"

Before I could utter another sound, his lips were on mine, gentle and warm, searching. My breath caught in my throat as his lips pressed down harder, with more intensity. He crushed my body close to his in his strong arms. I wound my arms around his neck and kissed him back with a ferocity I didn't know I possessed. My heart pounded against the tight muscles of his chest. Stars exploded behind my closed eyes as I forgot to breathe. The kiss became softer again as his tongue gently explored and tickled my lips.

Exhaustion was forgotten in the miracle that was our first kiss.

After I reluctantly stopped the kiss, we stayed in the circle: me in Johnathan's lap, my head on his shoulder, nose pressed into the groove where his neck met his collarbone, breathing in his perfect scent. I marveled at the touch of his skin on mine. It'd been a long time since his skin was a normal temperature and it felt so good to be able to be near him. The scorching heat of the curse was now lifted; the tortuous fire within him was now healed. But—as with all good things and wonderful feelings, it had to end.

"Paige," he whispered, his mouth grazing the hair above my ear. "Our friends are waiting for us to break the circle. We should let them share in our celebration."

I sighed and pulled away from him enough to look up into his amazing eyes—now pure dark chocolate again, with no flecks of gold. Gazing into his eyes seemed like a luxury I wanted to indulge in for the rest of my life. That thought led to another that made me shrink in fear. Johnathan saw it on my face, felt the sudden tension in my muscles. I felt like throwing up.

"What's wrong?" His eyes searched my face.

I owed him an explanation for what was about to happen. I just didn't know how to tell him. The bargain I'd made with Shalbriri was to be paid at the time the circle was broken.

"John... I... I had to make a deal... a bargain... with someone. To find out what to do... how to help you."

His face fell, flooded with concern. "What have you done?"

I shrugged. "What I had to do."

Not wanting to explain any further, not wanting Johnathan to look at me like the immoral Demon-summoner I was—I caught Halli's eyes outside the circle and gave a small nod. I took one last look at the gorgeous eyes of the boy I loved so much, reached over from where I sat in his lap, and Halli and I broke the circle.

The pain struck instantly and with the intensity of a rocket. My eyes were being pulled from my head by burrowing spiders with lava for venom and cactus-covered drill bits for fangs. The pressure was so intense I was sure the whole top of my head would implode and I would die by choking on my own brains being squeezed down into my throat. Those are the images that formed in my head during the intense sixty seconds of unimaginable pain.

I screamed, loud, long and piercing—the pain was too horrible to do anything else. Johnathan held me, bewildered, as I writhed in agony and tore at my eyes with the temporary insanity caused by the pain. Outwardly, the only signs anything was happening to my eyes were the tears flowing from them and the damage done by my own hands as my fingernails grated the surrounding skin. When Johnathan saw that I was drawing blood with the frantic tearing, he grabbed my hands and held them in one of his, his other arm wrapped like steel around my body.

The pain stopped as abruptly as it started.

I slowly, and with great reluctance, raised my eyelids and saw... darkness, nothingness. This was by far the most terrifying thing I'd ever experienced. The screams that had just ended were replaced with terrified sobs. Deprived of sight, the depression of darkness encompassed me.

Even still, as I felt Johnathan's arms holding me against his chest, rocking back and forth—as I felt his warm tears falling on my head then my face when I tipped it up toward his—I knew I would choose to do it again if I had to. The price was steep, but the stakes were too high not to pay it. I knew I would give anything to save him.

"Paige." One hand touched my face, tipped my chin upwards. Then both hands—I immediately missed the warmth of his arms around me and I clutched at his shirt, scared—his hands cupped my face. I could *feel* him staring into it—into my empty, dead eyes. "What did you do? Oh, Paige, what did you do?"

Another sob escaped my throat at the anguish in his voice and I could only shake my head. His lips pressed into the skin of my forehead, then onto my closed eyelids. His kisses traveled down my face—first one cheek, then the other, to each corner of my mouth, to my chin. All the while he muttered, "I'm so sorry. Oh, Paige, I'm so sorry," then, "I love you," as his lips found mine.

The kiss was gentle, sorrowful. Our tears combined—the saltiness intermingled with the sweet taste of his lips. My blindness and the ordeal of the long night were forgotten for one precious moment as his kiss melted the icy fear in my heart. The terror I felt was slowly replaced with the sure knowledge that this was where I belonged; in his arms, his lips pressed to mine. Finally. The kiss lingered, soft and gentle, never increasing in intensity as the first kiss had. It was magical, without any magic. His lips drew out the poison that was terror and uncertainty and filled the empty void with light.

Still, he continued to kiss me, until my grip on his shirt relaxed and my arms snaked around his neck; until his hands grew tired from holding my head and his arms circled around my back. Still, we kissed, until our tears were dried and my shaking ceased; until the warmth of his love enveloped me fully in a cocoon of security.

Still, we kissed, until...

"Geez, you guys, get a room or better yet, quit macking on each other and tell us what the heck is goin' on." Leave it to Alec to interrupt my paradise.

I heard a smack and Alec's "Ow!" I assumed it'd been Halli that slapped him.

"Take your time, Paige. When you're ready, we have a warm fire going and some breakfast ready for you. Then you can tell us what's going on."

Joe's voice was touched with concern, but, behind that, I heard contained anger. I was sure he'd guessed at least part of what I'd done—who else besides a malevolent creature would take my sight in a bargain. Joe had been around a long time; he'd lived through more battles with creatures of all kinds than I could even imagine. He knew, or at least had an idea, what I'd done. And he wasn't happy about it.

I shivered, just then realizing how cold the morning air was.

"Come on, Paige. Let's go get some of the heat from that fire," Johnathan said quietly.

We stood, his right arm wrapped tightly around my waist so our sides melded against one another. He also gripped my left arm in his left hand and guided me toward the fire where the others were. It was a very strange feeling, not being able to see, not knowing where to step. The slight dips in the ground that were easy to navigate when you could see them, caused my steps to jolt and falter. I clung to Johnathan the short distance from the circle to the fire. As he helped me sit, it hit me like a slap in the face that this was real—I wasn't just closing my eyes to wait for a surprise or wearing a blindfold for a child's game. The darkness was the same with my eyes open or closed, there was no blind-fold I could rip off at the end of the game. Total blackness. No shapes, no shadows, no light.

The Demon had taken it all.

Johnathan and I sat inside a small booth of a restaurant, in a small town somewhere between Seattle and Utah. He sat next to me instead of across the table like most couples sat. When we'd reached this town, Joe gave us some money and told us to do something *normal*.

The smells wafting around me literally made my mouth water. The sounds of utensils clinking, ice hitting the sides of glasses, and people chatting was intensified as my remaining four senses tried to make up for the loss of my vision.

Our meals came. Rib-eye steak, crab legs, and garlic mashed potatoes for me; steak, fried shrimp, and a baked potato for him. He cut my steak and placed the fork in my hand. I was still learning how to get food from the plate to my mouth without making a huge mess. It was very brave of Johnathan to take me to a public place for our first *real* date. He had infinite patience with me and I felt his love in every soft touch and every spoken word. He'd rarely left my side since my sight was taken... or given away a few weeks ago.

"I love you," he said. He'd said it often since that time in the circle. And I knew he meant it.

"I love you, too, John." And he knew I meant it.

"I *will* find a way to fix this, Paige. I promise, you will see again. No matter what, I'll fix this."

I dropped my fork as the familiarity of those words hit me. And I was scared.

Because I knew he meant it.

THE STORY CONTINUES IN

ACKNOWLEDGMENTS

I seriously considered forgoing the acknowledgements for this book. So many people have helped me make this dream a reality and I'm really afraid I'll leave someone out—so please forgive me if I do, and know that I appreciate everything that has been done for me.

First and foremost I want to thank my husband, Steve, for his support and understanding when I disappear upstairs for hours or days to write while he takes care of everything else. Without him our house would be falling down around us.

I am so thankful to my Alpha readers for their insight and encouragement: Laura Bastian, who made my manuscript bleed, but who's critiques are spot on; Heather Lyman, my friend and fellow book lover; Shay Lloyd, my beautiful niece; Re'Nae Metz, the greatest sister-in-law in the world; Cheri Jacobson, a life-long friend, my biggest cheerleader, and a true inspiration to me; Stacey Atherley, my daughter-in-law—your enthusiasm for reading is contagious; and last but certainly not least, Emeri Hansen, my young adult alpha reader who's love for my book makes me happy beyond description.

I must acknowledge Dr. Russell Bradley who's donation of my first laptop helped get me started down this road to authorship.

Todd Ellis, photographer extraordinaire, for taking such an amazing photograph for my cover. And, Alexandria Thompsen for the graphic arts magic that resulted in an amazing cover. And to the 'models': Lexi Paige Anderson, Halli Henwood, Alec Anderson, Seth Anderson, and Johnathan Morton—you guys rock!

Thank you to my Editor, Jessa Russo for helping me make my

book into something I truly love—you've been so awesome to work with (I still think 'sand puppy' was a good reference).

To my Project Manager, Jade Hart. You did a wonderful job of keeping us all on task. I especially want to thank you for answering my many questions and never acting exasperated while doing so.

To everyone at Curiosity Quills Press for giving me this opportunity of a lifetime and being so wonderful to work with.

And lastly, to my family. My sisters Brandi Anderson and Misti Sparks who are there whenever I need them. My brothers Troy Lloyd and Shawn Lloyd who love to tease but I know I can count on them for anything. My parents, Duane and Sandi Lloyd for their support and love. My boys Riley Atherley, Wayne Atherley, Alec Anderson, and Seth Anderson for giving me the inspiration to begin writing and not give up. And, my beautiful and amazing granddaughter, Harley Lynn Atherley for being the joy of my life.

ABOUT THE AUTHOR

 Holli Anderson grew up in a small town in Utah where she read anything she could get her hands on--mostly from the scant selection offered by the BookMobile that came around once a week. Her love of books grew from there and often became a means of escape from the real world. During an especially difficult time in her life (it involved teenaged sons...), reading was no longer giving her the escape she longed for, so she decided to write her own stories in order to visit different worlds when the real world was in too much chaos.

Holli is the author of the FIVE trilogy, a young adult urban fantasy/paranormal; and Saved, an adult romantic suspense; and Myrikal, a YA dystopian/superhero. She has many other projects in the works. She is the Chief Editor for Immortal Works, a Registered Nurse, wife of a very supportive husband named Steve, and the mother of four boys.

ALSO BY HOLLI ANDERSON

FIVE: Out of the Pit

FIVE: Out of the Ashes

Myrikal

Saved

Valcoria: Awakenings

A Mighty Fortress

Under the Viaduct

The Bar Killer

Georgia Rain

The Specials